Eliane started awake. She had been dreaming of slaughter. The demon stalked through the village, tearing apart the innocents. He tore them limb from limb, eating their flesh as they watched with dying eyes.

Was I really dreaming? Eliane thought. *Or am I seeing through the demon's vision?*

It was not likely that she had fallen asleep. She knew he came for her tonight. This was not natural sleep. It was a spell, a trance forced on her.

She had seen evil deeds before this, although never quite so vividly. Indeed every night since the vampires came she had dreamed of the village. She had witnessed the horrors committed there, the men and women tortured. But this time, Eliane was spared no detail.

Eliane knew why the demon was sharing each sensation with her. The vampires wanted her. The innocent villagers were simply bait, there to lure the Slayer from her home.

She stood. She would wait no longer. She would go to him, and bring death with her.

The Slayer would take the bait.

Buffy the Vampire Slayer™

Buffy the Vampire Slayer (movie tie-in)
The Harvest
Halloween Rain
Coyote Moon
Night of the Living Rerun
Blooded
Visitors
Unnatural Selection
The Power of Persuasion
Deep Water

Here Be Monsters
Ghoul Trouble
Doomsday Deck
Sweet Sixteen
Crossings
Oz: Into the Wild
The Wisdom of War
Little Things
These Our Actors
The Cordelia Collection, Vol. 1

The Angel Chronicles, Vol. 1
The Angel Chronicles, Vol. 2
The Angel Chronicles, Vol. 3
The Xander Years, Vol. 1
The Xander Years, Vol. 2
The Willow Files, Vol. 1
The Willow Files, Vol. 2
How I Survived My Summer
Vacation, Vol. 1
The Faith Trials, Vol. 1
Tales of the Slayer, Vol. 1
Tales of the Slayer, Vol. 2
The Journals of Rupert Giles, Vol. 1
The Lost Slayer serial novel
   Part 1: Prophecies
   Part 2: Dark Times
   Part 3: King of the Dead
   Part 4: Original Sins

Child of the Hunt
Return to Chaos
The Gatekeeper Trilogy
   Book 1: Out of the Madhouse
   Book 2: Ghost Roads
   Book 3: Sons of Entropy
Obsidian Fate
Immortal
Sins of the Father
Resurrecting Ravana
Prime Evil

The Evil That Men Do
Paleo
Spike and Dru: Pretty Maids
   All in a Row
Revenant
The Book of Fours
The Unseen Trilogy (Buffy/Angel)
   Book 1: The Burning
   Book 2: Door to Alternity
   Book 3: Long Way Home
Tempted Champions

The Watcher's Guide, Vol. 1: The Official Companion to the Hit Show
The Watcher's Guide, Vol. 2: The Official Companion to the Hit Show
The Postcards
The Essential Angel
The Sunnydale High Yearbook
Pop Quiz: Buffy the Vampire Slayer
The Monster Book
The Script Book, Season One, Vol. 1

The Script Book, Season One, Vol. 2
The Script Book, Season Two, Vol. 1
The Script Book, Season Two, Vol. 2
The Script Book, Season Two, Vol. 3
The Script Book: Once More,
   With Feeling

Available from Simon Pulse

Buffy the Vampire Slayer™

Tales of the Slayer, vol. 2

A collection of original short stories based
on the hit TV series created by Joss Whedon

SIMON PULSE

NEW YORK   LONDON   TORONTO   SYDNEY   SINGAPORE

First Simon Pulse trade paperback edition January 2003

™ and © 2003 by Twentieth Century Fox Film Corporation. All rights reserved.

SIMON PULSE
An imprint of Simon & Schuster
Children's Publishing Division
1230 Avenue of the Americas
New York, NY 10020

The text of this book was set in Minion

Printed in the United States of Ameica
2 4 6 8 10 9 7 5 3 1

Library of Congress Control Number 2002114583

ISBN 0-7434-2744-0

Contents

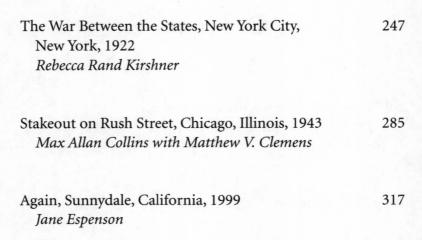

All That You Do Comes Back Unto Thee

Todd A. McIntosh

SUNNYDALE, CALIFORNIA, 2000

When he opened his eyes, the world was reversed. His back was against cold hard earth, and his nose tingled. Looking up, the Aryan football jock's face glared at him with a mouth worn upside-down like Bette Davis in *The Little Foxes*. Josh giggled inside his head. Here he was getting bashed for being gay, and all he could think of was a Bette Davis movie. Bruce had probably never heard of the divine Bette and might have killed Josh if he understood the reference. Josh curled himself into a ball in an instinctive move to protect soft inner organs from further damage. This move also saved him from seeing the tennis-shoe-clad foot of Bruce being lifted and reared for a good solid kick. Josh also never saw that foot continue rising to an impossible height as Bruce himself joined Josh on the unyielding topsy-turvy earth.

"Did I do that?" Buffy Summers asked innocently. The small group of UC Sunnydale students that had gathered couldn't help giggling at the situation. Buffy, smart as ever in a cream top, mid-length gray skirt and shiny, black Prada boots, had flipped Bruce with one hand simply by using the two-hundred-pound football player's ill timed kick against him. Buffy just smiled and let the humor build until every giggle had turned to a laugh at the tiny girl's upturn of the brawny butt-head.

Josh was quick to realize that the situation had just changed, and he was able to uncurl enough to take stock.

"Hey, Bruce, wanna go to the prom?" He managed to wheeze out. "After all, the principal said I was only allowed to bring a *girl*." This caused a fresh wave of laughter. Josh rose slowly, leaving the supine Bruce behind. Josh nodded a little thanks at Buffy, who had saved his ass more than once in the time he'd known her since high school. Buffy nodded back with a grin and continued on her way with her best chum, Willow. Josh and Willow had been friends in high school too.

As the two girls walked off laughing and chatting, Josh's little smile of triumph quickly faded. Thankfully, Bruce was too occupied nursing his wounded ego to pay attention as Josh limped quickly away. It was just beginning to get gray with that odd Sunnydale twilight. Josh faded into the crowd and made his way back to his dorm.

An hour later Josh sat in his darkened dorm room nursing his nose. How much could he take? His thoughts were as dark as the early black outside. It was 2000! A new century! But Sunnydale was slower to get on the progressive bandwagon. Josh had just successfully negotiated with the campus authorities to organize a Gay/Straight Alliance meeting. He was just putting up the first flyers when Bruce had sauntered by with his little gaggle of geesey girls and gassy guys. As ever, spotting Josh was the perfect excuse to macho it up for the crowd.

Of course Josh knew, even back in high school, that he had done a lot to draw the jeers on himself. Like most kids at that rebellious age, Josh had tested the waters; it was just that his waters seemed a little more tropical that everyone else's. It was easy for everyone to spot the fag when he was wearing white makeup, lipstick, and black nail polish. It was a Goth period. Not the best makeup application; those skills would come with practice. Josh laughed to himself.

Well, that was years ago. Josh had tested those exotic waters and being gay was the right fit. He'd actually always known he was gay, and coming out to his parents had been easy; what a surprise that had been!

"Hey Mom, I've got something to tell you. . . ."

"That's okay dear. We knew already. What would you like for breakfast?"

Home was cool, and Josh realized how lucky he was to have such rare and wonderful parents. Of course they had tried to tell him the Goth look might exacerbate any trouble he was likely to encounter, and they'd been right, of course. More than one bully had moved in to make Josh's life a little tougher. But support at home and from friends he made along the way had eased things. Most everyone else seemed to be more interested in his or her own life than in Josh's sexual preference. *Almost* everyone; Bruce was the leader of that other constituency, and had been a thorn in Josh's side ever since the first day of junior high. Today's fight had only been one in a long line of confrontations, but somehow to Josh this had been different. This time Josh was really fed up.

Naturally Josh had already noticed that Sunnydale wasn't your *usual* small town. Of course most small towns had their demons; it was just that Sunnydale's were somehow just a little more Demon, with a capital *D*. Like the kind of fishy high school swim team that Xander had joined or principal Flutie's disappearance. Willow was the one who had first brought to Josh's attention all the supernatural stuff going on around them. At first Josh didn't believe her. Who would? But little by little he started to see evidence of it himself. There was the time the whole town went on a witch-hunt. Willow and Amy had been the focus of a lot the town's anger, and Josh himself had almost been expelled because of some herbs found in his locker. *That* his parents had been angry about! And the same night, Amy had vanished, just like her mother before her. No, Josh knew something was going on. It took very little to make a malodorous flower blossom in quiet little Sunnydale.

How long would it be until Bruce sprouted claws, or hair in some less attractive places? How long before a little scuffle over a Gay/Straight Alliance poster became a nocturnal feeding of the wolf pack? And who might be the first meal that pack set out to find? How about the tasty, teensy, and toasted fairy in cell block Kappa Kappa Gay?

Josh paced his room much like a caged wolf himself, working himself into quite a state. In Sunnydale a simple baseball bat didn't do the trick. If you weren't Buffy, you had better be her friend. And although Josh felt protected by Buffy, his own macho pride was a little hurt by that.

"Funny. Perhaps Bruce and I have a little more in common than I thought! Well, damn it. How do I protect myself when Buffy's not there?" He muttered to himself.

Josh slumped onto a pile of pillows on his floor-height mattress. The room was a little too residual Goth and a little too cluttered with homework. Books piled everywhere, on top of black stuff also piled everywhere. He lay back on the bed and allowed the pillow to rest under his back and stretch his spine. Looking up at the ceiling he let his mind wander over high school memories, things that had happened since he'd first been rescued by Buffy. He liked Buffy, but he adored Willow. She was so cool. Sometimes he thought Willow might be gay too. Way back when Josh had first met her he remembered sensing *something*.

Willow and Josh had spent a lot of time together back then. They started as study partners. Another stereotype : the studious mama's boy. He couldn't help it if he *liked* learning! And Willow was just great. She had a wonderful, intuitive mind, able to jump from idea-spark to another spark, making connections that left Josh bewildered, but caught up in the excitement of learning.

What a great teacher Willow would make, he thought.

Josh remembered too how they would get off track with their studies and start talking about all the weird stuff happening in Sunnydale, and with Buffy and Xander, too. That's when they had started to research magick. Not magic like on stage, but real magick like witches practiced. They borrowed books from the reserved and tight-lipped librarian, Mr. Giles, and really got into it. Sometimes Josh got the feeling that Willow didn't actually check out those books. In fact maybe Mr. Giles didn't even know she was "borrowing" them. Anyway, the two of them spent a lot of time together reading, then later trying out the things they had read.

Josh remembered the last time that they had worked a magick spell. It had been an ordinary night—a school night—and he and Willow were in her bedroom studying for some class or another. In fact the ordinariness of the room with its girlie decorations, and the mundane task of learning facts they both knew they would never use in their future lives, made the results of their spell seem even more dangerous.

Willow had said that it was a perfect night for a conjuring. The planets were in a specific configuration that was conducive to bringing entities over from other dimensions. Josh was more than a little fearful about this. Conjuring was pretty serious stuff. He had read enough to know that Willow was suggesting a dark magick working—way beyond floating pencils! In fact Josh had once read a story about two witches that had conjured the god Thor to come down into a statue of the God that they had placed outside their circle. Then the statue blew up—shattered into little pieces. The power the witches were playing with was too strong for them. No one was hurt, but the potential for evil was always there.

Despite his misgivings, Josh gave in to Willow's enthusiasm. He trusted that she knew what to do. They darkened the room and assembled the ritual ingredients. There on the floor, by the light of a single candle, Willow began her chant. She had memorized the Latin words and had given the book over to Josh so he could follow along. Willow's voice became louder (but not loud enough to disturb her mother downstairs), and her chant became faster. Josh could feel the energy they were raising. Now he began his part of the chant, faster and faster until at the height of speed they both shouted "Come!" as loud as they dared. For a few minutes it was silent and they thought they had failed. Then everything got darker. That was all. An already dark room just got darker, like someone had turned off *another* light. Josh and Willow stared at each other in the smothered light of their candle. They began to shiver, then to sweat, then to shiver again. It was cold and dark and just as surely as Josh knew that there were things that lived outside of our reality, he knew that one of those things was there in the room with them.

Willow stood up very abruptly and commanded in perfect Latin, "Be gone!" She grabbed a little pinch of sulfur from their altar and sprinkled it into the candle flame; a nasty smell followed.

"Sulfur burns and fire cleanses! No evil things can stay here. Be gone!" she commanded. Josh was surprised to see how forceful the usually mousy Willow was in that moment. He would always remember that image of her. As soon as the smoke of the burning sulfur had filled the room, they felt the light return. It wasn't physical light, but it was a light-ness. A lessening of the dark.

Josh quickly gathered up his schoolwork and they made awkward good-byes, both knowing that something had been left unsaid. Josh felt he knew what that unsaid thing was. He now realized that the missing piece was the acknowledgement that Willow had been doing much more magick than the little experiments they had tried together. She was playing with magick way beyond the benign wicca they had been studying together, and even though Josh knew her intentions were innocent, he wasn't sure where her practice was headed.

That night had marked the end of their friendship. Not with any harsh or final words, but little by little Willow and he had drifted in opposite directions. Willow was seeing Oz then, and that relationship took up most of her free time, along with the tight little group of friends that revolved around Buffy Summers. Then they had become freshmen and recently Willow had begun to hang with Tara. Josh was happy for them, because he suspected they might be more than just friends, although she hadn't really said anything yet. He saw the way they looked at each other and the way that they were always so close. He was envious of what they had. If his suspicions were correct, Willow was in her second full-blown relationship and was accepted everywhere on campus, and he was still the geek being beat up by the campus jock! He hadn't even had a boyfriend yet! And that was exactly why he had to find that book he had taken from Willow's room that night. *Now.*

A fierce rummage around the room produced no results. Where was it? Josh remembered unpacking it when he had moved into his room. He stopped and surveyed the tiny area again. There! He had used the thick volume to prop up his computer monitor! He looked at it every day and never even gave it a thought. Josh extricated the book from the wires and connections of his computer and sat cross-legged on his black sheets to read. With the help of this ancient tome perhaps Josh could find a way to protect himself. Willow had used these powers without hurting anyone, so he could too.

It was quite late by the time Josh returned from the Magic Box. The old proprietor, Mr. Samson, seemed disgruntled at having to serve a customer so late in the day—after nightfall, in fact. He kept looking over Josh's shoulder through the shop window like something unpleasant might be lurking just outside. Despite being rushed, Josh had found the ingredients for an interesting spell he had chosen from the old book. The walk back from the Magic Box to the campus was dark and eerie. It wasn't just the anticipation of what he was about to do. No, it was something in the wind that was starting to shake the branches, making a parchment whisper sound that is the language of trees. It was something unsettling in the scent of wood-fire smoke from someone's chimney. Just average things on an average night, but to Josh they felt different. He was almost running by the time he reached the warmth of the entryway for his building. The door was heavy and resisted opening. He took the stairs two at a time.

Outside the window of his room the wind had picked up and the trees were bowing and nodding for all the world like they anticipated the magick about to be performed. Josh kept the dark at bay with plenty of candles; he wasn't going to relive the last experience with too little light. The spell was a simple conjuring involving the spirit of a high priest of Anubis in Ancient Egypt. The Anubis cult was concerned with judgement of the souls of the dead, and Josh figured that a *dead* priest might just be interested in judging a few living souls. If he could find a way to have the spirit judge who was good and who was bad and then protect Josh from them, he would never need Buffy Summers to look after him again.

It only took a half an hour to lay out the tools for the spell and to reread the difficult text. He tried to memorize the incantations and the order of gestures.

Josh sat in silent meditation for a moment or two, then began his spell. The chant was hard, as the unfamiliar Egyptian sounds were unintelligible to him, though he thought he understood their gist. For good measure he added an invocation of his own in English between the Egyptian prayers.

"Great Sesostris, Priest of Anubis, come to me this night! I supplicate myself and ask for your intervention in the lives of men. Sunnydale has many souls who need to be weighed against the feather on your eternal scales. Come. Help me. Be here with me. I ask. I beg. I command. As I will, so must it be!"

By this time Josh was flushed and breathing heavy. His concentration on the invocation was tightly focused, so he hadn't noticed the deepening gloom in the space about him, the gloom that he had tried to keep away with so many candles. A soft, damp mist had settled over the room—smoke really. Josh noticed the scent of sandalwood incense and realized the cloudy force was real.

Josh held his breath and watched as right in front of him the fog became denser and took form. His peripheral vision caught flickers of movement all around him, but the dense column of gray didn't jump or waver; it just became more real and more human-shaped. Josh could see condensation form on the walls of his room. Drips trickled down the inside of the window. The temperature was dropping.

In moments (that seemed like an eternity), the figure in front of him was as complete as a negative image from a piece of film. Josh could clearly see the figure's white linen Egyptian skirt and robe. Hints of gold glittered mutely in the candlelight and the triangular headdress so associated with Ancient Egypt held its starched form to frame a long and severe face. Even in half-light the priest of Anubis was hard. His face was like translucent alabaster with clearly apparent lines that looked too smooth not to have been drawn. His eyebrows were highly arched and seemed to portray mocking humor at the same time as a haughty superiority and condemnation. But Josh's attention was riveted to the coal-black eyes that stared into his own. Those eyes did not blink or waver, but held Josh rooted in place.

"Thou hast called Sesostris from Side. Where is my body?" The ghostly being's image may have been in half-light, but his voice was deep and immediate. "You are no priest, mortal. Why have I been returned to this place and time? What has become of my mortal shell?"

Josh sat in stunned silence.

"Speak!" demanded the priest.

"I . . . I'm not sure," came Josh's tiny voice. *Was that me?* Josh wondered. Swallowing, he stood and tried to regain some control.

"Great Sesostris, Priest of Anubis of old, I have summoned you this night. I do not know of the body you seek, but I have called you forth to do my bidding." And Josh waited, trembling.

The granite face of Sesostris didn't move, but an expression of outrage suffused his eyes. "Fool! Meddler!" finally burst out of his mouth, too loud in the little dorm room. "You are no magician. What point is there in my being here now? The great God Anubis granted me the power of life over death, then the cowardly priests of Aten separated my soul from my body and placed the shell in a hidden space so that I could no longer drink the blood of men, but must wander eternity as a spirit lost between worlds."

Josh's trembling increased as he realized he had little control of this entity.

"Look at you, bloodling! You are not even a fit sacrifice for me, let alone my *master*. Where is your ritual circle, oh powerful one? Where are the sigils and protections that would give you domination over the spirit realm? Do I do bidding just for the asking?" Sesostris thought for a moment, then said, "But you could not have brought me here without powerful help, and my body must lie nearby for you to have succeeded. What is this place?"

Josh blinked. "S—S—Sunnydale," he ventured. Of course that wouldn't do. Josh quickly grabbed some of his homework books lying nearby where he had tossed them earlier. He found a map with a flattened view of the world. Pointing a shaking hand to the Giza plateau he said, "This is Egypt." Then, sliding his finger over the double page, he stopped over northern California. "This is where we are now," he said, and waited.

"The world has changed shape many times since I walked as a mortal man," came the least threatening thing the priest had yet voiced, "but even in my time we knew the entrances to the underworld. Geb placed the doors to his domain carefully, but Anubis entered them all, and at his will. As priests, we too knew the mouths of the Earth. This place you call Sunnydale is near a door to the netherworld. That explains how you might have power to draw me here, and there may I gain strength and form to move on this plane and interact with will here. Take me there. Now!"

"But I don't know where this door is," Josh said, thinking wildly.

"Look to your past," said Sesostris. "There will be ancient and modern disaster associated with this place. All manner of chaos is drawn to its power. Think."

And suddenly Josh had it.

"The old high school!" he blurted. "If there was a weirder

place in Sunnydale, I can't think of it. The ruins are only a few miles from here."

"We go now, whelp. I am helpless in this form. Bring me to this place and restore my power, and I will do what I can to repay you. Our priestly judgements were harsh, but we were priests of honor."

"No way. Nuh, uh. I know all I want to about mummies. You said, 'A nice cultural trip to the museum.' You didn't say anything about mummies. Not going." Xander protested defiantly while walking through the door to the museum. "They date you, then they suck you, then you're Folger's instant coffee."

"Come on, Xander. It's educational, and you promised," coaxed Willow. "We all agreed that we haven't been seeing enough of each other lately. Buffy's off patrolling every night and you work all the time. Even Anya doesn't get to see you much. I thought this would be a good, non-Scooby, non-end-of-the-world gathering."

"Besides, this mummy is a daddy," offered Buffy.

"I don't care what gender he-she-it-them is. Let me just say I'm not ending up as astronaut food!"

By this time the troop had made it to the main hall of the Sunnydale museum. Surrounded by marble and huge dinosaur bones, they were naturally awed into whispers. Besides, the guard was eyeing them suspiciously.

"But I'll never be able to finish my report without this field trip credit," said Willow. "I promise, we'll be quick. In, out. Like that," she snapped her fingers.

"Hi, everyone," said Tara, approaching from the museum cafeteria to the left. She handed Willow an ice blended mocha. "I, uh . . . did anyone want anything?" she asked, embarrassed. "I didn't mean to just get one for us." she added lamely.

"Hey, no," said Buffy. "Caffeine a nervous slayer makes."

"That's okay," added Xander. "I'm already all a twitch over this mummy thing."

"Oh that's right. You had a supernatural mummy experience once, didn't you?" Tara's stutter faded as the spotlight was off her for the moment.

They moved farther into the lobby and sat at the visitor bench while the girls finished their drinks. The guard by the entrance to the traveling Ancient Egyptian exhibit looked dubiously in their direction. He clearly had visions of sloppy coffee fingerprints on exhibit glass.

"Ampata," intoned Xander blankly.

"It was a little rough for an infatuation," said Buffy. "She almost killed Xander before we managed to stop her."

"As soon as she kissed me I felt the life just leave me. It felt like I was dehydrating," Xander mused, lost in thought.

"Oh, did you guys hear about Bruce Carter? The jock guy you flipped yesterday?" asked Tara.

"I told Tara about how you helped Josh Headly with that stupid jock . . . again," said Willow.

"That's what makes having superhero powers worthwhile. Just so I can come to the rescue of the underdog. What freshman girl doesn't dream of whooping some jock ass now and again? Anyway, Tara, you were saying?" Buffy asked as she realized they had just run right past Tara's news.

"Well, he's dead." Tara offered meekly. "His mom found him in his room this morning. They think it might have been one of those freak sports accidents. You know how it's always the young guy who is in top shape that dies of the unexpected clot or something. The only thing is they said he was all dehydrated like Xander was just saying. That's why I thought of it."

"Whoa, whoa, whoa, now girl. This isn't the right campfire for dark and nasty-scare-Xander-to-death tales," said Xander, standing. "I'm led here to the Egyptian den by my bestest friends, on the excuse of a friendly get together, and just before I'm dragged into the maw of death I hear something like this? No, I'm scootin', Scoobies."

"Xander, I'm sure Bruce died from very natural causes. Even if they were unnatural, I'm sure they were perfectly natural un-mummy unnatural causes. Did anybody understand that?" asked Willow.

"I really hate to be the dropout again, but this has got me wigged. I'll see you all at the Bronze—later." With that, Xander stood up and peeled out of the museum.

"I guess we'd better get the viewing of ancient art and old bodies over with," said Buffy decisively. They gathered their things to go in, Willow carefully disposing of the drink containers in the trash. "You know, my 'Spidey sense' is tingling. Maybe when we're done here we should go tell Giles about Bruce's death?"

The Expresso Pump was one of Sunnydale's more modern conveniences. Even small towns in California could not escape the pervasive pleasures of the coffee craze. By the time Xander met Anya there, the afternoon was getting on, but the trade was bustling. Despite how close Xander and Anya were sitting, the waitress gave Xander a special smile as she delivered their drinks.

"She smiled at you," Anya said flatly.

"Ahn, people smile at each other. It's part of being polite."

"That was no 'your money is good here, thanks for the custom' smile. That was an 'I like your eyes' smile," she contested.

"Ahn, I didn't ask you to meet me so we could talk about the waitress."

"I'm glad you did call. I wasn't sure what to do with myself while you had your secret meeting," Anya said. "I think your friends might have included me. Where are your special friends, anyway?"

"Anya, there wasn't any secret meeting! Willow was just trying to make sure we didn't drift apart. I'm sure you were welcome to come to the museum too," he mollified. "I feel bad now that I bailed on them."

"I thought you were looking forward to your secret meeting. What happened?"

"Anya! It wasn't a secret meeting."

"Whatever you say."

Ignoring her jealousy of his friends, Xander said, "It turned out the trip to the museum was to see a *mummy*. I chickened out."

"That's right. Your last girlfriend was an ex-demon too."

"She was not a girlfriend! And she wasn't 'ex' when I met her; she was very much the demon-demon. Thanks to Buffy, she's an ex-everything. She really freaked me out."

"Well, I know that mixed relationships can be difficult. The last human boyfriend I had is an ogre now."

"Not making me feel better, Ahn. In fact, queasy now."

Josh came running up to the couple.

"Xander, I'm glad I found someone. Do you know where Buffy is? Or Willow? I've got to find them!" He wheezed, out of breath.

"Whoa, Josh. Cool down. What's the matter?" Xander asked.

"Would you care for a caffeinated beverage?" asked Anya, being helpful.

"No, I haven't got time to explain. I think I've done something really bad. Willow and Buffy might be the only ones who know what to do." Josh was less breathless, but seemed to be getting more agitated. He hadn't sat down and was shifting his weight from foot to foot.

"Well, I left them all at the museum, but I'm sure they've finished there by now," said Xander. "We were all going to meet at the Bronze in a little while, so they probably went to Giles's place to check in." Xander rattled off the address. "Look, we'll come with you."

"Xander Harris. You cannot invite me out for coffee then just run off any time someone mentions your Buffy. You're with me now and we will meet your little friends at the Bronze tonight." This was the most assertive Anya had been in quite a while, and Xander began to realize just how deep their relationship was becoming. He had already been beating himself up over bailing on one group of friends; he couldn't bail on Anya, too. Besides, Josh wasn't waiting for the lovebirds to sort it out. He had already begun to take off in the direction of Giles's apartment.

"Okay, Ahn. I hear you. Buffy can handle it. I bet Josh is just freaked out about Bruce Carter dying so weirdly, especially after that fight Buffy broke up yesterday. Probably blaming himself."

"That's my sweetie," said Anya, brightening up. "Understanding and funny, and so cute! Here's the bill."

"Yes, well, I think it is precipitous to act on this just now. Mr. Carter's death may have been perfectly normal for all we know," said Giles as he cleared the cluttered desk in his cozy living room. Giles's apartment had become the Scoobie Gang's meeting place since the high school was demolished by the Mayor-snake. "Buffy, why don't you take an extra patrol around the campus and neighboring streets tonight, and

Willow, you see if there is anything of interest on the computer."

The little group of girls had met in Giles's home as soon as they had finished with the museum. While Willow had been making her class notes and looking at ancient artifacts, Buffy had been feeling little tingles at the back of her ponytail. That's all it was sometimes: just a little discomfort or itchy spot that kept returning her to the idea of something not natural at work in Sunnydale. That was a part of her training—to listen and feel for these little signs. Giles said that was what would keep her alive. And so far he had been right.

The gathering was disturbed by a knock at the front door. Giles wiped some dust from his hands and answered the knock. Revealed on the sunny porch was Josh.

"Hello, young man. Can I be of assistance?" asked Giles.

"Josh! What are you doing here? How did you find us?" asked Willow coming forward.

"I saw Xander and Anya at the Expresso Pump. They gave me the address," Josh answered.

"Right, I remember now. Josh Headly. You were around for some of that difficulty with that odious little Principal Snyder. Weren't you suspended for some magick paraphernalia he found in your locker?" Giles asked.

"That's right."

"Well, you look a little upset. Why don't you come in and I'll make some tea. That always settles me a bit." Giles moved to the Spanish style apartment's tiny tiled kitchen. Buffy closed the front door and showed Josh to the couch. Willow sat down next to him with Tara and Buffy perching opposite.

"What's the sitch?" asked Buffy, all business. She knew that little tingle of hers had just come calling.

"I really didn't mean for it to get out of hand. Willow, you'll understand," he started, searching Willow's face for signs of their old friendship.

"Uh-oh. What did you do?" Willow asked. Her guard went up as she remembered their last spell attempt. Willow watched carefully as Josh began to squirm a bit under the girls' combined stare.

"I just wanted to have some protection. You know, so I could look after myself without Buffy." This came out almost as a whine. Josh plunged into the story, recalling his encounter with Bruce. "So I began to think about some of the stuff we used to try. I thought if I used magick to protect myself I would be more independent. Less trouble for everyone."

Josh then described the spell and its shocking results.

"What was the spirit's name?" jumped in Giles as he placed the steaming tea down in front of Josh.

"He called himself Sesostris, and said he was a priest of Anubis," Josh explained. "Anyway, he made me take him to the old high school. Something about a door to the underworld, but I was so scared I don't remember all the details. Sesostris went away somewhere, I think down a tunnel near where the old library used to be." The group exchanged significant looks. "But when he came back it was like he had been colorized! Like an old black-and-white movie gone all TNN. He was Technicolored. But he was even scarier. I could sort of see his eyes glowing in the dark, and he seemed more solid somehow."

"The Hellmouth revivified him." Giles pondered. "If that's the case then we can now expect this spirit to be able to affect things on our plane of existence."

"But that's what happened!" Josh was getting visibly more upset now. "I wanted protection, but I didn't want him to kill Bruce!"

Buffy leaned in closer. "What happened?"

"Sesostris told me that I had been a good servant; he called me his jackal. Then he said he was created to judge the souls of man. He would drain all the life from those he found wanting. He must have read my mind then and gone right to Bruce. I don't know what happened after that, because he just left me there at the ruins. I heard about Bruce at school today and I know it was Sesostris!"

"Josh, what you have done was decidedly unwise," Giles admonished softly. "There is a coven of witches in England—very grounded, Earth worshipers. They taught me at an early age, not that I listened naturally, the basic rule of the universe: 'Ever mind the rule of three. All you do comes back to thee.' We shall yet see what you have released on us, Josh, and what the repercussions will be." Giles stood and, wiping his glasses preparatory to reading, he approached the locked glass cabinet. "If my suspicion is correct we have a difficult situation on our hands—but not impossible."

Giles leafed through a book, replaced it, and tried another. There was a little silence in the room behind him and glances were exchanged between Willow, Josh, and Tara. Buffy didn't miss this, but though it best to keep her suspicions about a burgeoning magick circle to herself.

"Ah," Giles called from his desk, "here we have it. Yes indeed, this Sesostris is mentioned." Giles addressed the group as if giving a lecture. "There is much speculation amongst early watchers about the origins of vampirism, and a great deal of clues seem to point to Ancient Egypt. Sesostris was a very powerful priest of the Anubis cult, much feared in the ancient world. They seem to have been connected with an older Osirian cult with overtones of death and resurrection. According to an ancient Greek scroll, probably translated from an earlier Egyptian papyrus, particularly conferred on

Sesostris was a benediction of *ankh er neheh,* or 'living forever.' If this were vampirism, as some suspect, rather than simply a 'benediction,' we could be dealing with a very ancient and powerful vampire. It would seem, though, that we are fairly safe and he should be easily disposed of despite the Hellmouth's power. You see"—Giles lifted his folded glasses to his lips while he shifted his thoughts into his own past research—"the ancient Egyptian's entire religion was based on a sort of 'cult of the dead.' In preparation for a return to the physical body after death, the body was preserved by mummification. Of course with mortals there was no return of the soul to the flesh, but the texts point to vampirism in the case of Sesostris because they go on to state that Sesostris was so feared for his judgements and the subsequent deaths of many, that the priests of Aten, the sun God, disposed of him. More pointedly this Sesostris was too powerful to simply kill, so they vanquished his soul from his body, then mummified the body."

Giles smiled as he mentally returned to the room. The group waited, but he was putting away his books as though the lecture were complete.

"But, the spirit?" asked Willow.

"Hmm? Oh well, there should be little to hold him to this plane without his body to return to, even with support from the local Hellmouth. I expect his powers will fade all on their own. His true search, you see, is for his body, and as there are no Ancient Egyptian burial sites in Sunnydale, we may not even have to search him out." He looked at the ground and then sidelong at Josh. "Our young man here may have a little to answer for, though." Giles looked long at Josh, measuring, but said nothing further.

"Oh boy. There *is* a mummy in town," said Buffy suddenly.

"That's right. We just came from seeing it!" said Willow, lighting up. "Let me get my notes." She pulled out her backpack and found a spiral-bound notebook. "Here: 'Remains of a first dynasty mummy, as yet unidentified, though the spells and incantations on the wrappings and outer casings suggest a connection to the priesthood of Anubis.' That's what the display said."

"Oh, God," came from Josh, sinking into his chair. They all swiveled to look at him with one movement. "Sesostris said that he thought he would be drawn down if he were near his body! I just remembered that."

Giles light attitude had faded during these revelations and he now looked quite ashen.

"Rather a different light on things," he muttered, then added more forcefully, "If we are indeed to be facing this spirit vampire reunited with his Earthly remains, we could be preparing for a difficult battle. This is a very ancient creature, and may be almost indestructible."

The gang was quiet for a moment, then Buffy, always preferring action, grabbed her pack and started for the door. "Right. I'm off to fight mummies again. I can get to the body before the spirit does."

"Wait," said Giles rising. "I'll join you, Buffy. Willow, Tara, and Josh, go back to Josh's rooms and see if you can find a way to reverse the conjuring. Try to use the same formula Josh began with. Perhaps between you, you can send him back before he reaches his body. And for Heaven's sake, protect yourselves!" He opened the door for all to leave and Xander jumped back, his hand outstretched to knock.

"Yikes! I was just seeing where everyone had got to. I left Anya at the Bronze to come find you. Why do you look all apocolyp-ty?"

"Explain on the way," clipped Buffy. "Got a mummy to rebury." She grabbed a bewildered Xander by the shoulder of his jacket as they filed out the door.

"*Noooo!*"

• • •

"So you two knew each other in high school?" Tara ventured.

"Yeah, we used to hang." Josh said, a little quietly—quietly enough that Tara knew there was a little more to the story. They were in Josh's room back at the campus, and Tara and Willow were sifting the piles of belongings for a place to settle.

"It was kind of my fault," Willow spoke up. "I really didn't mean to freak you out with that spell that time."

"It's okay. We just sorta drifted. No biggie." Josh shrugged off the apology.

"No, really. I want you to know that I really liked spending time with you." There was an awkward pause. Tara looked around.

"Well, we should get started. Do you have any ritual supplies left?" Willow asked, mainly to ease away from the conversation that seemed to be going nowhere. "We'll need salt and sulfur, and copper sulfate if you have any. I think three rings of protection should do it."

They went to work quietly. The process wasn't hard, and the two girls seemed to really have the system down. Soon they all sat inside the protective circles strewn with herbs and were ready to start.

"Call the quarters," said Willow, and Tara responded, going to each direction and inviting the protective spirits of the elements to watch over them. Josh held the old grimoire and handed it over to Willow, who seemed to be in charge.

They began the ritual and reversed the incantations from the order Josh had used. This time the results were instantaneous. As soon as the word "Sesostris" passed into the air the creature itself appeared. Josh had not exaggerated; Sesostris was much more "present" than the girls had imagined.

"Jackal! Again you play with your tiny sparks of magick," boomed Sesostris. "And whom have you brought with you?

More mortal souls for me to judge?" The tall, lean figure of the Egyptian priest stepped forward but suddenly stopped. His foot lay outside the first of the three circles on the ground. "Sorceresses? Be you high priestesses? Be you servants of Aten?" He shot the questions out rapidly, not giving the stricken girls a chance to answer. "What manner of trickery is this, jackal?"

"Spirit of low order, spirit of ill intent, you cannot enter this circle," spouted Willow. The three rings on the floor began to glow first a deep violet-blue, then the color intensified. At the same moment, the room began to fill with smoke and wind, like the elements from outside had just begun a polite little gale inside Josh's room. Books and papers, socks, and furniture began to spin around the room.

"Fools!" thundered Sesostris, who suddenly morphed into his true vampire face. "Look at you, animals waiting to be butchered in a slaughter-tent. Tiny sparks of life will not threaten me. That one is mine already! He called me forth from the spirit realm but had no pretty circle of sulfur to burn arrant ghosts. I claim what is mine."

Suddenly Josh made a little croaking noise and fell to the ground. He lay there blinking and shivering as Sesostris watched and conjured from the center of the storm.

"What's this?" said Sesostris abruptly. "I have his thoughts! There is more trickery here! There is a *slayer* in this place. So the lineage of demon-blooded fighters for humanity still lingers. Where, boy? Where?"

Josh began to turn white and his skin began to show tiny little wrinkles. It was like a frost descended on this face and the veins and tendons were peaking through the cold parchment covering.

"What connection have you with a slayer? There! I see it." The monster's furrowed brow reddened with his concentration; his gold jewelry glinted in contrast to his white skin. Suddenly he leaped back and cried, "My body! You know where it lies. And this secret you would keep from me. You work to separate me once again from the mortal world. A jackal is but a dog after all." Sesostris raised his arm and made a grasping motion in the air with his hand.

As suddenly as Josh's fit began . . . it stopped. Josh didn't move again. A thin line of spittle leaked from his open mouth to the floor. Willow and Tara pulled back from cradling Josh's body and held each other in the center of the three protective circles. Sesostris turned to face the two girls.

"You are true sorceresses then. I cannot reach you now, but I judge you vile tools of Aten, and you shall feel the price of your chosen path after I have been made flesh once again." And with that, the spirit was gone, and all the flying socks and debris dropped to the ground as silent and still as their owner.

The Sunnydale Natural History Museum rose up rather more menacingly at night than it had in the warm California sun that afternoon. The reddish bricks looked somehow rougher, with more of a sandpaper finish, and the wood frames to the old doors and windows seemed dingy with crackled paint. The entire building had an abandoned and disused feeling. Giles, Buffy, and Xander veered from the streetlights and the open entryway to creep along the side of the building, flattening themselves against the wall.

"Just a nice cool beer at the Bronze with my buds. That's all I wanted: good friends, my girl Anya at my side, a pleasant never-another-school-night evening," said Xander, continuing the constant stream of chatter he had kept up since they told him where they were going. "But no. Alexander Harris has to be a hero. Has to fight the mummy-monster. Has to look after his Buffy-friend. . . . Anya is going to kill me. She thinks I'm having secret meetings."

"Do be quiet, Xander," snapped Giles from ahead of him. Xander looked around. The trees on the grounds were wagging and waving. One looked just like a dragon's head. He could see the crest of scales surrounding the leafy neck and the tongue wagging around in the yawning mouth.

"*Gotta* get a grip."

They had reached the back entry to the museum. From here it was an easy path through the delivery bay. They just needed to get in.

"Okay, Xander. Do your military shtick," whispered Buffy.

"What? You mean I'm supposed to get us in?" stammered Xander back.

"Of course. Who else?" said Buffy. "Now get to it."

"Oh, for Heaven's sake." Giles pulled out a lock-pick kit. "I will attend to this. You two watch for the security guard." The lock was undone with alacrity.

Xander looked at the coffin shaped opening in the rough wall facing him, seven feet by four feet. He froze. "I'm not facing another mummy. One mummy is all anyone could ask me to fight, right?"

"Well you could stay and guard the door, but it hardly seems of much purpose, and you're sure to encounter the guard on his rounds," Giles said.

"Really, Xander, you're safer with us than waiting here," Buffy added as she dropped her pack and began pulling out an armament of stakes and a stout ax. As always, Xander had to smile to himself to see the petite girl he'd known since high school, wielding an incongruously huge ax. But he knew she could use it, too.

"Okay. A priest of Anubis, you say. I'm in. How bad could it be?"

• • •

The Sunnydale Hospital was one place Willow had seen just a little too much of. She was glad to have Tara there with her. Of course, in a town where a Hellmouth happened to yawn open in the ground, the hospital would naturally be a bit busier than most.

As soon as Sesostris had vanished, the girls had hastily taken down their protections, cleaned up the salt and chemicals on the floor, and removed the magickal trappings from the room. They knew that they needed to call the police and an ambulance and Josh's family, but things would just be difficult if there was evidence of a witchcraft ritual all around. Josh's withered state would be oddity enough.

The two girls worked very fast to tidy the room but not move the body. They also took the big book out of Josh's hands. It was only a few minutes to Tara's room from Josh's, so she went to drop off the stuff while Willow made the calls and waited for Josh's family to arrive. It had been a long wait and unsettling to be in the room with the body of someone who had once been a friend, lifeless now and awfully still.

The girls had done their best to come up with an explanation about what happened, how Josh had had a sudden seizure and collapsed. Josh's mother was taking the news very badly, and it broke the girls' spirits to see the family's grief in such a raw display. Josh had always told Willow about his parents' extraordinary support.

Willow and Tara had gone to the hospital on their own, letting the family take charge and following along after. Now they sat outside the emergency ward in the little reception area. It was odd how the colors, textures, and low lighting in that room were deliberately set to induce calm, but achieved the opposite. The atmosphere was edgy. Maybe it was that ever-present hospital smell. Whatever it was, it made the mood somber, and Willow and Tara sat together on the stiff couch, not talking.

"I guess this was what Mr. Giles was talking about," ventured Tara.

"Oh, sweetie, I don't think he meant that Josh would *die* from working that spell. He just meant that there would be a negative reaction of some kind."

"I know, but the whole thing makes me worry. You know. About us. The magicks we've been experimenting with." Tara's eyes were beginning to well up with tears. Willow realized for the first time how terribly sensitive Tara was to the events the Scooby Gang was forced to witness. It came with the territory. She thought about how much she herself had been through since the little gang had formed. Was she getting immune to the deaths and the violence? No, seeing Mr. and Mrs. Headly tonight had assured her that wasn't the case. She turned and gave Tara a reassuring hug.

Tara just sat looking down, but she kept speaking. "You are really strong, Willow. I mean, you've survived the end of the world. A couple of times." She sniffed and made a little laugh at how impossible that sounded. Looking up to meet Willow's eyes, she said, "I didn't know Josh. We'd just met, and now he's gone. And that creature threatened us. I guess I'm a little over-whelmed."

Willow loosened her hug just a little bit. "Tara, we're going to be fine. There is nothing to worry about. What happened to Josh was because he mishandled his spell. He didn't use any protection and that allowed the spirit in. Josh was under the spirit's control because he was careless. That will never happen to us, because we know how protect and defend ourselves. Right?"

Tara nodded but didn't say anything.

It was a quick climb past the labeling and sorting offices, with their trestle tables of artifacts, and up into the main gallery of the museum. Buffy, Giles, and Xander entered the marble hall single file from the opposite side from the cafeteria and got their bearings.

"Now, if all is as it should be, the protective bindings and amulets hidden within the mummy's bandages should hold the body of Sesostris inviolable. Before he gained strength from the Hellmouth, he would have been unable to affect anything in this dimension, thus preventing him from ever removing the protections. Now we must reach the corpse before he does, since he is substantial enough to take action here. This will be a battle of wits and timing, Buffy. In his semispirit form he will be too insubstantial for you to inflict any real damage with traditional fighting techniques," relayed Giles.

"Great. Do I talk him to death?"

"While I have little doubt about the efficacy of your skills in that area, I hardly think it necessary."

Buffy blinked. "Did you say what I think you said?"

"Never mind," Giles continued. "Here is our approach. I will try to reinforce the protective spells and keep the spirit at a distance. You will stand prepared to fight the creature should my efforts fail."

"What do I do?" asked Xander earnestly, caught up in the planning. Giles and Buffy just looked at him.

"No, no. Not bait. I'm not the bait. Been there, was almost eaten."

"Don't be silly. The spirit is here for the body he once inhabited. There need be no bait but that," Giles said. "You will be the second line of defense should Buffy and I need assistance."

"I can do that. Assist in the mummy snuffing. Then back to the Bronze to explain everything to Anya, which is the really scary task."

"Very well then. On we go." Giles took the lead and they filed across the entrance hall, made cavernous in the half-light, toward the featured exhibit. Once inside the faux tomb entrance, it seemed as though they were a thousand miles away in Egypt, ascending an ancient stairway to the king's chamber. At the top of the stairs the way was barred by another stage prop entrance, and Buffy pushed aside the Styrofoam stone doors to allow them passage to the tomb proper.

Inside, the elaborate museum display gave all appearances of being a real underground tomb. Piled in the corners was rubble and broken crockery. The only giveaway was that the artifacts themselves were encased in display boxes artistically built into the walls. Here and there would be a freestanding display with a pinpoint spotlight making the treasures they contained appear to be lit from within.

At the far end of the room, and partially hidden by a turning in the stone wall, was the mummy itself. The stone casing and protective sarcophagus were lovingly presented in *situ* as if they had just been uncovered. But the body of the high priest himself was eerily propped on a slanting board, protected in its glass case, and made to look particularly creepy by the overhead light—like a kid might hold a flashlight over his head.

"Nice," said Xander.

Buffy stood on her tiptoes to look down into the casing at the mummy's face. The skin was nearly black and stretched like saran, taut over the bones of the face. The mummy's features were aquiline, with a high bridge of nose making him look regal and noble somehow. The neck had shriveled down to look like that of a vulture, but the effect on this long-dead body was aesthetic, bookish—like they were looking down on a sleeping scholar who had neglected his meals in favor of his studies.

"Look, here . . . and here," said Giles as he pointed out the little amulets hidden in the bandages and revealed only by the telltale bulges against the tight wrappings. "We are in time; the body hasn't been touched."

Before any of the trio could prepare for it, however, there was an explosion of wind and smoke. The room shook as if to make room for the sudden intrusion of mass in it's confined space. Giles was thrown against a display cabinet where he slumped unconscious.

Buffy and Xander were on the other side of the mummy and received less of the blow. They landed together in a heap.

"Slayer!" bellowed Sesostris. "Prepare to die. You will witness the rebirth of an ancient, then give up your blood to me in sacrifice."

"Do we know each other?" quipped Buffy. Xander crept over to Giles and pulled him into a far corner near the door.

"I know your kind, born as I was in the *Zep Tepi,* the First Times. You are mortal, but made from other-than-mortal. Your kind emerged from the dim times to plague us who were rightful rulers. I was given the strong blood of Anubis himself, and through him I have many memories from the before-times. If you understood your powers you would find these memories too, for your blood is like unto mine. And your blood will swell my dead skin and invigorate my petrified tendons."

Buffy didn't wait for this speech to reach its conclusion. "I've heard it," she said as she threw a powerful kick into the spirit's midsection. As Giles had predicted, the kick landed, but felt like it went through thin Jell-O.

Sesostris swung a blow at Buffy's head and it connected with an unfair strength. *What happened to the Jell-O?* Again she got up, took her stance, and waited until he was moving toward her to add his momentum to her blow, but again it connected with less force that she would have wished.

"You tire me, Slayer," said Sesostris as he turned away from

her. With a blow of his fist he smashed not Buffy, but the display
case containing his mummified body. Glass flew everywhere,
and Xander and Buffy had to cover their heads from flying
shards. Sesostris picked up a large piece of the broken glass and
began slicing away at the mummy's wrappings. The brittle cloth
shred easily, and dust, threads, and little stone figures fell to the
ground.

"We could both rush him," said Xander low to Buffy. He had
sidled around the display room until he was standing beside her.

"It wouldn't work. He isn't formed enough," Buffy whispered
back. "I don't think we have any choice. I can't kill him in spirit,
so I'll kill him in the flesh. If Willow, Tara, and Josh can't stop
him, we'll have to wait until he's in that body, and then . . ." She
let the idea of the fight ahead hang there.

The specter of Sesostris was hacking through the last wrappings, seeming not to care if he damaged the body beneath. He
was in a frenzy of excitement, jabbering to himself in his own
ancient tongue. He abruptly stopped and stepped back. Buffy
and Xander could see the shriveled body now revealed. All the
clothing left to it was shreds of cloth. They could see the deep
scars of the ancient embalmer's knife, the oddly flattened ribs
fighting for release from their leathery covering, the body en-
gendered both awe and sadness.

Now Sesostris raised his hands to the sky and intoned, "Great
Anubis, Lord of the Underworld, I return to the realm of the
flesh as you promised me I would. I will act in your name. Let
judgement begin."

And with that, the room seemed saturated with shadows and
movement, like all manner of spirits had arrived at once and were
dancing around a fire. Buffy and Xander watched as the flickering
image of Sesostris stepped forward, then *into* the archaic body. As
the spirit merged with the flesh, it drew all the jittering dark

shadow-forms in with it, and the thirsty corpse absorbed them in an instant. There was a silent pause, and then the dried thing on the slab began to move.

At first it moved slowly, tentatively, with a sound of twisting leather. Then all at once it jumped up and came forward like a predatory spider. The illusion they had seen of a starved scholar vanished, as did all pity for the abandoned corpse. That body was very much inhabited now.

"At last! I am flesh. Let the mortal world quake before me." Sesostris's voice seemed as strong as ever, giving lie to the desiccated form in front of them. The two watched in horrified fascination as the muscles and tendons of that ancient mummy strove spasmodically to respond to the instructions of its owner. Then the face morphed. The exaggerated brow of the vampire was exceptionally horrid to see fashioned from the grainy dried skin. The withered creature looked almost burnished with a soft shine that rendered each harsh line unnaturally clear in the dim light.

The sight of the vampire face made Buffy come out of her spell.

"Okay. Just a bag of twigs. I can do this." She leaped toward the half-naked monstrosity, finding a sure two-footed landing in its midsection. Buffy had expected the skin would crumble and she might even punch through it, but it was more like fighting beef jerky. The body was very tough, and she fell sideways from the reflected blow. She was up in a second and coming again. Sesostris swung and connected with her shoulder and chest, flinging Buffy against a wall. The wall fell away to reveal the chicken wire and foam understructure. Buffy was up again. This time she tried to thrust a stake forward, but the stringy arm of the mummy swung and knocked the weapon out of her hand. Next he was holding her shoulders and trying to bring his fangs toward her throat.

Xander threw himself on the creature's back hoping to pry its hold loose from Buffy. It worked for a second, until Xander found himself looking up from the floor on the other side of the room.

"Such insignificant lives, and yet you struggle so," Sesostris whispered intimately into Buffy's ear as his attention came back to her. He had his taloned hand about her throat now and Buffy was definitely in trouble.

Xander shook his head clear and stood up.

"Alright, fighty-fight not working." He started to look around the floor for a weapon, running a list in under his breath. "Stake, not here. Sun, hours away. Fire would be good." Then he noticed the little amulets and protective images that had fallen from the mummy's bandages. "A cross?"

Buffy was struggling in the crispy grip of the vampire when Xander flung the little amulets at Sesostris's back.

"Ahhh!" The vampire dropped Buffy and turned to face this new distraction. There were little smoky burned patches on his skin where the amulets had done their thing.

"Buffy, the stake!" Xander cried. Buffy, bent and coughing, spotted the stake and made a grab for it. Just as Sesostris was about to return to her, Xander held out an ankh.

"Looks like a cross. Hope it works like a cross."

"*That* is a symbol of eternal life, child, not a weapon." Sesostris sneered, grabbing the ankh from Xander's hand and tossing it aside. Sesostris was distracted just long enough for Buffy to retrieve the stake and lunge, but the wood couldn't penetrate the mummy's rubbery hide. Sesostris turned his attention back to Buffy, which gave Xander the time to retrieve a shard of glass and wade into the fight.

Buffy was alternating left and right punches and saw Xander coming in. She grabbed Sesostris and spun him about so the loathsome vampire was facing Xander.

"Cut him!" she shouted. "Over the heart, so I can get the stake in!"

Sesostris was thrashing wildly in her hold, but she had successfully pinned his arms back and had him immobile.

"Me?" was Xander's reply. "Okey-dokey." With his eyes half squeezed shut, he lunged. It took a little hacking, but he managed to saw a little rip in the creature's chest, when suddenly Sesostris made a violet jerk forward in a bid to free himself from Buffy and Xander found his arm buried half way into the dead thing's chest.

"Heart! Heart!" squeaked Buffy.

"Oh, man." Xander wiggled his fingers in the dried innards. He gave a quick search with his hand of the stringy insides and feeling something like a shriveled plum, he yanked. The room filled with a loud thrumming that resolved into an ascending scream that faded into a ghostly echo. Sesostris's body exploded into skin fragments, bone chips and dust and the room was silent.

In the moments following, both Buffy and Xander, breathing heavily, became aware of another wailing noise: an alarm.

"Can you carry Giles?" Buffy asked urgently.

"Fireman style."

"Leaves me free to fight if I have to. Let's go." Buffy helped Xander heave Giles over his shoulder, and they made their way as fast as they could to the rear entrance they came in by.

"So Josh didn't make it?" asked Anya. She had gone to Giles's place to find Xander when no one showed up at the Bronze. The gang was all assembled now to help Giles, who had come around with the sunrise.

"I . . . I'm sorry to say, we had a casualty," ventured Tara. Willow and she looked gloomily around at their friends.

"I'm sorry about your friend," Giles offered, replacing the damp padding on his forehead. "The universe mandates that there be consequences to all actions, particularly magickal actions. Those witches who abide by the these universal laws strive to act in ways that cause the least harm to themselves, to others, and to the Earth and its inhabitants." He recited the last words of the wiccan rede: "Eight words the wiccan rede fulfill. An ye harm none, do what ye will."

"I'll call his mom today," Buffy said, breaking the silence following Giles's lecture.

"Do you think there's anything we can do?" Anya asked. "I don't know how to handle these things. Xander?"

"No, we spent all night with his family. We went to the hospital with them," Willow answered. "Let the family have some time."

Although he didn't say anything, Xander pulled Anya a little closer. He was relieved to find she wasn't still mad about his sudden disappearance last night. Things were good. He might even really be in love, and that thought brightened the sadness and made his terror of mummies feel very far away.

There was another quiet moment.

"Well, I seem to be getting quite adept at this," Giles said, hoping to lighten the mood. "I'm making an art of being knocked unconscious. Can I assume that, as I remember nothing of last night, and the sun is indeed shining this morning, that we have averted disaster once more?"

"I think it's safe to say civilization is going to last a few more days," Buffy answered.

"If that's what we may call it," added Giles getting up to make tea.

Lady Shobu

Kara Dalkey

SAGAMI PROVINCE, JAPAN, 980

Whistling Arrows

"Ai! Ai! Ai!" Kishi Minomoto yelled to her pony, digging her knees into its flanks. She dropped the reins on the pony's neck and held her bamboo bow at the ready. The pony's hooves pounded the Kanto Plain, releasing the scent of damp summer grasses. The air was heavy with the promise of another evening storm, and thunder rumbled in the distance.

Kishi stood in the stirrups, taking the pony's gait on the balls of her feet and in the bend of her knees. She drew the bowstring taut, pulling her hand back by her ear, as she rode closer . . . closer. Then, just before passing the straw-man-in-armor, *twang!* She let loose her arrow.

With a satisfying thunk, the arrow lodged in the chest of the target. "Hai!" Kishi raised her fists into the air as the pony carried her toward her waiting brothers. She was glad they were letting her practice with real arrows today, instead of the blunt whistling arrows whose only use was to signal the beginning of battle. Now she *knew* she would be ready for the tournament.

"Very good, Kishi!" said her elder brother, Higashi. "If I were a man made of straw, I would be very afraid of you. Now we had better go home. The storm is coming in."

"One more run!" said Kishi, flushed with her success. "I will do it again, and this time I will hit the neck." The neck was a small but prime target, least likely to be armored, most likely to be fatal.

"But it's getting dark," complained her younger brother, Hiroi.

"That only makes it a better challenge," said Kishi, turning her pony for another run past the target. "I want to be ready for the Dragon Horse Tournament."

Higashi sighed and shook his head.

Hiroi said, "You're not a boy, and you're only fifteen, Kishi."

Kishi looked over her shoulder at him while she nocked another arrow to the bowstring. "I will compete in a mask. People do it all the time. Besides, I'm tall for my age. No one will know. Don't be jealous, little brother. You will have your turn someday."

"And what will you do if you win your dragon horse, Kishi?" asked Higashi. "Hide it? Give it as a bride-gift to your husband-to-be, Matsuo?"

"Nonsense," said Kishi. "I will . . . I will donate it to the Hachiman Shrine. Maybe Bennin will let me visit the horse sometimes." She made sure her wide sleeves were still tied securely back.

"Have you told papa you're going to compete? Maybe someone ought to," said Hiroi.

Kishi glared at Hiroi and then smiled a ferocious grin. "Why don't we wrestle for it after I'm done here? If you win, you can tell Papa. If I win, you don't."

"No," moaned Hiroi. "You always win."

"Right." Kishi nodded once and cantered her pony into position at the far end of the field.

"Sometimes I think you forget you're a girl!" Hiroi called after her.

"That is the whole *point*, little brother," Kishi muttered to herself. She held up her bow in the ready position and nudged the pony forward with her knees. "Hajime!"

The pony began to run, and again Kishi rose off the saddle, standing in the stirrups. *Blessed Hachiman, let my arrow find my enemy,* she prayed. Kishi aimed her arrow as the target neared. She let fly—

"Lady Kishi!"

"Yi!" Kishi herself went flying as her pony stopped suddenly. She landed in a muddy puddle as thunder boomed and rumbled overhead.

Her two brothers erupted in peals of laugher as Kishi grunted, stood, and tried to brush the mud off. In front of her was the family chamberlain sitting on his plain brown horse. "Lady Kishi, are you all right?"

"Yes, of course I'm all right, Sankumo-*san*." Kishi had fallen off her pony many times and never broken a bone . . . unlike her brothers. "What do you want?"

"You have a visitor at the mansion. You must come at once."

Kishi sighed. "Oh, not now! Who is it? Is it Matsuo?"

"It is an important personage. That is all I know," said Sankumo. "A bath will be waiting for you."

"Thank you. You are living up to your name and clouding my day," said Kishi.

"If it will make you feel any better," said Sankumo, "look there, my lady." He tilted his chin toward the target.

Kishi looked. Her arrow had penetrated precisely between the helmet cord and the breastplate of the target. Kishi smiled.

An Important Personage

As Kishi soaked in the barrel of hot water, steam rose like wraiths around her and floated out to the rainy courtyard beyond. Kishi poked playfully with a finger at the steam ghosts, as if stabbing each one with a sword. Thunder rumbled almost continuously outside, and Kishi remembered her grandmother's stories of how thunder was caused by the sky dragons snapping their tails.

The servants had been evasive about her visitor, but their anxious, intense glances suggested that something had changed. They had behaved this way when Kishi's grandfather had died. *I hope it is not bad news. Perhaps Matsuo's father has come to discuss our marriage with my father.*

Kishi was content with her father's choice of bridegroom for her. At least Matsuo had seemed to enjoy her tales of how she mastered the short sword at nine years old and could now throw a spear farther than her elder brother. Kishi thanked Hachiman that she had been born into a noble warrior clan. She didn't have to play at the social niceties that girls of higher—or higher-striving—families did in order to be ladies.

Her handmaid arrived with towels and evening-informal kimonos to wear. As Kishi dressed—first the white under-kimono, then a layer of yellow, then an over-kimono of green shading to golden brown—she said to the maid, "It can't be a *terribly* important personage if I'm not asked to wear brocades."

"I was told there wasn't time for formality," said the maid. "Your visitor is an old friend of the family. You won't even need a screen of modesty."

"Thank Hachiman for that," said Kishi. "The only good thing about a *kicho* is that you can make silly faces at someone without them seeing you." Kishi tied her long hair back with a simple silk ribbon and followed the maid into the mansion. She was led to the lesser formal dining hall, where her father and mother were already seated on floor cushions with teacups and bowls of rice. Kishi's stomach growled.

And then it clenched as she saw the fourth personage in the room: an old man in the white hunting kimono of a Shinto priest and wide green trousers that showed he was of Third Rank nobility. He wore a broad, round straw hat from which hung a veil of black silk netting to keep off the bite of summer insects.

"Kishi, you remember Bennin-*san,* don't you? From the Hachiman Shrine?" asked her father.

Kishi said, "Yes, of course. You helped bless our new stables when they were built. And you performed Hiroi's trouser ceremony when he turned seven." She bowed low in greeting, but also to hide her distress. *Bennin is here because he has somehow learned that I intend to compete in his shrine's tournament. And he has told Father. I am in big trouble.*

"Bennin has had that honor, yes." The old man's voice was lower, more resonant than she had remembered. But it had been a long while since she'd last seen him. "And now I hope I shall perform a task to bring even greater honor . . . to you."

"Honor? Me?" On a flight of fancy, Kishi wondered if word of her archery prowess had already spread so far that she was going to be allowed to compete openly. Exceptions were made, on rare occasions—especially for the nobility. Perhaps she could win her dragon horse after all. Kishi looked at the faces of her parents and saw a mixture of pride and sorrow . . . and a bit of fear. "What is it?"

"Kishi-*chan,*" said her father, his voice breaking so that he had to clear his throat, "Bennin has informed us that you are called to serve as a lady-in-waiting in Heian Kyo, at the Imperial Palace."

Thunder cracked and boomed overhead. "The heavens themselves congratulate you, Kishi-*san*," said Bennin. Kishi had the impression that, behind his black veil, he was smiling.

Kishi's stomach now felt as though it had fallen to the floor. "The . . . the Imperial Palace?"

Her mother added, "You are to serve the Great Lady Ankimon-in. She is a *Fujiwara* and a cousin of the *emperor*."

Kishi's mouth fell open. "A *Fujiwara*?" Fujiwara was the highest ranking nobility next to the imperial family itself. "W-why me?"

"All will be explained as we journey to the capital," said Bennin.

"When will I go, then? This autumn?" Spring and autumn were traditional times for new ladies to be presented at court.

"I am afraid we must leave at once. Tonight, in fact," the old priest said.

"Tonight?" Kishi looked again at her parents and now the sorrow in their eyes was understandable. "But—I must say proper good-byes."

"You may send all the letters you like from the palace," said Bennin.

But the competition! "Forgive me, holy one, but . . . but I . . . had plans!" Kishi protested. "What about . . . what about Matsuo?"

"Your service at the palace," said her father, "will enhance your noble reputation. Matsuo will consider himself most fortunate for this rise in your status, even though it means the wedding must be postponed."

"And if he does not," her mother added, "what better place to find another suitor, possibly of even higher rank?"

But I don't want another suitor of even higher rank! thought Kishi. She'd seen glimpses of high noblemen from the capital on trips to the shrine. They were plump and pasty-faced and weak and simpering and the Minomoto made fun of them, just as the noblemen sometimes called the Minomoto "barbarians." "But—," she started to protest.

"Kishi," her father said, a roughness to his voice. "Surely you cannot be thinking of bringing dishonor to this family by refusing this summons?"

"Your father is correct," said Bennin. "A great destiny lies before you, Kishi-*san*. And if you are half the brave spirit you are said to be, you will embrace this destiny with the renowned strength of those with Minomoto blood."

Kishi felt her cheeks flush with shame. She bowed low again. "Of course I will go, Father," she heard herself say, for she knew she had no choice.

On the Tokkaido

Two hours later, as the thunderstorm eased into a constant, dismal rain, a lone ox-carriage bearing the Minomoto crest began its journey down the great eastern road, the Tokkaido.

Kishi sat within, feeling distinctly cheated. When a girl was called to the Imperial Palace, there would usually be many long good-bye parties. There would be lavish gifts to help the girl start her new life in style. Other girls from the area would be clamoring to be picked as her ladies-maids. There would be a grand procession of family and well-wishers to accompany her to the capital. But Kishi shared the ox-carriage with only one person, the priest Bennin. The only "procession" with the carriage were four outriders, consisting of the best available warriors in her clan, all cousins. *At least I am given that,* Kishi thought, sourly.

The last words her father had said at her departure had disturbed her. "May your courage and sacrifice bring honor to our blood." These were words spoken to a warrior going off to battle, not a girl who would serve as a handmaid in the Imperial Palace.

Already she was missing her parents, her servants, her brothers. Kishi tugged aside the curtain of the ox-carriage's window for a last glimpse of the Kanto Plain.

A gnarled hand stopped hers. Bennin gently pushed the curtain closed again. "There is no point in dwelling on what you have lost, Kishi-*san*. You will lose so much more—your old way of life, your innocence, even your name." He had not removed his hat and veil inside the carriage, and his wrinkled face was obscured, unreadable.

"Forgive my disrespect, holy one, but *why* is this happening?" Kishi demanded. "Why now? Why this way? This is all improper and wrong, I know it!"

Bennin inclined his head. "It is so, Kishi-*san,* because you are different. Did you never wonder why you, a girl, were consecrated at the Shrine of Hachiman, a god of war?"

Kishi paused. "I am a Minomoto. He . . . is our clan god. And I was told I might serve as a shrine maiden for a year."

"You might have, but it was decided that would not be the best training for you."

"Training? Decided by whom?"

"The Council of Watchers could not be open about it. The danger was too great. Fortunately your competitive brothers have accomplished it even better."

"Who is the Council of Watchers? What are you talking about?"

"You are no ordinary girl, Kishi-*san*. You were born to be a *oni-goroshi,* a slayer of demons. In every generation, there can be only one—a girl. The council provides one watcher to guide each slayer. It is Bennin's honor to have been called to be your watcher. And you, the new slayer, are now called to your duty."

"My . . . duty? Demons?" Kishi had not given much thought to the existence of supernatural spirits in the world. The Shinto shrines taught of gods being present in stone and water, and Buddhist priests spoke of demons that lured the unwary to bad behavior. Many in her land took it for granted that such creatures as ghosts and demons were ever-present, a part of life. A rarer few gave such beliefs public lip service and privately called it superstition.

Kishi wondered for a moment if Bennin were mad. But this was the trusted priest of their clan shrine. Her parents must have known of his beliefs. And surely a high priest would know of mysteries she did not. Kishi looked down at her hands. "Is this like those girls who are possessed by spirits, the mediums? Something I do for the shrine?"

Bennin's eyes glittered behind the veil. "It is something slayers do for the *world*, Kishi-*san*."

"The world," Kishi said, trying to understand. "Why am I summoned to this duty now, so suddenly?"

"Because your predecessor is dead, murdered by the foes you are to fight."

Kishi looked up at him in shock. "Dead? There was another slayer and she is dead?" Her heart nearly stopped in her chest. Warriors were taught to accept early death as their natural fate, even to consider themselves dead at the moment they take up the sword. In Kishi's dreams, she imagined herself invincible in battle, free from any fear of death. But real life was a different matter. Her hands began to shake and her mouth went dry.

"There is little time to prepare you," Bennin went on, "especially given that the task before you is so dangerous and dire. But you are a slayer-born, and of Minomoto blood, and there is no doubt of your courage and strength. All are counting on you to bring honor to your warrior heritage."

"I am expected to . . . kill things. Demons." Now her father's final words to her made sense. Kishí felt a cold prickle steal over her as if her skin were putting on invisible armor.

"Just so."

Kishi sat up straighter, feeling her bones take on the burden that she recognized and accepted as her destiny. "What must I do?"

"You will serve as a handmaid to the Great Lady Ankimon-in and learn all the proper arts of a lady of the Imperial Court."

"But—"

Bennin held up his hand. "This is just a cover. Someone has opened up a rift to the spirit realm in the Imperial Compound itself, threatening the very life of the Emperor and his court. Your secret appointed task is to kill any demons or evil spirits that come through the rift, find the rift, and close it."

"But—"

"Yes, others have tried," Bennin continued, "monks and priests and guardsmen. They have failed. Only a demon slayer can accomplish this task. And that slayer is you."

"Will I have warriors from the Imperial Guard to help me?"

"No, you will receive no official help. Not even the emperor knows your true identity. Your duty must be kept clean of any political taint. There are many noblemen, even within your own clan, who would like to gain power over the emperor or supplant him. If they learned who you were, they might try to use you and your powers to serve their ambitions. You can trust no one. Remember, whoever killed your predecessor, once he or she discovers you are the new slayer, will try to destroy you as well."

Kishi swallowed hard. "Why wasn't I told to bring my bow and arrows, then? Or my *tachi*? Will I be given weapons at the palace?"

Bennin's eyes opened wide. "Dear me, no! Your weapons will

have to be improvised. or extremely well hidden. To carry a weapon in the presence of the emperor is highest treason, punishable by instant execution. You must not be caught with a weapon near the imperial residence. The Council would try to intervene on your behalf, of course, should there be trouble. But many zealous men serve the emperor, and they might exact their justice before the Council could assist."

"Forgive me, holy one," said Kishi, with a sigh. "But this task sounds impossible."

"Nonetheless, you must strive to do your utmost, Kishi-*san*," said Bennin. "Bring honor to your blood and your family. For that is the duty of any warrior. Particularly a slayer."

Those Who Dwell Above The Clouds

The journey to the capital, Heian Kyo, took two days with only brief stops at inns for rest. Bennin graciously gave Kishi his servings of rice and fish, saying she had to gather her strength. They stayed secluded in either the carriage or an inn room, hidden even from the moon and sun. Bennin never removed his hat and veil, and even Kishi only got the occasional glimpse of his wrinkled face.

As they traveled Bennin instructed her in the types of creatures she might face; *oni* warriors with horselike heads, *kappa* with the body of a monkey and a turtle's shell, *tengu* in the shape of large black birds, dragons that can emerge from any body of water, and the omnipresent ghosts, who seem like the living, but who have no feet, who suck blood or life force from those they prey upon.

By the time they reached Heian Kyo, on a misty, muggy evening, Kishi was weary from travel and jittery from the knowledge of horrors she had been given. She glanced out through the ox-carriage curtain and saw the shops they passed were shuttered and the grand streets lined with willow trees were largely empty. "Where is everyone?"

"Home for safety, I expect. The Buddhist temples have been rioting again," Bennin said wryly. "For such a quiet, contemplative faith, they behave like tigers defending their patch of forest. I do not understand why this new faith has caught on with the nobility. The old ways of the gods of nature, of rock and water and air, the *kami*, are better."

"Might it be monks from one of these Buddhist temples who are bringing the demons into the palace?"

Bennin shrugged one shoulder. "Holy men who have turned to evil are not unknown. You must consider it a possibility. If that is the case, however, you must take special care. Such a foe would be formidable indeed. Ah, we are near the entrance. Look there."

Kishi peered out and saw a tree with large round fruit. No, the "fruit" was severed heads hanging by their topknots in various stages of decay. Some were mere skulls hanging by hunks of skin and hair. Kishi wanted to tear her gaze away but could not. "Is this the demons' work?"

"Oh, no, Kishi-*san*. This is the Imperial Guard's work. This is the Traitors' Tree, where those accused of plotting against the emperor are displayed to shame their families. Note that some of the skulls are misshapen; traitors are tortured by bands being tightened around their head until they confess their crimes. Pray you do not run afoul of those close to the emperor, or your head may end up here."

Kishi swallowed hard. "My predecessor, did she . . . ?"

"No. She died honorably and in secret. But even if she had not, after the foes she faced were through with her, there would have been nothing left to display."

Kishi looked down at her fingers making knots in her lap. "If you are trying to frighten me, you are succeeding, Bennin-*san*."

"Frighten you, Kishi-*san*? You have not even begun to know fear."

The ox-carriage bumped over a threshold beam and rolled into a graveled courtyard.

"Ah, we are here," said Bennin. "Remember to cover your face until you are inside. Let Lady Ankimon-in instruct you. I will inquire about your progress from time to time."

Kishi was halfway out the carriage door when she stopped. "You aren't coming with me, Bennin-*san*?"

"This is a woman's wing. I may not enter unless one of the ladies specifically requests my presence."

"I see." Kishi stepped out of the carriage, one of her warrior cousins helping her down. Lifting her wide sleeves to hide the lower part of her face, she turned to say thank you. But the door to the carriage was already closed and the carriage pulling away.

Fighting her feelings of being abandoned and alone, Kishi went up the nearest flight of wood steps onto the broad verandah. Night birds trilled nearby, and the air was heavy with the scent of wisteria blossoms. The paper sliding door before her clacked open. "Ah. There you are," said the girl standing there. Her face was painted pure white, like a porcelain doll. Her teeth had been fashionably blackened with berry stain, and her voluminous kimonos flowed to the floor.

How would I know if she were a ghost? wondered Kishi. *I can't even see her feet.*

The girl gave Kishi a disapproving glance. "This way. The Great Lady awaits you."

Kishi followed down a long cedar-floored hallway lined with gold-leaf paper sliding doors, the girl ahead of her gliding almost as if she were floating. The girl stopped and slid open a door. "In here, if you please."

Kishi entered and stopped at the doorway. It was an enormous room, as big as the largest hall in her family home. Ladies lay sprawled about on cushions on the floor, their colorful kimonos splayed about them like the fins of giant fish. Some were playing *go*, some were writing with brush and ink, some were playing musical instruments such as *koto* and *biwa* and flute.

All looked up at Kishi with the same white-painted, expressionless faces . . . until one giggled behind her sleeves. "Look how brown she is," that one whispered.

A large woman at the back of the room turned around. She was wearing a brocade outer-kimono embroidered with gold thread. Her face was noticeably lined, despite the white makeup, and her obsidian-eyed gaze bored hard into Kishi's face. "Come here," the woman commanded.

Kishi walked forward as gracefully as she could. At what she deemed to be a proper distance she knelt and bowed low. "I bring you greetings from my family, Great Lady, and they hope you will accept this unworthy one into your service."

"Hm," the Great Lady said, and then nothing more for long moments. Then, "Do you play *koto?*"

This was not what Kishi expected as a first question. "Um, no, but I will learn, Great Lady."

"Do you write poetry?"

"Poetry?"

There were more giggles behind her.

"Have you memorized any of the important Buddhist sutras?"

"Um, a line or two. But my family—"

The Great Lady interrupted with a loud sigh. "Do you know the art of the fan? Can you dance?"

Kishi swallowed hard. This wasn't fair. She was a warrior. Her family sneered at the noble arts.

"I suppose all they taught you in Sagami was how to ride horses and shoot arrows, then."

More, louder giggling. Kishi did not know how to answer or whether this was a ritual humiliation she would have to bear as young warriors sometimes did.

"Listen to me," the Great Lady intoned. "You must learn these arts swiftly and well. The behavior of a lady-in-waiting reflects upon the one she serves. If you irritate or disobey me, you will be sent back to your family. If you embarrass me, you will be sent to a Buddhist temple to take vows. If you shame me or my clan's honor, you will be imprisoned in far exile, never to see Heian Kyo or your family again. I trust this is clear."

Kishi bowed lower. "Yes, Great Lady." *And my mission would be over and the world ended, returned to the rule of the demons. What did I do in a previous life to deserve this fate?*

"Now what shall we call you? Ah. You have arrived near the Iris Festival, so you will be called Lady Shobu."

"Does that mean," giggled one of the other ladies-in-waiting, "that she will keep away demons, as the Shobu Iris Festival talismans do?"

Kishi held her breath and said nothing.

Lady Ankimon-in narrowed her eyes at Kishi a moment. "Given her present appearance, perhaps so."

Tales in the Dark

Kishi was shown her sleeping chamber, which she would be sharing with another lady-in-waiting. *Could my situation be any more impossible?* Kishi wondered as she lay down on the reed mat. Light spilled in from the many lanterns hanging on the eaves, making sleep difficult.

Her roommate came in through the sliding door, and fortunately she was not one of the girls who had laughed at her. "Hello. I am called Lady Usagi, but you can call me Aikiko."

"Usagi? Rabbit?"

"I was even more frightened than you when I arrived a year ago, always hiding my face. So the Great Lady gave me that name. She's really not so horrible as she seems, you know. She is stern, but she will look after you. If you behave well, she will see to it that you prosper here at the palace."

Kishi felt like a complete fraud. How could she behave well with such a heavy duty?

"She has even been known to arrange advantageous marriages," Aikiko went on.

"I have a betrothed."

"Ah. Someone of good family, I trust?"

"Yes." But Kishi did not wish to think about the boy she might never see again. "Aikiko, are there places in the palace where . . . where people do not go?"

"What a curious question. Why do you ask?"

"So that I will not go there," Kishi lied.

"Ah. Well, do not worry. If you stay in the woman's wing, leaving only on errands for the Great Lady, you will avoid trouble completely."

"No, truly, please tell me about the Imperial Compound. I have never been here before and it is so big, and I am so afraid of . . . doing the wrong thing. Please tell me what you know. I am too anxious to sleep tonight anyway."

Aikiko laughed gently. "Good, because there is a lot to tell." And for the next hour or so, Kishi heard of a bewildering array of Ministries-of-this and Ministries-of-that, the Bureau of Medicine and the Bureau of Divination ("Both very important," said Aikiko), the Office of Female Dancers and Musicians and the Office of Imperial Wine, the Court of Abundant Pleasures, and so forth. "But do not go near the northern gate, the Ikanmon. That is the direction of ill fortune. But all that is there are storehouses anyway, so you will have no need to."

This is sounding promising, Kishi thought. "What is in the storehouses?"

"You *are* a curious one, aren't you? Well, I don't know. Costumes for festivals. Old books. The guards keep some of their weapons and armor there."

Even better, thought Kishi. "Do you ever hear stories about . . . oh, ghosts and demons and things in the palace?"

"You do ask the oddest questions. It is bad luck to speak of those things. Besides, great care is taken by the Office of Divinations and the Imperial Guards to make sure the imperial family is protected from evil."

"Oh. Then you know nothing of any mysterious occurrences in the compound recently."

A long pause. "Well, . . ." Aikiko began. And then she rolled closer to Kishi's mat and in excited whispers began a torrent of stories that made Kishi's hair stand on end. Tales of illness, first servants and then minor nobles becoming sick with symptoms never seen before. Children, particularly girl children, and young maids disappearing. "Just last month," Aikiko said, "there was a girl, very strong and curious like you, who died mysteriously. Only her bloodstained kimonos were found. The Great Lady had looked after her like a daughter, and she was most distraught."

My predecessor, thought Kishi. "And no one knows who, or what, killed this girl?"

Aikiko sighed. "There are so many stories. Who knows what to believe? Apparitions of pale, skeletal women have been seen in the tea garden, and horse-headed men in the Banquet Pine Grove, and *tengu* near the Treasury Ministry. Or perhaps the poor girl was just of the wrong family, fell in love with the wrong man, offended the wrong person. It happens."

"Surely you cannot believe her death was ordinary?" asked Kishi.

Aikiko paused a moment. "I saw her kimonos—before we burned them. They looked as though they had been torn by some giant animal. No, I do not think her death was ordinary."

"Ah." Kishi shivered. *Bennin had said there was not much left of her.* "These monsters that have been seen, were they all in the north end of the Imperial Compound?"

"Yes! So you see why you mustn't go there."

"Of course," said Kishi, thinking precisely the opposite.

Preparations

The next morning, Kishi rummaged through the one trunk that had accompanied her on the journey. It contained her newest kimonos and a few of her personal things. Kishi looked through these with a different eye. The ebony hair sticks could be made sharper and turned into stakes or arrows or throwing stilettos, as could the writing brushes. The fans had edges that could be sharpened for slicing and cutting. Her brothers had taught her the warrior's art of making arrows. She would simply have to apply those skills to somewhat unusual materials.

At the bottom of the trunk, Kishi found a black *hakima* jacket and black leggings such as a warrior wears under his armor. There was a note from her brother.

Father suggested you might want these as a keepsake. Never forget your warrior blood, despite what the pasty faces may do to you.

—Higashi

Kishi hugged the black garments. Now she might be able to move about by night unseen and unhindered by the many layers of robes. The warrior garb would be suspicious if she were caught. But she did not intend to get caught.

Aikiko came in from the open verandah. "Ah, I see you are enjoying yourself. I brought you something." She held out a handful of little spheres of dried purple flowers and silk streamers. "These are old decorations from last year's Iris Festival. We'll be replacing them in a few days with new ones. But, given your new name . . . I thought you might like these, to put in letters and things."

"Do they really protect against demons?"

Aikiko shrugged. "So they say. And where is the harm in having pretty flowers hanging about the palace if they do not?"

"Thank you," said Kishi, and she put the iris balls into the bottom of her long wide sleeves. *Perhaps I can throw them at demons,* Kishi thought. *Or take them apart and grind the dried petals into a powder I can blow through a bamboo straw.*

"Oh, and here is one more thing. A letter." Aikiko held out a folded piece of plain white rice paper. "Perhaps it is your first love poem from a secret admirer."

Kishi blushed, hoping her roommate was wrong. Fortunately the note was from Bennin.

How fares our newest iris blossom?
Does she prevail against the weeds yet?
May this one clear any ground for you?

A knothole in the willow by the koi pond will receive your
reply. I will retrieve it from there this evening.

—Bennin

After Aikiko had left the room, Kishi wrote out a hasty reply
on the back of Bennin's letter. She didn't have time to think of
fancy allusions, so she stated matters simply.

I think I have learned where the demons are.
And I think I can find or make weapons.
I should be able to do battle soon.
A map of the Imperial Compound would help.

—Kishi

She folded up her note and stuck it in her sleeve until she had
a chance to slip away and find the tree by the koi pond.

But that chance did not come. Hour after hour Kishi had to
spend at Lady Ankimon-in's side, arranging the Great Lady's
hair or kimonos or curtain of modesty, handing the Great Lady
a teacup, or a writing brush, or a fan. Kishi sat patiently as the
Great Lady chanted the Lotus Sutra, repeating the words as the
Great Lady demanded that she join in. Midday slid into afternoon into late afternoon, and Kishi was nearly frantic. At last
she decided she would have to trust someone else to make the
delivery.

When a child-page of perhaps eight years came to deliver a
note for the Great Lady, Kishi pulled him aside. "Listen, could
you deliver this note for me to the willow tree by the koi pond?"

"Deliver a letter to a tree?" said the boy, in the too-loud voice
that children sometimes have.

"No, no," said Kishi, trying to shush him. "Put it *in* the tree."

"Where in the tree?"

At this, Great Lady Ankimon-in glanced up from her correspondence. "What is she asking you?"

Kishi hurriedly answered, "Forgive me, Great Lady. I merely wish a note delivered to my . . . spiritual advisor. Since I cannot leave your side to deliver it myself—"

"Come here, both of you," ordered the Great Lady.

Oh no. Kishi felt her stomach curdle, but she obeyed. She followed the page over to the Great Lady and knelt before her.

The Great Lady held out her hand. "Give me the note."

"But, Great Lady, it is merely a reply to my—"

"I heard you. But it would be delivered by *my* page, along with *my* correspondence. Have I not said what you do reflects upon me? Let me see it so I can determine whether it is appropriate."

I am done, thought Kishi as she handed over the letter with a trembling hand. She stared at her lap as the Great Lady read, the room filled with an awful silence. The silence was broken by the sound of tearing paper. Kishi's letter fell in black-and-white streamers to the floor.

"Your calligraphy is terrible and your poetry is worse," declared Great Lady Ankimon-in. "Leave us in privacy," she said to the room, and the other ladies-in-waiting hurried out whispering, even their kimonos whispering. "You too," she growled at the page, who fled running.

Kishi felt the obsidian gaze fall upon her and linger there long moments.

"Who was to receive this note?" the Great Lady asked, her voice low and rumbling like an earthquake.

Kishi hoped no unfortunate secrets would be revealed by telling the truth. "A priest named Bennin, Great Lady. He is from the Hachiman Shrine in my home province."

"Hmmm. I am acquainted with a Bennin, though I have not seen him in a couple of years. Why did he not come here if he wished to speak with you?"

What was it Bennin had said? Kishi tried to remember. "He . . . felt it would not be proper."

"Hm." The Great Lady paused in thoughtful silence. "Lady Shobu. I will assume that because you were born to a warrior clan, that words such as weapon and battle and map come naturally to you. And that you were writing of personal battles of the spirit. But remember where you are. There is no peace in a royal household. There is constant fear of treachery. Think how your words might be misconstrued if read by the wrong eyes."

Kishi bowed her head lower. "*Hai*, Great Lady."

Another long silence passed, and then, "I will forgive you this once. But you must not make so foolish a mistake again, or I will be forced to dismiss you."

"Yes, Great Lady. May I rewrite my note, so that it is more acceptable?"

"No. I think it best you forgo your . . . spiritual advice, and meditate upon what I have said instead. From now on, *any* correspondence you plan to send to *anyone* must have my approval first, is that clear?"

"Yes, Great Lady," Kishi whispered.

Perseverance

That night, Kishi knelt in her room, alternately fuming and frightened.

"You are very fortunate," Aikiko said. "I have rarely seen the Great Lady so upset, and yet she did not dismiss you. She must think you have hidden talents worth cultivating."

Kishi's hands made fists. "I . . . cannot continue like this. I have duties."

"We all have duties, no? From the moment we are born."

"I meant particular duties. I was consecrated at the shrine of Hachiman. I have . . . things I must do. Sacred things, which I cannot speak of."

"Perhaps if you explain to the Great Lady, she will understand."

Kishi shook her head. "I may not speak of them to *anyone*."

"Ah. That would make matters difficult." After a long pause, Aikiko continued softly, "I know where the koi pond is, and the willow tree. The Great Lady is not so concerned where I go or what I do. If you write a more circumspect note, I will deliver it for you."

Kishi stared at her in amazement. "You would?"

"Why not? If you are miserable, it will be difficult to sleep. And these days we need protection from all the gods, no? That is why the Great Lady insists we learn the sutras. So the Amida Buddha will protect us. Why not Hachiman as well?"

"I would be most grateful," Kishi said, and she hastily took her brush and ink and wrote out a new note. This one merely read:

I am preparing my spirit against the dangers ahead.
I wish your guidance to set me on the correct path.

"I hope he understands this," Kishi murmured as she folded the paper and handed it to Aikiko.

"Priests and monks are good at understanding in my experience," said Aikiko as she put the note in her wide sleeve. "Often more than you intend them to." She departed, and Kishi lay down to try to sleep.

Kishi awoke some time later with a sense that something was very wrong. It was still dark. Moonlight slanted in through the slats of the bamboo blinds, and Kishi could see that Aikiko was still gone. She heard the barest of sighs somewhere outside, drifting in on the night's breeze. "Kishi . . . Kishi . . ." It was a girl's voice.

Is it the wind and my imagination?

"Kishi . . . Kishi . . ." A hiss of cloth being dragged. Thump. Hiss. Thump. "Kishi . . . Kishi . . ." It was coming closer.

Kishi's skin prickled. She shivered and sat up. *Are the demons and ghosts coming for me? I am not ready!*

"Kishi . . . Kishi . . ." Hiss. Thump. Hiss. Thump. It was on the verandah. Very near now.

Kishi ran to her clothing trunk, reached in, and rummaged until she found one of her long, pointed hair sticks. *I am of Minomoto blood. I am a warrior, a slayer-born. I will not be afraid.* She lifted the bamboo blinds and stepped out onto the long verandah.

"Oh . . . Kishi . . . Bennin . . ."

Kishi turned. Not far down the verandah, Aikiko lay in puddle of moonlight, her pale face agape in pain and fear.

Kishi ran as swift and silent as she could to Aikiko's side. But as she arrived, Aikiko's eyes turned up and her head fell to the wood planking in a final, soft, thump. Kishi could now see the dark, dark blood oozing out of Aikiko's torn neck, spreading over the back of her kimono. A small piece of white rice paper fluttered in her hand. Kishi fought back her sorrow and rising gorge and picked up the paper. It was a roughly drawn map of the Imperial Compound.

So Bennin gave her a map for me, Kishi thought. *But the demons attacked Aikiko on her way back. Oh, Aikiko, this is my fault. I should have known the danger and gone myself. You were as brave as a warrior, Aikiko. I will see that you are avenged.* Kishi felt cowardly, running back to her room instead of properly seeing to Aikiko. But if she'd been caught with the body, too many questions would arise and her restrictions would be even greater. *It is time for Lady Shobu to disappear.*

She removed all her kimonos and put on the black garments her brother had sent. Working mostly by feel, Kishi found the fan and the other hair sticks and combs and placed these in the deep sleeves of the black *hakima.* She found the bottle of crushed dried iris petals and pocketed that, too. She pulled on the black hood and slipped out into the night.

In the moonlight, she stared long and hard at the map that Aikiko had so dearly paid for. Kishi memorized every building shown, especially those near the north gate. Then she folded the map, placed it in her sleeve, and hurried north.

In the Storehouses

Despite her fear, or because of it, Kishi reveled in the freedom— being able to run with no long kimonos to trip her; being invisible, blending in with the night. She ran through the gardens, over the ornamental foot bridges and crossing stones of the streams. She felt light as a spring-flower fairy. She would pause behind a tree as the occasional nobleman strolled by on his way to a lover's tryst. She lay low in the shadows when an Imperial Guard walked past in his red cloak, confident that he would not see her.

At last, Kishi came to a row of large buildings, too plain and inelegant to be living quarters or offices of imperial business. *These must be the storehouses. Good. I will have a better chance if I have real weapons.* She ran to the nearest one. Its entry was a huge wooden sliding door. Kishi expected it to be bolted, but pushed against the door anyway. To her amazement, the door rumbled aside with merely a firm shove. Kishi paused, breath held, to see if anyone would come running at the sound. No one did.

Kishi hopped up onto the raised flooring and shut the door behind her. It was very dark and smelled musty. Something fluttered in the eaves overhead—birds or bats. There were holes in the roof through which some moonlight filtered in. *How can a building in the palace be in such disrepair?* But she remembered her father once saying that emperors were capricious when it came to spending their wealth.

Once her eyes adjusted, Kishi saw an untidy clutter of cloth and wood and rope and things whose form and function she could not determine. A glimmer of light caught her attention, perhaps metal reflecting the moonlight. She crawled toward it. it looked like a sword! She grabbed the hilt and lifted, but it was so light it nearly flew out of her hand. It was a child's toy or ceremonial prop, made only of painted wood. Disappointed, Kishi sat on a pile of canvas and silk cloth.

She sensed that something was staring at her and sharply looked to her left. There! A horrible face in the shadows by the wall. But it was only a dancer's mask, hung in a line with other masks. A painted dragon head hung limply from a roof beam. Once lavish but now tattered kimonos littered the floor. *No wonder this storeroom has been allowed to fall apart,* Kishi grumbled to herself. *It is filled with useless things.* She considered leaving to search for the weapons storage.

Voices were coming closer outside. "The noise came from over here. I'm sure of it."

Ah. So I was heard. Kishi sat very, very still.

"What sort of noise was it again?"

"A low growling, I told you. Beasts are prowling out here. Yoshi says he was attacked. You saw the cuts on his arm. You saw all the blood near the ladies' wing."

"Yoshi was drunk."

"That does not make him wrong. We should double the patrols along these storehouses for the next few nights. Some of these structures are falling to pieces. Anything could have crawled into them."

"Very well. We can bring some men down from the parapets so that these walkways have constant surveillance, for tonight at least. Then we'll see what the Captain suggests." The men's voices drifted away again.

So the monsters that got Aikiko attacked a guard, too, Kishi thought. *I should be out there killing demons. Instead I'm stuck in here with no weapons but some sharpened hair sticks and a fan. If only I had my bow and arrows! But I can't leave if they're going to double the guard. And what if they search this storeroom?*

Kishi looked up at the sad, painted dragon head. Dragons, in the ancient stories, were protectors and granted gifts, though often at high price. *Would you protect me?* she thought at it. *What price would you ask for your guardianship?* It did not reply.

Kishi stood and walked cautiously around the storeroom. By the masks, she saw a *sakaki* branch lying on a lacquered trunk. She picked up the branch, which still had some dry leaves hanging from its twigs. Shinto priests, such as Bennin, used *sakaki* branches in their rituals. *Has its sacredness been used up, or might there be a little left?* Kishi wondered if it would be suitable for a bow and she bent it. The branch snapped. *Not for a bow, then. But perhaps an arrow or two.*

She explored further. On the floor below the hanging dragon head was a bit of its "body," a partially rotted tube of cloth stiffened with curved slats. Kishi picked it up and pulled out one of the slats. It was whale bone, only as long as her upper arm and hand, and still pliable. It bent but did not break. *Perfect!* Arigato gozaimas, she thought at the dragon above.

On another wall she found some rusted carpentry tools. She took down an awl, a broken knife, and a hasp. From the tresses of one of the masks, she cut a length of horsehair.

The rest of the night she spent turning the whale bone into a small bow that could be concealed in her wide *hakima* sleeve. She cut as many arrows as she could from the *sakaki* branch, pausing only when footsteps went by.

Proving Grounds

As dawn arrived, Kishi became hungry and tired. *I will have to steal food from somewhere.* Voices and footsteps approached again.

"Try them all. The trail of blood came from this way. To the north and east. The same monster that got Yoshi got the girl, I tell you."

"Really? I'd heard that was a botched suicide. The girl had probably been discarded by a lover, Lady Ankimon-in said."

"And what about her new maid who disappeared, eh? Beast probably got that one, too."

"The Great Lady said she'd been temporarily sent away for disciplinary reasons."

Strange, thought Kishi. *Did the Great Lady lie to spare herself shame? Or was she somehow involved in Aikiko's death?*

"I'm not so sure we'll find anything other than where Yoshi wandered drunk and bleeding last night," the guard went on. "It was this storeroom you heard noises in?"

They were right outside the sliding door. Kishi looked wildly around and saw a small boat carved in the shape of a koi fish. She leaped into it as the heavy door slid open and she pulled a couple of the old kimonos on top of her.

"That's interesting. Is that a footprint in the dust?"

"Small, if it is." Floorboards creaked closer to the koi boat. "Look, wood shavings. They seem fresh. And look, a toy bow."

Kishi cursed silently. *They found it. Blessed Hachiman, now what will I do?*

"That explains the noise, then. Boys have been slipping in here to play. The shavings are probably from rats gnawing at the ceiling beams. I'll bet the boys were shooting at them."

"I can see one. Think I can hit a rat with this?"

"We don't have time for such nonsense."

"There it goes." *Twang. Thunk.*

"Good shot. You hit the drag—watch out! It's coming down!"

There was a massive crash. Kishi's boat shuddered as the dragon head hit the floor.

From farther away, near the door, she heard, "All right, that's enough foolishness. There's clearly nothing in here. Let's keep searching."

"That thing almost hit me." The huge sliding door rumbled shut.

Kishi waited for ten long breaths before she emerged from beneath the kimonos. Shaking, she stepped out of the boat. To her amazement and relief, she saw the whale bone bow on the floor, just beside the dragon head. She patted the carved dragon on the snout. "Again, I thank you." Kishi gathered up her bow and all the arrows she had made and put them in the koi boat. Then she curled up beneath the kimonos again and tried to sleep.

But she slept only in fits and starts, and by the time the sun was setting, her stomach was protesting its emptiness loudly.

Kishi consulted Bennin's map again. She was too far from the Imperial Kitchens, but there was a small Shinto shrine noted not far to the north and east. Often offerings of food and drink would be left in shrines. *Once I have eaten, I can try to find the storehouse with the real weapons. Too bad Bennin did not note which one it is on the map.*

Kishi gathered her new bow and arrows and her newly sharp-ened fan and hairsticks, placed them in the bottom of her *hakima* sleeve, and slipped out into the gathering gloom. Hiding in the shadows in the airspace underneath the storage buildings, she made her way north and east across the palace compound. Curiously, this was also the way the guards had said the blood of their comrade had led.

Kishi easily found the Shinto shrine, which resembled a small thatched house. On its little "porch" were evening offerings of a bowl of rice and a small ceramic bottle of plum wine. Kishi looked around. No one was in sight. She gobbled up the rice, eating with her hands, and drunk down the wine. Wiping her mouth on her sleeve, Kishi bowed to the shrine. "Please forgive my sacrilege, and I promise to repay you—"

"Oh, you'll pay all right," someone growled, and laughed nas-tily behind the shrine.

"What?" said Kishi, stepping back. "Who is speaking?"

"She's right upon her hour. These slayers are so predictable," growled another voice to her right. Kishi whipped around, but whoever had spoken was hidden behind a cluster of ornamental pines.

Someone has found me out! "What are you talking about?" Kishi bluffed to the air as she fished in her sleeve for a weapon. "I am Lady Shobu. I have been lost and could not find my way back to the women's quarters."

"Awww," the first speaker jumped out from behind the shrine. Its skin was dark scarlet and its head was that of a horse from hell on the body of a man wearing only a loincloth. It held a long spear in its hands. "She's lost! Did we scare you?" It circled around Kishi and before her fumbling hands could pull out her bow, the *oni* stabbed with the spear. Kishi shifted aside, but the spear pinned her left sleeve against the wall of the shrine.

The other *oni* came out from behind the pine. It breathed fire from its nostrils and its eyes glowed like hot coals. "You have her piked already? This one is no fun. She is unworthy."

The heat of anger joined into her flush of shame, and Kishi felt white-hot energy flow into her arms and legs. She yanked on the shaft of the spear . . . and broke it. "Awww, cute little horsie," Kishi mocked. "Do you give pony rides?" Her legs kicked up, her left foot striking the *oni's* groin, the right its chin. She pulled the fore-half of the spear out of the wall of the shrine and leaped up onto the stunned *oni's* shoulders, knocking him down. She jammed the spearhead deep into the creature's left eye. The *oni* dissolved into a puddle of green goo. "You were no challenge," she said to it. "You were unworthy."

She heard a roaring snarl from the one behind her and spun. As the *oni* charged her, Kishi pulled the sharpened fan from her sleeve. She danced aside as the *oni* lunged past, and tripped it with an out-stretched foot. Kishi snapped her fan open and sliced the *oni's* neck with the sharpened edge as the demon fell. Blood spurted every-where as the *oni* clutched its neck and staggered, crumpling dead to the ground. Kishi shook her head. "Your dancing would shame the Great Lady. A good thing she did not see you."

Kishi spun around, looking for the next opponent. She felt ex-hilarated, alive. She lusted for more combat as though the spirit of Hachiman himself rode her. "I am Minomoto no Kishi, daughter of Hiragashi, Lord of Sagami Province. Where is the fighter who is worthy of me?" she called out, as a true warrior would.

"Kishi . . ." A whisper in the twilight. "Kishi, beware." It came from the pines.

Kishi went closer, feeling a chill in her blood. "Aikiko?"

A dim, pale form emerged from the trees. "Kishi, I have come to warn you. You are in great danger."

Kishi looked down. Beneath Aikiko's flowing white kimonos, there was only air. She had no feet.

"I thank you, Aikiko's spirit, for the warning. But I am prepared for the danger."

"No, you are not," Aikiko's ghost sighed. "There is so little you know. They will take you, as they took your predecessor. They will turn you, as they have turned . . . me!" Her face contorted into a demonic mask and she flew at Kishi.

Unprepared, Kishi felt Aikiko's fingers, like icicles, rake against her skin, the cold flowing through to her bones. Strike after swift strike, to her face, her arms, her back, Kishi cried out as Akiko's ghostly talons ripped through her, drawing out her life force instead of blood. *How do I fight an opponent with no form, no substance?*

Kishi suddenly remembered Aikiko's gift, from what seemed so long ago. She sank to her knees and pulled from her sleeve the bottle of dried iris blossoms. She pulled out the tiny cork stopper and waved the bottle in a circle around her, flinging the crushed petals.

The attack stopped at once. "Ai," sighed the ghost of Aikiko. "You best me with my own gift. But beware, my once-friend. I am not the worst opponent you will face." The ghost faded into nothingness.

Kishi fell forward onto her arms and panted, trying to resummon her strength. *I cannot lose heart now. My duty is not fulfilled. I have not found the hell-rift. I must not disappoint Bennin and my family.*

Slowly, Kishi stood. She staggered ahead, not yet certain where she should be going. She tripped and fell over a log into a sticky puddle. She looked back. Not a log. The body of one of the Imperial Guards, his chest slit open. His face looked very surprised. "Yoshi-*san*?" Kishi inquired, but the guard did not answer, not even his spirit.

Kishi heard a noise ahead of her. *Swish-swish. Voop-voop.* It was a sword moving through air. Kishi crawled to the base of the nearest tree and peered into the twilight darkness. In a bed of chrysanthemums, a man in a black robe stood in fighting stance, holding a long *tachi* sword. The man turned. He had a raven's head.

A tengu! Kishi thought. *Tengu* were the finest swordsmen of the demon realm, Bennin had said. Kishi had no training in swordsmanship. She would be lost against such a fighter.

The *tengu* tilted its head, listening. To buy herself time, Kishi climbed halfway up the tree.

"Ahhh," cawed the *tengu*, "sounds like the Slayer has arrived."

"What are you doing standing in the emperor's flowers?" Kishi said, knowing there was no point in trying to hide. "Have you no shame?"

"Ak ak ak!" laughed the creature. "I am a *tengu*! Of course I have no shame. Unlike you, who hides among the maple branches."

"I am just trying to get a better look at you, so I can kill you," Kishi said.

"Gaze in admiration all you want, little slayer," said the *tengu*. "Meanwhile, I will allow you a closer look." *Whack, whack!* With spinning strokes, the *tengu* sliced off the two lowermost boughs of the maple tree. "Do you think the Great Lady would like *my* dancing?"

"She very well might," said Kishi, inching higher. "But she doesn't grow trees in her entertaining hall."

"Oh, heads will do instead of branches," said the *tengu*. "By the way, I should tell you that no matter how high you go, that tree does not reach to heaven. But if you come down, I promise to get you there quick as breath. It would be in your best interest, you know. We *tengu* are relatively kind, as demon folk go."

"Thank you for your generous offer," said Kishi. "But I am not yet worthy to visit heaven. How about if I chant a few sutras first?" And she began to chant the first few lines of the Lotus Sutra, just as the Great Lady had taught her.

"Ow!" cried the *tengu*, clapping his hands over his ears. "Stop that!"

But Kishi did not stop. She chanted as she reached into her sleeve and pulled out the whale-bone bow and one of the sacred *sakaki* arrows. As the *tengu* screamed in rage and raised its sword again to attack the tree, Kishi let fly. The arrow took the *tengu* right through the neck. With a sad caw, the *tengu* vanished and the black robe drifted empty to the ground.

Kishi placed the little bow back in her sleeve and climbed down. She poked carefully through the robe . . . and found the *tachi* sword. *"Hai!"* she whispered.

She looked around, trying to get a sense of where she was. From the shrine, she had been heading south, toward a vast open area of gardens and groves. *Should I turn and go back northward?*

She heard another strange sound, like the chirping of late summer cicadas. But it was growing louder. She held out the long sword in a double-handed grip. In the dim twilight she could not see anything approaching. Until she saw the flowers and their leaves, in the entire garden, moving. Whatever approached were . . . small. And there was a horde of them.

With a high screech, something jumped up, landed on her leg and bit hard. It had a turtle's shell and webbed feet like a frog, but with claws. *Kappa!* The long sword was too awkward to swing at the creature without cutting her leg, so Kishi had to ignore the pain. She swung wildly as more of the creatures leaped up and grabbed her, biting through her clothing. Kishi sliced through the rain of *kappa*, killing many, she was sure. But just as many survived, armored by their turtle shells. More and more sets of tiny teeth were taking hold on her back, her legs, her arms. One latched onto her left cheek and Kishi felt blood running down to her chin. Frustrated, Kishi dropped the sword and tried to pull the *kappa* off her. But each one she pulled off took a chunk of skin with it. More and more of them kept piling on, chittering and screeching, blending in with Kishi's cries of pain.

Kishi fell to her knees. *No, this cannot be how it ends! This is unworthy, to die at the hands of such loathsome little creatures.* She remembered that *kappa* needed to keep their heads upright, or the water that they carried on their cuplike heads would be spilled, weakening them. She crawled forward, remembering there was a long slope downward ahead. She did a somersault, flipped, and began to roll and roll, faster and faster. The *kappa* screeched and fell off one by one until, by the time she got to the bottom of the hill, there were no more *kappa* clinging to her. She got up again and looked around. Ahead she saw a moonlit pond with a large willow beside it. And beside the willow stood someone in a broad round hat and veil. *Could that be Bennin? He must be waiting for a message from me! I must warn him!*

Kishi staggered forward, every muscle aching from wounds, straining to fight off weakness. She could feel blood running down her arms, legs, and face. No matter. Didn't Bennin say she would heal quickly? But her duty was not yet finished.

"Bennin-*san*!" Kishi gasped as she came up to him. She fell to her knees from exhaustion. "Bennin-*san*, I am here."

"Ah, there you are, Kishi-*san*. Excellent. It would seem you were well chosen."

"I have done as well as I could, Bennin-*san*. But you are in danger. There is an army of *kappa* just over that hill. I could not fight them all off."

"Oh no, I am in no danger at all. I am protected."

"But—," and then Kishi stopped, chagrined. He was a Shinto priest, no doubt the master of many magickal ways of keeping away demons. "Forgive me, Bennin-*san*. That was foolish of me. Please allow me to take shelter within your protection while I heal. I need some rest before I continue my mission."

"Oh, do not worry, Kishi-*san*. Your duty is nearly ended."

"But I have not yet found the rift through which the demons come."

"Why, yes you have. It is right here." Bennin gestured at the pond.

Kishi stared at the calm, dark water. "Ah. And it is your magick protecting us,"

"Ah, no. The protection extends only to me. Alas, you have one more monster to face. Or two."

"One or two more? I don't think I can at this moment."

"Oh, but you must." Bennin raised his arm and the pond behind him began to bubble and ripple and bulge. Something enormous was emerging from the middle of the dark water. Something with great golden eyes, a long, bumpy snout, and cavernous, fang-rimmed jaws.

Kishi's own jaw dropped open. "It is a dragon," she whispered.

"You have absorbed my lessons well," said Bennin-*san*.

Up and up the dragon head rose on its long, long neck. Kishi was certain the pond was too small to have contained the whole creature. "Of course. The dragon is your protector."

"Very good. You are very smart. What a pity that it is your time to depart the world."

The dragon loomed over her now, jaws wide, its hot, wet breath stinking of pond moss.

"I . . . I do not understand, Bennin-*san*."

"Ah, poor Kishi-*san*." The priest took off his round hat and veil. "I am not really Bennin. I am his brother, Migoto. But

Bennin was chosen to be a member of the Council of Watchers while I was not, even though I was also a priest and had greater mystical powers than he did. I was determined to demonstrate this to the council, and so I used my powers to kill my brother a year ago, take his place, and summon the dragon. And I learned how to achieve immortality, albeit as a blood-sucking demon." Migoto's face changed, wrinkling over the brow and cheekbones.

Kishi's heart nearly stopped beating. "You . . . did not tell me of this sort of demon," she said, trying to hide her terror. She realized that she had never seen his feet either. Or watched him eat. *I have been tricked. How could I have been so foolish?*

"For obvious reasons, of course I did not tell you. But I do recall mentioning that I favored the old ways. In ancient times, our ancestors would repay the gifts of the dragons with a sacrifice."

"The sacrifice of a young maid," Kishi said, remembering tales her mother had told.

"Exactly so. And what more worthy sacrifice than a maid who is also a warrior, blooded in battle?"

"Is this how my predecessor died?" asked Kishi, feeling the anger grow hot in her again.

"It is. And just as I did her family, I will tell your parents that you died honorably and that your name should be remembered as a hero in the annals of your clan. They will be very proud of you."

Kishi turned to the dragon. "Please. You protected me in the storehouse. Protect me here. Do not kill me."

"What?" asked Migoto, frowning in irritation.

"The bargain has been struck," said the dragon in a voice as low as the booming waves of the ocean. "You are the payment. He bears the truth in his heart. So long as he has immortal life, maids must be offered to me in sacrifice."

"I see. Thank you." Kishi bowed, her hands in her sleeves, letting her forehead touch the cool grass.

"Dying with gratitude," sighed Migoto. "It is touching how noble you slayers are, even in your final moments."

"You are too kind," said Kishi, suddenly sitting up. She drew the string on her whale-bone bow and let fly with a *sakaki* twig arrow. It neatly pierced the priest in the center of his chest.

"But . . . this isn't right!" said Migoto with a glance of hurt betrayal at the dragon before exploding in a cloud of dust.

"Ahhhhhhh," the dragon sighed, as if relieved of a burden as large as the world.

"You wanted my help."

"It was a shameful bargain," said the dragon.

"But you did eat the former slayer."

"Her soul has been taken to the undersea palace of the Dragon King, where chosen heroes may go. I will offer you that choice. But not today. Not until fate overtakes you some other way. *Sayoonara*, Kishi-*san*." The dragon sank down, back into the pond.

"But wait!" cried Kishi. "What about the other demons, the hell-rift . . ." But the dragon was gone.

And then Kishi heard a sound more terrifying than any other she had heard that night.

"Are you certain you heard a noise this way, Lady Kabu?" It was the Great Lady Ankimon-in.

"We should call the guard, Great Lady."

"No, no, I am sure it is nothing. Wait here."

Kishi held very still, hoping she would not be seen in the darkness, hoping the Great Lady would go some other direction. She wished she could call upon the dragon's protection again, but she knew that bargain was complete.

Soon she heard the heavy susurrus of brocade silk and

smelled the Great Lady's perfume. *I am done,* thought Kishi, hanging her head. *They will behead me as a traitor.*

"Well, Lady Shobu. I thought I saw you speaking with a priest. Was it Bennin?"

"I had thought it was Bennin, but it was not. It was his brother."

She heard the Great Lady's sharp intake of breath. "Indeed? Migoto was it? Where did he go?"

Kishi nodded at the little pile of dust that was already fading away. Since she was doomed anyway, Kishi told Lady Ankimon-in all that Migoto had said.

The Great Lady knelt down beside her and her warm hand grasped Kishi's arm. "We on the council had been concerned about Migoto. But Bennin was reclusive himself, so we did not notice any change a year ago. Naturally we assigned him to be your watcher when"—she hung her head—"when my slayer failed. And I failed at my duty as her watcher. As the Council has failed you."

"What is done is done," said Kishi. "How could anyone have known that such an alliance had been made, that such evil deeds had been committed?"

"Evil deeds are the council's business, Shobu-*san.* Let us speak no more on this. I will ask that abundant bandages be sent to your room, and say that you will be staying in isolated meditation for a few days. I will apply to the council to become your watcher now, though that may not be approved. It is highly ir-regular for a watcher to serve two slayers in a row."

"What am I to do?" asked Kishi.

"Why, Lady Shobu, I will expect the same service of you as be-fore. As I have said, you are not to disappoint or shame me in any way in your duties as a lady-in-waiting of the Imperial Court. Life will appear to have a comforting normality. For without that, we all live in nightmares, no?"

The Great Lady stood and walked away, her kimonos hissing like sea foam.

Kishi remained where she was. *I am not dead. I am not imprisoned or exiled. I am still to be a slayer. I am to continue serving the Great Lady.* Endless days of arranging hair, arranging clothing, *koto* and calligraphy and poetry. Endless days of acting like a foolish woman of no substance, no power, no strength. More fearful of the humans around her than of the demons she was born to slay. Free only at night, when her warrior nature could be allowed to fully express itself.

A tear rolled down her cheek. *Blessed Hachiman, what did I do in a previous life to deserve this fate?*

Abomination

Laura J. Burns and Melinda Metz

BEAUPORT, BRITTANY, 1320

"Tonight I kill him," Eliane whispered.

Across the small room, Isabeau began to cry.

"In a moment, dumpling," Eliane called. She used her teeth to tear a strip from the hem of her underskirt. "In just one moment." Eliane used the piece of cloth to tie a stake behind her back.

Isabeau's cries turned to wails. And Eliane's blouse grew wet with milk. She ignored the dampness. She slid the stake free, then replaced the weapon. Drew, then replaced. Finally satisfied, she rushed to the cradle by the hearth and scooped up her daughter. "Oh, my big girl," Eliane whispered, summoning the will to keep her voice calm and soothing. "Soon your toes will be pushing between the slats. You're much bigger than your brother was when he—"

Gervais. Oh, God, Gervais. *It seemed like only a few days ago that she held him in her arms just as she held Isabeau now. Her sweet baby boy. Her firstborn, now five years old, with a laugh that sounded like a jaybird's squawk. How many times had she woken to that sound, followed by Gervais pouncing on her, waking her with smacking kisses and demands for porridge with lots of honey?*

Gervais is gone, *Eliane told herself.* I must accept that. *Isabeau started rooting around her bosom like a hungry little piglet.* Life continues, *Eliane thought. She sat down in the rocking chair Michel had carved and freed one breast for her daughter. It felt wrong that it should, after all that had happened, but life did continue. Eliane began to rock slowly as Isabeau fed, a sensation that was half pain and half pleasure coursing from her breast to low in her stomach.*

Is she taking more than nourishment from me, my innocent sweetling? *Eliane wondered.* Is she taking in my horror and revulsion at what I must do? Does Isabeau know that before morning breaks I will become a killer, taking revenge on those who stole my son from me?

"*It is a curse for what your father and I did,*" Eliane murmured, gently stroking the down on Isabeau's head. "*We knew it was wrong. But Michel and I felt powerless to stop it. And this is our punishment, more horrible than we ever could have imagined. The price of our love was the child Michel and I made together.*"

"Eliane, pay attention!" Michel shouted as he slashed the sword toward her gut.

Eliane easily twirled away from him, her bare feet slicked with the meadow's early-morning dew. How was she supposed to pay attention on a day like this? It felt as if this were the first day ever created, as if she and Michel were the first humans ever to experience the soft, warm sunshine, the cool grass, the song of the stream in the distance.

"Eliane! This is serious work," Michel scolded.

"Serious work, I know," Eliane answered, stifling a giggle. When Michel tried to sound like one of the strict old priests at the orphanage where she was raised, it always made her feel like laughing. Her watcher was only three years older than she was. And so handsome. No one with lips as soft-looking as Michel's should ever bother to say a harsh word. All the words that came out of that mouth were sweet. It was no use trying to make it otherwise.

Eliane fisted her hands in her skirt and pulled it up above her knees, then whirled around and expertly kicked the sword out of Michel's hand. She swooped it up, but instead of lunging at Michel, she used the blade to slice through the stem of a daisy. "For you." She tossed the flower to Michel.

She'd never been quite so playful with her watcher before. But there was something about the day, the glorious day, maybe simply that after such a long cold winter it was so delicious to feel the sun on her face again. "Isn't spring wonderful?" she cried.

"Concentrate, or I will double the length of your training session for the rest of the week," Michel barked out with his soft, soft lips.

Eliane didn't attempt to hold back her giggles this time. They flew out of her mouth, tickling her throat on the way up.

Exasperated, Michel put his hands on his hips and stared at her. "What, pray tell, is so amusing?"

"Your pretty face doesn't match your sour words," Eliane blurted out. She felt a blush race all the way up to her forehead. Had she actually said that aloud? Sometimes, lying on her pallet at night, she would allow herself to imagine that Michel wasn't her watcher, allow herself to imagine flirting with him the way she'd seen girls flirt with boys in the village. But she'd known she should never attempt to act out her daydreams. She was his slayer. He was her watcher. Love was forbidden for both of them.

"Pretty face," Michel repeated. His green eyes bored into her. Was he angry? Had she pushed him past all limits?

"Yes," Eliane answered, deciding the best thing to do was get back to work immediately. She swung the sword out in a smooth arc in front of her, forcing Michel to jump back. He was not fast enough, and the blade cut through his linen shirt, lightly scratching his chest.

Eliane had a wild desire to put her mouth on the scratch and lick the thread of blood away. The thought had her blushing again. What was wrong with her?

Lightning fast, Michel reached out and freed the sword from her hand. She should have been able to stop him easily, but her hand felt suddenly boneless. Michel dropped the sword onto the grass, grabbed Eliane roughly by the waist, and kissed her.

From the first day we met, this has been wanting to happen, Eliane thought. Then her mind was taken over by a flood of pure sensation: Michel's hands moving slowly up her spine, then tangling in her hair, Michel's tongue brushing against hers; the heat of his body flowing into hers until she couldn't tell where he stopped and she began.

Then the world turned to ice as Michel wrenched himself away from her. "This is wrong," he told her, the words coming out thick and harsh. "We share in a sacred trust. Watchers, slayers must be focused only on the fight against the darkness."

It was what he had told her every day since he brought her here from the orphanage at the age of thirteen. For two years they had trained and studied, but there was no darkness in their little village. Even the Great Hunger had passed them by. Eliane felt blessed here as if no shadow could cross their doorstep. The evil things Michel described did not seem to exist in Beauport. She did not believe she would ever be the Chosen One.

Instead of preparing for the darkness, she would embrace the light.

"It can't be wrong," Eliane said. She took his hand and then sat down in the meadow, pulling him with her. "Not when it feels like this."

"But your destiny—," he protested.

Eliane slid her arms about him. "My destiny is you."

"Our destiny," Michel agreed, his face so close to hers that his lips brushed against her mouth with each word.

Isabeau's mouth slid free of Eliane's breast. Although the baby slept, Eliane continued to rock in the chair that Michel had made. Perhaps if she didn't move from this spot, the day would remain where it was, the sun suspended in the sky.

"Foolishness," Eliane whispered. "Cowardice."

Already the shadows on the stone floor were lengthening. Night was coming. He would be here soon, the monster who had taken Gervais. Her little boy with the jaybird laugh.

My darling boy is dead and cold, *she thought.* And that has made me into a monster too. Tonight I will make the town run red with blood. *Eliane closed her eyes and pictured the small village of Beauport. She had not been to the village center in years now, but still she could see its semicircle of stone cottages in her mind's eye. Is there anyone left alive there? Have they all been murdered by the demons too?*

Eliane rose slowly and managed to return Isabeau to her cradle without waking her. There was much to do before dark.

Eliane gathered her long, pale hair in to a tight knot. Then she began stretching out her body the way Michel had taught her. How long had it been since they trained together? Years. Lovemaking had taken the place of training, and still no evil threatened. The Watchers Council never even sent messengers. She and Michel had grown complacent. Happy. Did Eliane any longer possess the strength and agility she would need this night? She glanced at the cradle, at her sleeping daughter. "I will protect you," Eliane vowed. "Even if I must die to do it."

Isabeau was all she had left. Michel was gone. Gervais . . . Gervais was gone too. Eliane would not allow Isabeau to be taken from her as well. A whimper escaped Eliane's lips. She clamped her teeth together hard. This was a time not for tears, but for fury.

Tears streaked down Eliane's face, mingling with the sweat. "What if they find out?" she asked Michel, panting between each word.

He used a damp cloth to bathe her cheeks and forehead. "They won't," he promised. "They won't venture out this far. And we will be very careful."

"But the priest must have registered our marriage. Surely they will become aware—"

A fresh bolt of pain sliced down Eliane's back, cutting short her words. Her stomach tightened until she wanted to scream.

"I see the top of the head," Michel cried. "It's our baby! Our baby's head!"

Eliane choked out a laugh. She'd been so worried about giving birth, especially because she hadn't been able to talk to any women in Beauport about it. She'd kept her pregnancy a secret, not venturing away from home after her condition could no longer be concealed. She and Michel lived in the cottage farthest from the center of the village, and because they had always kept to themselves, unexpected visitors were not a problem.

And it turned out that she hadn't needed any advice from the village matrons. Her body knew what to do with no instruction. Without actually deciding to do it, she began to bear down, pushing the baby along.

Michel grabbed her hand so hard she felt the small bones grind together. "Eliane, wait! Stop!"

Stop? Has he gone mad? Eliane thought. It was well past the time that anything could be stopped. Her muscles tightened, pushing, pushing.

"Eliane, no! The cord. It's wrapped around the baby's neck," Michel explained. "You have to stop pushing or it will choke." Michel pulled his hand free of Eliane's. "I'll get it. I'll fix it. Just stay still."

Eliane dug her fingers into the blanket beneath her. She clenched her jaws until it felt as though her teeth would snap. She curled her toes tightly. And she willed the rest of her body to relax. What was happening? She couldn't see Michel's hands over the slope of her stomach. Had he freed their baby? Did it still live? *It couldn't have died,* she told herself. Not without her knowledge. She and the babe had been connected for too many months; it was almost as if she could hear the child's thoughts, as if they dreamed the same dreams. It would be impossible for it to die without Eliane feeling it to her core. But why wasn't Michel saying anything?

Her body begged to be allowed to push down. It was the only thing that could stop the agony. Eliane tightened her grip on the blanket. One of her fingernails broke free, and she savored the small pain, focusing on it to keep her mind off the horrible urge to push and push and push.

Michel muttered under his breath. Eliane couldn't make out the words. She wanted to ask him what he had said, but she was afraid to loosen the muscles of her jaw. If she did, she might push without meaning to, might squeeze the breath from her child.

"Almost," Michel called. "Almost, Eliane. Yes! Yes! The cord is out of the way. Push! Push now!"

Eliane let her fingers and toes and jaw go slack. All that tightness rushed into her belly, and she bore down with a strength she hadn't been aware she possessed.

"I have him!" Michel exclaimed. "A boy, Eliane. Our baby boy."

Eliane struggled up onto her elbows. She couldn't wait a moment longer to see their child. Michel lifted the boy by his tiny feet and smacked him on the rear. Silence. There was no comforting wail from the baby. Another smack. Silence.

"Do something," Eliane begged.

Michel lay the baby on Eliane's belly. He used his little finger to clear the baby's throat and tiny nostrils. "He's not breathing."

"He can't be dead. I'd feel it! I know I would!" Eliane cried.

Michel lowered his lips to the baby's tiny mouth. He blew in a puff of air. Another. And the baby let out a glorious shriek. "We have a baby," Michel said, sounding awestruck.

"We have a baby," Eliane repeated. "Our little baby, Gervais." She raised her eyes from the baby to Michel. "This is our family, Michel. This is the most important thing to me now."

"I know, my love," Michel replied.

"More important than being the Slayer," Eliane whispered. "If they tried to come between me and my family, I would go mad." Eliane felt a sort of hysteria growing within her. "What would they do if they knew about him, Michel? Would they—"

Michel silenced her by putting a finger to her lips. "The Watchers Council will never know."

Will Michel ever know what happens here tonight? *Eliane wondered.* Does he know they've killed Gervais, and that I let it happen? I've betrayed not only my own calling, but his calling as a watcher. Will he be able to forgive me?

It's no time to indulge yourself with questions such as those, *Eliane admonished herself. She began to perform the pattern of feints, jabs, rolls, and spins that Michel had devised to keep Eliane's slaying skills sharp. There had been a time she'd gone through the routine several times a day. Now caring for the baby and amusing little Gervais—*

Eliane stepped on the hem of her skirt and stumbled. She fought back tears as she thought of Gervais. The demon, *she decided. She would only think of the demon who had taken her boy. There was nothing she could not do to a demon, no pain she could not inflict.*

She had been born to be the Slayer. Tonight the demon would discover what that meant.

"What do you think of this funny little creature?" Michel asked Gervais. "Do you think maybe our real baby was switched with a wood sprite?"

"Don't say that to him," Eliane protested. "Isabeau's your little sister," she told Gervais. "Not something out of a fairy story."

"She looks like a troll," Gervais answered, then he gave his caw of a laugh. "Beau the troll!"

Eliane smiled, pushing back the strange feeling that had crowded her all day. She'd slept ill; that was all. She'd had dreams, ghoulish dreams, like nothing she'd ever known before. Still she could feel the dreams, licking at the edge of her thoughts.

But the sun was warm and her children were radiant with life. She breathed in the sweet air and determined to ignore the uneasiness in her gut. Eliane reached out and tickled Gervais under the ribs, his best tickle spot. "Do you think you didn't look the same when you were less than a year old?"

"You always said I was the most beautiful baby in the world," Gervais reminded her. "Tell me that story again. About how I almost died when I was getting born."

"You didn't—," Michel began.

He was interrupted by a knock on the door. Eliane's eyes flew to Michel, the old fear of discovery springing up inside her. It had been five years since Gervais was born, and the fear had faded every year. She hadn't received the call to become the Slayer, and both she and Michel had grown more and more convinced she never would. Almost all slayers were called before they reached Eliane's age, never experiencing marriage or motherhood.

"Who is it?" Michel called as he strode to the door.

It must simply be someone from the village who needs our help, Eliane told herself. But people from the village rarely came to them for any reason. She, Michel, and the children lived a solitary life.

"Gaston Roux," came the answer.

Eliane had never heard the name before. But the grim expression on Michel's face made her suspect that her husband had.

"Who is that, Maman?" Gervais asked.

"We'll have to wait and see, won't we?" she answered, struggling to keep her tone light.

Michel swung open the door. Three men stood outside.

"Eliane Ward?" the tallest man asked.

"Eliane de Shaunde," she corrected him, using her married name. All the little hairs on the back of her neck stood up. The nightmare images from her dream invaded her mind once again. This man was her enemy. She could feel it.

"I am Gaston Roux, your new watcher," the man announced. "The Slayer is dead. You have been called."

Heavy silence filled the room. Eliane realized she was not breathing.

"I . . . I am Eliane's Watcher," Michel said. "She has no need of a new one." But his voice sounded high and frightened, and Eliane knew it was useless. They had been found out.

Gaston Roux now turned his cold eyes on her husband. "Michel de Shaunde, my associates will escort you to London, where you will be required to stand trial for your offenses before the Council."

"Offenses?" Eliane exclaimed. "Is it an offense to have a family? To love your wife and children?"

"You know it is!" Roux snapped. "At least you should know. A slayer with children—it is an abomination. Your watcher should have taught you this much."

He gestured to the other two men and they moved forward slowly, positioning themselves on either side of Michel. He clutched baby Isabeau tighter, and a soft moan escaped his lips.

"There is no abomination here," Eliane whispered. "Only happiness."

"The position of Watcher is a sacred one," Roux answered, his eyes on Michel. "The rules of conduct were well known to your watcher."

"My husband," Eliane corrected him.

"What is a watcher?" Gervais asked, his little voice trembling. In Michel's arms, Isabeau began to fuss.

Eliane couldn't tear her attention away from Roux to answer her little boy. Even last evening's nightmares paled in comparison to this. These men wanted to destroy her family! "What if he refuses to go with you?" she demanded.

The two other men stepped closer to Michel, threatening without saying a word.

"He cannot refuse," Roux said.

Michel kissed Isabeau's forehead and gently placed her in her cradle. The baby immediately began to wail. The sounds shredded Eliane's heart. "You're not really going to leave her, leave us?" she asked Michel.

His eyes gave her the answer. They were flat and dull, as if Michel's soul was already absent from his body. "I have no choice," he said. "But I swear I will come back to you." Michel wrapped Gervais in a tight hug. "Papa has to go away for a little while. You be a good boy and take care of Maman and baby Beau."

Gervais's little chin quivered, but he nodded. "I will, Papa."

Michel took a step toward Eliane, then froze. She knew why. He was afraid if he touched her now he would never be able to let her go. It was how she felt as well. Eliane wanted to hurl herself at him, to press her body against his so hard that they would become one, inseparable. But Michel had to go; he had no choice. So she would do nothing to make this harder. She would not give the council members that satisfaction.

"Come back to me soon," Eliane said quietly.

"I will." Michel turned toward the door. Roux's two associates escorted him outside. Eliane stared after them for a long moment, then shut the door behind them.

Her mind reeled. She had closed the door on her entire life. There was no living without Michel. She was not even sure the sun would rise tomorrow over her half-empty bed.

"We must begin training at once," Roux announced. "It is my sad duty to tell you the last two slayers were killed by the same vampire, a demon called Tatoul. He seems to have acquired a taste for slayer blood. Tatoul will soon know your location, and he will come for you, bringing others with him."

Eliane stared at him, shocked. A vampire coming here? Looking for her? She could not fathom such a thing. *He wants me to be terrified,* Eliane thought. *This bitter man has destroyed my family. I will not allow him to frighten me.*

"There has never been a vampire in Beauport. I know of them only through Michel's descriptions," Eliane said. "There is no need for a slayer here. Your council has made an error."

"The council is never wrong," said Roux. He held a stake out to her. "Come. Let us train. You will need all your skill to face Tatoul. He is an old one. His powers have been growing for many years. It is said he can move like the winds of a hurricane, so fast that he is almost invisible to the human eye. Soon he will be here, he and the others. You must believe me. You should feel the call within yourself."

Eliane took this in. She could not deny a certain quickening in her body, almost as if her instincts had been sharpened since yesterday. And there were the dreams, those which haunted her even now. She knew in her heart that he spoke the truth: She had been called.

"I refuse the call," she said simply, trying to ignore the wild rushing that now filled her ears. She almost fancied that she heard evil voices on the wind. But she turned away from Roux, from the stake in his hand.

"That is not your choice to make," Roux replied, his words tipped with steel. "Would you let the people of your village die when you have the power to prevent their slaughter?"

The image of humans being slaughtered like pigs filled Eliane's mind. Poor creatures. Poor helpless creatures. She blinked rapidly, trying to free herself from the gory picture. She had to be strong now, no matter what the price. All that mattered was her family, and her family could not exist without Michel. "When my husband is returned to me, I will take my position as Slayer. Not before."

"I am the Slayer. I will do what I must," Eliane said aloud to reassure herself.

It was almost time. The last rays of the sun were lingering on the horizon.

Eliane heard a rustling in the trees outside the cottage. Not almost time, she realized. Time. *She dipped her finger in the small vial of holy water and made a cross on Isabeau's forehead. If the priests were right, the holy water might help keep evil at bay.*

"Be strong, my darling," she whispered. "I pray this is enough to protect you."

Eliane checked the stake tied to her back and picked up the crossbow lying beside Isabeau's cradle. A supply of arrows fit neatly into her waistband—arrows Michel had carved to perfection over the years. The sharp wood of the arrows would slide easily into the monster's flesh.

Without hesitation, Eliane moved to the door and opened it. She scanned the small clearing in front of the cottage and the woods that surrounded it. Yes, there was movement in the underbrush. She could see the movement of the demon.

Eliane slid an arrow, wickedly sharp, into the crossbow and raised the bow to her shoulder, aiming at the trembling leaves of the blackberry bushes. She pulled in a deep breath and waited for the demon to show itself.

The rustling grew louder. The leaves shook harder. And a hoof stepped out into the clearing.

The hoof of a doe. She cautiously moved through the blackberry bushes and began to graze on the tender grass at the edge of the clearing. A moment later, her fawn joined her, the hair on its spotted rump looking as downy as Isabeau's wispy locks.

The air left Eliane's lungs in a whoosh. She forced herself to survey the woods again before she lowered the bow. Then she picked up a small rock and tossed it toward the deer. "Run away, Maman. You and your baby aren't safe here."

"Think about the safety of your children, if the fate of those in the village is not enough to soften your heart," Roux said.

He'd been talking for hours as the day turned to night, and all the time a feeling of nausea had been growing in Eliane's stomach. Now it was almost unbearable. "What my children need is their father," Eliane answered, shooting a look at Gervais—still napping, as was Isabeau in her cradle. "You would do best to return to the council yourself. When Michel is brought back to me, I will gladly take on the duty I was trained for." *They will bring me my husband before they let harm come to any of the people here,* she told herself. *I must stay strong.*

There was a knock on the cottage door. Eliane's heart seized up. More trouble come so soon? She straightened her spine, determined not to show Roux even a hint of fear, and swung the door open wide.

A corpse stood outside, bones almost poking through the skin of its face, deep furrows in its brow, and a mouth crammed with fierce, jagged, deadly sharp teeth.

"Tatoul," Roux whispered.

"Vampire," Eliane said, the word spoken involuntarily. She had heard many stories, and even studied sketches, but this was the first time she had ever seen one of the creatures in the flesh. It was so close to her, she could smell the coppery scent of blood on its breath.

Eliane took a step backward, her gorge rising in her throat. She had not been prepared for this, the horror. Michel had never told her of the smell.

"He cannot enter if you do not invite him," Roux reminded her, as if she could ever forget such a basic fact, as if Michel had taught her nothing. His condescending tone roused Eliane. She shook off her feelings of fear and disgust. Before she dealt with the vampire, she must deal with this odious man, Roux. He was merely a watcher. She was the Slayer. She held all the power, and she must not forget that.

The watcher tossed her a stake. She let it clatter at her feet.

The vampire raised an eyebrow. "Clumsy for a Slayer," he commented, showing even more teeth as he smiled. "I came tonight hoping for some amusement, but—"

"I'd have caught it if I wanted to," she answered. "Caught it and killed you where you stand."

"Easy to say. Much harder to do," Tatoul answered.

"Not if I chose to," Eliane answered, pleased that her voice came out firm and strong. "And if things go as I hope they will, I will soon choose to." She shot a glance at Roux. He stared back at her, his eyes as hard as rocks. "But until then, you and your kind are free to do as you will, without fear of the Slayer."

Tatoul hissed in a breath. "Even if what I will is to sink my teeth into your pretty white throat, taste your sweet slayer blood?" he asked, his hunger-filled eyes sliding to the point just above her collarbone where Eliane could feel her pulse beating.

"Have you lost your mind?" Roux began, running toward her. Eliane shot out a hand and caught him by the throat. In one swift move, she pinned him against the wall next to the door. Now he and the vampire stood side-by-side, one in the cottage, one outside. Her twin enemies. She held Roux still as she addressed the vampire.

"There are some limits to my generosity," Eliane answered. "Me and mine—my son, my daughter—are untouchable." *Surely Roux will order my husband home now,* she thought.

"I don't make bargains," Tatoul told her, sliding his tongue across his cruel incisors.

"And I don't ask for favors from your kind," Eliane replied. "I occasionally give warnings, if I'm in the mood."

The vampire inclined his head. "I'll spread the word, pretty Slayer. And here is a warning for you. You choose not to fight. Do not imagine that we will do the same."

Eliane started awake.

It was dark in the cottage; the only light came from the last dying embers of her cooking fire. Her hand flew immediately to Isabeau, and she breathed a sigh of relief at feeling the babe's chest rise and fall in sleep.

She had been dreaming of slaughter. The demon stalked through the village, tearing apart the innocents there. This time he did not even play with them the way a hunter toys with its prey. This time he tore them limb from limb, eating their flesh as they watched with dying eyes.

Was I really dreaming? Eliane thought. *Or am I seeing through the demon's vision?*

It was not likely that she had fallen asleep. She knew he came for her tonight, and as the Slayer she did not need sleep the way others did. No, this was not a natural sleep. It was a spell, a trance he forced on her.

She had seen evil deeds before this, although never quite so vividly. Indeed every night since the vampires came she had dreamed of the village. She had witnessed the horrors committed there, the men and women tortured. The vampires did not kill the villagers right away, preferring to draw out the agony.

But this time, Eliane was spared no detail. This latest vision was so powerful she could actually feel a lump of flesh sliding down her throat. Worse, the sensation was enjoyable.

Eliane knew why the demon was sharing each sensation with her. The vampires wanted her. The innocent villagers were simply bait, there to lure the Slayer from her home.

She stood. She would wait no longer. She would go to him, and bring death with her.

The Slayer would take the bait.

The scream came from only inches away.

Just on the other side of the door, Eliane thought, pressing her hand against the wood. *Someone is being attacked right outside.*

Isabeau answered with a wail of her own. Gervais had given up on screaming. He just sat in the corner now, rocking to and fro and watching Eliane with big, terrified eyes. *Michel's eyes,* Eliane thought, smoothing the fair hair back from her little boy's forehead.

"Try to be brave, my love," she murmured, leaning in to kiss him. "Soon Papa will be back, and then the monsters will all go away."

"You foolish wench," snapped Gaston Roux. "The demons have just slaughtered a man on your very doorstep. The undead frolic among the cottages of your town. Your children are on an island surrounded by blood and gore, and yet you tell them stories of salvation?"

"Be silent!" Eliane growled. "I've told you I'll not listen. You've taken my husband, and until he's returned, I will not hear a word you say."

The words were strong, and her voice did not waver. But Eliane knew she could not hold out much longer. She had thought refusing the call would be a simple matter of standing up to the Watchers Council. She hadn't realized that the call came from within her. Her very blood sang with the desire to be out in the night, stalking her prey, destroying the undead who roamed Beauport, stopping the slaughter of the innocents. During the sunlight hours, all was calm. But come sundown, the unsettled feeling in her stomach returned, and her senses were heightened almost beyond bearing.

The vampires had taken the village. Though her cottage was almost a mile from the center of Beauport, Eliane could hear the screams on the air, could smell the stench of death. It was impossible, she knew, and yet the noises and the odors plagued her. Her pulse seemed to pound against her skin, pushing for release. Sleep brought her no solace, for with sleep came the dreams— dreams of the hunt, the freedom and power of tracking her nemesis. In these dreams, all her heightened senses were put to use—to smell the beasts, to hear their undead footfalls, to sense with her body the nearness of the demons.

The call was so irresistible that when she woke, it was all she could do not to fling open the cottage door and throw herself into slaying just to satisfy the needs of her body. And to avenge each and every one of the innocents the evil ones had taken.

But then she would look at Gervais, her darling boy, and see in him her husband. She could not abandon Michel. She would not give up on their love, even though it cost the life of every person in Beauport. She looked at Gaston Roux. How could he be allowing all this slaughter to happen?

"Do you know why the demons haunt this town?" Roux asked. "It is because they know you are weak."

"I am not weak," Eliane said, though she felt faint with the need to hunt. "I will not weaken."

"You fight your own destiny," Roux pressed. He moved toward her as if he could sense that her slayer's instincts were battling with her reason.

"Michel is my destiny," Eliane gasped. "And our children—"

"Maman! Maman!" Gervais's shrieks filled the room. "Maman, there's blood!" He sobbed uncontrollably.

Eliane rushed to her boy and pulled him into her arms, turning his face to her chest to spare him the sight. There was indeed blood. Running under the doorway and pooling at a low point in the dirt floor. And the puddle was growing. So much blood.

Eliane felt sick. She raised her eyes to meet those of Gaston Roux. "Where is it coming from?" she whispered.

"The vampires cannot come inside your dwelling," Roux said. "But they can invade in other ways. They are teasing you, showing you just how horrific their power is when they are unchecked by a slayer."

Eliane frowned. "I do not need a lesson. You are not my watcher, and I am not the Slayer."

"You deny your sacred duty. You are no better than those soulless wretches out there. We are all doomed." For the first time, Roux sounded frightened. "This is but your first taste of true evil. I tell you, Eliane, there is much worse than what you have seen. Tatoul, the leader, has walked the earth for centuries. Your heart would stop if you knew all that he has done in those years."

There was a moan from outside. Eliane's breath caught in her throat. Whoever had been attacked out there, just inches from where she stood, was still alive. Was this the blood of that poor unfortunate? Maybe she could still help him. She rushed to the door and pulled it open, ignoring Roux's yell of protest.

With the door came the body. A young woman's body, held fast to the door by means of a knitting needle stabbed through her stomach and into the wood. She was nearly naked, and had clearly been tortured. The telltale wounds of a vampire's teeth marked her neck, her wrists, even her leg. Her head lolled about as if her neck could no longer support it, yet still she lived.

Eliane retched, but now Gaston Roux grew eerily calm.

"This is your work," he said. "Are you proud?"

Eliane peered into the darkness outside the door. Who was he talking to?

"This maid was your neighbor, a lass from your own village. A lass whom it was your duty to protect."

Eliane stared at him. He was talking to her. He was blaming *her* for this atrocity.

"How dare you?" she cried. "I have not done this! I am no monster! It is your fault the village is unprotected. You had only to bring Michel back to me—"

"Silence, selfish wretch!" he thundered. "You were born to be a protector of the people, a force of light, one who sacrifices her own needs for the benefit of others. Yet you, mindful only of *your* wants, have left the people vulnerable. You've brought the undead here like vultures to a funeral. Here they are free to wreak their evil. Here they feast and grow strong—"

"And don't think we don't appreciate it," a smooth voice broke in.

Eliane whirled back to the doorway. Outside stood the vampire, the first one she had seen, Tatoul. He looked stronger now, his pale skin firm and his lips red from drinking blood.

"We've been frolicking in your little hamlet for two weeks now," the vampire said. "It's rare that we have such a prolonged period of feeding."

Kill him, a voice inside Eliane urged. *Take the needle from the girl's belly and stake him through his unbeating heart.* Eliane held tighter to Gervais, fighting the urge. She must think of Michel. She must put her family first.

"But I must confess we are getting bored," Tatoul went on. "We want the Slayer to come out and play with us. How many more corpses do you need to see before your anger gets the better of you?"

"I will not give in," Eliane whispered.

"Then you are killing these people yourself," Roux told her, his voice shaking with fury. "The undead horde will move on to the next village and the next. All those people will be murdered just like the people of Beauport, and their deaths will be on your head."

"He's right, you know," the vampire remarked.

The need to hunt was almost unbearable. "I will not give in," Eliane repeated.

"As you wish." Tatoul reached out and lifted the arm of the girl on the door. He raised her limp wrist to his mouth and slowly bit down, his yellow eyes never leaving Eliane's. The girl moaned again, too weak to do anything more.

Eliane was struck dumb with horror. But Gaston Roux was not.

"I will kill you myself, you damned creature!" he yelled. Before Eliane could move, Roux leapt through the doorway, leaving the protection of the cottage. He did just what Eliane had thought of: grabbed the wooden needle from the girl's stomach and pulled it out.

For Eliane, it was as if time itself slowed, but the actions of the others sped up. All at once, she heard the girl's scream of pain as her body fell to the ground, the wound gushing blood like a fountain. She saw Roux lift the wooden needle, heard his roar of anger. She saw the vampire's smile. Saw his hand move with the speed of lightning, catching Roux's arm and snapping it in half. She saw the vampire spin the watcher, pulling him close, bending to his throat.

She saw Roux's eyes meet hers, filled with terror and a silent plea for help.

Then the vampire bit down. Blood ran everywhere—down the Watcher's neck, over his white shirt; down the vampire's chin as he drank hungrily.

Gervais squirmed mightily, trying to escape the horror. But the Slayer within Eliane did not even register the movements. Forgetting her son, forgetting all other concerns, the Slayer leaped forward, through the door. She hurled herself at the vampire, heedless of the child who still clung to her neck.

They were outside now, no longer protected by the dwelling. The vampire roared with pleasure and dropped Roux to the ground.

"You join the fray!" Tatoul cried, dancing away from Eliane's assault. "You have become the Slayer!"

The words hit her like cold water running down her back.

"No," she gasped, reining in the Slayer instincts. "No, not without Michel."

She stared about her as if seeing through new eyes. She stood outside, unprotected. Gaston Roux lay at her feet; his lifeless eyes would no longer watch. Her little boy screamed in her ear, terrified beyond all reasoning. From inside, baby Isabeau's cries matched her brother's. And the vampire stood not two feet away.

"No?" he repeated. "Not even killing your watcher will make you accept your call?"

"No," Eliane whispered.

Tatoul studied her. "I think you have lost your way, Slayer," he murmured. "But no matter. Once you tried to bargain with me. I told you I make no bargains."

He seemed not to move. Yet suddenly Gervais was gone from her arms. The weight of her darling boy, the heat of his skin— gone. The vampire stood ten feet away now, though Eliane had not seen any motion. *It is said he can move like the winds of a hurricane, so fast that he is almost invisible to the human eye,* Eliane heard Roux's voice whisper in her memory.

"You and yours are not untouchable," Tatoul said.

In his arms he held Gervais—her child, her baby. He still screamed. He still looked at her with his father's eyes.

The vampire bit him. The monster's deadly sharp teeth sank into the babe's soft neck. Her child's lifeblood spilled out, feeding this unholy hunger. From inside, Isabeau's wails grew louder.

It is an abomination, something whispered inside Eliane. *A slayer cannot have children, a slayer and a watcher cannot know love.*

They were being punished.

Eliane flew at the vampire, but he was gone. Again she had not seen him move, but now he stood behind her. He smiled, fangs dripping the blood of her son.

"You have let me grow strong," he mocked her. "And you yourself are weak and untrained."

She ran at him again; again, he eluded her. Eliane let out a sob. Gaston Roux had been right: She had not truly understood evil until this moment. She had not seen the villagers killed, had not had to watch them die. Not like this.

"Your child's blood is sweet," Tatoul murmured. He stood now near the edge of the clearing around her cottage. Gervais lay limp in his arms. Isabeau's screams were fading. Eliane's head swam. She watched helplessly as the vampire leaned again to her son's throat, sipped again of his life.

The vampire moaned ecstatically.

Eliane moaned in response. She wanted to shake off this dream of horror, but could not. She seemed rooted to the ground now.

"Intoxicating, the death of a child," Tatoul said. "His final moment of life." His yellow eyes held Eliane's own as he drank the last of her son's blood.

Then he turned and melted into the darkness, Gervais along with him.

Eliane collapsed to the ground as if only the vampire's will had been holding her up. The Watcher's body lay in a pool of blood. The village girl's twisted corpse lay across the doorstep. Inside, Isabeau cried softly. Gervais was gone.

"My baby," Eliane gasped, unable to breathe through the pain that filled her soul. "My darling child."

Suddenly she heard him behind her, only a few steps away. "I will come back for the other one," he whispered.

By the time Eliane turned, he was gone again.

"Farewell, my beauty, my sweet one," Eliane whispered. Isabeau played with the rattle Michel had carved and watched with wide,

innocent eyes as Eliane tucked cloves of garlic into the cradle. Finally she lifted the cross off her own neck and placed it over her daughter's head.

"I have let innocent people die." She leaned forward and kissed Isabeau's forehead. "But maybe God will have mercy on you if I pay for my sins," she murmured. "I go to face the demon."

"There is no need," said a voice behind her. "The demon has come to you. Tonight we will take your second child."

Eliane straightened, still looking down at Isabeau. Her senses were sharp, almost painfully so. She could smell the demon at the doorstep, and she could smell the others who had come with him. They were outside, at least fifty of them, surrounding the cottage.

They wanted the baby. Their hunger was so intense that Eliane could almost taste it. He still wove his spell, sharing everything with her.

"More than the baby," the vampire said. "We also want you. Blood of the Slayer is the strongest blood there is, I hear. When I have drunk you dry, I will dance in the air, I will survive even in the sunlight, and I will be unstoppable. The babe is simply a whet to my appetite. You are my true desire."

"I am not prey," Eliane told him. "I am the hunter."

"You are no hunter," he spat. "You are weak, a miserable slave to your emotions. So you have ever been."

"No longer. Now I understand true evil. Now I know that I have the blood of innocents on my head. I have learned the error of my ways," Eliane said. "I am the Slayer. Tonight I will kill you . . ."

She turned to face the demon. His pale hair fell across his tiny forehead, and he watched her with his father's eyes.

". . . Gervais."

"I do not believe you," said her son. He smiled a cherub's smile. "You put your family first. I heard you say it over and over to the Watcher."

Eliane looked over his shoulder. Behind him stood the vampire who had killed him, Tatoul. Before her mind had recognized the creature, her body took action. Moving quickly, fluidly, she reached behind her back and removed the stake from its sheath of cloth. A jerk of her wrist, and the sharpened wood streaked across the room, embedding itself in the monster's chest. Once more, his yellow eyes met hers.

"Slayer . . ." Tatoul whispered. Then he exploded into a fine, ash-like dust.

"Do you see?" Eliane asked Gervais. "My first kill. Now I am truly the Slayer."

The little boy laughed. It sounded like the harsh caw of a crow, no longer like a jaybird. His tiny features transformed, thick ridges marring his perfect forehead, Michel's beautiful green eyes turning to the yellow eyes of the undead.

"Did you think he was still the leader?" Gervais mocked her. "Why should I care if he's gone? He was a thorn in my side."

He stepped forward, and Eliane hesitated. She had thought seeing her boy's living corpse would be difficult, but in truth, seeing this transformation was even harder. How could it be possible that this was the child she'd held in her arms?

"Has there ever been a vampire sprung from a slayer before?" he asked. "I don't think so. I take after you—my blood is strong."

"It was you today," Eliane said, "weaving a trance about me. The dreams had always been just dreams before, but today I saw clearly. I saw the atrocities. It was you. That's why the dream was different."

"I share your blood, Mother," the vampire said. "I see your heart. You and I dreamed together when I was still in the womb. Don't you remember?"

Eliane did remember the connection she had felt to Gervais, even before he was born. But she also remembered the dream of today—*the monster tearing peasants apart, no longer as a hunter but now as a senseless butcher. No longer drinking blood, but now also eating flesh.*

The creature that wore Gervais's face smiled as if he could hear her thoughts. His full baby lips were deep red, his cruel fangs as sharp as the stake hidden in Isabeau's cradle.

"Yes, I have eaten them all," the vampire said. "I grow tired of Beauport. I will move to a larger village now, and then on to the cities. There is no one to stop me. But first I will take the rest of your blood."

He stepped forward, his small feet teetering on the very brink of the doorway. He could come no further.

Eliane reached for the baby's cradle.

"I will keep the family together, Mother," the vampire said. "Your blood will join mine. And Isabeau's blood. And when I find my father, I will take him as well. You two created me. You shall share in my crimes."

"Our love created you, and it was wrong," Eliane whispered. "It is my duty to correct that mistake." *She closed her fingers around Isabeau's rattle and pulled the toy from the baby's hand.*

"Mother—," Gervais began.

"Stop," she said, moving toward him. "I will give myself to you if you spare the babe."

The vampire smiled, revealing his fangs. He held out his chubby little arms. "Then come and hug me, Maman."

Eliane had reached the doorway. She stepped across the threshold and knelt to hug her son. His baby arms went around her neck, his mouth seeking her vein. As his fangs pierced her flesh, Eliane felt again the sense of seeing through his eyes, of feeling his sensations. Triumph, she felt, and insatiable hunger. Her blood filled his mouth, coursed through his body like a drug.

He is an abomination, *Eliane thought.* A vampire sprung from the Slayer . . .

His gaze fell on the baby's cradle, and the hunger increased. Eliane saw what he saw, felt his desire for Isabeau.

As darkness crowded her vision, Eliane yanked the ball off the top of the rattle, leaving only the sharpened wooden handle. Michel had whittled it to a deadly point. It was so with most of his carvings; he had wanted Eliane to be always prepared.

She plunged the stake into her son's back and through his heart.

"Your father and I love you, Gervais," she whispered into his soft hair.

The blood within her grew hot, too hot. She felt what Gervais felt: fire running through his body, white-hot like the fires of hell, burning him from the inside out. So hot . . .

As Gervais turned to dust, Eliane felt the heat within her own body. The heat which consumed her as it took her firstborn child. Flames filled her vision, and she realized that they came from herself.

Eliane fell forward on the ground, watching the fire spread from her body. "I have paid for our mistakes," she whispered.

Then all was fire.

LONDON

The cold stone hallways echoed with footsteps for the first time in the month Michel had been here. He leapt off the straw pallet he slept on and hurried to the thick iron door of his cell.

The watchers didn't consider this a dungeon. They called it a retreat, a place for him to meditate on his transgressions until he was ready to ask forgiveness. But all he could think of was Eliane's smiling lips, the way her breathing matched with his as they lay on their bed. The way baby Isabeau's soft skin smelled, the sound of Gervais's impish laugh.

Would they let him out now? He already knew the answer: No. Eliane was the Slayer. He had never doubted that she was truly called. He'd seen the strange new light in her eyes on the morning that Gaston Roux came. And as the Slayer, she had a duty that transcended her duty to him or even to the children.

Had Eliane understood that duty? He wasn't sure that he had made it clear to her. Those years when they were so happy together, had he let his own duties as a watcher slip? He feared it was so. He feared that Eliane would put him first, put their love before her calling. But surely if there were vampires, she would fight them. Surely if the villagers were in danger, she would know that her first duty was to protect them.

Michel tried to swallow his fear. He had not taught Eliane the importance of her post. He had let her believe that love was the greatest calling of all.

They had made a terrible mistake.

The door swung open. A woman stood outside. Michel stared at her, then slowly sank to his knees.

"But what became of her?" the Elder asked impatiently. The Watchers Council was depending on him to bring back a satisfactory answer. He did not like to rely on the occult, but in the present situation it seemed the only option. The council hadn't received any news of the Slayer or her watcher, and at such times they turned to people such as this medium for help. It was an errand little to his liking.

"I cannot see clearly," replied the medium. "It seems there was a great fire. The villagers are all dead, and there was a tremendous amount of blood, but no bodies. They all must have burned, dead and undead alike." She shivered—it was indeed cold in the tiny hut where she lived—but she did not open her eyes or break her trance.

The Elder ground his teeth, staring at the medium as if he could force the woman to see all that had happened in that far-away place. "How did the fire start?" he demanded. "Where did it start?"

"At the Slayer's cottage," the medium said.

"And Gaston Roux?"

The medium was silent for a moment, her eyes moving under closed eyelids. "He was not there. I cannot see him." She gasped. "There is an intense heat. It scalds me from within." She opened her eyes and stood. "I will not seek there again," she announced.

"But my council has no records," the Elder protested. "We watchers must find out what happened. We do not know how it's possible that the one life was spared among so many—"

"Eliane the Vampire Slayer is dead," the medium snapped. "Another is called. That is all you need to know, and I will not seek there again."

Michel wept on his knees before the woman.

"You are free to leave here now," she said. "The Watchers Council has found you a position in Ireland."

"My wife?" he asked, though he already knew the answer.

"There is a new slayer," the woman said. "The village of Beauport has been burned to the ground."

Eliane was dead, then. Michel hung his head and sobbed. "I should have been there to die with her," he cried. "Her transgressions and mine were the same. Why should I be spared rather than Eliane?"

"Because you are needed here," the woman said gently. She held out a small bundle. "She was found in a circle of destruction. The land was burned for a mile around, but her cradle was untouched. The Watchers Council says it is a sign of forgiveness."

She placed baby Isabeau in his arms. Michel gazed down at

his daughter's face, looked into her big blue eyes. "She has her mother's eyes," he whispered.

"It's no small thing, to be the child of a slayer," the woman said reverently. "And your wife killed a village full of vampires, from what we can tell. This little girl will have a blessed future."

The medium left Michel alone with his baby daughter, his entire family. "You will have a blessed future," he promised Isabeau. "I will devote my life to that."

Isabeau smiled up at her father, as if she understood his words. Then she opened her lips and spoke a word of her own, her first word:

"Demon."

Blood and Brine

Greg Cox

THE CARIBBEAN, 1661

One-legged Jack Tyburn was a blackguard when he was alive. Dead, he was a monster.

Animal eyes, the color of Spanish gold, glared at the Slayer from the buccaneer's transformed countenance, which now resembled that of an enraged jungle cat. Fangs jutted from his gaping jaws as he snarled at Robin Whitby from the rear of the quarterdeck. The peg-legged pirate stood aft of the tiller with one taloned hand on the eight-foot-long steering bar and the other clutching onto the scalp of the unfortunate helmsman, Jeremiah Pyle. "Help me, Cap'n!" the terrified old tar entreated Robin, unable to escape Tyburn's demoniacally powerful grasp no matter how frantically he thrashed. "For mercy's sake!"

Fangs like daggers dipped toward Pyle's neck. . . .

"Avast ye!" Robin called out sharply. Her husky voice testified to considerable acquaintance with rum and tobacco. Cutlass in hand, she strode across the main deck to confront her former crewman. Her vibrant auburn hair was pigtailed in the back, sailor-style, while a blue woolen frock coat flapped open to reveal the striped linen shirt and canvas trousers beneath. A cravat of crimson silk, knotted around her neck, added a touch of color and flair to the captain's ensemble. "Strike yer colors, Jack Tyburn, or I'll feed yer scurvy flesh to the sharks!"

A gibbous moon silvered the sails of the double-masted schooner, *Neptune's Lady,* and sharpened the argent gleam of the pirate captain's upraised cutlass, which had once been blessed by an honest Puritan minister. A brace of pistols was slung across Robin's chest, but she knew better than to waste good powder on hellspawn such as this. She was the Slayer after all, and this was hardly the first leech she had run alongside.

I knew it was no mere fever he caught, she thought, *carousing in Port Royal with that doxy Darla.* Seeing her suspicions proven all too seaworthy provided meager satisfaction at this perilous juncture, and a surfeit of opportunities to rue her own foolhardiness. *I should have never set sail with him aboard, all pale and trembling below decks. Now the sun has sunk beneath the waves, and here I be, many leagues to sea, with a God-cursed leech at the tiller!*

"Ye hear me, Jack Tyburn?" she challenged him. Fierce eyes, as blue as the sea, admitted no trace of fear or trepidation. Her boots pounded decisively across the tar-caulked timbers of the deck as she marched past the mainmast toward the stern, deftly avoiding the working sheets of the ship's fore-and-aft rigging. A warm Caribbean breeze blew from the northwest, rustling her hair and filling the billowing white sails above her head. "Leave that salty old dog be, his blood's not yers to quaff!"

Provoked by her scornful tone and cognizant of her flashing blade, the leech shoved Pyle aside and fixed a ferocious gaze on the approaching captain. A trickle of spit ran down his unshaven chin as he licked his lips in anticipation. "As ye command, Cap'n Whitby, sir," Tyburn answered her, flashing his newly acquired fangs. His foul breath reeked of both rum and the grave. "I have a powerful thirst, I do, but a captain's blood will suit me fine!"

Robin had not truly expected the mutinous devil to surrender, her sole intent having been to distract the leech from his intended prey by diverting his sanguinary attentions to herself. Now, meeting Tyburn's blazing glare with a fiery broadside of her own, she watched out of the corners of her eyes as Pyle, ashen-faced and quaking, scrambled toward the bow, where he joined many of his fellow crewmen, who hung back in fear and dumbstruck awe as their captain vaulted onto the quarterdeck to face the unholy thing that Tyburn had become. Yet more seamen watched tensely from the rigging overhead or crouched anxiously behind the silent cannons mounted along the ship's bulwarks.

Robin did not fault her men for their terror in the face of evil incarnate. They were brave enough, she knew, when squaring off against mortal foes or while daring the tempestuous caprices of the sea, but a genuine fiend, straight out of purest nightmare, was another tankard of grog altogether. Even the wildest seawolf might quail before Perdition's own children, unless they were Chosen to the task—as she was.

Tyburn gave the tiller a violent yank, causing *Neptune's Lady* to lurch sharply to starboard. Despite her sea legs, Robin had to grab on to the nearby taffrail to steady herself. "You'll have to do better than that, Jack!" she called out defiantly, eager to separate the leech's head from his shoulders. "I'm comin' for ye, you fetid bilge-rat!"

"Aye, aye, Cap'n!" he mocked her. Robin braced herself for battle, anticipating that Tyburn would lunge at her like the beast he was, slashing and tearing with fangs and claws. Instead he took hold of the main boom with both hands, then shoved it with all his hellborn strength.

The swinging timber struck Robin full on, knocking her onto her back. A queue of tightly-bound red hair scarcely cushioned the blow as the back of her skull collided thunderously with the floor of the deck. Worse, her silver cutlass slipped from her fingers and went sliding athwart the deck into the scuppers. *My blade!* she thought in dismay, cursing her luck.

Seizing his advantage, Tyburn sprang forward, his oaken peg clattering against the planks as he moved with preternatural speed and agility, especially for one so crippled. In a heartbeat, he stood astride Robin's supine form, ivory fangs at the ready. She reached instinctively for her sword, but found it tantalizingly out of reach.

Very well, she resolved coolly. *We'll make do without.*

Without hesitation, she wrapped her fingers around Tyburn's peg-leg and snapped the tapered wooden pin from its lodging beneath the one-legged buccaneer's knee. Deprived of the peg's support, Tyburn yelped and toppled forward. Robin swiftly turned the point of the captured peg upwards, so that the leech fell squarely upon the makeshift stake. He let out a startled cry as his own leg pierced his heart.

Jack Tyburn had spent his entire mortal life at sea; no surprise then that the grave-dust that suddenly rained down on Robin, powdering her face and hands, had a distinctly salty taste.

Argh! Robin's face wrinkled in disgust. She clambered quickly to her feet, spitting out a mouthful of briny grit and brushing the rest of Tyburn's disintegrated remains from her face and clothes. An enormous roar accompanied her rising, as dozens of onlooking buccaneers cheered their captain's victory over yet another stinking leech. Their heartfelt cries, born of sheer amazement and relief, drowned out even the sound of the surging rollers crashing against the schooner's sturdy hull.

Sailors being a superstitious lot, not one of them was troubled by the existence of such as Tyburn had become; in their voyages, she and her crew had encountered all manner of hellspawn, from Aztec mummies to flesh-eating zombies.

Jeremiah Pyle hurried to Robin's side and tugged at her arm in grateful supplication. "Thank ye mightily, Cap'n!" he exclaimed. Admiration beamed from the old salt's weathered, sun-baked features. "By the powers, ye're the bravest man I ever sailed under!"

Or woman, Robin imagined, although scarcely a man aboard knew as much.

Presently, in the great cabin beneath the quarterdeck, the ship's surgeon took an inventory of her injuries. "Your skull appears none the worse for its abrupt rendezvous with the deck," Dr. William Henry Pratt announced sonorously. Gentle fingers probed the sore spot at the rear of her cranium. "The swelling already looks to be abating."

His cultured accent betrayed his Oxford education, as surely as his sepulchral tones betokened his grave and prudent temperament, particularly where the Slayer was concerned. For the physician, whom had contrived to be taken aboard *Neptune's Lady* many long voyages ago, was not just the ship's doctor; he was also her watcher.

"Hah!" Robin laughed, reveling in the glow of her easy victory over the bloodthirsty seaman. "The day I cannot cross swords against the likes of Jack Tyburn, dead or alive, is the day the council needs must press a new slayer into service." She grinned exuberantly. Resting her back against the chair facing the captain's desk, she glanced at the locked door leading to the deck outside. Sunlight entered the narrow cabin through a pair of open windows at the stern, while the everyday sounds of sailors at work penetrated the varnished pine walls. "Did you hear the men a-cheerin' for me just now?"

Although Pratt's neatly-groomed hair was a uniform silver, his bushy eyebrows had remained black as pitch. "I wonder if they would trumpet quite so loudly," he asked, raising one such sable brow, "were they knowledgeable of your true gender?"

His somber query dampened Robin's high spirits. That her shipmates might discover her womanly nature was a constant worry; a pirate captain ruled only at the sufferance of her crew, and Robin lived in fear that her loyal brethren would turn against her should they learn the truth about their captain.

Mind, she ofttimes suspected that many of the men already knew the way of things, but were content to feign otherwise—a sort of willful blindness, comparable to that which allowed ordinary mortals to blithely ignore the presence of leeches and demons in their midst. And, although familiar with vampires, the crew were unacquainted with the notion of slayers; it would never occur to them to think that a female might be more proficient at battling leeches than a man.

Yet the question of how the crew would react should the exact particulars of her sex be forced upon them was one that often troubled her mind; in truth, she feared the exposure of her masquerade far more than any of the foul hellspawn that she had vanquished during her years as Slayer.

"Have no fears on that score," she assured her watcher, with greater bravado than she genuinely felt. She reflexively reknotted the silk cravat about her throat, which served to conceal the absence of her Adam's apple, just as her heavy coat and mannish attire conspired to hide her feminine proportions from the world. Only here, in the exclusive privacy of her cabin, did she dare shed any of her sartorial camouflage. "I've played the man too long and too well to let me secret slip through any chuckle-headed blunder."

"True enough," Pratt conceded, fully aware that Robin had

posed as a boy ever since her twelfth year, when she first ran away to sea in search of adventure. He stepped away from the captain's chair, circling around to address her face-to-face. Unlike the garish and exotic attire flaunted by the rest of the pirate ship's crew, he preferred a conservative gray suit, always impeccably pressed and tailored. "Let us pray that circumstances never converge to give the game away."

"Sail, ho!"

The cry from the crow's nest brought every man jack onto the main deck or up into the rigging in search of a better look. Leaning out over the port gunwale, the balmy tropical sunlight warming her face, Robin felt her heart beat faster in anticipation. Could this be a prize worth taking, sailing near enough to catch the avaricious eye of the lookout? *Neptune's Lady* had been prowling the sapphire waters off the Spanish Main in pursuit of just such an unwary vessel, laden, perhaps, with tobacco, wine, or stolen Inca gold.

"After her, me hearties!" she called out to her crew, who eagerly threw themselves into the task, trimming the sails and hauling lines. The deck of the schooner became a hubbub of activity as the avid buccaneers readied both the ship and themselves for battle. Tattooed seamen, their bodies likewise marked by scars won in bloody frays on both land and sea, scurried fore and aft. Pistols and muskets were primed and loaded, while the *Lady*'s eight cannons were freshly rammed with round-shot.

The sun was high and the wind was steady. Robin couldn't have asked for better conditions.

She strained her eyes to catch a better glimpse of the ship on the horizon. Joining her at the rail, Dr. Pratt offered her a spyglass, which she gratefully accepted. The scope brought the mystery ship closer into view, showing her a vast, three-masted, square-rigged vessel nearly twice the length and perhaps five times the tonnage of *Neptune's Lady*. Robin whooped excitedly as she recognized the unmistakable lines of an imposing Spanish galleon. "Look lively, lads!" she shouted at the top of her lungs. "We've got a golden fish on the line!"

A cacophony of lusty cheers greeted her declaration, as the jubilant buccaneers realized that they had lucked upon the richest prize of all: a Spanish treasure ship transporting the plunder of the New World back to Europe.

Robin grinned wolfishly. Despite the lofty nature of her calling as Slayer, she felt no compunctions against preying on the sea-faring transports of the hated Dons. Spain was the enemy of England, after all, not to mention the oppressor of the native Indians, who had suffered greatly under the sword and lash of the merciless conquistadors. As well was Spain the bastion of the dreaded Inquisition, whose untender mercies had, according to Dr. Pratt, already claimed the lives of at least one slayer and her watcher. Robin saw nothing wrong in depriving the Spanish crown of gold and silver that the Dons themselves had savagely looted from the fallen Incan and Aztec empires.

"Congratulations, Captain," Pratt said sincerely. A patriotic Englishman, he shared Robin's enmity toward imperial Spain and had never objected to her piratical ways, provided they did not interfere with her duties as Slayer. Thankfully the West Indies held more than enough black magick and bloodsuckers to keep her suitably employed on mankind's behalf. Why, the voodoo cults alone more than evidenced that Providence had been wise in placing a slayer at large in the Caribbean.

At this moment, however, Robin looked forward to business of a less eldritch sort. Peering into the spyglass, she scanned the horizon in search of any other vessels that might be escorting the slow-moving galleon; given the popularity of piracy in these parts, it was not uncommon for ships carrying large amounts of valuable cargo to sail in the company of other armed vessels, with perhaps even a man-of-war or two for added protection. Robin had no wish to lead her crew into battle against vastly unequal odds.

To her delight, she espied no such ambush. The solitary galleon appeared to be just that. *A straggler,* she speculated, *left behind by a larger fleet?* If so, then the galleon's tardiness was the pirates' good fortune; the ponderous treasure ship could not possibly elude the swifter and nimbler schooner.

Already, *Neptune's Lady* was closing on the other ship, cracking on all sail as the warm trade winds sped the schooner toward her prey, like a wooden dagger hurled at the undead heart of a blood-gorged leech. "Raise our colors!" she shouted, and within minutes her own singular banner flapped atop the mainmast.

A skull-and-crossbones against a field of Stygian black, Robin's flag resembled the celebrated Jolly Roger except in one respect: the bone-white death's-head bore the fangs of a newly slain vampire, thus serving as a warning, of sorts, to the living and the living dead alike.

Soon the towering stern of the galleon loomed before them, and Robin no longer needed the spyglass to keep her prize in sight. Gleeful pirates, brandishing cutlasses and boarding axes, crowded the bow, yowling like demons and thumping their feet upon the deck in hopes of chilling the blood of all aboard the Spanish vessel. Sharp-eyed marksman peered down the barrel of their muskets, ready to pick off any gunners who might entertain notions of deploying the galleon's own cannons against the approaching schooner. Robin caught a whiff of burning matches on the air and knew that the pirates were ready to fire the six-pounders at her command.

Much to Robin's surprise, the galleon made no attempt to outrun *Neptune's Lady*. Was the treasure ship's captain, she wondered, a man of uncommon good sense? She hoped as much; it would spare much bloodshed if the galleon simply surrendered without a fight, as many a cornered ship had been known to do. Indeed, what else was the Jolly Roger for, if not to frighten God-fearing captains and crews into submission? For herself, Robin was always willing to grant quarter to any mortal man or woman who wholeheartedly requested it. Leeches, of course, were another story.

"Bring 'er alongside!" Robin called to the helmsman. "Make ready the grapples!"

Infinitely more maneuverable than the bulky galleon, *Neptune's Lady* came abreast of the larger vessel, whose name was emblazoned upon her starboard bow: *El Dorado*. A carved mahogany figurehead, in the shape of an Aztec princess, paid no heed to the pirate schooner even as Robin's ship glided within boarding distance of her quarry. The *Lady*'s strakes all but scraped against the galleon's hull.

In contrast to the schooner, whose deck was positively over-crowded with raucous buccaneers, the *El Dorado* appeared curiously unpeopled. Staring up at the mighty ship's tall bulwarks, Robin expected to see human faces—frightened, fierce, or both—peering down at her, yet not a single countenance did she see, save for the painted profile of the wooden princess. "Benjamin Fancy!" she yelled to the lookout, whose lofty vantage point offered him a better view of the galleon's upper decks. "Do ye see hide or hair of the crew?"

"Nary a soul, Cap'n!" Fancy shouted down, raising his voice over the flapping of the sails. He spit rudely onto the undefended Spanish ship. "The cowardly swabs must be hidin' below decks!"

Perhaps, Robin thought, *or perhaps not.* A sense of foreboding fell upon her like a sudden squall as she eyed the galleon with the wary instincts of a slayer. Looking more closely, it was clear that the *El Dorado* was floating adrift upon the sea, following no particular course or compass. Her huge white sails were arrayed haphazardly, without regard to the fickle play of the winds, while her intimidating gunports remained shut and silent, like the lowered eyelids of a corpse.

She cupped her hands around her mouth, in order to be heard by any ears that might be listening aboard the *El Dorado.* "Heave-to!" she commanded, ordering the galleon's masters to bring their vessel to an immediate halt. "Do ye hear me, ye cringin' curs? Heave-to at once, or risk the vengeance of Captain Rob Whitby!"

Her name, she knew, was spoken with fear and respect from Barbados to the Carolinas; nonetheless, there came no answer from the errant treasure ship, only the creaking of the masts as they struggled under the strain of the untended sails.

"This bodes ill," Dr. Pratt intoned in a hush. Ordinarily it was his custom to go below ere the fighting began, the better to insure his own safety so that he might afterward tend the wounds of all those injured in the fray. On this occasion, however, no imminent danger to life or limb appeared to be in the offing.

Which was not to say, Robin realized, that the mysterious galleon did not hold hidden perils far more malignant than armed and defiant Spanish sailors. "Aye," she agreed. In her time as Slayer, she had learned to trust her intuition where the unearthly was concerned, and right now a clammy prickling upon her skin warned her that there was deviltry at work here. "This has the stink of Satan about it."

"Satan, yes," Pratt surmised, "or evils even older and more obscene." He was never one to look to the sunny side of things, her watcher.

"The sooner I get to slayin', then." Seeing nothing to be gained by further prattle, she hooked her cutlass to her baldric and clambered into the rigging, briskly climbing the ratlines until she was able to look down upon the barren deck of the galleon. Grappling hooks, thrown by her excited and impatient freebooters, arced over the *El Dorado*'s gunwales, binding the galleon to the schooner. Both ships shuddered as they came together atop the waves. "After me, mates!" Robin exhorted her crew before somersaulting off the forward gaff to land flatfooted upon the spray-splashed planks of the galleon's waist.

Benjamin Fancy had spoken truly. From where she could see, standing amidship fore of the mainmast, the upper decks of the *El Dorado* appeared as deserted as those of any abandoned hulk left rotting in some lawless Caribbean harbor. Her keen eyes hastily examined the capstan and coiled cables for any damning splashes of blood, as might be left by some shipboard massacre or mutiny, but nonesuch was to be found, although she spotted ample evidence of past tumult and disorder: hatches left open, tarpaulins torn asunder, shrouds and stays dangling uselessly, and tar-smeared ropes strewn about the deck like seaweed. Drunken buccaneers, at the height of their revels, could not have left the galleon in a greater state of disarray, let alone a shipload of fastidious Dons in charge of their empire's treasure.

Robin scowled. *Something* untoward had transpired here; that was for certain. But what?

Already she had her suspicions.

Howling and hollering more from habit than need, her boisterous crew of cutthroats boarded the galleon in Robin's wake, climbing up and over the rails with their dirks and cutlasses gripped between their teeth. As their bare feet dropped onto the deck, they glared about them ferociously, accustomed to raising

Cain with sword and pistol. Today, alas, they found themselves sheepishly lowering their weapons due to a lamentable lack of Spaniards to threaten. The baffled buccaneers looked so abashed and discomfited that Robin would have laughed had she not been on guard against supernatural evil.

"Luff'er smartly!" she instructed the nearest crewmen. Floating freely, the *El Dorado* was a danger to both herself and *Neptune's Lady*. "Bring her to a halt instanter." Robin raised her voice to address each and every boarder. "The rest of ye, keep a weather eye out for trouble. This lumberin' barge may not be as empty as she presents herself."

While obedient seamen hurried to the task of curbing the galleon's wayward drifting, Robin carried her investigation forward. Cutlass in hand, she stalked the unswabbed planks, climbing onto the railed deck atop the forecastle. From there she observed that the *El Dorado's* boats had not been launched, but remained secure in their berths upon the spar deck. The missing Spaniards had not fled the galleon in their own boats, then. So where were they?

Robin had heard tell of death ships such as this, found empty and abandoned upon the sea. Indeed, if her watcher were to be believed, the annals of his predecessors were fair to bursting with accounts of such star-crossed vessels. More often than not, she recalled, 'twas a leech at work, feeding on the crew by night and consigning their bodies to the deep to avoid detection. . . .

"Cap'n!" An excited voice, carrying an unmistakable undercurrent of fear, called to Robin from the stern. She bounded off the forecastle, descending the steps in a single leap, and dashed aft, where she found a cluster of her own men gathered below the quarterdeck within a shallow compartment just before the great cabin. "Hell's bells," one battle-scarred buccaneer said in a horrified hush, "have ye ever seen the like?"

At first, Robin could not discern what sight held the men so transfixed. "Clear the way," she grunted, roughly elbowing her way through the packed throng—until she came nigh face-to-face with the mortal remains of the only Spaniard still remaining at his post.

Standing upright at the helm, his lifeless body lashed tightly to the whipstaff, the dead man stared blindly forward, his bearded face contorted into a rictus of perpetual agony. His garments had been shredded from his corpse, making it impossible to determine his rank, and his throat and torso were marked by a multitude of strange, circular impressions, like the puckered kisses of a devil. These livid, ringlike blemishes were the only wounds Robin saw upon the unfortunate Don, the exact nature of whose death she was at a loss to explain. As elsewhere aboard this accursed vessel, not a drop of spilled blood could she see or smell, although the deceased seaman was markedly pale beneath his typically swarthy complexion. *What rendered this unlucky mariner so bloodless?* she pondered. *Some new and unfamiliar breed of leech?*

"Leave him to the sawbones," Robin ordered. Dr. Pratt would almost certainly want to examine the Spaniard's remains. "As for me, I'm goin' below to flush out the vermin that done for this poor soul. Ye're all to stay above deck until I give the word to commence with the pillagin'." She swept a forbidding gaze across the faces of the assembled freebooters. "Are we clear on that, me brethren?"

On any other raid, a blistering fusillade of grape shot would not have deterred the greedy buccaneers from immediately inspecting the contents of the galleon's hold. But the *El Dorado*'s eerie silence and desolation, along with the ghastly spectacle of the doomed helmsman, had cast a pall over their unslaked lust for Spanish gold. "Aye, Cap'n," said the boatswain, Jonas Pugh.

Like his fellows, he appeared well content to let the captain brave the shadowy recesses of the galleon's lower decks before the rest of them. "Just as you say."

"Very well then," Robin confirmed. She paused a second to take her bearings before ducking her head to enter the companionway leading to the gun deck. She fully expected to find one or more leeches lurking below, far from the purifying rays of the sun, and was not so naive or inexperienced as to expect the hidden bloodsuckers to be completely dormant just because the sun had not yet sunk beneath the horizon. She knew too well that the living dead need only shun direct exposure to daylight; indoors, sealed away from the sun, leeches were just as dangerous as they were at the blackest hour of the night.

At first she had little need of the lamp she carried, as shards of daylight penetrated the darkness through open hatches and cracks between the planks over her head. It required only a heartbeat for her azure eyes to accommodate themselves to the sunless murk of the cramped gun deck, which was fetid with reek of unwashed men crammed together for weeks or months a time. Rats and roaches scurried away at the sound of her approach, but Robin paid them no heed; it was a fouler breed of infestation she sought.

The footsteps of her crew, milling about upon the spar deck above her head, grew ever more faint as she headed deeper into the bowels of the ship, which thus far had proven to be as deserted as the upper decks. Here at last, far from the sun, she depended on the flickering glow of an oil lamp to see by. The lower she climbed down the companion, the more the noisome stench of the bilge polluted the air, permeating her nose and mouth. So, too, did her awareness of the presence of some diabolic evil increase the nearer she came to the galleon's secluded hold. Her skin fairly crawled from its proximity to the unnamed abomination.

Arriving at last at the dank and dismal entrance to the hold, she took a deep breath, near gagging at the malodorous reek, then kicked open the hatch and, cutlass drawn, sprang into the compartment beyond.

"By Davy Jones's goddamned locker!" she exclaimed aloud, her jaw dropping at what she beheld.

Gold, lustrous and unmistakable, packed the spacious hold from top to bottom, reflecting what scant light filtered through the remains of the sundered hatch high above, as well as the paltry glow of Robin's lamp. Priceless Incan jewelry and sculptures, all seemingly forged of solid gold, glittered atop open casks overflowing with shining yellow doubloons, as well as flashing silver pieces of eight. The pagan idols, sporting jagged fangs and bestial features, stood out amidst the scattered riches by virtue of their blasphemous, albeit artfully rendered, grotesquerie; Robin's eye was caught by one bizarre graven image, roughly the size of a half-gallon tankard of rum, whose beaklike jaws and coiled tentacles gave it the look of a squid or octopus perched regally atop a throne of skulls. Polished rubies, red as wine, served as the seabeast's eyes.

Who in heaven's name would venerate such a loathsome thing? she wondered, repressing a shiver of revulsion, before such philosophical concerns were driven from her mind by the sheer magnitude of the gleaming hoard before her. *It's a king's ransom, by thunder!* she exulted silently, unable, for the nonce, to tear her spellbound gaze away from the glittering treasure trove. *No, an emperor's!* Even the Watchers Council, whose wealth was legend, might envy such a fathomless sea of swag.

Greed threatened to usurp the prudent caution required by her present circumstances, yet wiser counsels prevailed; Robin forcibly diverted her attention from the lavish spoils to search the hold for the leech she felt certain was hiding there. "Show yerself, ye bloodsuckin' rogue!" she taunted, holding her sanctified cutlass at the ready. "I know ye're in here!"

Her mind's eye envisioned the voracious vampire draining the crew of the *El Dorado* one by one, then tossing the bloodless corpses over the rails into the waiting brine, the murdered seamen consigned to the deep with neither rite nor reverence. The grisly images filled the sails of her righteous fury; even popish Spaniards deserved better deaths than that. "What be the matter?" she mocked the anonymous darkness. "Have ye gorged too much on hot Spanish blood to crave a taste of me own salty brew?" She slashed at the foul, pungent air as her angry gaze swept the hold, which was, she observed, notably devoid of skulking rats, as though even those pestilential vermin feared to associate with the unnatural monstrosity she sensed nearby. "Ahoy, ye maggoty glutton! Rise and face a slayer's vengeance!"

A furtive gasp reached her ears, drawing Robin's attention to a closed teak casket, suspiciously akin to a coffin, lodged against a starboard bulkhead. Sea-blue eyes narrowed and a knowing smile lifted the corners of her lips as she closed upon the casket and placed her free hand palm down upon the timber lid, where she felt the telltale vibrations of someone—or something—stirring inside the rectangular wooden chest.

Thought ye could hide from me, did ye? Robin thought smugly. Her left hand gripped the lid of the casket while the other raised the cutlass high. Her sly expression turned to one of unbending resolution. *Well, many's the leech that has thought the same afore I made dust of his unbreathin' carcass!*

Exerting her more-than-mortal strength, she flung open the heavy teak lid, in full expectation of discovering a fiend-faced revenant cowering below, only to find herself staring into the frightened brown eyes of a dusky young Spanish woman whose trembling hands were clasped together in a fervent prayer of supplication. *"Socorro!"* she pleaded desperately in her native tongue. *"Madre de Dios, socorro!"* Fresh tears gushed onto cheeks already streaked by much weeping. Her panicked heart pounded so loudly that Robin would have known the terrified maiden was alive and not a duplicitous leech posing as human, even if she hadn't spied the silver crucifix resting upon the other woman's lacy bodice.

"Her name is Carmelita Aponte," Dr. Pratt revealed after a rapid perusal of the *El Dorado*'s log. "She is the captain's half-Indian daughter, who was accompanying him on his voyage back to Spain." The physician sat behind a heavy wooden desk in the captain's private office beneath the galleon's poop deck. Chart-sized glass windows at the rear of the cabin admitted more than enough light to see by. "Furthermore, should there be any doubt, my examination confirms that the young lady is quite entirely mortal."

Not for the first time, Robin thanked Providence that she had not beheaded the unfortunate girl by mistake; only her supernal reflexes had allowed the Slayer to check the fall of her cutlass in time to spare the other woman's life.

Robin glanced at the captain's daughter, who now sat tensely on the velvet cushions atop a timber sea chest. Although quieter now than when Robin first discovered her, Carmelita clearly remained in a state of dire agitation. Her birdlike gaze darted about fearfully, ever on guard against some unnamed peril, while she hugged herself tightly and whispered fretful prayers without cease. She started skittishly at the slightest unexpected sound, and she trembled within an elegant saffron gown that was now hopelessly rumpled and frayed around the edges. The silver crucifix still hung from a delicate chain around her neck; Robin wondered if the cross had played any part in keeping Carmelita alive where so many others appeared to have perished.

"Has she told ye what transpired here?" she asked Pratt, having, for appearance's sake, permitted the doctor to examine his patient in private. "What became of her father and his crew?"

A thorough search of the *El Dorado,* conducted after Robin gave her crew of buccaneers leave to explore the vessel, had found no other survivors aboard the deserted treasure ship. Nor any bloodthirsty stowaways, for that matter.

Pratt shook his head. "I fear that Senorita Aponte's reason has not yet fully recovered from her ordeal, whatever it may have entailed. She is far from lucid, barely able to utter more than repeated prayers for deliverance, and a few fragmentary words and phrases."

Robin nodded in understanding. She had often witnessed the shocked reactions of ordinary men and women to an attack by diabolic forces; such a hellish encounter could shake even the strongest soul to its foundations. "Has she been driven mad?" Robin asked, heartfelt sympathy making her throat to tighten.

"I think not," Pratt replied. "With time, and by the grace of heaven, she may recover, but, for the present, I am reluctant to press her too strenuously on whatever tragic fate befell this vessel. To stir up such grievous memories now would do her more harm than good."

Robin knew better than to ask the doctor to violate his Hippocratic Oath, which took precedence over even his duties as her watcher. "And did she tell ye *nothing* of what claimed her father and the rest?" The persistent nebulousness of the threat frustrated Robin immensely. "Have we no clue at all?"

"Just one," Pratt divulged. A pensive scowl deepened the furrows above his hirsute brows. "When questioned, as gently as possible, about the fate of her countrymen, she could only whisper the same puzzling phrase, over and over: '*Muchas bocas.*'"

"'Many mouths,'" Robin translated. *What the devil?*

A knock at the cabin door startled Carmelita, who sprang to her feet, her eyes wide with fright. Robin rushed to calm the distressed senorita. "Easy now, lass! All's well. Nobody's goin' to hurt ye." Lapsing in and out of Carmelita's native Spanish, Robin gently took the other woman by the shoulders and eased her directly into the sunbeam entering the cabin through the stern windows. "See? Sunlight. Nothin' can get ye, nothin' from the dark."

Robin's soothing tone, in concert with the comforting warmth of the bright golden light, quieted Carmelita. *"La luz del sol?"* she repeated uncertainly, looking from Robin's face to the illuminated window and back again. *"La luz del dia?"*

"Aye, that's it," Robin assured her. "You're safe now, in the light." *Best to get her off this cursed ship before nightfall,* Robin decided. *She may feel safer aboard* Neptune's Lady.

The rapping at the door came again, now accompanied by the raspy voice of her quartermaster, George Newgate. "Beggin' your pardon, Cap'n, but the crew be wonderin' what your orders is, now that we made sure this vessel's been swept clean of Dons." His inquiry carried a subtly hectoring edge; Robin had long suspected that Newgate harbored ambitions of usurping her as captain some day. "The crew's chafin' to get back to port and divvy up the spoils."

Hardly a surprise, Robin thought with some amusement. The pirates' uneasiness aboard the death ship had been much allayed by the discovery of the stupendous fortune stowed away in the galleon's hold. She had no doubt that, within their fevered imaginations, her gleeful cutthroats were already spending their shares amidst the copious taverns and brothels of Port Royal.

"Hold yer fire!" she called back, taking care, after speaking so softly to Carmelita, to deepen the timbre of her voice once more. "I'll be with ye directly." Casting one last look at the disturbed

Spanish damsel, she headed for the door. "Watch her, William," she urged her watcher, "and keep readin' that damned journal. I want to know what manner of devil we're dealin' with."

A hasty council upon the El Dorado's main deck rapidly yielded a consensus concerning how best to take advantage of the buccaneers' newly-won prize. At Robin's suggestion, it was agreed to split Neptune's Lady's crew between the two vessels and sail them both back to Port Royal without delay. As a caution against treachery, half of the captured Spanish gold was transferred to the schooner's own hold, with the remainder left stowed away in the bowels of the galleon. With some reluctance, Robin turned over command of Neptune's Lady to George Newgate so that she could remain aboard the death ship, the better to confront whatever evil might yet lurk unseen within the El Dorado's shadow-haunted hull.

Dr. Pratt, on the other hand, accompanied Carmelita Aponte over to the pirates' schooner, where Robin hoped she would rest more easily, safely distant from the site of her fellow Spaniards' mysterious disappearance. Robin also took pains to spare Carmelita the dreadful sight of her father's stripped and bloodless corpse; only after the faltering senorita had been taken aboard Neptune's Lady did the Slayer cut down Capitan Aponte's body from the whipstaff and, purely as a precaution, sever the doomed mariner's head before, with a bowed head and a moment's prayer, consigning the unfortunate man's body to the deep.

Many mouths, she mused, recalling the obscene stigmata branding the dead captain's flesh. Aye, but whose?

Night fell quickly in the tropics, and soon the blazing Caribbean sun dipped beneath the waves. Heavy clouds, pregnant with unshed rain, obscured the moon and stars, rendering the night as black as a leech's heart. Choppy seas and strong winds made lamps too dangerous, so the *El Dorado* sailed by the light of a single candle, lodged in the wooden binnacle fore of the tiller so that the helmsmen could read his compass by the candle's flickering glow.

Alone in the crow's nest, overlooking the night-shrouded galleon, Robin cursed the clouds concealing the moon. How could she hope to watch over the ship and her crew when the elements themselves conspired to hide her faceless adversary from sight? Even her superb eyes had their limits.

A warm, salty wind blew from the northeast, stirring the fabric of her loose frock coat. Robin felt the roll of the ship, almost a hundred feet below her current perch. Keeping lookout from atop the mainmast was not a captain's duty, but it was a slayer's; in truth Robin was more concerned with watching out for whatever might be prowling the ship's decks than in surveying the turbulent seas through which they sailed.

From the crow's-nest the upper decks of the galleon appeared deceptively quiet. Only a handful of men worked the sails in concert with the helmsmen; the bulk of the crew, some four and twenty men, had retired to their freshly-acquired berths within the forecastle. Pacing impatiently, Robin stared down into the shadows, her concentrated gaze sweeping the *El Dorado* from stem to stern. Although the day's searches had yielded no clandestine nest of leeches, she felt certain that some foul and loathsome bloodsucker still dwelt aboard the captured galleon, hungry to feast upon the lifeblood of her loyal buccaneers.

"Where are ye, you soul-lackin' lubber?" she muttered. The toe of her boot tapped restlessly against the floor of the nest. "I've better things to do with me time than wait upon your vile pleasure."

Glancing away from the ship below, she looked out past the

bow. If she strained her eyes, she could barely glimpse the tops of *Neptune's Lady*'s familiar masts. The treasure-laden schooner, sparing no effort in her haste to return to port, had easily outdistanced the much slower galleon. Robin felt a stab of irritation at being so blithely left behind by her own ship. *I shall have to deal with George Newgate in due course,* she resolved with a scowl. Alas, the duly-elected quartermaster was popular with the men, if not with their captain.

She turned her gaze toward the sea behind her. Lambent phosphorescence, glowing like faerie fire atop the cascading rollers, trailed behind the *El Dorado* in her wake. Robin wondered about the dead Spanish captain they had buried at sea many leagues astern. Did light of any sort penetrate the abysmal gloom of his watery resting place, or had his unfettered soul already ascended beyond such concerns?

Feeling a kinship toward a fellow seaman, regardless of his nationality, Robin vowed to avenge the other captain's wretched death—if only the guilty party would show its hideous face!

Too restless to stay still, too weary to bear easily this endless nocturnal vigil, Robin yawned and returned to watching over the placid decks below, which remained maddeningly free of leeches, zombies, witch doctors, were-beasts, succubi, Flying Dutchmen, or any other malevolent emissary of Erebus. Her fingers hovered expectantly over the grip of her silver cutlass, yet hours passed without incident, and, as dawn approached, Robin began to suspect that her vigil had been in vain—until the echoes of a distant shriek caused her head to jerk upright and her sword hand to tighten around the hilt of her weapon.

"What the devil?" she swore, for the faint-yet-tormented keening came not from the ship below, but from somewhere just beyond the horizon. *The schooner!* she deduced at once, realizing to her horror that she had chosen to guard the wrong ship.

A heartbeat later she remembered just which vessel her watcher and Carmelita were sailing upon.

"William!"

They caught up with *Neptune's Lady* just before dawn. The schooner was lying-to upon the aquamarine sea, its sails artfully set in opposition to each other so as to keep the ship more or less stationary. Robin chose to take this as a good omen, proof that, at the very least, *someone* remained alive aboard the other vessel.

Drawing nearer, she breathed a sigh of relief as she spied clusters of seemingly unscathed seaman milling about upon the schooner's upper decks. Nonetheless, she wasted no time boarding *Neptune's Lady* as soon as they overhauled the pirate craft, leaping over the galleon's gunwales onto the planks of the smaller ship. Her boots touched down just forward of the mainmast, where the majority of the crew appeared gathered.

She knew at once that something was amiss. A foreboding silence greeted her arrival, while the faces of the men, which had positively shone with triumph and lustful anticipation when last she saw them, now seemed drawn and discontented, their sour expressions composed of equal parts fear and anger.

"About time ye got here, Cap'n," George Newgate said with a sneer, as though he had not expressly chosen to place long, rolling leagues between the schooner and the *El Dorado*. A great hairy bear of a man, with a livid white scar over one eye, the quartermaster leaned insolently against the mainmast, his beefy arms crossed atop his naked chest. His bristling, blond beard had been bleached nearly white by the West Indian sun. "Ye fairly missed all the commotion!"

Robin ignored Newgate's flagrant insubordination . . . for now. Craning her neck to peer over the head and shoulders of the motley throng crowding the schooner's waist, she spotted

Dr. Pratt and Carmelita standing apart from the others, in the shadow of the quarterdeck, their backs against the forward wall of the captain's cabin. The physician had one arm draped protectively over the senorita's shoulders while his other hand clutched the grip of a ready flintlock pistol. His countenance was, if possible, even more somber than customary.

"Well?" Robin demanded, striding across the deck toward the doctor and his charge. An empty bottle of rum, its neck snapped off by an impatient pirate, rolled fore and aft between the sailors' feet. "What ill tidings do ye have for me?" Her probing eyes surveyed the crowd of sailors, finding certain faces disturbingly absent. "Where be Ezra Davies . . . and One-Eyed Ned?"

"Gone, Captain!" Newgate growled, stalking away from the mast. "And an 'alf-dozen others besides. Vanished without a trace in the dead of night!" He shoved his way through the mob to confront Robin face-to-face. Spittle flew past his tawny whiskers as he hurled his words at her like smoldering grenades. "Just like the Dons on that God-accursed galleon you led us to!"

Damnation! Robin thought bitterly. She blamed herself for not anticipating that the faceless evil upon the *El Dorado* might transfer itself from one vessel to another. "This be a dark, dastardly business, I grant ye," she said, shaking her head mournfully before assuming a more determined mien, "but fear not, maties. I'll track this contagion to its root, ye have me word on that!"

"Why, ye needn't look very hard, Cap'n." Newgate drew himself up dramatically and shook an accusing finger at Carmelita Aponte, still cowering beneath Dr. Pratt's arm, her tremulous lips mouthing a ceaseless plea for deliverance. "There's the baneful albatross that cost our shipmates their lives: that damned Spanish witch!"

"Belay that talk!" Robin barked. "Are ye mad? Look at her! She's no more dangerous than a wisp of seaweed. Less so, I warrant!"

"So ye say, Cap'n, but I 'ave me doubts." He raised his voice so that all present could attend to his words. "Be it just a coincidence that this slip of a girl survived where so many able-bodied soldiers and seamen perished? We brought 'er aboard the *Lady,* out of the goodness of our 'earts, and now eight of our brethren have been spirited away to the Good Lord knows where." A smirk betrayed his seditious designs as he stared pointedly at Robin. "'Tis well known that a woman aboard a ship brings nothin' but ill luck!"

Robin swallowed hard behind her knotted silk cravat. A gaping pit formed in her stomach as she felt the mood of the men turning against her. Loyal crewmen, who had fought beside her through fire and steel, now looked away, refusing to meet her gaze. *How many of them know my true sex,* she wondered anxiously, *and for how long have they known?* Angry muttering mixed with sullen glances and sneers seemed to surround Robin as she backed warily toward Dr. Pratt and Carmelita. "Toss the Spanish whore overboard," a scowling buccaneer snarled, spitting in the senorita's direction, and Robin heard truculent voices murmur in agreement.

Her spine stiffened and she drew her cutlass. Although her deepest, most private doubts and fears appeared to be coming true before her eyes, she was not yet ready to cede command to the likes of George Newgate. "Stay back!" she warned, cutting a swath through the air with the blessed blade of her cutlass. "I've never sacrificed a defenseless hostage before, and, by thunder, I'll be hanged if I'm startin' now!" She snorted contemptuously at the panicky buccaneers. "The Spaniards' gold came aboard this here ship as well, same as Senorita Aponte," she reminded them.

"Yet I don't hear anyone suggestin' that we heave all that glitterin' booty over the sides!"

Her slashing blade drove the crowd of pirates back a few paces, so that they formed a half-circle around Robin, the doctor, and Carmelita, with the front of the quarterdeck at their backs. Robin hoped her stinging rebuke would take the wind out of this incipient mutiny, but George Newgate, damn his perfidious soul, pressed the issue further.

"Whose side are ye takin', Cap'n?" he challenged her, all but flinging that last word. He drew his own sword and snatched a loaded pistol from his belt. "Maybe if ye'd worried more about yer own shipmates and less about some papist slut, Ezra Davies and the others would still be walkin' these planks beside us, not condemned to suffer for all eternity in some unholy limbo!"

I thought the danger was aboard the El Dorado, she thought, racked with anguish and regret, *else I would never have left* Neptune's Lady *without a slayer!* Her heart bled for the squandered souls of the missing buccaneers.

She knew better, though, than to justify herself to a rebellious crew. "Quite the orator ye've become, George Newgate, but do ye care to test me mettle with more than just empty words?" A murderous smile upon her lips, she beckoned him with her free hand while holding her silver cutlass aloft. "Come then, if ye have the stomach for it. I can always find another quartermaster."

The scar-faced man blanched behind his beard, perhaps recalling Robin's preternatural strength and speed. "This isn't about takin' command," he blustered, lying through his teeth. "It's about the safety of this crew!" He looked about him expectantly, seeking support. "Isn't that right, lads?"

"I'm not riskin' my skin for some halfbreed jinx!" another crewman called. Newgate's cronies seconded the sentiment, crowding forward to lend their tattooed and sunburned weight to the quartermaster's defiance. Of the rest, none seemed willing to stand up to the rebels for the sake of the captain or Carmelita. *Be their fear that great,* Robin had to wonder, *or be it that we're naught but mere women?* It despaired her to think that her crew's loyalty ran no deeper than her slender facade of masculinity.

In any event, it was clear as fresh spring water that more than a one-on-one duel with Newgate was in the offing. Her azure eyes narrowed as she coolly assessed her position.

Even counting Dr. Pratt's flintlock, the odds were woefully against her. *Very well,* she thought, resolved to sell her life dearly if needs be. She smiled bleakly at the dark humor of it; after battling the ravening legions of hell for all these many voyages, in the end it was her own merry band of cutthroats that slipped her the Black Spot!

"Watch me stern," she sharply instructed Dr. Pratt, concerned that furtive mutineers might attempt to drop down on them from atop the quarterdeck or perhaps from the spider's web of rigging strung out above them. "And, pray, keep your eyes lifted."

"Understood," her watcher intoned solemnly.

Robin kept her own gaze squarely fixed on Newgate and his belligerent cohorts. "So," she dared them, "shall we get to fightin'? Let us see whose blood will flood the scuppers!"

An uneasy silence ensued as Robin faced off against the encroaching pirates. None, it appeared, wanted to be the first to tempt the captain's cutlass. "Damn ye all!" Newgate finally howled in frustration. "She's just one scoundrel, by the powers, and a goddamned woman to boot! Rush her!"

An icy chill stabbed Robin's heart as Newgate unfurled her most tightly wrapped secret. *So be it,* she concluded resolutely. After the initial shock, she felt strangely relieved to have the matter dredged up to the surface at last. *No more flying under false colors.*

"Wait!" another voice cried out, belonging to Jeremiah Pyle, the helmsman whose leathery neck Robin had but recently rescued from a leech's fangs. "There be no need for bloodshed, mates! We have two ships, don't we? Let each man choose with whom he sails, then let us go our separate ways!"

A chorus of approving shouts and exclamations applauded the proposed compromise, and even George Newgate appeared to welcome the chance to duck a battle to the death against Robin and her allies. "The ayes 'ave it!" he declared with magnanimous shrug. "But I claim the *El Dorado,* by virtue of me clear majority."

Robin was more than willing to cede him the grander vessel, whose ominous history had now been overshadowed by the yet fresher depredations aboard *Neptune's Lady.* For once, she found herself in agreement with the scheming quartermaster; as Newgate himself doubtless did, Robin prayed that the curse of the doomed galleon, which had seemingly shifted to the luckless schooner, would not move on again.

In the end Newgate and the *El Dorado* got the lion's share of the crew. He therefore insisted that the bulk of the treasure be transferred to the galleon as well, an onerous and back-breaking chore that took up the better part of the morning. Soon enough, however, both vessels unfurled their sails and set course for the pirate refuge of Port Royal.

Now it was Robin's turn to leave Newgate behind. Even with naught but a skeleton crew to man the sails, *Neptune's Lady* quickly outpaced the lumbering galleon, ploughing the waves as nimbly as a leaping porpoise. The schooner's own figurehead, carved in the likeness of a comely mermaid, with chiseled golden ringlets tumbling down her back toward a fishy emerald tail, looked out, as did Robin, over the churning expanse of sea before them. With a favorable wind drawing her sails, the *Lady* might well come within sight of Jamaica in two days' time.

Robin wondered if any aboard the schooner would still be alive to see land again.

After ensuring that all was shipshape, and thanking the remaining crew for their steadfastness, she retreated to her cabin beneath the quarterdeck, where she found Dr. Pratt engrossed in his studies. The dead captain's logbook was spread open atop the lacquered walnut desk, while ancient volumes of arcane lore were piled high upon the floor beside his chair.

Carmelita Aponte, fallen into an unsettled sleep, occupied Robin's cozy berth in the side compartment, visible through an open doorway. By the piteous moans that escaped her lips, and the spastic twitching of her limbs, it was heart-breakingly apparent that slumber offered the poor maiden no relief from the nightmare visions and hellish memories plaguing her troubled mind. *"Muchas bocas,"* she whimpered, not quite so softly that Robin's keen ears could not hear her cryptic lament. *"Tantas bocas!"*

A shudder passed through Robin as she translated the foreign phrases into proper English. *Many mouths. So many, many mouths . . .*

"Have ye found anything?" she asked Dr. Pratt. Barely literate herself, she depended on her watcher for any scholarly assistance that might be required.

"I fear not," he answered, raising his eyes from the handwritten text before him. He glanced cautiously at Carmelita's sleeping form and lowered his voice before continuing. "The late *Capitan* Aponte's log describes how, night after night, his entire crew gradually disappeared. It's a classic pattern, which nearly always signals the presence of a lurking vampire aboard the afflicted vessel. This undead stowaway lurks in the lower reaches of the ship by day, emerging at night to prey upon hapless crew members, whose bloodless bodies the vampire then heaves over the rails, thus concealing his own presence." Puzzlement was written upon his saturnine features. "And yet you say you found no evidence of an infestation aboard either ship?"

Robin shook her head. "I searched the *El Dorado* from stem to stern when we first found her, and just did the same for the *Lady.* I'll prowl the ship again if ye like, but I'll tell you plain that it would be a fool's errand." She paced restlessly about the narrow cabin. "If some foul thing be aboard, it's beyond mortal eyes to see."

"Hmm," the doctor said thoughtfully, stroking his chin. "Invisibility. I had not thought of that." He nodded at a stack of venerable tomes tottering precariously upon the swaying floor. "Pray, fetch me Ambrosius's *Chronicles of Realms Unseen.* That gilt-edged volume there," he added, noting Robin's blank expression.

She located the desired text, which felt strangely cold and slimy to the touch, like an algae-covered rock at low tide. Intending to hand it over to Dr. Pratt forthwith, she took one step toward the desk when, without warning, a numbing shock flowed up her arms, from her fingertips to her shoulders, causing her to drop the unhallowed book as though it were ablaze.

"What is it?" Dr. Pratt asked, springing from his seat so abruptly that the chair toppled over behind him. His bushy black brows lifted in alarm. "Are you unwell?"

Robin heard his anxious inquiries, yet her attention was elsewhere. As the feeling returned to her arms, nigh as swiftly as it had departed, she stared in wide-eyed amazement at the book upon the floor, which had fallen open to reveal two of its myriad pages. "Shiver my soul!"

She could not read any of the words inscribed upon the pages. Why, even the very alphabet of which the writing was composed bore no resemblance to any language she had ever encountered before, making the ornate and inscrutable hieroglyphics of the Far East look like a child's ABCs.

But there was no mistaking the grotesque illustration, engraved with exacting if abominable precision, that accompanied the indecipherable scribblings: a tentacled monstrosity with eyes the color of rubies, reigning atop a throne of skulls. "I know this ugly devil!" she blurted loudly. "There was a golden effigy of the very same creature stowed in the hold of the *El Dorado,* with the rest of the treasure!"

"Good Lord!" the doctor gasped. "Are you certain?"

"As ever I was!" *This be no chance event,* she realized; Providence, in its wisdom, sometimes gifted slayers with prophetic dreams and hints of knowledge beyond their ken. She felt very clearly the hand of fate at work here.

Gently, taking care not to lose their place, Dr. Pratt lifted the supine volume from the floor and laid it upon the desktop. A beam of radiant sunlight, entering the cabin through a glass porthole, fell upon the exposed pages, permitting her and the doctor to behold the telltale portrait in all its repugnant detail.

Upon closer inspection, Robin saw that the squidlike beast was not alone. Tiny figures squirmed within the coils of the monster, while others fell helplessly into the creature's gaping beak, their paltry arms and legs extended in all directions. With a start, Robin realized that the minuscule figures, so small and insignificant with respect to the many-armed colossus, represented grown men and women.

Mere symbolism, she wondered, *or a portrait drawn from an all too hideous reality?* Robin suddenly recalled wild stories she'd heard, in seaports all around the globe, about a mythical sea monster called a kraken. . . .

"What became of this golden idol you spoke of?" Dr. Pratt

inquired, urgency coloring his voice. His careworn visage seemed to age visibly as he contemplated the dreadful illustration. "Where is it now?"

"I cannot say for certain," she admitted. There had been so much gold aboard the Spanish treasure ship, so many priceless baubles. "But I'll wager you a hundred guineas that it spent last night in the hull of this very vessel!"

"Yes," Dr. Pratt agreed, his mind speeding in concert with her own. "It must have been brought aboard the schooner during the initial division of the spoils." His gaze dropped to the floor, as though to peer through the solid wooden planks. "But is it still below? That scoundrel Newgate claimed most of the treasure for himself."

Robin tried to remember if the pagan idol had been among the booty returned to the *El Dorado* before they parted company with Newgate and the rest, but her foggy recollections were interrupted by the unexpected sound of a hysterical woman crying out in mortal terror.

"*Muchas bocas!*" Carmelita Aponte shrieked, staring with thunderstruck eyes at the open book. Intent upon the revelatory pages, neither Robin nor Dr. Pratt had observed Carmelita bestir herself from sleep, then rise from the portside berth to approach them. Now the sole survivor of the *El Dorado*'s original complement, her ashen face contorted in abject fear, pointed at the finely rendered kraken and its guppy-size victims. "*Muchas bocas! Tantas bocas!*"

"Faster! Faster, by God!"

Racing the setting sun, Robin stood atop the forecastle, urging her crew and her ship to greater speed. Every square inch of sail had been unfurled and *Neptune's Lady* was virtually flying atop the waves, but Robin had not yet caught sight of the *El Dorado*'s lofty masts. Glancing to the west, she winced as she watched the tropical sun plunge toward the horizon, trailing blood-red streamers across the twilight sky.

A rapid inventory of the schooner's hold had yielded no sign of the blasphemous idol, suggesting that the accursed sculpture once more resided upon the captured galleon. Consequently Robin had immediately turned *Neptune's Lady* around and set out in search of the other ship. Although the faithlessness of the mutineers still galled her soul, she knew she had no choice but to try to save Newgate and the others from the hellish fate in store for them. She was, after all, the Slayer.

A briny spray splashed against her face as she peered out over the prow. The schooner's tapered bowsprit stabbed at the cresting swells ahead of them, in rhythm with the persistent susurrus of the blue-green waters breaking against the stem. A strong northeast wind blew at cross purposes to their course, forcing them to tack back and forth in order to make any headway against the opposing gusts. Robin ground her teeth in frustration and clutched her spyglass so tightly that her powerful fingers indented the scope's metal casing.

"Step lively, ye sea dogs!" she demanded, even though the schooner had to be making ten knots at the very least. Dr. Pratt held tightly to the forecastle rail behind her, his pale lips pinched together. "Trim 'em closer, by God!"

The sun sank like an anchor beneath the Caribbean, casting everything above the seas into darkness. Last night's gravid clouds veiled the moon and stars once more, giving Robin not a jot of light to sail by. "You did your very best, Robin," Dr. Pratt offered by way of meager consolation. "Those rogues brought their doom upon themselves through their own base avarice and duplicity."

"Petty sins," Robin opined, unwilling to accept such solace. A pirate captain, she knew, was hardly one to pass judgment over her fellow mortals. "Undeservin' of so loathsome a fate."

As though unwittingly conjured by her doleful pronouncement, the screams of dying men erupted from the night, reaching the schooner from somewhere across the waves. Robin peered anxiously through the spyglass, but distance and darkness conspired to hide the source of the screams from her view.

That the horrible shrieking came from the *El Dorado* she had no doubt. "No, damn my soul!" Robin cursed. "Not again!" From the din of the strident cries, she judged that the besieged galleon could be only minutes away at top speed. "Helmsman!" she called out to faithful Jeremiah Pyle. "Set course for those poor, tormented souls!"

Although many a crewman blanched at the prospect of drawing nearer to the genesis of that fearful cacophony, they hastened to obey Robin's shouted commands. The elements, alas, were not so obliging, as, just at this most crucial juncture, the wind abruptly failed, causing the sails to sag lifelessly from the gaffs and *Neptune's Lady* to slow to a halt.

"No!" Robin stared at the listless sheets in disbelief; it was as though fate itself were intent on preventing her from coming to the rescue of the imperiled buccaneers. "Confound it!" she yelled. Hopelessly becalmed, the schooner bobbed upon rolling swell; more than a few of the men looked distinctly relieved to have been so stalled in their progress toward the fearful wailing.

But Robin refused to surrender. If nature herself would not be willing to provide the wind required, then she would just have manufacture one herself. "Get to your magicks, doctor!" she instructed her watcher, who hurriedly scrambled aft toward his library. Meanwhile Robin resorted to the time-honored tradition of the sea, pursing her lips to whistle loudly for a wind, pausing only to command all in earshot to do the same. "Whistle!" she ordered vehemently. "Whistle as though yer scurvy lives depended on it!"

Hesitantly at first, then with increasing enthusiasm, the staunch buccaneers whistled at will, producing a discordant babel of sharp toots and trills. The raucous whistling competed bizarrely with the agonized shrieks issuing from the unseen galleon. "Aye, that's it! That's a proper racket!" Robin encouraged her men. "Keep on warblin'!"

Invoking another hallowed superstition, she drew a dagger from her belt and drove it into the foremast, indicating the direction of the wind she sought. Even as she did so, Dr. Pratt came running forward, gripping a dilapidated, leatherbound volume. Robin was surprised to see Carmelita Aponte emerge from the stern cabin as well, trailing nervously behind the doctor like a dinghy cruising in a flagship's wake.

"Unto Eurus, scion of Astraea and Eos," Pratt recited sonorously, reading aloud from the mystical tome. "Unto Ehecatl, Vayu, Itzamna, and Aeolus; I beseech thee, Lords of the Air, grant us the blessing of thy divine and beneficent exhalations." Bracing his back against the foremast, facing the bow, he raised his right hand in supplication. "Breathe, breathe, *exhalare!*"

Was it the pirates' whistling or Dr. Pratt's more arcane incantation that did the trick? Robin neither knew nor cared as, with a resounding crack, the flaccid sails billowed outward and *Neptune's Lady* charged forward like a cannon shot, so swiftly that Robin had to grab on to a standing line to steady herself. *Aye!* she exulted triumphantly. *This be more like it!*

Then those same powerful gusts blew the overhanging clouds away from the moon. A silvery lunar radiance fell upon the nocturnal sea, revealing at last the unspeakable horror Robin had already envisioned.

The *El Dorado,* nearly half a league away, was under attack by an immense sea monster identical to the one depicted in that gruesome illustration. Monstrous tentacles, the size of soaring masts, rose from the turbulent white froth surrounding the galleon. Black as ebony and glistening wetly, the mammoth limbs snatched the panicked mutineers off the towering upper decks of the besieged treasure ship, just as they must have silently plucked last night's victims from the more modest environs of the schooner.

But those furtive abductions had clearly only whetted the kraken's voracious appetite, which now was aroused to gargantuan proportions. Heavy tarpaulins were torn asunder and battened hatches thrown carelessly open as the questing tentacles, endowed with grasping palps at their tips, probed below decks in pursuit of fresh human meat. Shuddering at the purgatorial tableau before her bulging eyes, Robin well imagined how an equally ravenous assault must have emptied the galleon of its previous crew, save for the captain lashed to the whipstaff and the terrified senorita cowering down in the hold, inside the closed teak casket.

For certain, it's the fault of that damnable idol, she realized angrily. The cursed statue surely acted as a beacon to its demonic inspiration, luring the kraken up from the dark, abysmal depths. *I should have hurled that ugly bit of ballast over the side the minute I laid eyes on it!*

Through the magnifying lens of the spyglass, Robin watched, aghast, as her former shipmates fought desperately and futilely against the invading tentacles. Slashing blades and smoking pistols, along with frantically-wielded axes and marlinespikes, inflicted little damage on the enormous limbs, whose leathery hide appeared all but impervious to harm. Robin saw a merciless tentacle wrap like a boa constrictor around the writhing form of

George Newgate. Ringlike suckers the size of doubloons, abundantly arrayed upon the underside of the relentless tentacles, affixed themselves to Newgate's bare throat and chest; despite his perfidy, Robin's eyes widened in dismay as she watched the traitorous quartermaster's lifeblood drain out of him, leaving him as pale and lifeless as the late *Capitan* Aponte. Robin instantly recalled the puckered stigmata upon the dead Spaniard's flesh, and an icy shiver of comprehension ran down her spine. *Not even Newgate,* she thought ruefully, *deserved so deplorable an end.*

A heartbeat later the hungry tentacle dragged the bearded man's bloodless carcass beneath the roiling foam, to be devoured, no doubt, by the kraken's crushing beak.

Her face white as well, Robin mutely passed the spyglass over to Dr. Pratt so that her watcher might also comprehend the full malignancy of the hell-beast assailing the galleon. A sharp intake of breath, followed by a whispered "Good Lord," announced that he, too, had witnessed the thirsty suckers at work.

"*Vampyroteuthis infernalis,*" he identified the beast, slowly lowering the spyglass. "The vampire squid from hell." He shook his aged head in awful wonder. "But I never dreamed it could grow so large!"

"*Muchas bocas,*" Carmelita Aponte confirmed. Hugging tightly to the sturdy trunk of the foremast, she nodded gravely in recognition of the multiple-limbed monstrosity that had sucked the life from her father and his crew. Robin knew now the nature of the "many mouths" that haunted the young woman's memory.

An occult wind carried them quickly toward the kraken's appalling feast. Within minutes Robin and the others no longer needed the telescope to behold the atrocity taking place upon the galleon. Desperate to escape the insatiable tentacles, the frenzied mutineers took to the rigging, climbing higher and higher in a last-ditch bid to evade the horrid death that had already claimed their shipmates.

But the gluttonous beast would not be cheated of its prey. Wrapping two of its mighty arms around the *El Dorado*'s bow, it pulled itself up onto the ship's prow so that its remaining tentacles could reach all the way to the tops of the masts. Clinging to the galleon's prow like a grotesque, fleshy figurehead, the kraken's entire body was now exposed, granting Robin a fuller look at the monster.

At least thirty feet long, the giant squid's bulging mantle was a mass of black, palpating meat and muscle, like the beating heart of some even more colossal archdevil. Seen in profile, as *Neptune's Lady* approached at a ninety-degree angle to the galleon's starboard side, the kraken's lurid red eye was the size of a seawitch's crystal ball. Its chitinous beak clacked hungrily as it chawed down upon the blood-drained corpses of the slain pirates. Robin counted ten tentacles in all, including the two that now held the beast glued to the prow. The ponderous weight of the monster was such that the bow of the mountainous galleon dipped into the sea, raising the stern, along with the rudder, many yards above the foaming brine. Dislodged seamen spilled from the poop and quarterdecks as the forward tilt of the treasure ship catapulted them into the air, to land clumsily upon the rigging or timber planks below.

A burly freebooter, Francois Leveau by name, repeatedly jabbed a wooden marlinespike at the sinuous tentacle now lifting him from the beakhead of the askew galleon. But his fear-crazed efforts were in vain; the vicious prong did little more than scratch the kraken's tough and slippery hide. Seconds later his gray desiccated body joined the others disappearing down the squid's yawning maw.

As *Neptune Lady's* closed on the horrific scene, coming within a thousand yards of the galleon's bow, Robin contemplated her own trusty cutlass, which struck her as starkly inadequate against so gigantic a behemoth. She briefly considered bringing the schooner's cannons to bear, but quickly discarded the notion. The havoc inflicted by a blazing barrage of round-shot would most likely devastate the surviving buccaneers more than the unstoppable kraken.

What then was she to do? Robin had slain many a leech, but never one so much larger than herself. *I can't just stab a stake through its filthy heart,* she lamented silently.

Or can I?

Inspiration struck, and, cutlass in hand, she crawled out onto the bowsprit, gripping the angled wooden spar between her knees. Spume splashed against her, drenching her clothes, and splinters of pine flew like sparks as she hacked away at the tip of the bowsprit, sharpening it to a jagged point.

The *El Dorado*, held tight in the kraken's embrace, loomed before her, so near that Robin could smell the putrid stench of the sea monster, which reeked like heap a of rotting fish left too long in the sun. Beneath her, only a few yards back, the *Lady's* undinal figurehead looked on impassively, offering Robin a measure of sisterly support.

"Dead ahead!" she called out over the roar of the sea. Finished at the spar's tip, she slid back down the bowsprit onto the forecastle. "Aim this goddamned ship right through that devil's heart!"

Pyle did not falter at the tiller. Galloping over the waves, her close-hauled sails pinched tightly to the wind, *Neptune's Lady* slammed into the kraken, driving the sharpened bowsprit into the vampire squid like the world's largest wooden stake! ·

A crimson geyser gushed from the impaled beast, the gory Vesuvius adding to the salt-spray dousing Robin's face and garments. Letting go of the *El Dorado,* the kraken writhed in agony, its tentacles flailing wildly. The schooner tilted forward as the weight of the creature pulled the prow down. Robin held her breath, then exhaled in relief as the kraken slid off the pointed spar, back into the brine. Before her grateful eyes, the wounded monster disappeared beneath the foam, leaving a thick cloud of stolen blood behind.

Can it be? she wondered. *Did I truly kill it?* The creature had surely seemed mortally injured, but how could she be sure?

Leaning over the main rail, she peered into the deep . . . just as the tip of a vengeful tentacle burst from the bloody froth and wrapped itself around Robin's right forearm. Greedy suckers bit into her flesh, drawing out her blood even through the sleeves of her soaking coat and shirt.

The clammy palp tugged on her with inhuman vigor, threatening to yank her over the rail and into the sea. Grunting in pain, Robin clung to the gunwale with her free hand. "Help me!" she cried out. "I can't hold on!"

Heedlessly dropping the valuable spellbook onto the swaying deck, Dr. Pratt scrambled to his slayer's aid. His bony fingers pried at the stubborn tentacle coiled around Robin's arm, but he could not extricate the imprisoned limb from the kraken's grasp. "Dear God, it's too strong!" he gasped.

Aid came from an unexpected quarter. Clutching an ax she must have found discarded upon the deck, Carmelita Aponte raced forward and began chopping at the tentacle with unexpected fury. *"Liberala! Permita ir!"*

The kraken's hide was too tough and impenetrable, however, so the valiant senorita labored to no avail. Her feverish blows barely scratched the surface of the unyielding tentacle.

"No," Robin groaned. *Devil take me,* she realized, *there be only one course left to us.* Her strength fading, she stared urgently into

Carmelita's eyes, then shifted her gaze down to where her upper arm emerged from the tentacle's coils. "*Comprende?*" she pleaded, praying that the Spanish girl would realize what was necessary.

Understanding dawned upon Carmelita's face. "No . . . no!" she protested, shaking her head.

"You must!" Robin entreated. Her feet slid perilously upon the deck as she fought to stay aboard. Darkness encroached on her vision, dimming the moonlight, as her blood fed the submerged sea monster. A sickly lassitude beckoned, and she struggled to keep her eyes open. "Now!"

Carmelita nodded. Biting down hard on her lower lip, she raised the hatchet high, then chopped off Robin's arm just below her elbow.

Robin screamed as the tentacle disappeared into the sea, taking the Slayer's right hand with it.

"There," Dr. Pratt said approvingly. "A perfect fit."

Resting in the cabin of *Neptune's Lady,* Robin inspected the physician's handiwork: a custom-made timber stump with an empty cavity sufficient to bear a wooden stake, a silver spike, or any other implement that might be deemed necessary. She swung her arm experimentally, imagining it in battle.

'Twill do, she decided, wincing slightly as she recalled the rough amputation that had preserved her life at the expense of her hand. Although Dr. Pratt had swiftly cauterized the wound by sealing it with boiling pitch, the brutal shock, along with the attendant bloodloss, had taxed even her prodigious powers of recuperation. "Thank ye, doctor," she said sincerely. "I figure it be a miracle we came through that fray alive, if a trifle less than intact."

"Indeed," her watcher agreed. "It is not every day or night that one encounters such a formidable denizen of the deep. From my reading, I believe it to have been no less than a chthonic remnant left over from the primordial days when the elder demons ruled the Earth . . . and the seas."

Robin tried to picture a bygone age when the likes of the blood-sucking kraken dwelt in abundance throughout the oceans of the world. An icy shiver crept down her back. *Thank heaven that wretched idol be gone at last,* she mused; despite her injury, she had personally seen to it that the golden effigy was tossed over the sides of the galleon, and had watched with profuse relief as the idol sank under the waves, where, if Providence was kind, it would remain lost for all time.

So much for matters infernal, she concluded, rising from her chair and marching out of the cabin. Now there was but one more bit of business to dealt with.

The deck of the schooner was alive with the sun-baked bodies of busy buccaneers tending to the sails as *Neptune's Lady* journeyed back to Jamaica. Off the starboard rail, the *El Dorado,* somewhat the worse for wear but still seaworthy, lumbered alongside the schooner, manned by a newly contrite crew of former mutineers. A warm tropical breeze helped speed both vessels on their way.

Robin climbed onto the quarterdeck and, placing two fingers to her lips, whistled to get the men's attention. "Ahoy!" she hollered, raising her truncated right arm. "Give me yer ears, every man jack of you!"

All eyes turned toward the captain, curious and dutiful. Among the upturned faces, Robin was amused to see Carmelita Aponte's exotic features. Having traded in her bedraggled saffron gown for much more practical sailor's garb, the orphaned senorita, whose bruised wits and spirit had mended considerably since saving Robin from the kraken, appeared to be blending into the pirate crew with remarkable ease.

Encouraged by Carmelita's example, Robin doffed her heavy woolen coat. With but one set of fingers at her disposal, it was awkward work, but soon the bulky garment dropped limply onto the spray-stained planks. Robin then fumbled with the bottom of her striped linen shirt, knotting it tightly beneath her bosom, so that her unmistakably feminine contours were made manifest. The strangling cravat was the next to go, carried away by the wind as Robin tossed it heedlessly aside.

"Well?" she demanded, daring all and sundry to make an issue of her sex. "Here I be, in all me unmasked glory." She posed with arms akimbo, looking out over the length of the schooner. "Does anybody care to question me command?"

A rousing cheer dispelled her doubts once and for all. "Hurrah for Cap'n Rob!" Jeremiah Pyle called out boisterously, and the rest of the beaming pirates took up the cheer. Even Carmelita, despite her scanty command of English, joined in. "Cap'n Rob forever!"

The Slayer basked in the acclamation of her crew, ready at that moment to take on a score of leeches and Spaniards alike. *It feels good to be a woman again,* she reflected. A steady breeze blew past her, ruffling her trim auburn locks while filling her nostrils with the intoxicating aroma of the open sea.

Perhaps I'll even grow me hair long.

The Ghosts of
Slayers Past

Scott Allie

LONDON, ENGLAND, 1843

The Vampire Slayer was dead; of this Charlton Muzzlewit was sure. I do not mean to say that his particular slayer had met her end, that this West End watcher had found himself suddenly without charge. For what would that matter, anyway? Of what importance is the life, or in this case death, of one child? No, the tradition of the Vampire Slayer is a grand history of ghastly deaths visited upon heroic girls; but it was that very history that the watcher this night mourned. For surely his young slayer, now fiercely engaged with a common gutter vampire, marked the ultimate decline of the fine tradition.

Charlton Muzzlewit stepped back an inch from the precarious stack of empty crates, from which paper labels peeled back at the corners in the damp night air. The labels bore the name of a popular spirit from an out-of-town distillery; Muzzlewit and his young charge faced their prey—she moreso than he—this thick and pressing evening behind a public house in the neighborhood off Blackfriar's Road near Lambeth Palace. He held his hands lightly against the crates, not so much to brace himself as to brace the haphazard pile from crashing down upon him. In his simple and worn—though nonetheless fine—brown suit, he blended perfectly into the murky scene in the alleyway. Beneath the suit, he wore a gold-colored vest, the only accent in his typically drab presentation. Beneath the vest the shirt was brown; even the collar was brown. A great swirl of brown hair spiraled from the part (combed as straight and flat as the gentleman could manage without the benefit of wife nor maid), curling sharply under the ears. A great nose distinguished an otherwise forgettable face, and a great bump adorned the nose itself, too high to support spectacles, which instead tended to slide toward the tip. Unbeknownst to Charlton Muzzlewit, his few adult associates found him a somewhat comical character.

Young Catherine Hogarth drove a short, pointed holly branch into the head of her opponent. Not merely the head; the dull end of the stake now bobbed horribly from the fiend's eyesocket, which disgorged a red froth upon the cheek. It was almost too much for poor Muzzlewit. As the creature bellowed, echoing down the canyon of riverside buildings, Catherine offered cold comfort.

"No eye at all's better than an evil eye, dark master," the girl barked in her heavy East End accent, so that for a moment Muzzlewit thought she said "dock master."

"That," he muttered, "is too much."

As if hearing her lord, Catherine Hogarth produced another stake of holly and pounded it through the screaming beast's heart, returning him to the dust from which we all come.

"Well, sir, I kilt another for you. That's, what, four this week, no? Must put me in some kind of vampire hunter record book!"

"You're a vampire *slayer*. And while we keep many books, I'm afraid there's no tallying of scores."

"Oh, right. You're just here for lookin', yeah?" Catherine said without guile as she picked up her drab bonnet from where it had fallen at the start of her skirmish. The chin strap had torn away, so she gathered her tangled hair and pulled the bonnet tightly over it, then looked round as if to claim any lost articles. Finally remembering that both stakes had turned to dust with her victim, she set her hands on her broad hips and let out a deep "harrumph."

"Furthermore, Miss Hogarth, you undertake these nightly missions not for me. It is your destiny, and it is this calling alone which elevates you above your peers in this wretched neighborhood."

"But that's just why I say I'm doin' it for you, m'lord. Most East End girls don't have no destiny. You've done me a right favor bringing this whole thing to my attention like."

As they went their separate ways that night, Charlton Muzzlewit happened to turn, and he fancied he saw a cloud of doom hovering not inches above the ignorant young thing's head.

It had often been pointed out over the years, by those outsiders familiar with the Watchers Council, that though the Slayer might save the very world itself and stave off the hosts of hell, she could never enjoy remuneration for her efforts. So it was, and so it should always be, that at the end of each night, the valiant slayer retires to her slum or crude hut, either on the wrong side of town or outside the town entirely. Perhaps it was with this sense of tradition that Catherine Hogarth proceeded to sidestep clots of human waste that floated down the streets running out of London's lower East End and into the pungent Thames.

Watchers, however, tended to be educated men from good families who accepted their calling after some success in life—all of which explained the roomy, two-story house to which Charlton Muzzlewit retired that late evening on Marlybone Road in the pleasant neighborhood of Regent's Park. Though we flatter Miss Hogarth to suppose she pondered the history of the slayers and watchers on her way through Whitechapel, Mr. Muzzlewit thought of little else.

His father, Hayward H. Muzzlewit, had been actively engaged as a watcher for only ten short months back in 1842, in the foggiest recesses of Charlton's memory. Of his father's slayer he remembered nothing, but in the thirty years since, he'd had the opportunity to meet many of the other girls to serve—each with less skill and grace than the last. His discouragement reached its peak when the last girl, a young tart from a medieval village in the south of France, followed her watcher to the great city of London. She liked nothing more than to play games and to grin suggestively, as though she held some secret regarding everyone she met. Her backwoods demeanor compounded the accident of her birth into that most loathsome class of creatures: the uneducated French.

With a shudder, Charlton Muzzlewit closed the curtains of his bed on such harsh memories and laid himself to sleep.

Sometime in the unknown and uncounted hours of middle night, Muzzlewit woke to see the curtains of his four-post bed drawn back by the hand of his father, whom he'd laid to rest some fifteen years ago. While this might not, for whatever reason, surprise the reader, one can rest well assured that it surprised Charlton Muzzlewit. He shot out of his bed, backward and at great speed, tripping on the hem of his nightgown and tearing the entire bed curtain off the bedposts and out from his father's withered and unlikely hand. The light scrim flipped up from over the top of the structure, settling upon the trembling and gaping watcher.

The apparition leaned forward and pressed a hand on the mattress, as if to test for firmness. The dead man looked nothing like his son. He was admirably bald with a peaked crown to his head, making his forehead appear flat. A similarly pear-shaped torso featured narrow shoulders and a gut that bore down menacingly over the belt. He shifted his hips stiffly and lifted one leg up onto the bed, like an injured rider sitting sidesaddle, and rested his hands on one knee.

"Damn it, boy, you've not learned a bit of coordination in all these years I've been gone."

"F-father," observed Charlton Muzzlewit, before collapsing in a spasm of chills.

"Come, now, Charlton. You spend your every night chasing down the undead. Surely the sight of your own father cannot take the starch out of your shorts."

The younger, livelier Muzzlewit gritted his teeth, set his brow, and mustered up what dignity he could, as he fought desperately to unwind himself from the lightweight bed curtain. His own muffled grunts and groans spared him his father's rattling chuckle. When finally he stood free of the linen prison, the ghost walked round the bed and stood with his thumbs hooked into his front pants pockets, a stance all too familiar to the heir whom he now sized up.

The dead man frowned, the lower lip jutting out past the chin, which Charlton knew did not necessarily indicate displeasure. The gentle nodding of the fruit-shaped head, in fact, suggested the most overwhelming approval for which the son could have hoped.

"You've grown up straight and tall, my son, and I'll even admit that you've turned out a bit stronger than I'd dared hope. You never filled out, not to speak of, and I see by the state of the place that you didn't manage to secure a wife. But neither did you gamble off the family home, so I must thank the good Lord for these small favors. I have to say that in this respect I'm somewhat surprised, and not nearly so disappointed as I'd prepared myself to be." Charlton Muzzlewit took the compliment in the spirit it was intended; he flinched slightly, as from a sharp blow to the cheek.

"But you haven't a heart, boy. Oh, you watch young Catherine in her nightly service, but you've no compassion for the girl. You press her to lay down her very life for the council, yet you know nothing of that life she'd so gladly give. As I hear it, you even strike her if she botches a kill."

Charlton frowned; he'd always loathed the old man's colloquialisms. "Father, you taught me to be stern with my charge. And I remember you striking your girl, Samantha."

"Well, if I'd wanted to discuss any indiscretions of my own, I needn't have returned from the afterlife to do so here with you, need I? Might be I've spent the last fifteen years worrying about all that, and my son should be glad to hear whatever it is I've learned. You think?

"Now, if you're done your babbling," the ghost said, gathering up the bed curtains from the floor, "I've only got a few words for you, and then I leave this house to your further abuse. Though you listened with nearly as much fear when I lived as you do tonight, not a word of mine ever sunk in to that mop-head of yours. So the powers that be figured you'd need to hear it from someone else." Hayward H. Muzzlewit pinched the corners of the curtain with the thumb and forefinger of each hand, and lifted it as a sheet before him, his visage even more ghostly now through the transparent fabric. "You'll be visited this night by three spirits, and it should be God's mercy if you learn a damn thing from any of them."

With this the elder Muzzlewit released the corners of the scrim, which settled slowly to the ground, revealing an empty spot where he had, it seemed, just stood. The younger Muzzlewit was alone again. But only for a time.

• • •

Being of a naturally nervous temper, thanks in no small part to the manner of his father, Charlton Muzzlewit spent the next little while in a dead panic. He hated the dark, which made him not the most effective watcher, always shambling home shortly after midnight, as he had this very eve. Yet now he paced from window to door and back, well past twelve, but well before the dawn, when no decent company was to be had and no proper activity could adequately pass the time. Bunching and stretching the front of his nightgown in nervous fingers, the cursing of his father's name so preoccupied him (though he did this under his breath, lest someone take him for a madman) that he did not spy the lithe form of a girl passing behind him; she even had time to reset the slightly torn bed curtains before he noticed her. He turned, screaming to high heavens in a voice good for shattering glass.

Not waiting for the shriek to die on his lips, the girl fought to be heard over his falsetto solo. "A good evening, Mr. Muzzletwitch. I am Carissa the Vampire Slayer."

Muzzlewit clapped a hand over his mouth, cutting off the uncontrollable tone. The trapped cry became a momentary pressure at the back of his eyes, after which the sound abated altogether, except for a certain ringing in his ears. He worried momentarily about the servants, then remembered that the servants had been let go fourteen years past. Ah yes; it all came back to him.

"Carissa. Carissa Avenhaus, the Dutch slayer of . . . 1670?"

"That is 1673, sir."

"I meant your starting date, not your, ah, finishing date," he said, attempting to flatten the front of his wrinkled nightgown.

"They are not so far apart for the most of us, as you know well," the girl said, lowering her chin and brushing back the golden curls that fell before her eyes.

"Fascinating," he said, courageously approaching the deceased fifteen-year-old virgin, examining her simple, yellow dress and white laced apron, her cloth shoes tied at the ankle. "Another girl of low station selected for a short but dignified service to mankind . . ."

"Yes," she snapped, his head snapping backward in response. "Well, it was a real honor, and you are most certainly welcome." She looked down her short, pert nose at the hunched man inspecting her, and crossed her arms over her bosom. "But we have no time for you to be staring at me like some mad doctor. There are other things which are to be seen this night," said Carissa the Vampire Slayer, waving a thin, fair hand before his face. Speckled moonlight from her fingertips lulled Charlton Muzzlewit toward a sudden state of peace, into which he gratefully swooned, his eyes drawing slowly shut.

The inviting dark resolved to a red glow permeating his closed eyelids. He opened them to a sight he'd never previously seen, but he recognized immediately from the stories of military acquaintances: a village on an African plain in the dead of night. He choked on the thick air, smoke and dust riding the slight breeze in equal parts. The crude and ever so primitive huts were made of straw held together with clay, now dried enough that the flames consumed the squat hovels. Perhaps the clay did not so much hold together the fronds and blades of grass; perhaps the thick earth coating was spread to keep the harsh desert sunlight out of dark interiors.

Charlton Muzzlewit never had an inspired thought in his life, and this one had been cued by a singular image: three hideous vampires bursting out from the cover of their grass-hut hideaways, their hair aflame, fangs shining in the blaze. A little better accustomed to the harsh contrast of the fire and the night sky, the Watcher could now see that color still clung to the western horizon. Wearing only his nightclothes, the proper English gentleman found himself at dusk on the Sahara—or so he assumed his location to be, knowing little to naught about the geography of the dark continent.

He turned to the girl at his side, who looked every bit as out of place as he in the sweltering African night. "Did you take me here so I could bear witness to your final, posthumous slaying?"

"This work is not of my hand, Herr Muzzletwitch. And she who did it, did it not after my death, but even before my birth."

Suddenly another African appeared, white markings on her jet-black skin glistening in the fire. Though nearly as monstrous as those beasts now running for cover from the setting sun, Muzzlewit knew at a glance that he beheld the arsonist responsible, the slayer of her day, and that this day was in no way his own. This primitive slayer snapped a flaming branch from the lower roofs and drove the jagged end into the chest of the fleeing vampires, one after another, their ashes mixing with the smoke and the clay dust lifting off the burning huts. She howled as she worked, her head and her filthy hair whipping round with great excitement. The Watcher frowned at the barbaric spectacle, his lower lip jutting out over the chin; indicating acute displeasure.

"This is where it starts, this tradition that you will live by, by which I am to die—by which your young Catherine Hogarth will also die."

"If its roots are with these coarse savages," Muzzlewit said, looking away, "perhaps it's best that such a *tradition* die too." Turning, he didn't see the Dutch girl scowl, then wave a hand at the moon.

The sky suddenly lit up as though at midday; Muzzlewit spun on his heels again, bare feet nearly tripping over one another in the sand. He now faced not just the ghost of the Dutch slayer, but a magnificent wall. Stones, each of them bigger than the rooms of his luxurious house, were stacked high into the pale arid sky, each one painted with a different mural of some winged god, an unidentifiable (though beautiful) beast, or a heavenly woman, performing acts which in England would be reserved for saints and kings. Muzzlewit gaped at the fantastic facade, which stretched hundreds of yards in either direction; when his eyes came to center again, Carissa walked away from him, toward a grand doorway in the wall, leading into a bright blue chamber. It was not merely a wall; Muzzlewit stood at the foot of a most enormous building. Unsure what to fear more, the world within or without the mammoth structure, Muzzlewit did what he trusted, and followed a few feet behind the Slayer.

Past the door, pillars as grand as those before the church of St. George Bloomsbury lined the entryway. This was merely the entryway! Each great shaft was covered by an exquisite mosaic, which Muzzlewit imagined would reveal, if he were to take the time, the entire history of the strange people occupying this palace. The mosaics and paintings all bore the signature style of the ancient Egyptians, whose crumbling relics had recently arrived in the British Museum. The wonders before him, however, put to shame the scraps that Schliemann and his plunderers had scavenged. But if archaeologists had not been able to unearth such wonders as this . . .

"Who could've *built* it?"

The ring of his own voice in the vast hall surprised even him, and he whipped round to check on his astral guide. Carissa proceeded along the vast hall more quickly, so he raced now to catch up, doing so just in time to enter another room at her side.

If the outside of the building had the quality of a mirage in the vast desert, this room delivered on that promise. A great pool filled most of the place, and two long-necked birds, unlike any swan, coasted gently in an arc across the calm water. At the near end of the pool four nude Africans stood with arms crossed, backs to the European arrivals. Despite skin as black as night, Muzzlewit had to admit a certain handsomeness to these brutes; they were certainly more pleasing in appearance than either the vampires or the Slayer to whose skirmish he'd just been subjected. For a moment he couldn't take his eyes off them, until he realized two things, the first being that Carissa again walked away from him.

"They don't see us, do they?" He shared this second revelation as he followed her along the left side of the room. Only as she answered did Muzzlewit notice the two women at the far end of the pool.

"It is needed that you see these sights. Do not be surprised that they have nothing to learn from *you*, sir."

Wading through water up to the hip, a naked Egyptian girl moved with inhuman grace and beauty; Muzzlewit knew at once that this was the Slayer. What fantastic contrast, what immeasurable variation in that term "slayer," could be seen when turning from the proper Germanic girl at his side to the Nubian child in the water.

Sitting at the edge of the pool—and the two Europeans now approached quite closely this far end—an older Egyptian woman kicked her feet in the water, her skirt pulled up to her thighs. Naked above the waist, with an enormous bosom, she had nonetheless almost the bearing of a man. Her jaw was set proudly, her nose broad, but with a bridge as thick as a Frenchman. Although her appearance could not have been more in contrast to that of Her Royal Majesty Victoria, it surprised Muzzlewit not at all when Carissa gave the woman's title as queen.

"She lets the Slayer live in the palace because the people worship the girl as a living goddess. She is to them as much a savior as He whom you and I acknowledge upon bended knee, though these people collect many a goddess in their halls. Certainly this is not so coarse, not so savage, as to offend your fine British senses? Do you not look at this young girl and bemoan her doom as the Slayer of a wondrous age?"

Muzzlewit, now a little less horrified at these leaps through time and place, fairly spat, "Pttf! All this talk of goddesses, my blasphemous slayer? Are you so quickly swayed by this heathen temple, the obvious lack of male discipline? Of order? Do you take one of those brutes by the door for a watcher? Nay, I wager yonder 'queen' deigns to fill the shoes which in any civilized age have been worn by one such as I." He paused a moment to consider his condemnation of an admittedly beautiful place, but decided that what must be said would be said. "I'm sorry, dear girl, but this impresses me not at all."

This time Muzzlewit witnessed the rage clouding Carissa Avenhaus's eyes, the scowl, and the quick wave of the hand. This caused him to take a quick step backward, and, were it not for the sudden disruption of space and time, he'd have unhappily joined the beautiful Nubian "goddess" for a swim.

Their next destination Muzzlewit recognized immediately, not in any great specificity, but with comforting certainty: He found himself in England. Beyond a long, well-maintained field, an enormous country house glowed with a golden light from within, warming the edge of the night sky. The estate appeared to host a great party; on the terrace a young lady—finally, a real lady—in a beige evening gown and white gloves looked round curiously, kicking at what seemed to be a pile of dust. Within the terrace doors, pairs of partygoers engaged in conversation, while through another tall window Muzzlewit could see a grand ballroom alive with dancers. A fine blue greatcoat had been discarded in the yard by Muzzlewit's feet, and at this proximity he could see that, though clearly brand new, this coat, and probably everything else he saw, belonged to a slightly older England than did he himself. He nonetheless breathed an audible sigh of relief to be, for most purposes, home.

Scanning the scene to find Miss Avenhaus, he first spied two men disappearing into the wood that surrounded the field. His Dutch slayer also observed the pair slipping between the trees, and, after a guttural "Ach," waved her hand in the manner Muzzlewit had come to recognize.

Now he found himself in the thick of those same woods, the stars barely visible through the dense treetops. Just when he thought he'd gotten used to their mode of travel, this shortest of all jumps left him dizzy. He whirled slightly and looked to the ground to steady himself. A cough startled him, (or perhaps the Slayer laughed) and was followed by some sharp movement across the forest floor. He collected himself, fearing that he'd be abandoned out here, untold miles from London. But Carissa had not taken a step away; the two figures they'd just seen leaving the field now ran toward them through the trees.

In the lead by a dozen feet, the younger of the two sprinted in shirtsleeves and a powder-blue vest, short blond hair plastered back over his forehead by the swiftness of his stride. Behind him pursued an older man in a handsome brown waistcoat and vest and a purple ascot coming loose at the throat. To this man, the London watcher felt an immediate camaraderie.

"I would suppose," Muzzlewit said, taking a deep breath and trying to look bored, "that these are hapless victims? We've come to witness an attack by fiends and subsequent rescue by your counterpart of this age?" He tried to muster an air of superiority, looking down over the prodigious bump on his nose at the girl; until, remembering that he wore only a nightgown, he let his shoulders fall noticeably.

At just that moment the two men ran by Muzzlewit and his guide. They did not run round the stationary pair, but ran directly through them, and our hapless protagonist was surprised to find the sensation not particularly unpleasant.

"You did recognize the Slayer in a 'savage' and a 'heathen' with no help of mine, but in your own country you are blind to her?" She pointed to the smaller and younger of the two receding figures, disappearing again into the shadows of the forest. "In the council's incomplete records of these days, she is Elizabeth Weston, but in her day went by the name *Edward* Weston. Only by wearing the clothes of a man could she move through your English society with the freedom necessary to a slayer. Maybe this is why in our time the Slayer tends so often to be of low station. No one is batting eyes at dirty fingernails on a peasant girl.

"This, Mr. Muzzletwitch, is the courage of the Slayer. This, the ability to adapt to any situation, any obstacle—"

The Watcher covered his mouth and cleared his throat softly, politely interrupting. "Has it really been so hard for these girls, through these long ages?"

"More often than not, yes, it has. My own parents died when I—"

"Then what I've always suspected is true. It was an accident— a misstep in the history of our order! The Slayer should have been a man—!"

Carissa's eyes flared at this, and her hand whipped under her white laced apron, drawing a short chunk of wood with one end carved into a long point. This she raised, and she stepped toward the befuddled Watcher, who fancied he heard a soft and sonorous voice from above offer a subtle reproach: "Uh-uh."

But it was probably just the wind.

Or nothing at all, for he found himself suddenly sitting bolt upright and partially under the covers of his own bed. The bed curtain hung where it belonged atop the four posts (he did not remember that the Dutch slayer had put it back before taking him away), and for a moment he believed the entire thing had been a dream. The small tear in the scrim, made when he'd pulled the whole affair sharply out from the hand of his dead father, made it once again real to him.

His father had spoken of three spirits. Muzzlewit tried to quell the pounding in his thunderous heart by counting off the three girls he'd observed, but under all the heavy beating in his breast was the knowledge that it was the visitors to his chamber who would number three before the night was through. So it was with more chagrin than surprise that he noticed another girl in the room with him.

The word "chagrin," borrowed from the French, can imply anything from distress to disappointment, and it is the whole spectrum of the word that I call upon for the current moment. Noticing another girl meant only mild disappointment, as he'd somehow known that the night would not end so soon. But as he recognized her—"Not you!" he cried—matters drifted into the more unpleasant meanings of the word.

"*Oui, m'sieur.* And I am not happier than you to be here in London again."

"Marie Siegner, the most recently deceased of the Slayers."

"Yes, *m'sieur* Muzzlewit. I am certain that I am the last girl you would choose to see on this night. However, know that I have forgiven you your cruelty, although I am sure you shall not ever forgive me. Fortunately we have not far to travel together, and it is only one girl I am to show you."

With those words, the few minutes of comfort he enjoyed in his own bedchamber ended, and Charlton Muzzlewit found himself in the East End, a place he recognized chiefly by its stench.

He scowled at Marie, who bowed slightly and pressed a finger to her lips; he believed he detected a smile. She leaned toward him, and he noticed with some relief that though a corpse certainly stinks worse than the French, a ghost leaves its body odors at the grave.

"Be very quiet, *m'sieur*," she whispered. "You'll see now the hovel in which lives that girl who you are meant to look after. Maybe this sight will teach you compassion."

"Oh, why are you whispering? They can't hear us!" he shouted, and pushed open the front door of the crude shanty.

His experience bore out, as their impolite entry failed to wake even the bum asleep at the foot of the stairs. Muzzlewit had never been here before, had never even seen the outside. It occurred to him that this might be an oversight in his responsibilities as a watcher, but he had no time for self-reproach. Marie stepped over the snoring drunkard and started softly up the stairs, giving Charlton Muzzlewit a clear view of her uncovered calves and the hem of her skirt, muddy now as in life. He rolled his eyes and ascended after her.

The stairs going up were perhaps hazardous, many of the boards either split or with the nails pulled up. A window would have helped to ease the horrid smell of the narrow passage, but there was none. He breathed a sigh when Marie indicated the first door they came to as Catherine's.

In a small front room, two older East Enders slept under a sheet on the rough floorboards, which had suffered slightly less wear than the crumbling staircase. This pair looked too old to be Catherine's parents, but Muzzlewit knew that the workers of the East End often appeared old for their age; also, the woman resembled Catherine—the weak chin, the eyes too far apart. A bedpan sat on the windowsill, conveniently next to a broken pane, where the smell from within and the smell from without battled for dominance. Beside the window was a doorway without any door. Marie stood in a corner and gestured that Mr. Muzzlewit should look within.

"Oh, you can do without the bloody pantomime," he shouted, waving a hand over the sleeping couple. "They can't hear us!"

So the Watcher stepped through the open doorway, peering into the dark room. Clothes hung from a rod over the window to block the dim light from the street, and it took him a moment to make out the bed. Upon a stained mattress slept three children—Catherine had perhaps once mentioned younger brothers—but they were all too small to be his wide-hipped slayer. A torn wool blanket lay over the boys, wrapped round one of their ankles, and the urge to straighten the covering to better serve the boys took Muzzlewit quite off guard; he pushed the thought away easily enough.

Standing closer to the bed, he at last saw his teenage charge. She kneeled, saying her prayers, on a small pile of towels and clothes in the corner, surely her approximation of a bed. The clothes she'd worn that night made up her pillow, and the raw destitute honesty of the scene, as though from an engraving, spared Muzzlewit any unease at seeing his apprentice in her underclothes. Still, the spectacle of poverty inspired a certain discomfort which, he wondered, might have been akin to sympathy.

Soliciting a nod of approval from Marie, still in the doorway, he squeezed past the foot of the bed to get a closer look at the child. He'd known she was poor, but he never knew that she lived like this. She whispered her prayers so as not to wake her brothers, her head bowed toward the wall. Muzzlewit almost thought to kneel, but instead just leaned over her.

". . . needs a new crutch or she ain't goin' to work no more," the girl said in words as soft as breath. "The boys, they need proper beddin'. Me, Lord, I don't need much. Ain't me needs lookin' after. It's Muzzlewit."

In some strange way these words tickled that discomfort which was now lodged just between his belly and his throat. He shifted his weight, although he in fact had none in this spectral form, and leaned yet closer to his charge, who continued her prayers, unaware, of course, of his attention.

"And the best lookin' after he could get would be by one of them plague of frogs, or summat like what you did to that Job fella. Give him some real painful-like affliction of the skin—a real slow, tortured death. I could do it meself, Lord, but I got this whole destiny bit I need to keep up on. I tell you, though, what I wouldn't do for Scotland Yard to declare open season on stuffy old used-up spinster-blokes from the West End."

Charlton Muzzlewit set his jaw and stuck out his bottom lip so far that even in his father it would have indicated strict displeasure. "*Merde,*" said Marie the Vampire Slayer; with a wave of her hand they were gone.

Alone in his room again, Charlton Muzzlewit, from a long line of watchers and a fine London family, sat in a plush armchair, wishiing the dawn were upon him. His teeth had taken to chattering, as they often did if he went too long without sleep. He gripped the arms of the chair and tried to push himself deeper into the soft cushioning, to make himself as steady as that fine bit of furniture, which, he couldn't help thinking, probably cost more than a month's rent for Catherine Hogarth's family—a sum which they no doubt scraped together with great pains sometime well after the first of each month. "Still, let the ungrateful peasant be damned," he muttered. "Hadn't she said herself that I'd done her a favor bringing to her attention the destiny of the Slayer? What hypocrisy, then, for her to curse me for it to God Himself!"

And cursed he'd be, as cursed he was. He had not known happiness in all the years of his adult life, and so no happiness had he brought to others. His misery held no glory, as in Job's refusal of Satan; Charlton Muzzlewit was a living martyr to the secret cause of vampire slaying. He had not a heroic bone in his body. Would an eternal reward come to him for his lackluster service, his joyless isolation from all but a doomed fifteen-year-old girl? Throughout these shadowed hours between midnight and dawn, he tread the yawning chasm of his own existence, and that empty feeling which had made him always shun the dead of night—thereby allowing poor service of his duty and his Slayer's duty—only reflected his deficient soul.

Then, by the window, he spotted a short but trim figure, its back to him. Wrapped in a long black sheath of leather, with yellow hair tied up on the head in the manner of the Chinese, the creature did not move, just stared out to the street below.

"Speak, O Spirit!" he cried. "What revelations do you have for me?"

"London?" said this third girl in a questioning tone, but from which Muzzlewit could infer no actual inquiry. "I *so* believed the hype. And this is like the upscale hood. Why the Mr. Hanky swimteam backstroking down the street?" With this she turned to him, extending a hand. "Howdy, trembly British guy. I'm Buffy."

"You . . . what . . .," he stammered, as uncertain of what he wanted to say as he was of what she'd just said. The black leather coat she wore clung tightly round her narrow hips, and from underneath poked pantlegs; this most bizarre of slayers, whom he could only assume came from some disastrous future, had resorted to the same subterfuge as Edward/Elizabeth Weston, but with present company any such illusion was compromised. The hair was as yellow as Weston's, but long and tied in an Eastern fashion, the face lovely but painted in a style slightly more gaudy, or perhaps clownlike, than that of a London lady—though decidedly feminine. Just who did this slayer mean to pass herself off as? And what, dear God, *what* on earth was she trying to *say?*

"I got a big dumb century to show ya, so pull it together, big guy."

"What are you saying?!"

"Mm, whatever. You're the one who's been at it all night. We gotta make with the magic-carpet ride, so let's get it in gear, 'kay?" said the girl.

"What?!"

"Ooh, sorry, mixed metaphor, right?" she said, wincing insincerely.

The crimes this girl perpetrated upon the English language went well beyond this "mixed metaphor," a phrase not to be coined until some date equidistant from Charlton Muzzlewit's death and Buffy Summers's birth. The language of his homeland remained the only thing intact this night, the one true guide in his journeys. Though he'd heard it abused by Germanic and French accents, he could not bear to hear it slayed outright.

"Jumpy much?" the girl said as the Watcher burst out through his bedroom door, down the hall, and into Marlybone Road, taking care to hop—he had put on his slippers while waiting for the third apparition—over a narrow trickle of offal in the gutter before his house.

He ran down Baker to Oxford Street, along High Holborn north of Piccadilly Circus, down past St. Paul's. All that he had seen tonight left him with only one kindred spirit, one possible companion, the one to whom he'd been drawn by shared destiny. Muzzlewit ran through the warren of streets of Whitechapel to where he could smell the nearby river over the smell of the homes themselves, finally coming to the newly familiar tenement.

Two of the stairs broke underfoot as he bounded up the narrow passage, then banged the door against the head of the father, who did not stir in his sleep. Muzzlewit hopped over the lame mother and into the children's room, startling Catherine from the prayers upon which she still concentrated with such devotion. Her siblings woke slowly to this frantic and partially dressed man begging her forgiveness.

"I'm sorry, Catherine. I had no right to treat you as I have. I vow to you that never more will I take you for granted! Please forgive me. You must understand—I'm a man of certain breeding, and we of my class are accustomed to fraternizing only with our own kind. But, oh, if only I'd been told sooner what else there was in this world, I'd have thanked my lucky stars for a real London girl!"

Any unfair assumptions made by the young masters Hogarth regarding their sister and this undressed gentleman caller could certainly be excused.

"The horrible past of our shared tradition," continued Muzzlewit, "the terrifying places I fear it shall go! We must be grateful. Yes, Catherine, grateful that it is in this day and age that we fill our roles as watcher and slayer!"

He said all this as he grasped her shoulders in his hands, shaking her lightly in his excitement. The girl positively beamed at his newfound interest in her. Suddenly he released her and urged her to kneel again as he kneeled by her and lowered his head. The Hogarth parents stood in the door dumbfounded, the mother leaning heavily on the father.

"Dear God," Charlton Muzzlewit said, "I beg your forgiveness, sinner that I am, and I thank you, and Catherine thanks you, for the graceful mercies you have allowed us—for pairing us with one another, instead of someone far, far worse." He glanced up to see Catherine's confused face as she tried to unravel the exact meaning of those last few words. Sensing possible offense, he put his arm round the girl's shoulder, and called out, "God bless us!"

"God bless us *everyone*!" she answered, smiling at him.

Charlton Muzzlewit looked up at the faces of her parents and of her brothers, and returned his slayer's smile. "Well, God bless us *both*, anyway."

The New
Watcher

Kristine Kathryn Rusch

ATLANTA, 1864

Deep beneath the half-dismantled Atlanta roundhouse, in tunnels designed and later abandoned by men fleeing the Union Army, Frankie Massey staked her fifteenth vampire of the night.

The foul-smelling dust blew over her, caking onto her face and coating her hair. She kicked sideways—the Chinese kick that Reed had taught her—and slammed another vampire into the stone wall.

She'd found the nest, and she was getting tired after hours of killing all alone.

Another vampire snuck up on her. She could smell it, that stench of blood mixing with rotted teeth and clothing that hadn't been changed since the grave. She whirled, stabbed the vampire's unbeating heart, and whirled again before the dust fell to the tunnel's wooden floor.

Another vampire and another, her arm stabbing, staking, dusting while her leg kicked and her other arm blocked. She wore her collar up, guarding her neck, and still she could feel the pointed teeth grazing her skin, the cold hands against her collarbone, hands so cold they felt like they'd been dipped in snow on a frozen Illinois day.

She whirled faster, staked harder, surrounded by dust and dirt and death. She fought in a frenzy, until she was the only one left.

Frankie climbed out of the remains of the roundhouse as the first tendrils of dawn pinkened the night sky. She sat on the steps—once indoor steps—and wiped her face, feeling the granules left by people who had died days, weeks, maybe years ago.

Her body hurt, her arm ached, and her boots were stained black from all the filth below.

She had never felt so all alone.

Six months ago Reed would have been sitting beside her, offering her water from his canteen, his own face coated with vampire dust. He'd guided her. She was the weapon, he used to say, and he was the historian. He provided the information, and she chose whether or not to use it.

Sometimes she helped with the information.

Sometimes he helped with the weapon.

They had been partners, even at the end.

The real end, not the one she tried to forget, the one that occurred a few nights later, when he had crawled off a Georgia battlefield to hunt her down personally, as if his mission had changed overnight from that of protector to destroyer.

She supposed it had. Viewed coldly, his determination to slay her, to make her one of them, made complete sense.

Except that he had smiled when his new mission failed, as if a part of Reed remained in the undead thing he had become.

"Cheeky girl," he had said, admiration in his voice as her stake pierced his sternum. "Cheeky bloody girl . . ."

Frankie wiped her face again and felt dampness on her skin, probably from the heavy morning dew.

Then she stood, headed back to camp for a quick cleanup and a pretend shave, and maybe, just maybe, one precious hour of sleep.

• • •

She got two.

Two restless hours with vampires and long-past conversations haunting her dreams. Reed, following her on her way to enlist, whispering his objections, his fears: *They'll know you're a woman. They'll know you're unusually strong. They'll figure out that you're someone different, someone dangerous.* Vampires in boxcars, hiding behind ammunition boxes marked with the address of Atlanta manufacturers. Dead boys, sprawled in the Tennessee countryside, not a single toothmark on them, only the marks of Minié balls, buckshot, and bayonets.

Then, suddenly, she was being shaken, hands gripping her shoulder, warm hands—the hands of someone living—and she opened her eyes to see Private McCutcheon frowning at her.

"The major-general needs you."

The major-general always needed her, but that was not, apparently, the point McCutcheon was making. The major-general had sent for her, and she needed to be at her best.

Frankie told McCutcheon she'd be right there, then wiped her face again. The dusty feeling never left her, hadn't for years, even though she washed more than she probably should have. Most men didn't wash as much as she did and many of them were as shy about their privates as she had to be.

After she enlisted, she learned fast to keep her breasts bound, even at night, even when she had the luck to sleep in her own tent—or next to Reed who had somehow managed to enlist beside her, despite his obvious foreignness.

He'd stayed beside her the entire war, until they got him. And it was her fault that they had, no matter what he had told her. She was supposed to protect him, too, and that night, she hadn't. She had her back to him; she hadn't even seen them drag him off. And because the vampire fight blurred with a night fight against the

Rebs, she thought Reed was deep in the battle.

Instead they had turned him. She hadn't known that at first, and she tried not think about it—how they must have gripped the back of his neck, forcing him to drink their blood; that foul, awful stench as his face moved closer and closer . . .

Frankie shook the thought away. It had happened because of her, because she believed in the cause. She didn't want to be some pretty girl staying at home, not when the Rebs were breaking up the Union—and doing it to keep people enslaved. She was a fighter, and she meant to fight, whether she fought vampires or Rebs.

Both were wrong.

But it hadn't been Reed's fight. He had adopted it for her, and somehow the vamps had known it. They had even left his body for her on the field, for her to find, and they had shot him—or someone had—to hide the fact that he had also been bitten. She had only looked at the cavity in his chest, clearly caused by an exiting bullet. She hadn't even thought to look at his neck.

Not until he showed up a few nights later, smiling, seeming just like himself except for the emptiness in his eyes.

Frankie splashed the leftover shaving water on her face, then turned the dish upside down. The water and soap turned the red Georgia clay into a pinkish mud. She'd never known land could be this color, never known that places as desolate as this so-called city could exist.

Four thousand buildings here, four thousand of them, and most of them uglier than the vamps they still hid. She'd been in most of them, searching for the source of the nests she'd been finding. Somewhere in Atlanta was a vamp who turned Rebs, deliberately, so that they'd become their own supernatural fighting force.

And despite all the southern whining about the rules of war, these Rebs didn't fight by any such rules. They attacked good soldiers in their sleep, crossing to the Union camps in the darkness and sucking on the blood of the living, careful not to turn them (or most of them, anyway. She always sensed they had treated Reed differently because of her)—killing them instead, before the blood was fully drained, snapping necks or stabbing them (so damn symbolically) through the heart.

No one talked about it, except in private. She wouldn't have known until she stumbled on a cadre of them, doing their crazy nightly deeds outside of Vicksburg, and she knew then that all the rumors she'd heard had been true. Reed had even found how the vamps were coming into battlefields: via railroad direct from Atlanta, along with the percussion caps, canteens, and corn bread—everything needed to sustain a Rebel Army—food, materiel, and some undead bodies as well.

Frankie slipped her blue coat over her long underwear, slapping the vampire dust off as best she could. Everyone serving in Atlanta was covered in dust, although most of it was red, not gray. The soldiers, some of the best fighting force in the Union Army, hadn't been fighting these last two months. They'd been disassembling a city, brick by brick, train track by train track.

Atlanta, which had fed the armies of the Confederacy, wasn't going to feed them any longer.

Frankie finished quickly and then hurried to the major-general's headquarters. The major-general had a few makeshift headquarters, but his favorite of late was Atlanta's City Hall. Frankie walked past the scores of men yanking ropes to pull up spikes that held in the metal tracks; carting dried goods from the basements of stores to the supply wagons; and scattering coal and other combustibles inside the munitions factories, waiting for the order to move out to some other battlefield, deeper in Reb territory.

The City Hall building, made of the same damn red brick that filled Atlanta like a plague, rose above a hundred tents that had been pitched in its yard. The Second Massachusetts Infantry had camped there, as if thumbing its collective nose at everything the Rebs and Jeff Davis stood for.

The camp was empty except for the cooks and the wounded, slowly healing thanks to the lull in the fighting. She touched the bill of her cap as she passed a few of the men, sitting upright despite bandaged legs or arms slung up, attempting a game of cards in the thin November sun.

Guards stood outside the hall, a sure sign that the major-general was inside. Frankie nodded at them as she hurried up the stairs, a spring in her step despite her lack of sleep from the night before. Staking a nest gave her a euphoria that she didn't admit to anyone, not even Reed when he was alive.

Laughter rumbled through the corridors. She climbed the interior staircase, its white railing now gray from the hands of a hundred dirty men, and stopped just outside the big office that had, just a few weeks before, housed Atlanta's mayor.

The major-general used that office when he was entertaining outsiders. He liked the statement it made—the proof that he was a clear victor in a war that had had too few winners and too many losers.

Two more guards stood outside, men she'd seen before but didn't know. Their gazes brushed over her, then moved back to the simple stare they were trained to use as if she were unimportant.

The other aides were already inside, along with one of the division commanders and a man she'd recognized as handling the prisoners of war. She had thought all war prisoners were gone now, shipped north in September to serve their sentences for betraying the laws of God and the Union.

She stepped across the threshold.

"There he is!" the major-general said.

Major-General William Tecumseh Sherman looked official that morning. His uniform had been cleaned, the deep blue wool almost sparkling in the light from the open window. His boots shone and his unruly dark hair had been combed.

He was leaning against the massive desk abandoned by Mayor James M. Calhoun. The desk, pristine when the major-general inherited it, was now scarred with burns and sulfur tracks, match trails deliberately made in the surface whenever the major-general lit one of his famous cigars.

The major-general sucked on one of those cigars now. "We were having such a fine time, and I was afraid you were going to miss it, Corporal."

"I'm sorry, sir," Frankie said. "Private McCutcheon hadn't mentioned any special hurry."

"There is none." The major-general's dark eyes seemed especially sharp this morning.

The probing look he gave her used to make her nervous; she was always afraid he could see past her woolen coat and trousers to the delicate female frame beneath. At least her voice was a rich contralto, roughened now by whisky and a few too many cigars of her own.

"But," he said, "we haven't had true entertainment in weeks, and I figured you would want to see this instead of hear about it."

She frowned, stepped deeper inside the massive office, and realized there was one man in the group whom she had never seen before. He stood before the open window, his hands cuffed in front of him. He was the only other person in the room who had no facial hair; unlike her, it was clear to anyone who looked that he could grow a beard if he wanted one. His brown hair had a stylish cut—obviously not Army issue—and his gray suit, stained though it was, pegged him for a civilian of some means.

"This," the major-general said, sweeping his hand toward the man near the window, "is Edward Landers, who claims he has traveled all the way across the Atlantic in search of his ward."

Frankie frowned. She didn't understand why this was amusing. "I'm sure we could find the boy, sir," she said. "We're not in the midst of any great battle at the moment."

The major-general turned toward Landers. Landers towered over the major-general by half a foot, but the major-general's square body held a lot more power than Landers's lanky one.

"Finding the ward should be even easier than you think, Corporal," the major-general said, "since Mr. Landers's ward apparently goes by the name Pauline F. Barnard."

Frankie froze. The seizure was involuntary and—fortunately—brief. Pauline F. Barnard—Pauline *Francis* Barnard—was the name she had been born with. She had kept the Francis and her childhood nickname, Frankie, and used her mother's maiden name to enlist. Massey. Frank Massey.

No one could know that Pauline Barnard and Frank Massey were the same person.

And yet Landers was here, claiming to be her guardian, which was the closest he could probably come to explaining his real relationship with her.

He had to be her new watcher.

The last thing she wanted was a new watcher. She knew her job, and besides, no one could take Reed's place.

But Reed had warned her that if anything happened to him, another watcher would come. "And," Reed had said, "he might not be as sympathetic to this course we've taken. The Watchers Council believes that women were chosen as slayers for a reason—and one reason was to keep them away from the petty conflicts of mankind's wars."

She had just figured that a new watcher wouldn't be able to find her, or if he did, he would come to her and they would find a way to keep her in the Army. But if she went with Landers, she would have to go as a woman—in a frilly dress, her hair down.

She didn't want to do that. She wanted to fight.

The major-general had paused. He was looking at her as if her reaction surprised him.

It probably had. She was sure everyone else had laughed when they learned that Landers was searching for a woman. Landers's eyes narrowed, and she thought she caught suspicion in them.

"Why," she said, trying to figure out how to account for her behavior, "would Mr. Landers believe that a young woman would still be here in Atlanta? Didn't he know that we evacuated the city in September?"

Landers blinked, the suspicious look gone.

The major-general shrugged. "Apparently, Mr. Landers's ward—"

"Is an unusual young woman," Landers said.

A gasp rose in the room. No one interrupted the major-general, especially not a man with a high voice, a snotty British accent, and a stained suit.

Landers apparently didn't notice. "She's quite strong and rather mannish. I am under the impression that she has enlisted under a male name."

Frankie forced herself to laugh even though she had trouble catching her breath. "And you think we wouldn't know right away that we have a female in our midst?"

"As I said, she's quite strong, and—"

"And unattractive, I'm sure." Frankie nodded, trying not to let her irritation show. The boys back home hadn't found her unattractive, back when she wore skirts and her hair was long. "She would have to be, though, wouldn't she, to hide out as a man?"

"I told Mr. Landers that we've been in the field a long time," the major-general said. "We've seen a lot of combat. A female wouldn't have made it through the first week at Vicksburg, let alone all the gore we saw in Shiloh."

Frankie's cheeks felt warm. A cliched female might not have made it. Many of the men didn't either. They said they opposed the major-general's policies when, in truth, they hadn't the stomach for them.

The major-general believed that war needed cruelty. Indeed war thrived upon cruelty. Without cruelty, without utter destructiveness, the major-general felt there would be no call for peace.

"Pauline is quite unusual," Landers said. "She knows and handles what you have called 'gore' rather well. I'm certain she's among your ranks. I would simply like a chance to see if she's here."

Frankie stared at him, wondering if she could work with him. She doubted it. Besides, he wouldn't be able to stay here now, not after telling everyone he was looking for a girl.

If he stayed beside her, it would take no time at all for the Army to figure out who she was.

"Doesn't sound like any female I know," one of the other aides said.

"I believe some of you will be startled to discover that you have been serving side by side with Miss Barnard and believing her to be male," Landers said.

Of course they would. They would be shocked, especially when they realized she was standing right next to them.

Frankie had a reputation for being one of the fiercest fighters in Sherman's Army. He had brought her in as his aide just after

Reed died because, he said, he needed warriors beside him. Working directly for the major-general had helped her deal with the grief and the loneliness, but she really felt as if she were living a double life.

And now that life could end. All because of one man, one man who didn't understand who she was.

She had never fit in anywhere like she fit in here. No one questioned her strength. No one tried to treat her as if she could break at any moment. She could cuss and ride a horse properly and shoot a rifle. She could punch a man in the face if he deserved it and smoke cigars when she could afford them.

"What's going to happen to this girl when you find her?" the major-general asked.

"I shall return her to her home," Landers said. "She's needed there. She certainly doesn't need to be here, fighting in a man's war."

He placed an emphasis on the word "man" and Frankie caught the double meaning. Man's war had nothing to do with the supernatural war she'd been born to fight in.

But both wars were connected—more closely than she had imagined when she joined up.

The levity seemed to have bled from the room. Apparently Frankie's serious reaction and the Major-General's questions took the humor from the situation.

"I should like to find her," Landers said, "and I would appreciate any help you give me including and starting with removal of these irons."

"Those irons," the major-general said slowly, "are a common treatment for spies. I would think, Mr. Landers, that you would come up with a better story for your presence here than the one you have."

"I don't understand how you can believe me a spy," Landers said. "I am who I say I am. Your men confiscated my travel papers. I—"

"Describe her." The words escaped Frankie's lips before she had time to think.

"I beg your pardon?"

"Miss Barnard," Frankie said. "If you describe her, we might be able to figure out who she's masquerading as."

She lent the last part of the sentence some sarcasm so that the officers in the room would know she didn't believe Landers's story either. This would trip him up, she knew. She'd never seen him before, and he'd never seen her. If anything, he might have had the miniature her father had painted on her sixteenth birthday, but that had been a flattering portrait, with no basis in reality.

"She's . . . ah, well . . . she's rather small boned and delicate, somewhat tall for a woman, with thick brown hair and dark brown eyes." As Landers spoke, his voice shook.

"You sound uncertain," the major-general said.

"Well, sir, I suspect she would look different after four years with the Army."

Someone laughed nearby, but Frankie didn't look to see who it was.

"What makes you think she's here?" Frankie asked.

"I've heard stories about her. People have seen her kill . . . ah . . . the . . . ah . . . enemy, and through those reports, I have tracked her to this place."

The enemy. How coy. Frankie's cheeks felt even hotter. So he'd tracked her through the vampire slayings, not through her female identity, knowing only the Slayer could handle that many vampires for that long.

She turned to the major-general. "You're right, sir. This is a ludicrous story, and it's insulting to think this man believes we are dumb enough to accept it."

"You heard my aide, Mr. Landers," the major-general said. "We aren't bumpkins, no matter what you people think of us."

"I'm not a spy," Landers said. "I do know my story is out-landish, but it is true. You cannot think I'm a spy because I tell you something you fail to believe."

"That's not why we think you're a spy," the major-general said, his tone deceptively light. "We think you're a spy because you're British and you're in the South. It's no secret, sir, that the English have been looking for a way to regain your so-called colonies. We also know your government has been considering an alliance with the Rebs for some time now. I truly don't know if you're spying for your homeland or if you're working for Jeff Davis, and I don't care. All I care about is that you're in my city attempting to disrupt my troops with ridiculous stories and wild searches for phantom women. I have no time for this, and nei-ther do my men."

The major-general pulled the cigar from his mouth. The tip had gone out long ago.

"Take Mr. Landers out of here and send him north as soon as possible. Let someone in the War Department debrief him. I simply don't have time for this nonsense."

The guards standing beside Landers grabbed his arm.

"You're making a mistake," he said as he was being tugged from the room. "You don't understand the forces you're dealing with."

"And there you have it, men," the major-general said. "A threat is sometimes as good as a confession. Let's make certain he's gone by morning, shall we?"

He snapped his fingers at one of the other aides, and the man scurried out of the room after Landers and the guards.

She watched Landers go, his rangy frame hunched in defeat. Her new watcher, the man who would guard her and train her. The educated one, the one who understood the demons and the vampires and the powers of the night.

The one who thought he was responsible for her, who would record her deeds and make certain she was remembered after her untimely death.

She felt nothing but relief as they led him out of the room.

He would most certainly take her out of here and make her stop fighting this war. He was English; he had no idea how important this war was.

Nor, she suspected, did he know how so many vampires were involved, turning their abilities toward the Confederacy. If anything proved that Jeff Davis's Army had rot at its core, the vampires did.

"Well, Corporal," the major-general said. "This interrogation proved to be more serious than I had expected. All the humor was in the beginning."

He was, in his own way, apologizing to her. Frankie plastered a smile on her face before she turned away from the door.

"It's all right, sir," she said. "I wouldn't have believed anything anyone said about this man if I hadn't seen him for myself."

The major-general nodded. He too stared out the door as if he felt some opportunity had passed him by as well. Or maybe Frankie was reading too much into a situation that for the major-general was just another detail of command.

"Well," he said, raising his voice so that it was clear he was speaking to everyone in the room. "You all have some work to do. I plan to muster out of here in two days time. Let's make certain there's nothing left to salvage in Atlanta."

The aides saluted and headed for the door. Frankie waited, not wanting to rush out, not wanting to feel any temptation to talk to Landers, to find out what his plans for the Slayer really were.

"Corporal Massey, a word," the major-general said. His tone

had changed from friendly to harsh. Frankie's mouth went dry.

"Close the door."

She did, then turned slowly.

All the humor had left his face. He looked like a hawk, hunting its prey.

"I understand you got little sleep last night."

"I got two hours, sir," Frankie said. "I figure four hours is a good night, but two is good enough."

"You wander many nights."

"I've found it difficult to sleep, sir. There's much to do." She clasped her hands behind her back to prevent them from shaking.

"I've had you followed." His tone was flat.

"Sir?" The shock she felt ran all the way through her. He had had her followed? To what purpose? And how had she missed it?

She had missed it, she knew, because she had been focusing on the vampires, not on men.

The major-general walked back to the desk and leaned on it. "Your work at the roundhouse last night was impressive."

She felt her breath catch. She had not expected him to say that.

"How many did you kill?"

"I don't know, sir," she said, trying to keep her voice level. She wasn't sure what the observer had seen. Had he known she was killing vampires? Or did he just know that they were Rebs? "Eighteen. Twenty. Maybe a few more."

The major-general nodded. "They come from the countryside, you know."

"Sir?" She wasn't quite following the conversation.

"Your vampires. They come from somewhere south and east of us."

The flush she'd been struggling against all morning burned her face. "You know of vampires, sir?"

"Every branch of the Union Army is plagued with them," he said. "We've had discussions, General Grant and I, about how to protect our men from them. There's not much we could do. But it wasn't much of a problem for me, when all of my compatriots struggled with it. Don't you find that odd, Corporal?"

"I find this entire conversation odd, sir," she said.

He smiled. "I found the conversation with Edward Landers odd. He's going to escape, you know."

She shook her head. "What do you mean?"

"He's no more a spy than you are, Corporal." The major-general opened his cigar box. "Smoke?"

"Yes, sir," she said. "I believe I'd like that, sir."

He handed her a cigar and then scratched one of his box matches across the desk, leaving another sulfur mark. He lit her cigar and then relit his own.

She puffed, feeling the tobacco hit, adding to her lightheadedness. Maybe she was still dreaming. Maybe she was conjuring this entire scene, after the fight in the roundhouse and her memories of Reed. She was feeling guilty. She would feel guilty about Reed for a long time.

"If you believe Mr. Landers is innocent, sir," she said, willing her voice steady, "then why aren't you helping him find his ward?"

The major-general took two lazy puffs, then pulled the cigar out of his mouth. "They say I'm crazy, you know. 'Sherman is not suited to serve.' That was in all the Eastern papers."

She'd heard. She knew all the stories. And she knew why they thought he was crazy. He had a core ruthlessness. He didn't believe in being a gentleman, especially in battle.

"Years ago," she said.

"Years ago," he muttered. "Not so many."

"We've lived lifetimes since then." She wasn't sure if she was pleading his case or her own.

"I served in California in the Mexican War. Did you know that, Corporal?"

"Yes, sir," she said.

"Have you ever been to California?"

"No, sir."

The major-general smiled faintly, as if her answer surprised him. "I met a young girl during my posting. Delicate thing, strong as an ox. Stronger maybe. She saved my life once."

Frankie felt her breath catch. The cigar suddenly tasted foul. She pulled it from her mouth and struggled not to cough.

"The vampires come from the countryside," the major-general said again. "And there's a lot of them."

She shivered.

"But I have a plan."

She suspected as much. She was to set Landers free and leave with him, returning to the life everyone expected her to live. She would have no choice now. She would have to go north and wear skirts once again.

"Tonight, when you patrol, mark the nests."

She had so expected him to say something else, that for a moment she wasn't certain what he had said. "Sir?"

"Mark the nests. Don't wade into them on your own. I've finally got my confirmation back from Grant. We're leaving Atlanta in two days, and before we go, we're to burn everything of military value in the city. We'll start with the nests."

She gaped at him. She couldn't help herself. She had never been so shocked in her life.

"Then we'll head for Savannah. We're abandoning our supply lines and living off the land instead. I promised the president Savannah as his Christmas present. I think I might be able to do that."

The major-general took the cigar from her hand. He stubbed out the burning tip.

"Wasting good tobacco there," he said. "This probably isn't the right time for a smoke anyway."

But he didn't put his out.

"As we move south, I'm sure we'll find more nests. We'll burn them, too. In the daylight, when they can't get us."

He looked at her. She still couldn't move. Reed had warned her that others knew about vampires. She just hadn't expected it from the major-general, although she should have. He had that ruthlessness, the same kind that she had. The kind that got the job done.

"Fire does destroy them, doesn't it, Corporal?" he asked.

He raised his eyebrows, and she realized he expected her to answer him.

"Yes, sir. Yes, it does."

He was making plans, just like Reed used to. Directing her efforts, making them stronger. Better.

"Good," the major-general said. "Then we'll burn our way south. We will get more of them that way. Pity that we won't get credit for all of this."

"I don't need credit, sir."

He studied her. "No," he said after a moment. "I don't suppose you do."

Then he handed her the half-smoked cigar, and she tucked it in her breast pocket.

"I'm afraid this part of the plan must remain between us," he said.

"I figured as much, sir."

He smiled. It was a gentle smile. "Dismissed, Corporal."

She turned and walked away, feeling as if her world had tilted. She had felt this way when Reed found her, when he'd told her about slayers and how she might become one, when the previous slayer died. He'd talked to her of training, and showed her how to fight. And she had loved it, never expecting to become the Slayer herself.

The war had been her excuse. She figured it would give her a chance to live the way she wanted to, whether she became the Slayer or not. And when she had explained that to Reed, he had understood.

Landers would never have understood. Or maybe she simply didn't want to make him try.

Frankie stopped in front of the closed door. "Sir," she said, turning, "may I ask one more question?"

"Quickly, Corporal," the major-general said. "I have much to do before we begin our march to the sea."

She nodded. "If you knew who—what—I am, sir, why did you let me stay?"

"You're not asking about the vampires, now, are you, Corporal?"

"No, sir."

"You think I should have sent you home to your Mama, so that you could wear skirts and stitch quilts for the war effort?"

Frankie swallowed. "Others would have, sir."

"Others are short sighted," he said. "I am not."

"Indeed, sir," Frankie said. "Your vision is clearer than most."

He grinned at her, and she grinned back. Then she let herself out of the office and down the stairs into the feeble sunlight of the mid-November day.

Her heart was lighter than it had been in months. The major-general may not have been trained by the Watchers Council, but he would watch over her.

In fact, he *had* watched over her. Ever since she lost Reed.

She'd had a new watcher all this time, and she hadn't even realized it. But now she had a partner, and together they would solve the Union's vampire problem once and for all.

House of the Vampire

Michael Reaves

LONDON, ENGLAND, 1897

I

The sight of a gentleman ambling down the crowded and ill-lit alleys of the East End after dark was not unique, but it was certainly not common. This neighborhood, containing parts of Whitechapel, Spitalfields, Mile End, and others, was one of the most dangerous and poverty-stricken in all of London, and for someone of obvious means to venture into it on foot, even by day, was remarkable.

Nevertheless, down the narrow avenue the stranger walked, briskly but with apparent nonchalance, all heads turning to mark his passage. The cacophony of raucous voices slowed as he went by, then started up again with increased interest, the multitude of topics now having diminished to just one. Tatterdemalions paused from their endless pursuit of one another across the flagging and through the stinking gutters; shop owners lounged in recessed doorways, blinking amidst malodorous clouds of pipe smoke; and slatterns slowed their strolling to gaze in appraisal or frank admiration. The stranger ignored them all, walking as casually as if he were out for a constitutional in Covent Garden. He swung his ivory-tipped cane in rhythm with his gait, and his top hat was perched at a jaunty angle. He seemed utterly unaware of the area's unwholesomeness.

It was just after nine P.M., the dark of the moon, so not even that celestial body's effulgence could aid in dispersing the shadows. The only things keeping the darkness even slightly at bay were rubbish fires, candles, and the infrequent oil lanterns and naphtha brands. From all about could be heard the wailing of hungry children, the shouts and scuffles of various altercations, and the moaning of the aged and infirm. The winding lane was hardly wide enough to permit the passage of a four-wheeled cab, and it branched off into alleys and cul-de-sacs that were even more restrictive, barely serving to separate the ramshackle buildings. The stench of offal, waste, and things rotten was almost palpable, coiling through the streets like an invisible miasmic serpent. But of all this the gentleman took no apparent heed.

He turned down an alley narrow enough for him to touch the slimy walls of both buildings with his gloved hands. The darkness here was complete and utter; even the faint starlight was blocked by webs of laundry strung between the upper floors. But he did not slow his pace.

The alley, after turning sharply in several directions, opened at length into a small, deserted courtyard. Dark windows and doorways, many boarded over, punctuated the walls. The starlight was unimpeded here, and the crowded buildings loomed overhead at what seemed impossible angles. The court was empty, save for a single figure, dressed in white, standing across from him.

The gentleman moved forward quickly, his cloak flaring. The woman stood with her back to him. His shoes made no sound on the cobblestones. He pulled his gloves off as he approached, revealing long, pale fingers, and reached toward her.

"Elizabeth!" His whisper was husky with longing. "My darling, how wonderful to be with you again!"

At the sound of his voice she turned. Each paused for a moment, then rushed into an embrace. They held each other closely, murmuring mutual endearments, the dreary surroundings and cares of Lower London banished for a brief time. Then they backed slightly apart, still staring lovingly into each other's eyes, and began to stroll slowly about the perimeter of the square, not speaking, content for the moment in each other's presence. At length, as they passed the dark lacuna of a stairway entrance, he turned to her.

"It won't be long now, I promise you," he said. "Once the decree is issued I'll be free, and then you'll bid this disgusting welter of thieves and mendicants good-bye forever."

"Phillip," she murmured, her eyes bright with the promise of good fortune. She drew a breath to speak again—

And the night took her.

One instant she stood before him, young and happy and full of love for him alone . . . and then it was as if the darkness itself reached out hungrily and snatched her away. Paralyzed by shock, Phillip stood staring into the impenetrable gloom. He heard the rustle of something that could have been a cloak, or perhaps even the stir of sinister wings, followed by a brief, sharp cry from Elizabeth . . . then silence.

Silence, save for a rhythmic, measured sound, as of some liquid being drawn by suction . . .

The gentleman gave a shout of mingled horror and rage. He raised his cane and leaped forward into the stygian gloom, only to be met with a single blow of such appalling strength that it sent him sprawling halfway across the court. Dazed, he rolled over and managed to raise himself on one elbow. He stared back at the dark entrance. From it emerged a pale face with eyes red as embers; it seemed to float toward him on a column of darkness. Behind this apparition he could see the stairway entrance. From the shadows an arm, slim and cotton-clad, lay outflung on the cold stones.

The face loomed over Phillip. A line of crimson trickled from one corner of the scowling mouth. The gentleman's final cry was one of utter despair; it rose into the night, blending unheard with all the other screams and shouts of the city.

II

Springheel Jack fled for his life.

He ran in great bounding leaps over the pitched roofs and gables, jumping from tenement to tenement, clearing gaps of fifteen to twenty feet at a time. He hurtled over chimneys and skylights, cloak billowing out behind him like black wings. His speed was such that nothing human could hope to catch him.

Not even the Slayer.

Angelique knew she had no hope of overtaking Jack. That was not the plan. Accordingly she pursued at a somewhat less than breakneck pace, leaping over impediments with practiced ease, the fetid city air pumping in and out of her lungs. Though the life of a slayer was in many ways a difficult one, there were compensations, and chief among them were physical strength and reflexes surpassed by none—none of her fellow humans, at any rate.

She saw Jack put his boot on the edge of a cupola and hurl himself forward into space to land on a rooftop one floor down and a good twenty-five feet away. Had she taken the time to doubt, she might not have made it. Instead she gave herself up to her training, as the Professor had admonished her so many times. She leaped. Sooty night air fanned her raven tresses . . . then she landed, her legs absorbing the impact with no complaints.

It felt good to be alive.

Jack was still running. He would not be for much longer.

Angelique charged forward and saw the dark figure step out from behind a water tank. He aimed a device at Jack and fired. Before the surprised Jack could react, a net of hemp flowered before him. It enveloped him, brought him crashing to his knees. Angelique heard him roar in rage, a sound no human throat could make.

He surged to his feet. Blue fire erupted from his mouth, incinerating his bonds. But the delay had been enough; before Jack could escape, Angelique leaped onto his back.

Jack roared again and twisted about, slamming himself into a brick wall, with the Slayer between him and the barrier. The impact set off fireworks behind the Slayer's eyes. For a moment her grip slackened. He would have thrown her from him then, but in that moment a thin blade flashed, the point darting toward Jack's chest. Startled, Jack stumbled backward. Angelique wrapped both arms around his neck, gripped his head and twisted with all her strength. The *crack!* his neck made when it snapped was clearly audible.

Springheel Jack collapsed beneath her.

Angelique stood, brushing soot from her skirt and Zouave jacket as the Professor and Gordon approached. "That's that," she said briskly. "We should hear no more about the terrifying Springheel Jack in London, I think."

"Perhaps," the Professor said. "But do not be overly sure, Angelique. The legend of Springheel Jack has endured for decades. I think it likely more than one Tethyrian demon has contributed to the stories over the years." He picked up his bowler from where it had fallen during the slaying and dusted it off before carefully covering his baldness with it.

The Slayer frowned, but then smiled again as Gordon came to stand beside her, sheathing his sword cane in its camouflaging shaft of wood. "No purpose to worrying about that now," she said. "I trust, Professor, that you noticed the aid Gordon was able to give us a moment ago?"

The Professor scowled, the fingers of one hand tugging at his beard. "It is still not right," he said. "The Slayer walks alone, save for her watcher. The council has made its stance very clear on this, and I agree with them."

Gordon responded before she had a chance to speak. "All well and good for the council to huddle before warm fires and make pronouncements like Parliament, I suppose. But Angelique is the Slayer. It is her life put at risk every night—"

"Which is how it should be!" The Professor interrupted, brandishing an indignant index finger. "Hers and hers alone! This has been the way of it for centuries. Remember: 'She *alone* can stand against the vampires, the forces of darkness—'"

"Enough arguing," Angelique said. In the silence that followed, the tolls of Big Ben could faintly be heard echoing across the distant Thames. "It's three in the morning," she continued. "I think this has been a good night's work. Whether one hand or many did the deed, the important thing is that the deed is done. Another demon lies dead."

The three looked down at the recumbent form. "Professor," Angelique continued, "do you mind tidying up?"

The Professor nodded. "Of course, of course." He turned to the black leathern satchel a few feet away and retrieved from it a small phial. Unstoppering it, he sprinkled a bit of sparkling dust over the demon's corpse. "*Facilis descenus,*" he said. There was a rushing sound, a flash of green fire, and when it cleared the body of the Tethyrian demon had vanished.

They found a stairwell and descended to the street. A single gaslight provided scant illumination. "Little luck we'll have finding a cab at this hour," the Professor grumbled, pulling his Inverness closer around him against the chill night air.

Angelique and Gordon looked at each other and smiled. Her heart warmed at the sight of him, clean-shaven and thin in his ragland overcoat, breeches, and boots, all varying tones of gray. Angelique felt her skin tingle as his hand brushed hers. They had known each other for over two months now, and so far everything seemed to be going right. Gordon Mycroft was considered by some—most, in fact—to be a ne'er-do-well with a shady background and equally shady standards. Some thought him a dandy for carrying a cane, not knowing, for the most part, how lucky they were to be spared his skill with the blade it camouflaged. He and Angelique had met on a cold night in the heart of one of London's many cemeteries—he had been there, he'd told her later, seeking inspiration for his poetry—where she had found him fending off the attacks of two newly-risen vampires. She had thought to make short work of the bloodsuckers, but then seven more had erupted out of the darkness. She and Gordon had fought side by side among the timeworn marble slabs, beneath the brooding oaks and willows, and he had been by her side practically ever since.

Her watcher disapproved of her associating with a wastrel poet, of course; from what Angelique had been able to discern, Professor Peter van Helsing was considered somewhat old fashioned even by the stuffy and hidebound standards of the council. He had been vehemently opposed to her initial association with young Patch, though even he had had to admit that the ragged urchin's knowledge of the streets and what was happening on them was far more effective than the local constabulary's—or even Scotland Yard's, on occasion. And he had practically become apoplectic when Molly Carrington had entered the picture, despite the ex-novitiate's passionate hatred for the forces of evil. But in the end he had grudgingly accepted the three, though his objections still flared now and then.

And, Angelique reflected as they walked along the narrow deserted street, the Professor was right, in an academic sense. It was unheard of for a slayer to work closely with anyone except her watcher. She was violating rules and traditions that had been accepted without question for centuries. But Angelique Hawthorne cared little about rules, and she knew that even the hoariest of traditions are not immune to change. In the nearly two years since she had been summoned, she had proven to be one of the most successful vampire hunters in the council's memory. So let them grumble, she told herself. It is never prudent to question success.

And, no matter how dangerous or ultimately short-lived her career as a slayer might be, it was still better than the life she came from.

By the time they reached the Professor's manor in Regent's Park, it was after four, and even Angelique was tired. She climbed the stairs, changed into her nightdress, and collapsed gratefully upon the four-postered eiderdown bed.

But, exhausted though she was, sleep danced tantalizingly just out of reach. She was keyed up, anxious. Such restlessness was unusual for her. She had made her peace years before with her calling and the short life expectancy that usually came with it, and she had also learned to snatch sleep when and where she could.

Tonight, however, peace evaded the Slayer. For some reason she found herself growing uncomfortably warm, to the point of perspiration. Impatiently she kicked the bedclothes free, lying exposed to the air in her nightgown. Still the heat plagued her, almost febrile in its intensity. *This is ridiculous,* she thought.

Such a balmy night is unheard of this late in autumn. And yet the breeze does nothing to cool me.

With a start, she realized that the French doors to the balcony were open. When she had retired, she had made sure they were shut and locked, as she did every night. While it was true that a vampire could not cross a threshold unless invited, other species of demons were not as restricted. Yet now the doors stood thrown wide. The moon was new, only the faintest sliver of a crescent, yet somehow she could see clearly the dead rust-colored leaves stirring on the balcony, could see the lace draperies framing the doors, and the massive dark wood wardrobe against the far wall . . .

And the man who stood cloaked in darkness at the foot of her bed.

Angelique felt her heart frost over. The moment of fear was quickly followed by anger. How *dare* some creature of the night invade her private chambers! She sat up, reaching for the stake which lay on the bedside table—

Or rather she *tried* to. But, to her astonishment, she was unable to move. A paralysis gripped her as if she had been inoculated by some potent drug. Helpless, she lay there and watched as the silhouette moved slowly, even casually, around the bedpost and toward her. Although she could see the rest of the room clearly, his face and form somehow remained in shadow, even when he stood by her side, close enough to for her to touch him . . . and for him to touch her.

He leaned toward her. Angelique could see the twin embers of red that were his eyes and the pale slivers of fangs as he opened his mouth.

Hear me, Slayer. Did she hear the whispered words, touched by the hint of a Slavic accent, or did they echo somehow only within her head? *Do not seek to meddle in matters not of your*

*concern. Some affairs of the night are beyond your station. Keep to
your domain, or pay the penalty.*

With a gasp, she sat up. She looked at the balcony. The doors
leading to it were closed. There was no one in the room but her.

Angelique's hand shot to the beside table, seized a hand mirror lying beside the stake. Quickly she inspected her throat.

It was unmarked.

From the far distance, at the very edge of audibility, she
thought she heard the howl of a wolf.

The Slayer reached for the heavy duvet, pulled it back up over
her. She bundled herself in it, shivering. The night air was very
cold.

III

At mid-morning of the following day, Angelique stood in the
tiny East End courtyard, along with the Professor, Gordon,
Molly, and Patch.

It was Patch who had brought them the news. He had woken
them at dawn with his shouts of "Hoy!" much to the annoyance
of the professor's neighbors. Yet even at that early hour they had
nearly been too late to inspect the site.

When they arrived, the bodies had already been moved from
the court into the avenue. The normal din of costermongers and
their customers was subdued now as the man's sheeted corpse
was loaded onto the back of a wagon. The woman's body had
been turned on to her back, and her eyes were being photographed at close range. Simon Peasbody, a detective from the
Yard, was supervising. Professor van Helsing distracted him with
questions while Molly and Angelique pulled back the coarse
linen and examined the bodies. A quick look was all they were
able to obtain before the crowding of curious onlookers forced
them away. Even so, they saw enough.

"The marks are there," Molly said. "The fangs of the beast have drained them both." Her thin face, which remained pale no matter how much sun she was exposed to, was even grimmer than usual. Molly Carrington had been an Anglo-Catholic novitiate before having been cast out for defiling the church; she had scooped a hatful of holy water from a baptismal font to fling at a vampire. Now she fought against evil in a more unorthodox, but certainly more effective, way. Her hatred of all things unholy and the undead in particular was a whip constantly driving her.

"The bodies still have blood in them," Angelique said. "They will not rise again in three days."

Molly looked closely at her. "You sound disappointed. Surely you do not wish the curse of the undead upon these poor people."

"No, of course not. Still, those newly risen tend to seek the one that turned them. They might have led us to—"

Angelique paused. For a moment the wan light of the morning sun seemed to pale even more; her vision grew dark around the edges, and instead of Molly's concerned face, she seemed to see another more sinister countenance.

"Angelique! Are you ill? Speak!"

Angelique blinked. Gradually the street around her swam back into focus.

"I'm fine," she told Molly. "A bit of lightheadedness; that's all. Nothing that can't be cured by a plate of kippers and kedgaree."

Molly looked unconvinced, but before she could respond, they were interrupted by the approach of van Helsing and Peasbody. The Professor was shaking his head at the detective and saying heatedly, "Optograms indeed! How can anyone believe such tripe in this modern day?"

Peasbody looked bored. Angelique knew him to be a prissy and officious man who went about constantly swathed in the clinging scent of various pomades. She could smell the one he had used today, a faint paraffin odor. *As stiff as one of Madame Tussauds's waxworks, and about as bright,* she thought.

"Indeed, Professor," Peasbody said. "And how would *you* go about finding the murderer?"

"Fingerprinting. Specifically, the Galton Method. It is the only dependable way to identify a criminal. Even in twins the patterning is different."

Peasbody elaborately stifled a yawn. "I am aware of the process, thank you. But it has not yet been established as being useful in criminal investigation."

"Bah," the Professor said. "Perhaps you should avail yourself of the good offices of that fellow over on Baker Street. What's his name? The one your colleague Lestrade is always popping off for advice."

Peasbody drew himself up haughtily—*like a paraffin penguin,* Angelique thought, and had to smother her laughter. "Forensic photography," the Yard man said to van Helsing, "is a well-known practice, and, given the importance of this case, I see no reason for the Yard to deviate from procedure. Good morning." And, with a slight nod toward Angelique and the others, he turned away.

"Officious idiot," van Helsing muttered. He frowned massively at Angelique as if she were somehow responsible for Peasbody's dismissal of his suggestion.

"I'm sure Scotland Yard will recognize your genius eventually, Professor," Gordon said. Van Helsing looked suspiciously at him, uncertain if he was being mocked.

"So who's the toff?" Patch inquired, nodding toward the wagon.

"The past tense is more appropriate," the Professor replied. "He *was* Phillip Menzies, Viscount of Kentington."

"That explains why the Yard's involved," Molly said. "Vampires drain these poor souls down here every day, and no one gives a tinker's damn. But let one of their own be attacked, and—"

"Exactly so. This demon must be found, before there is a panic."

They began walking away from the crime scene. Already the normal sounds of the neighborhood were reasserting themselves: the rattle of sewing machines from a nearby sweatshop, an organ grinder's sprightly tune, the noisy horseplay of children. Violent death was nothing new in the East End.

Van Helsing looked at Angelique. "How do you suggest we begin?"

"With some questions," the Slayer replied. "And I think I know where to start asking."

She pushed her way through the crowd, van Helsing and her friends following. She led them through the crowded, redolent neighborhood, down one twisted lane and up another, until all but the Slayer were completely lost in the warren of cul-de-sacs and blind alleys.

At last they stopped before a side entrance to what appeared to have once been a lower-class lodging house, but which now seemed deserted. "That's a bit more than strange," Gordon mused. "The East End teems with people, yet an entire building stands empty?"

"Not entirely empty," Angelique replied as she kicked the door in.

Within, a long-unused vestibule was barely visible in the dim light. The entrances to still-darker rooms could be seen on either side. The destruction of the door sent lances of morning sunlight down the hall, luminous with dust motes. From within the closest room they heard furtive rustling and uneasy hisses.

Angelique, moving forward quickly, caught a glimpse of yellow eyes disappearing into the darkness.

"Professor, illuminate the situation, please," the Slayer said. Van Helsing brought from an inner pocket another of his many inventions: an ingeniously small but powerful electric torch, which bathed the entire chamber in stark, actinic light. The room was empty of furnishings, anything of value having long since been stolen, and even much of the wainscoting torn away for firewood. Dazzled by the glare were four vampires, freshly risen; she could see the rich dark loam of the grave still caked on their clothes and fingers. For an instant the tableau held . . . and then one of the undead ones lunged toward her, howling, fangs bared.

Angelique nimbly sidestepped the bloodsucker's rush; it stumbled forward, off balance, and was abruptly stopped by the wooden tip of Gordon's cane, which speared its unbeating heart. With a sound of muted thunder, it disintegrated. Without looking back the Slayer whipped a stake from a holster concealed by her skirt's pleating and leaped to confront the next fiend. It hurled a flurry of blows and kicks at her, all of which she blocked with the ease of long practice. She saw an opening and struck, lunging into full extension with the stake as a fencer might thrust an epee. Her aim was true, and the second vampire followed the first into dusty oblivion.

Two were gone, and two remained. *No, make that one,* Angelique corrected herself as, out of the corner of her eye, she saw Molly skewer the third gravespawn. The expression on her pale face was grim, but her dark eyes glittered with savage satisfaction as her prey crumbled to nothingness. Then Angelique turned toward the last vampire, which crouched snarling in a corner, held at bay by the cross gripped in the Professor's extended hand. Behind him, Patch took aim with a small but powerful crossbow.

"Stop!" The Slayer's command echoed in the empty chamber. The others looked at her in surprise. Angelique moved to face the vampire.

"You know who I am," she said.

The vampire nodded, its fingers kneading the air as if servilely twisting the brim of a doffed hat. "Aye."

"The one who changed you," Angelique said. "Describe him."

The creature's eyes filled with fear. "I can't. Not the Master. He'll know."

"Tell me," Angelique said, "and we will leave you unmolested."

She heard Molly gasp behind her and knew without looking that Gordon's hand was on her arm, restraining her.

But the vampire shook its head. "He'll know, I tell you. His eyes are everywhere! Even here!"

Angelique saw the thing's gaze shift to a dark corner of the room. The vampire shrieked in terror, then turned and leaped unhesitatingly toward one of the boarded-up windows, crashing through it directly into the glare of the morning sun. It was dust before it had time to hit the ground.

The five comrades stood staring in shock at the open window and the bright shaft of light.

"It knew," Patch said. "Lummie, it *knew* what it were doin'."

Angelique turned and looked at the thing in the corner that had triggered the vampire's suicide. The sunlight made it easy to spot. The others looked as well.

It was a rat. As they watched, it scuttled rapidly along the floorboards and disappeared into a hole in the wall.

Angelique looked at Professor van Helsing. He shook his head in bewilderment.

She looked back at the window. "The Master," she murmured.

• • •

IV

"'His eyes are everywhere,'" Gordon quoted. "That's what the vampire said just before it destroyed itself. What could it have meant?"

They were in the laboratory section of what was unofficially known as the Lair, the secret sub-cellar beneath the Professor's manor house that gave egress to London's labyrinthine network of sewers and tunnels. Gordon lounged in a somewhat thread-bare Morris chair, Patch and Molly leaned against one of the stone walls, and Angelique paced nervously. The Professor stood near a bookcase, leafing through a handwritten journal. On a nearby lab bench a complicated distillation apparatus circulated liquids of various hues through a glass maze of tubes and coils. A large detailed map of Greater London occupied one wall. The room was dimly lit by flickering gaslight.

"As I thought." Van Helsing's forefinger stabbed an entry in the diary. "It is all here in my brother's account of his dealings with the one called the King of the Undead: Count Dracula of Transylvania."

Angelique stopped pacing. "I've heard of him."

"Of course. If the undead have a potentate, a Prince of Darkness, it would be Dracula. Before his death, centuries ago, he was a national ruler and a potent sorcerer as well. His knowl-edge of the black arts makes him the most powerful of his kind. His gaze is mesmeric, enthralling. It is said that he can transvect from a man to a wolf, or to a bat, that he can change himself into mist, and"—van Helsing peered at them from over his rimless spectacles—"that he can use, as if they are his own, the eyes and ears of vermin, such as rats."

"But didn't your brother help to slay him in his homeland?" Angelique asked.

The Professor shrugged. "It seems Dracula was not quite as dead as Abraham had hoped. And now he has returned to London. This is a very serious matter. It will take all your skill to prevail against him, Angelique. None of us will be safe until he is destroyed."

Patch sniffed. "Sounds like a tall order, that does."

"He does appear to be well-nigh indestructible," Gordon agreed. "Is there no vulnerability in this creature to exploit?"

"Only one," van Helsing replied. "To gain his dark powers, he had to give up the daylight hours. Instead of simply avoiding the sun like others of his foul breed, he must remain insensible from sunrise to sunset, sleeping in a bed of his native earth."

Silence, save for the quiet bubbling of heated beakers, followed Professor Van Helsing's words. Unbidden in Angelique's mind there arose the memory of her dream: the cloaked silhouette, eyes burning in the shadowed face, the gleam of fangs drawing closer . . .

She shuddered. She was not overly concerned for herself; it was hard to imagine a vampire who could stand against her. But she was worried about her comrades' safety.

A dozen times she had opened her mouth to tell them about the vivid, unsettling nightmare—and its enigmatic warning—that she'd had the previous night. But each time the words seemed to stick in her throat. She wasn't sure why she was so reluctant. The Professor had told her many times that a slayer's dreams could be prescient, warnings of things to come. But she still could not make herself speak of this.

It was Molly who spoke next. "Our course is obvious, then," she said in response to the Professor. "We hunt this Dracula during the day. We find his lair and send him back to hell." She pantomimed thrusting a stake.

"Do not be overly confident," van Helsing said darkly. "Dracula has not survived for centuries by underestimating his enemies; neither should we underestimate him. He may be helpless during the day, but he can bend humans to his will, force them to be his myrmidons. We must be on guard constantly. In fact," he added, "until this evil has been put down, none of us should be alone for even a moment."

Once again uneasy silence reigned in the Lair. Angelique saw Patch, Gordon, and Molly look uncertainly at one another, and read their expressions without difficulty: How were they to know that one of them might not already be under Dracula's thrall?

Though they were anxious to begin the search, Angelique and van Helsing decided it was best to wait until the next day, as it was already less than an hour to sunset.

The Slayer spent the rest of the evening and long into the night training with Gordon in the Lair's makeshift gymnasium area. Van Helsing and the Watchers Council had spared no expense to see that her prowess in the arts of war was as thorough as it was eclectic. Among many other skills, she had been tutored in *Baritsu* and the French art of *La Canne,* as well as fencing, both classic and bayonet.

Gordon participated with gusto in the exercises, adroitly using both his walking stick and the rapier concealed within it to parry her quarterstaff mock attacks. As always, Angelique joyed in the smooth kinetics of her body, her muscles and reflexes working seamlessly at a speed and strength unknown to the strongest of athletes. It had not always been thus.

Before she had been called she had been the third of five children, raised by her mother and uncle; her father had left the country for a new life in the Colonies before she was born. They lived in Shoreditch, renting two rooms for eight shillings a week. At the age of seven she sold matches to help put food on the table, usually no more than a loaf, a penny's worth of hard cheese, and a penny's worth of tea. When she was twelve, her uncle lost his job as a boot-machinist. He supported them for a time in a wide variety of increasingly desperate ways, including making artificial flowers and helping to drive herds of cattle through the narrow city streets to the slaughterhouses, but eventually his savings were exhausted and he was sent to debtor's prison. They never heard from him again, and Angelique had to go to work at a blacking factory to help support the family.

In a way she was lucky, for by being at the factory she escaped the fate of her siblings and mother. The city officials blamed their deaths, as well as the deaths of several other families in the impoverished neighborhood, on a local outbreak of cholera. That gave them the excuse to quarantine the area. But Angelique, like most of the local children, knew more than one way to gain entry to their houses. The removal of some loose bricks disguising a hole in a wall was all it took.

It had not been cholera. Sick people did not smash pieces of furniture to kindling against the walls or stain the floor with spatters of blood. At the time, she didn't know what kind of horror was responsible, but she quickly learned. When she was called, one of her first acts as a slayer was to clean out the nest of vampires who had orphaned her.

Angelique had no illusions about what it meant to be the Chosen One. A short life with a brutal death at its end had been the fate of nearly all of her predecessors. Indeed it could be argued that the ephemeral nature of the calling made the office of the Slayer more effective, because rarely was another activated in the same city—or even the same country—as the last. Thus the power of the Slayer was distributed throughout the world, and, though individuals died quickly, the efficacy of one girl against all the powers of darkness had proven itself surprisingly well over the centuries.

A short life and a brutal death, then. But what of that? Angelique knew that was to be her legacy anyway, like as not. To grow up poor and a woman in the waning years of Victoria's London was to face a life of hardship and humiliation. With little education and no trade skills, most of her friends wound up going "on the game." It was that or starve.

Professor Peter van Helsing and the Watchers Council had taken her away from all that. Now she lived in a fine house in Regent's Park, she wore clothes of fine linen and wool instead of coarse burlap, and she ate food she had hardly known existed in Shoreditch. And her powers as a slayer granted her what even women of noble birth could not have: freedom from the fear of footpads, killers, and others who prey in the dark.

All this, she thought, *plus the comfort of boon companions . . . and true love.* There was no reason to fear death; compared to her old life, Angelique Hawthorne was already in heaven.

When the training period was finished, she sat beside Gordon. "It might behoove you to learn unarmed combat as well," she told him. "Suppose you encounter a sword-eating demon some day?"

"He'll have to eat me along with my blade," Gordon replied, "and then I shall carve my way back to you through his giblets." He pantomimed somewhat graphically to suit the words.

"There's an image to inspire romance," she said, grinning at him.

He grinned back, then looked serious. "This Dracula . . . the Professor seems very concerned by the threat he poses."

She felt a stab of unease, but masked it with a light tone. "You know the Professor. Every danger is a harbinger of universal doom. Hazards of the course. I imagine very few watchers are optimists."

He nodded but did not seem to take much comfort from this. "Still—"

She gently laid a finger across his lips. "Hush. We will find him, and I will slay him. He may be more powerful than the vampires we're used to, but we have faced demons and other abominations both powerful and well-versed in magick." She traced her finger along his jawline, raised his face to hers. "We have so little time together," she murmured. "Let's not waste it in worry over the unknown. The future must wait."

"The Slayer is as wise as she is mighty," he whispered, just before their lips met—

And they were interrupted by Patch's excited shouts. "There's been another one!"

V

The corpse of the latest victim lay half concealed in a patch of trees and tall grass near one of the Crystal Palace's Dinosaur Islands. The swarm of lookie-loos was thick, keeping Angelique and her friends from getting close enough to see anything in detail. By the murmured comments of the crowd, however, it was obvious that the unfortunate was a woman, another member of high society. They hung back on the fringes, next to a statue of a four-footed Iguanodon, half-hidden in thick, eddying ground mist silvered by moonlight.

Professor van Helsing had not accompanied them this time, choosing to remain in the Lair and conduct more research.

"The second member of the upper classes to be claimed in as many days," Molly said as they watched the body being removed.

"True," said Gordon. "Dracula appears to have fairly specific tastes. No doubt he prefers cleaner throats and blood less tainted with gin than he's apt to find in the rookeries."

"Which means," Angelique mused, "he must look enough like his prey that he can move among them and put them at their ease before he strikes."

"According to the Professor, Dracula's intent was to relocate to England permanently," Molly said. "No doubt it still is."

"Didn't the Prof say he was a nob before he got turned?" came from Patch.

"He did indeed—a Count, no less. He also said that it isn't enough for Dracula to simply avoid the sun; he must pass the daylight hours asleep, resting in his native soil."

Gordon pressed the knuckle of his index finger to his chin. "He'd be looking for a home near the toffs, then, with room enough to hide some boxes of dirt. Someplace private."

Angelique looked at Patch, who nodded in response. "Me 'n' me boys're on it," he said. "I'll hav't sussed out before dark, or me name's not Archibald Oglevy." He raced off into the night.

Even slayers need some rest, and so Angelique passed the remainder of the night in her bed. But she did not get much quietude.

She anticipated the possible return of her nocturnal visitor— whether he had been a dream or reality she still was not sure— tensely at first, a stake clenched in her hand and a cross and phial of holy water on the table nearby. But gradually, as the hours wore on, she found herself relaxing. This was due partly to exhaustion—the tracking and eventual slaying of the Tethyrian demon posing as Springheel Jack had gone on night and day for over a week—but she had to admit that there was something more: an eagerness, perhaps even a yearning, subtle but unmistakable. At one point she rose and opened the windows, looking out over the sleeping neighborhood. She could faintly hear the exotic cries of various animals in the nearby Zoological Gardens, but nothing else.

Just before dawn she dosed off out of sheer exhaustion. She awoke with a start to the maid summoning her for breakfast.

Patch, hands and face uncharacteristically scrubbed at Cook's insistence, was buttering a scone and grinning a self-satisfied grin. Molly, Gordon, and the Professor had arrived before her. "It appears Patch has come through for us again," Gordon told her.

Angelique listened as Patch described an old mansion in Mayfair, recently sold to an anonymous buyer who would only sign the documents after dark. He spoke with a "foreign sort o' way," according to the errand boy who worked for the mortgage company. The place was secluded, spacious, and had a huge wine cellar.

"Excellent," Gordon said. "So, then, a hearty breakfast, a glance through the morning *Times*, and then heigh-ho to kill the vampire before tea." He helped himself to another rasher of bacon. "We'll have this wrapped up in no time."

Van Helsing set his coffee cup down hard enough to spill it. "Again I counsel you, Angelique. This should be the work of the Slayer alone. You cannot risk having your attention divided by—"

"Calm yourself, Professor," Angelique said. "You will upset your digestion again."

The Professor cast a dark look at Gordon, who affected not to notice. When he spoke again, his voice was low and compelling. "Beware Dracula," he said to the Slayer. "He is never where you think he is. He is never who or even *what* you think he is. Do not put too much confidence in the rituals and strictures which bind him. His hypnotic abilities are stronger than anything Mesmer could imagine. He knows of all the forces which empower you. You cannot even begin to imagine those which empower him."

After breakfast the Slayer outfitted herself, making sure that the hidden holster belt was lined with stakes, that a cross hung about her neck, and that a silver throwing knife was easily accessible from a sheath in one of her kid boots. She also slipped into a pocket a small cruet of holy water. Then the four set out.

Angelique reflected much upon her watcher's words during their journey. She understood his concern, even shared it to a great degree. She felt very responsible for the welfare and safety of those who stood beside her against the night. But, as she had told herself many times, they had chosen to live this life. She had not.

The mansion was indeed as secluded as Patch had described it. Though it was not dilapidated, yet it gave the impression of being in disrepair. The mighty oaks and yews surrounding it blotted away the sun, creating a pervading gloom even though the morning was bright.

They moved cautiously, entering the huge house in a manner designed and practiced to minimize attack. Angelique kicked open the door, and Patch and Molly went in behind her, Patch crouched low with cross extended and Molly with her crossbow ready to fire. From behind them Gordon shined a torch, quickly and expertly illuminating the shadowy corners and nooks. Once they were satisfied no threat was in evidence, they moved on. In this way they gradually investigated every room of the manse's upper and ground floors.

They found no vampires. Nor did they find any boxes or containers of soil, which Professor van Helsing had said would be a sure sign of the vampire lord. At last the only place left to investigate was the cellar.

They slowly descended stone steps into the darkness, Gordon's torch barely serving to show them their way. The shadows seemed almost alive, crepitant and hungry, pressing in from all sides with malign force. Though Angelique was thoroughly familiar with crypts, sepulchres, and other underground domains of the dead, still she found this cellar as unnerving as any mausoleum. It seemed to whisper to her, the darkness did, in a cold thin voice she could not quite understand, no matter how she strained her ears. A glance at the white and set faces of her friends told her without question that they felt it too. There was no doubt that evil, ancient and unspeakable, had walked the mossy stone floors of this place.

They found huge and empty wine casks, furniture piled in corners, and other domestic detritus, but no caskets of earth. At last Angelique reluctantly declared the mansion empty of the undead.

Patch was disappointed that his lead had yielded no results. There were indeed other places to investigate, but only this one had fulfilled all the criteria. Angelique headed back for the stairs, motioning the others to follow. "Let's be about it, then," she said. "We can surely get one more place checked out before—"

They all heard the sound at the same time: the unmistakable creaking of long-unused hinges. They froze, then slid into formation with practiced ease. Gordon moved the light, letting its beam slide over the seeping walls, past a stack of wooden buckets, to come finally to rest on a thick, iron-hasped door that they had somehow missed previously.

The door was slowly opening.

Quicksilver-fast, Angelique plucked a cross from its sheath, twirling it momentarily around her fingers before letting it settle securely in her grip. To her right, Molly raised her cross bow; to her left, Gordon partially unsheathed his sword cane; crouched in front of her, Patch loaded a slingshot with a holy wafer.

The door creaked open further. An aperture appeared, revealing utter blackness.

Something leaped out of the darkness toward them.

Molly fired. The wooden shaft struck the wall just above the cat's head. The coal-black feline changed course with a yowl, fleeing into the dark cellar depths.

Angelique, Patch, and Gordon relaxed, looking at each other somewhat shamefacedly. "Bloody hell," Patch gasped. "Thought for sure it was Dracula at first."

"How do we know it wasn't?" Molly asked.

The vampire hunters looked at each other in sudden apprehension.

"He can change himself into a bat or a wolf," Molly said. "Are other animals in his repertoire as well?"

"The familiars of witches have been known to take the semblance of black cats," Gordon pointed out.

Angelique turned toward the stairs. "Outside, quickly, while we form another plan."

She felt somewhat better when they were out of the house. The sun rode through a high mist, its blaze obscured to the point where the disc was visible. But still it was sunlight, which meant they were safe for the moment from the undead.

"We must turn to our second choice for Dracula's lodgings, Patch," the Slayer said.

The lad looked chagrined, but before he could reply, they all reacted to a sudden sound, a sort of whistling crack, from beyond the trees. Looking up, the Slayer saw a small egg-shaped object hurtling overhead. It arced and then started to fall. "*Look out!*" she shouted, shoving Gordon to one side. "Take cov—"

Before she could finish the sentence, the object burst and a thick cloud of gas diffused rapidly from it. It settled like a pall over the yard, enveloping them. Angelique heard her friends coughing.

The gas was obviously a soporific of some sort. She saw Gordon and Patch collapse on the sward. She could not see Molly.

A figure loomed before her, indistinct in the mist. She lashed out with one leg, a high snapping kick that would have felled a quarryman. But the haze made it difficult to judge distances, and the strike missed.

She saw he had a gun.

Angelique performed a series of backflips that carried her into a sheltering copse. She heard the gun fire, heard the bullet sear the air nearby. She crouched, trying not to take deep breaths, feeling the numbing effects of the gas seeping into her lungs nonetheless. Her slayer stamina would keep her conscious longer than her friends, but ultimately she too would succumb.

The clouds were beginning to thin. Angelique heard a peal of demented laughter.

Through the diminishing vapor she saw the figure again. There was something familiar about him; she knew she had seen him somewhere before. Obviously he was not a vampire.

"You were warned, Slayer!" The cackling voice echoed about her. "My master is far too smart for you and your pathetic cadre! It was easy for him to anticipate your reasoning and arrange for me to meet you here. You will never find his resting place—he lies with the legends, and his power dwarfs even theirs. Take heed—there will not be another warning!"

The Professor's words echoed in her head: *He may be helpless during the day, but he can bend humans to his will, force them to be his myrmidons.*

A sudden breeze cleared the remaining mist. She could see her enemy clearly now.

It was Detective Peasbody, the Scotland Yard investigator.

Angelique stared in shock. The man was normally meticulously neat and something of a dandy. Yet now his clothes were torn and muddy, his hair matted, and the look in his eyes was that of utter madness.

She tried to launch herself forward, to grab him and force him to tell him where Dracula was. But her muscles would not obey her. The narcotic gas had finally had its effect, and the Slayer fell forward into darkness.

VI

Images of fire and ash . . .
   Graveyard dust, stirred in a forgotten tomb . . .
   Cruciform light strobing . . .

Angelique blinked against the light. After a moment she recognized the chamber she was in: a drawing room in the Professor's house. Van Helsing, Gordon, and Patch were looking down anxiously at her. "What is your name, my child?" the Professor asked.

Angelique blinked again, in puzzlement this time. "Angelique Hawthorne," she replied. "And what is the point of asking me that, pray tell?"

"Good, good," the Professor said in relief, more to the others than to her. "I feared an injury of the brain, but she seems whole. Now—"

She interrupted him, sitting up suddenly. "Molly?" The room seemed to shudder and shift, and she felt a stab of pain behind her forehead. It cleared quickly, however. "Where's Molly?"

Gordon and Patch glanced at each other. Van Helsing kept his gaze on Angelique. "This we do not know. We must assume that she has been taken by Dracula."

She pushed them aside and rose. "Taken? How?"

"No doubt to insure your noninvolvement in his affairs. It is as I have said before: a slayer is vulnerable through those she loves."

She looked at him, expecting to see rebuke in his eyes, but finding only compassion. "Then we find him," she said. "We find him, kill him, and rescue her."

"There's less than an hour to sundown," Gordon said. "We have no leads, no idea of where to search."

Angelique began to pace furiously. "We can't simply give up! If we don't find her in time, Dracula will—"

She could not finish the sentence, but she could tell from their expressions that there was no need to. Van Helsing had been right, she knew, and now Molly was set to pay the penalty for Angelique's defiance of the council's law.

She realized she was breathing rapidly. She tried to calm herself, seeking her center, willing her racing heart to settle, but with little success.

"Let us not lose our heads," the Professor said. "Even if we do not find him until after dark, the sooner is still the better. Dracula's power waxes during the hours before midnight, and wanes—"

Angelique stopped pacing abruptly and turned to van Helsing. "Wait! There was something that Peasbody said." She frowned in concentration. "'He lies with the legends, and his power dwarfs even theirs.'"

The others watched her, knowing better than to interrupt her concentration. "Back in the East End," she continued slowly, after a moment, "when we spoke with Peasbody, I noticed a curious scent about him. I thought it was pomade, but now I think differently. It was the residue of fumes clinging to his clothes."

"What kind of fumes, then?" Patch asked.

"Paraffin," Angelique replied. "Hot wax."

• • •

Madame Marie Tussaud had first brought her fabled wax museum to London in 1835. By 1884 it had settled in Marylebone Road. The spacious, multichambered structure featured many different scenes to tickle the public's fancy, all painstakingly sculpted in pliable wax. But its most popular attraction by far was a room set apart to protect those of nervous temperament, and called for many years simply the Separate Area—a collection of mannequins, death masks, and implements of torture culled mainly from the bloody history of the French Revolution. In 1846 a more appropriate sobriquet was given to it by *Punch* magazine, and it has been known by this name ever since: The Chamber of Horrors.

Angelique moved stealthily through the dark exhibition, one part of her mind marveling at how lifelike the wax effigies were even as she remained alert for possible attacks. She paused before an elaborate Grand Guignol exhibit, with a grinning executioner holding up the just-severed head of a French aristocrat. The images and scenarios within her vision included the aristocratic Dr. Henry Jekyll and his bestial alter ego, Mr. Hyde; the American Lizzie Borden, caught in the act of raising her ax over her terrified mother's head; and the recently finished reconstruction of Whitechapel showing one of Jack the Ripper's victims lying in a pool of blood.

Peasbody had indeed been right to call them Dracula's peers.

She had not reached the museum until after dark, due to the arrival of a heavy London "pea-souper." Within an hour of the east wind's rising, the evening light had given way to Cimmerian darkness as the air filled with a noxious combination of chimney smoke, marsh gases, and other effluvia. It had quickly become impossible to see more than an arm's length ahead, and her hansom's speed had been greatly reduced.

The museum had closed early due to the fog. Gordon and Patch had wanted to come with her, but Angelique forbade it. She would not take the chance of Dracula acquiring yet another of her friends as hostage.

Now she prowled, silently and cautiously, through the eerie corridors of waxen horrors.

The sound that alerted her could not have been heard by normal human ears, but the Slayer's hearing was attuned for such frequencies. A soft sigh of air above her—she dived forward, rolled, and came up with a stake in her hand.

Nothing. No sound, no movement. Unless . . . did she hear the faintest echo of an amused chuckle? Or was it only in her mind?

A velvet curtain masked an alcove to one side of her. A few steps put her within reach, and she grabbed the thick material, yanked it back.

And exposed a coffin resting on a small dais.

It was a plain and simple oblong box made of dark wood. No insignia, no description. She had thought the resting place of Count Dracula, Lord of the Undead, would have been more elegant, more impressive. Nevertheless Angelique suddenly felt her throat go dry. The sick taste of fear rose like bile. A sense of dread, undefined but no less powerful for that, enveloped her. She had to force herself to move closer. Stake poised in one hand, she lifted the lid with the other, tilted it slowly back.

Only her training as a slayer prevented her from screaming.

Molly Carrington lay in the coffin's silken embrace. Her hands were folded across her breast, her eyes closed. Her head was tilted slightly to one side, affording a clear view of the wounds in her neck.

Angelique staggered, feeling as though a stake had been plunged through her own heart. Her friend's ashen pallor left no doubt that her blood had been thoroughly drained. Angelique knew that Dracula had done worse than kill her; he had turned her. Her body would rise again, but her soul would be replaced by the animus of a demon. The fiend would use the remnants of Molly's psyche as a template for its own consciousness, but it would not be Molly, any more than one of the wax representations that surrounded them could be mistaken for the real thing. Even so, her soul would echo with the psychic reverberations of her body's possession. Molly had died the death she had feared the most, one that brought with it the most hideous afterlife imaginable. Until the vampire was destroyed, she would never know peace.

And who is responsible? she seemed to hear the Professor's stern voice asking. Dracula had performed the unspeakable deed, but who had put Molly in harm's way in the first place?

She blinked back tears. The only way to make even partial amends was to release her friend from this unholy limbo. She raised the stake.

Plunging it into Molly's heart was harder than plunging it into her own would be. She watched through tears as the corpse in the coffin transformed to dust and dissipated.

Molly. I'm sorry. I'm so sorry. . . .

In her state of utter shock and sorrow, she very nearly did not react in time. He made no sound; it was the movement of air against her cheek that alerted her. Angelique spun about in time to see darkness move against darkness. She saw the pale oval of a face, hideously familiar from her dream, as Dracula came at her with uncanny speed. She barely managed to dodge.

He turned, and now she saw him clearly.

He was younger than she had expected and startlingly handsome, but it was a cold male beauty, with no promise of human feeling in the eyes or the set of the mouth. His face was pallid beneath his black hair, eyes glinting redly, like that of a beast's. His attire was formal, a cravat and sash adding a continental touch, and he wore a flowing opera cape that seemed almost to possess a life of its own; it followed his movements more closely than a shadow, rippling restlessly even in the still air.

His gaze caught hers. She felt his eyes searing into her soul.

"Foolish slayer." His voice was almost a whisper, with the faint accent she remembered. "Now you see that I am serious. But now it is too late."

Angelique tried to move, to leap toward him, to bury the stake in the ruffled shirtfront, but she could not. She was as immobile as the statues all about them.

Dracula moved toward her with silken grace. "I have lived a long life and an even longer death. But I have yet to taste the blood of a slayer. I have heard that it is the finest wine the heart can produce."

He made a slight gesture, and Angelique, to her horror, found herself tilting her head back, exposing her neck. She fought her rebellious body, but it was futile. And deep within her she once again felt the urge to give in, the attraction to the dark side that she had experienced in her bedchamber the past two nights.

"Why do you resist?" he asked, honest curiosity in his voice. "For friendship? For loyalty? Human relationships are ephemeral, evanescent. I can offer you a true lifetime . . . one measured not by calendars or clocks, but by cycles."

He stood in front of her now. She noted that his fangs had emerged, though curiously enough, his face had not assumed the monstrous appearance that other vampires did. *The Professor will be interested in knowing this,* a small, detached part of her mind said, knowing that she would not be the one to tell him.

He took her by her shoulders, lowered his face toward her throat. "Your friend was a mere aperitif," he murmured. "She but whetted my thirst. Now—"

Molly. The name echoed in her mind, stirring tides of shame, loss . . . and rage. And with the rage came suddenly the return of her will. Angelique hurled the vampire away from her; he staggered back, stumbling into an exhibit of a torture wheel. She leaped after him, ready to take advantage of his surprise and quickly end the fight. But even as she drove the stake toward his heart he somehow *dissolved,* became insubstantial, a white mist that quickly disappeared.

Angelique stopped, almost unable to credit her senses. She quickly looked about. There was no sign of Dracula.

A cold breeze, as if off a frozen pond, wafted from behind her. She turned . . . and he was there.

With blinding swiftness he struck. It was a backhanded blow, delivered almost languidly, and yet it hurled the Slayer across the room with the force of a catapult. She struck the wall hard enough to break through it, crashing into the adjoining room.

The rich smell of molten wax assaulted her, along with a blast of warm air. She rose, dazed. This chamber was filled with waxworks too, but they were all in various stages of construction. Half-formed statues, human in shape but not in detail, stared eyelessly at her. Shelves lined the walls, filled with jointed wooden arms and legs, busts supporting deathmasks, cans of paint, and all manner of clothing from all eras. In the room's center was a large vat, simmering over a bank of gas jets. Two workers, wearing heavy smocks and gloves, were adding chemicals to the bubbling mixture. They stared at Angelique.

"'Ere, now!" one of them shouted. "What're you about—?"

His eyes widened, as did those of his comrades; then they both turned and bolted for a door in the far wall. Angelique turned in time to see Dracula stalking toward her, eyes blazing with fury.

She reached for another stake, only to find them all gone. She grabbed an ax from a table of medieval weaponry, but as she lifted it she realized it was merely a wooden prop.

Dracula stopped and raised a hand like a conductor demanding music. Angelique felt herself pulled toward him.

She all but flew across the floor in his direction, as though being drawn by an invisible rope. She had barely time enough to snap the head of the fake ax free from the shaft and hold it out before her.

It struck him full in the chest.

Once again, surprise thwarted his spell over her. He looked down at the makeshift stake protruding from his chest. Then he looked up at her and smiled, and she realized that the strike had missed his heart.

By then she was already in motion. She leaped, twisting in mid air as she sailed over him, and landed on the catwalk surrounding the wax cauldron. Thick waves of heat roiled from it.

Dracula pulled the stake from his chest and cast it away. Then, with a single graceful leap, he was on the catwalk next to her.

"You pathetic fool," he snarled. "I would have made you immortal."

The hardest part was knowing that she *wanted* it, that a part of her, deep down, would always wonder. And that the desire, that dark desire that had kept her quiet about his nocturnal visit instead of telling the Professor, might have made it easier for Dracula to take Molly from them.

"You could have shared the night with me for eternity."

He stepped forward, one hand thrust out from beneath his cloak, fingers reaching for her throat.

"Forgive me," she said, thrusting one hand into a pocket, groping for what she had put there earlier. "I'm just not ready for that kind of commitment."

Dracula snarled and lunged, and Angelique slashed the air between them with the open cruet of holy water.

The drops struck his hands and face, and even over the bubbling of the molten wax she could hear his undead flesh sizzle. With a cry, he staggered back and fell into the cauldron of wax.

On a sudden impulse she threw the phial in after him.

She was blown off the catwalk by a concussive wave of air as the cauldron erupted. Sprawled on her back, stunned by the blast, Angelique watched in mute shock as a column of wax, writhing sinuously as if possessed of some bizarre life, rose from its center, towering over her. Its plastic surface roiled, and the astonished Slayer saw Dracula's image take form from it, face contorted in pain, fingers clawing the air as if seeking release. Then the column congealed, as if suddenly frozen by some hyperborean wind. It loomed above her, the face and figure rough-hewn as if by some elemental artist, but still recognizable as the vampire count.

Angelique rose to her feet, moved forward, staring at the formation. She had no idea by what alchemy the holy water and the hot wax had combined to produce so effective a prison for Dracula. But that did not matter. A slayer trusted her instincts.

She found a serviceable shaft of wood among the debris, moved to stand in front of Dracula, and raised it like a cricket bat.

"Rest in peace, Molly," she said softly as she swung the shaft. It struck the column squarely. The pillar shattered, fragments of wax raining down around her. From a great distance—or perhaps again just from the depths of her mind—she heard a final scream of anger and defeat.

Then all was silent.

Angelique returned to Molly's coffin, knelt beside it, and wept.

VI

It was dawn when she left the museum. The fog still held London, or at least Marylebone, in its gray grasp. As Angelique walked the streets she might well have been the last live inhabitant of a dead world.

It was certainly how she felt.

Professor van Helsing had been right. She understood now the folly of letting anyone too close to her, of forming any relationships, even platonic ones. Such joys and comforts were not for her. There was room for only one on the path she trod.

She would have to send Patch and Gordon away, she knew. That would hurt—in Gordon's case, almost as much as driving the stake through Molly's dead heart. But it was the only way. Her conscience could not bear the weight of another loved one's death.

She alone can stand against the vampires, the forces of darkness . . .

She wondered if Dracula were really dead, if she had indeed put the Lord of the Undead to rest for the final time. She realized that it did not matter. If he returned, as he apparently had in the past, she would face him again, or some future slayer would. She could not predict how or why. There was only one certainty in her world now: As long as vampires walked the Earth, a slayer would stand against them.

Alone.

Angelique turned a corner, and suddenly a figure loomed in her path. She stopped short, recognizing it immediately. The red, glowing eyes, the taloned hands, the voluminous cloak . . . they could only mean one thing.

Another Tethyrian demon had taken up the mantle of Springheel Jack.

In that timeless moment, as they faced each other, Angelique knew with bitter certainty that this was to be the sum of her future: A lifetime, most likely very short, of battles and struggles, of victories and defeats, of sacrifice and anonymity. A war against the forces of darkness that would inevitably end in darkness. Without friendship, save for her watcher.

And without love.

The Slayer leaped once more into battle, alone.

The War Between the States

Rebecca Rand Kirshner

NEW YORK CITY, 1922

Through the window of the train, a transformation had been taking place. The lazy flats of Carolina marsh had dried away and swollen into rolling green hills, then stretched long into great gapes of land rooted with unfamiliar, proud-looking trees, and now had metamorphosed into ancient towns made of brick and shutters and copper steeples gone green with time and weather. Now she was only a few hours away from New York City. Time passed as the trained chugged forward, and she watched as the sky began to color, brightening into pinks and yellows like fireworks set off in slow motion, and then without ever seeming to reach its apex began to fade away into shades of gray and then blacks, until Sally Jean was left with nothing to watch but her own reflection.

She was a very pretty girl, eighteen last February, with soft brown eyes and soft blond hair that she wore piled on her head like cotton. In fact being soft was as integral to Sally Jean as her family name or their home on the Battery. It was the adjective most likely to be spoken, in conjunction with some feature of hers or another, when castaway beaux remembered their days in Sally Jean's favor, or when admiring friends sat with her at her dressing table. Sally Jean knew how people thought of her; she knew how the boys brushed their fingers against the skin on her shoulders as if she were made of clouds and spun sugar, things that would melt away if you touched them with your mouth. She knew how the girls admired her, just to the brink of envy, but not beyond. They couldn't really envy her after all, not in a jealous way, because she was so kind, so generous, so pliable—so soft. Sally Jean knew all of this and yet she held all their compliments at arms' length, at the length of one pretty, soft, white arm, because she knew that being soft, just like being young and beautiful, was part of her arsenal. A weapon that she could call upon later, when life really began.

Sally Jean sat alone. Her small hand rested proprietarily on the pink-papered hatbox that occupied the seat beside her, making clear to the boarding passengers that she had no interest in company. Ordinarily Sally Jean would have generously made conversation with any sort of seatmate. But this trip was different. It wasn't that she was afraid of being accosted by an unsavory character with hooch on his breath and bad intentions up his sleeve. And it wasn't because she had hoped to lie down for a bit during her journey; she was as awake and as happy as she'd ever been. She needed to sit alone because she herself was undergoing a transformation.

Sally Jean felt a certain anxiety that if she didn't change along with the world, along with the air that was being ripped through with aeroplanes, along with the oceans that were being swum by women covered with grease, along with the country itself that was getting smaller and faster and full of cars, she would be left behind like a moldy tombstone in St. Phillips cemetery. When she was a girl, she used to walk through the cool quiet graveyards, reading the epitaphs until tears would spill down her soft cheeks. Her face would be wet, but she wouldn't feel sad, just full and proud, as if she understood something. But in the last few years, things had changed. Women could vote now for goodness sake, not that she was twenty-one or had any intention of doing so, but the fact remained that she could do so many things. She was tired of sweet tea, tired of grits, tired of religion, and tired of the past. Maybe if the Confederacy had won its ancient war she could have stayed in Charleston, but it hadn't, and she was up to her ears with the melancholy of it all. The same languorous, long-rooted world in which she had grown up now seemed hopelessly at the periphery of life.

There were external manifestations of Sally Jean's transformation as well. With each stop of the train, she compared herself to the new passengers and made adjustments to her attire accordingly. Only a couple of hours into the journey she had realized that her hat, just purchased last week at Berlin's, was not going to make it to New York atop her head. A clever-looking girl with sleek red hair had boarded in Baltimore, and Sally Jean had immediately felt the frothy thing burning against her scalp. As quickly as she could, she had removed it and pushed it unceremoniously into the hatbox. Soon after, she had unbuttoned the top two buttons of her blouse, and at the next stop, casually removed her white gloves and stuffed them into the hatbox as well. About her hobble skirt and thick cotton stockings, she couldn't do a thing. She needed a short dress and, if she could somehow manage it, silk stockings.

Silk stockings seemed absolutely necessary, the more she thought about it. She couldn't hardly exist without them! Her legs began to itch under the girlish, old-fashioned cotton, and she wished that despite the hour the stores would be open when she arrived. How could she afford them though? Half a thought flashed into her mind: Brett. Brett would surely understand and take her to Saks Fifth Avenue.

And then the second half of the thought joined the first with a clap, startling her like thunder: Brett. Tall, handsome Brett with his neatly cut uniform and steel gray eyes. Brett whose neck smelled like limes and in whose arms she had danced, night after night, during all the summer dances, two years in a row. Faithful Brett, who had written her nearly daily all through the war. Sweet Brett, who had known her when she was just a girl and had waited for her, who had let her grow up while he fought his wars and earned his money. Dearest Brett, as she had called him when she wrote her perfumed letters back, filling pink pages with vague ideas about love and life that she meant more as musings than as professions. Brett, whose lips had kissed hers on the veranda of her parent's house late one June evening.

When the first shots of the Civil War were fired on Fort Sumter, the good people of Charlestown had sat on their porches and verandas, juleps in hand, and watched as the battle began. And then, some sixty years later, Sally Jean had sat in the very same place and watched with perhaps a similar interested detachment as a young man from Asheville declared that they would spend the rest of their lives together. Whatever she had said that night was true when she said it, but it had felt unreal, as if what she said could go nowhere in that heavy, unmoving air. But now, in the brightly-lit train car, with the city buildings growing sharply outside her window, the whole thing seemed horribly lucid. She was traveling to New York because she was engaged to marry Brett Blakely.

And before Sally Jean could reconcile that solid fact with the new self that was tentatively blossoming inside her mind, she was at Grand Central Station. She had arrived. She made her way through the crowd, hatbox in one hand, suitcase in the other, and though she held her head up proudly, she felt like everyone was snickering. Sally Jean bristled and walked as fast as her long tight skirt would allow. And then again she remembered Brett. She stopped, looked around, scanning the bustling figures for a tall gray eyed soldier. He was nowhere to be seen. Her indignation was tempered with hope. Maybe this was going to be easier than she had thought. As impossible as it was for her to understand how a gentleman would be willing to throw her over, it sure would simplify matters. She did hate scenes.

She heard thunderous footsteps and turned just in time to see a hulking young man in an ill-fitting green suit and a feathered hat running up behind her.

"Sally Jean!" the young man bellowed.

"Why, who on earth—Brett!"

The whites of her eyes grew at the sight of him, and it was only with conscientious effort that she softened them into a look befitting the occasion.

"Darling!" he said as he pulled her close to his sweaty cheek.

"Oh, honey," she said as she pushed him away. "Not here!" This with a smile and a look toward the oblivious crowd around them. "Oh! Let me just look at that extraordinary suit you have on. Somehow I thought you'd be in a uniform forever."

He spun for her, tipped his feathered hat and picked up her bag and her hatbox, and they began to walk toward the exit.

"Pretty sharp, huh? And you wouldn't believe the deal I got."

She hummed noncommittally. No deal could have been too good; the suit was dreadful. Thick, green, out of fashion, and it concealed quite effectively his fine figure. Sally Jean felt a flash of outrage at this costume, as if he had wooed her under false pretences, in disguise. She had kissed a soldier and awoke to find herself with a man who wore a feathered hat and a clumsy old suit. His face was flushed with excitement, the creases around his eyes and at his mouth white in contrast. He leaned in close and she could see tiny droplets of sweat clinging to his upper lip.

"You must be exhausted, darling."

And suddenly she was. Sally Jean feigned sleep as they rode to the hotel in Brett's creaky old Model T and didn't look out the window once; she wanted to leave it fresh for when the city was hers alone. Brett had arranged for separate but connecting rooms, and it wasn't until she was in her single bed with the door to the other room safely bolted, that she allowed herself to open her eyes fully. This wasn't going to do. She wasn't going to be the same girl who sat passively on that veranda. She wanted to feel things, to be things. She wanted to be a modern woman, and getting married at eighteen to a man in a feathered hat wasn't part of her agenda. Having confirmed this with herself, she closed her eyes and fell into a deep sleep.

The polite knocking at the bolted door awoke her from a deep dark sleep.

She called through the door, "Just a minute, honey. I seem to have accidentally locked this silly thing."

"Take your time. I'm going to go down and have a cup of coffee. I'll come back in twenty minutes and take you to dinner and a show. I know this really fantastic place."

He parked carefully along a curb, hemming and hawing the car into position while Sally Jean regarded him with barely concealed irritation. He seemed a little nervous, and she worried that he was taking her to a party to which they hadn't been invited.

"This is it," he said as they stopped in front of an unremarkable brownstone marked 333 with bronze numbers.

"You do know these people, don't you, honey?"

"Well, not exactly, but you'll see. I came here with a fellow from the office."

Oh, poor Brett, he clearly doesn't belong in the North, she thought, her pretty jaw clenching. They entered the unlocked door and instead of a parlor were greeted with a darkened staircase. She didn't want to go down; it smelled like spoiled milk and wet wood. At Brett's insistence, Sally Jean followed him down the rickety staircase and nearly ran smack in to a gigantic man with wide-legged trousers and a matchstick between his lips. The giant didn't say a word, just looked at them.

"I think we're in the wrong—"

"Texas sent me," Brett said to the giant. And to Sally Jean's surprise, the giant took one heavy step to the side and indicated the door behind him with a nod. As he did, Sally Jean thought she saw the flash of a gun beneath his dinner jacket. She was about to dash back up the rickety steps when Brett opened the door and she saw into the room beyond.

It was like looking into the peephole of a sugared Easter egg and seeing the miraculous jeweled world inside. A splendid dining room, all red velvet and chandeliers, spread out before her, filled with the most elegant people Sally Jean had ever seen. And there was a stage at the front where a tuxedoed band was playing. She couldn't have dreamed that such an opulent place could be hidden in the bowels of the world like this, behind such a door, beneath such a staircase.

They sat at a table right near the front. Brett ordered a very fine dinner for them and they were able to drink real cocktails. It wasn't moonshine or some stuff from someone's bathtub, but real liquor from real bottles. It tasted like freedom to Sally Jean. And the show! There was a comedian who made Brett laugh like Peony, her horse at home—her horse in South Carolina—and a juggler who juggled martini shakers and finished his act by pouring a drink for a bald-headed gentleman at the table next to theirs.

After that trick Brett looked over at her with a gentle, proud smile, and she felt a small part of her heart melting under his glance. She smiled at him sweetly and felt a sort of sleepy nostalgia for him. Brett was a good man, honest and true, patient and kind. The lights dimmed; a new act was coming on. Maybe she wouldn't be able to stay frozen after all; maybe she'd just soften and melt back into being his girl, being his wife. She wasn't even sad about it, just felt a kind of sweet remembrance as if she was being led into a dance that had been going on for years and years. Maybe she was going to lose the battle for secession all over again.

And then the woman came on stage: tall, all in blue, with black bobbed hair. She beckoned with one lean arm and then there was a whole crowd of them, leggy girls in sapphire-blue costumes with bands of diamonds strung round their heads like glittering crowns of thorns. Sally Jean sat straight up in her chair, forgetting for the first time that day what she looked like and what others must be thinking of her. Brett squeezed her hand, but she pulled away. There was a miracle taking place on stage. The music was deep and suggestive, full of sliding trombones and a timpani beat from a tightly pulled drum. And the dancers—they moved like mermaids, like horses at the Derby, like angels. They were made of lightning, flashing across the stage with their legs high in the air. The past seemed to dissolve around them as they set forth some sort of dancing manifesto, a vision of the future described in kicks and spins. When the act finished, Sally Jean clapped as loudly as anyone in the theater.

Brett turned to her.

"That wasn't too much for you, was it Sally Jean?"

His face reflected concern and, to her, an artificial sense of propriety. As if she hadn't seen women's legs every time she took a bath! She smiled at him in the same way she might smile at an old woman talking about the exorbitant fee for overdue library books. And then the next act began.

The women had changed their costumes, adding long gold skirts and Egyptian-inspired headdresses. Their eyes were rimmed extravagantly in kohl. Sally Jean drank her cocktail in one swift swallow without taking her eyes off the stage. The music was silky, Middle-Eastern, and the girls, the women, the dancing horses, were even silkier. Sally Jean's eyes flicked across the stage, looking for the woman with the black-bobbed hair—there she was, at the far left of the line. And though the black-bobbed woman wasn't in the center for this number, Sally Jean was sure that everyone was watching her alone. Everyone and everything was drawn to the woman, and Sally Jean felt that any second, the stage itself would tilt toward her and all the dancers would slide uncontrollably to the left, pulled by her immense gravity of being.

Unlike the others, the woman in the black bob didn't smile; her face was incredibly still, fixed in an odd expression Sally Jean couldn't name, and her eyes, which peered out into the crowd, seemed not to be looking at the enraptured audience but somewhere else, into the future or into the past, as if she could see angels and phantoms. This woman, this creature, this future-dancer, this is who Sally Jean wanted to become.

Two more acts followed, and then the lights went up and the air seemed to return to the room. On the ride home, Sally Jean kissed Brett twice out of pure exuberance. And then it was night and then it was day again. Sally Jean put off visiting Brett's aunt and, after getting a new short dress and a pair of silk stockings with seams along the back, claimed she was too worn out to shop for her wedding dress. But when eight o'clock came, her energy miraculously returned and Brett found himself driving to Forty-fifth Street once again.

The show was just the same as the night before: the comedians; the singers; the sketch about the man from New Jersey who found a cow in his closet; the lanky woman who swung a long string of pearls around her neck while singing the national anthem; the martini juggler (this time Brett was given the martini and Sally Jean joyously ate the olives from a tiny plastic sword); and then the real show, the dancers.

Just as the night before, the air thinned and the moment froze as the sapphire girls took their places. Sally Jean was fixated on the black-bobbed dancer, staring at her as if she were a ring in the window of Van Cleef & Arpels. And when the show was over, Sally Jean felt the same sense of rejoining time. There was another act afterward and Sally Jean relaxed back into her seat. She smiled at Brett.

"You've been really terrific to me, you know that Brett? It's like we're sitting here side by side and I feel like I'm with one of my best friends in the entire world."

"Best friends? I should hope we're—"

"Absolutely. Really the best," she cut him off. She didn't want to talk about who they were to each other or who they had been. Her world was splitting in two. Her future had two paths and she could only take one. "And I just want you to know how grateful I am for you taking me here."

"Why sure, Sally Jean, why sure. After all, you *are* going to be—"

"Look!" Sally Jean whispered insistently. "Look at the table next to us."

Brett saw an urbane bald-headed gentleman and recognized him from the night before. He watched as the man pulled out a chair for a young woman. It took Brett a moment to recognize her as one of the dancing girls.

"It's *her*," Sally Jean intoned breathlessly. "Let's watch."

Dutifully Brett watched as the dancer, now dressed in a low-waisted burgundy cocktail dress and a matching cloche, sat with the older man.

"Do you think that's her husband?" Sally Jean whispered into Brett's neck.

The older man and the black-bobbed woman talked quietly together. The woman leaned on one tanned arm, and Sally Jean could see lean, hard muscles flex beneath her skin. The man said something. The woman glanced toward the back of the theater, nodded to the man, and removed her necklace. It seemed to be made of pearls, black pearls alternating with white pearls, and Sally Jean had never seen anything like it. Handing them over to the bald man, she strode back, past the tables, toward the door where they had entered.

"Guess he wanted his stones back," Brett whispered loudly. "She's probably his mistress and his wife just showed or—"

"I wouldn't mind another cocktail," interjected Sally Jean with a kiss.

Brett suppressed his surprise, and without comment began to flag for a waiter. After a minute he gave up and went to the bar himself. There was a line, and he was gone some time. Left alone, Sally Jean fixed the elderly man under her soft-eyed scrutiny. Soon after, the woman returned and, sitting beside the man, retrieved her pearl necklace and allowed him to assist with the clasp. She conferred again with the man, her face almost hidden behind the swing of her black hair, and seemed to indicate that something satisfactory had taken place. As she drank her cocktail—what looked to Sally Jean to be a gin and tonic—another man approached the table.

The older man stood and shook the younger man's hand. He slapped him convivially on the back and gestured to the seat on the other side of the woman. A waiter came by Sally Jean's table and, without a thought, she ordered a gin and tonic. She watched as both men talked to the woman with the black-bobbed hair. The younger man was wearing a sharply cut suit and a peppermint green shirt, and she imagined for a moment that he was the man she was destined to marry. He and the black-bobbed woman laughed, and Sally Jean felt a pang of jealousy, of desire, fresher than anything she had felt with Brett since she was fifteen years old.

Soon Brett returned to the table.

"I got you an old-fashioned, darling."

"Well, aren't you sweet, but somehow I ended up with this."

She held up her almost empty drink. Brett looked at the lime in her glass like it was a rare goldfish.

"I didn't know you drank gin."

"Me neither. You know they used to think the juniper in gin drove women crazy. Isn't that funny?"

"I think I heard something about that, " he said grimly.

The hours passed and the crowd only seemed to grow. Sally Jean watched as different people stopped by the table next to theirs and paid homage, sitting with the group for a while, exchanging kisses, and then departing for another table like a jolly school of fish swimming wherever crumbs of gaiety and laughter were offered. She watched how the younger man stared at the black-haired woman. *He's in love with her,* she decided. Sally Jean sighed. *Nobody loves me like that. Nobody.*

Brett touched Sally Jean's arm tenderly but couldn't get her attention. He was beginning to grow restless; early the next morning he had to be back at the office where he worked as a copywriter. But Sally Jean gave no indication of readiness to depart and Brett didn't want to displease her. He began to work over some ideas for the ladies shaver campaign. *Sell the sizzle, not the steak,* he reminded himself. *What on earth sizzles about ladies' leg hair?* After what Brett counted to be her fourth gin and tonic, Sally Jean announced that she wanted to meet the black-bobbed dancer.

"I've just got to talk to her! Look what fun they're having."

"Aren't we having . . . a good time? This here is fun, isn't it Sally Jean?"

"Yes," she said, weighing the question. "But it looks like they're having some kind of important fun. Do you know what I mean?"

He had no idea what she meant. In fact, as he thought back over the last two days, he felt there were quite a few moments during which he had had no idea what she meant. And she was drinking so much. She must just be nervous about the wedding. Feeling a surge of love for her, he reached over to pat her hand reassuringly, and found it missing.

He spotted her standing at the adjacent table, the short skirt of her dress riding up past her knees. Brett blushed. But before he could jump to her rescue, she was seated at the table, clinking glasses with the dark-haired dancer. Brett sat back down and sipped at his drink contemplatively.

"Well, aren't you just a gem for saying so," said the black-haired woman in her breathy voice, shaking Sally Jean's hand like a man.

"I think you were just, I don't know how to say it, like an angel out there. Like an angel and also sort of like my horse, Peony—"

"Peony!" The whole table laughed.

"That's her name. It's a flower."

"Isn't she a gem," said the woman, turning to the older, bald-headed man.

"A diamond," he concurred.

"A diamond in the rough," said the younger man, looking at her with a flash in his appraising eyes. He winked at Sally Jean and the black-haired woman laughed.

"Ardita," said the black-bobbed woman looking directly at Sally Jean.

"Come again?" asked Sally Jean politely.

"Ardita O'Reilly, that's me."

"Oh, I'm so pleased to make your acquaintance! Sally Jean Baker, that's me."

Again the table laughed, but their laughs were friendly and warm.

"She's the real McCoy, isn't she? A gen-u-ine innocent."

"I know! Let's keep her! Why don't we just adopt Miss Sally Jean Baker here, and keep her all for ourselves?" This was Ardita, breathless, delighted. "How about it, Mr. Whiskers? What do you say?"

"Is that you?" Sally Jean asked the elderly man sincerely, "Are you Mr. . . . . Whiskers?"

The table roared.

"That's what they call me," he told her confidentially, "on account of my excessive hairiness!"

"But you don't have—"

And then they all laughed, including Sally Jean.

"I'm the proprietor, the owner of this particular establishment," said Mr. Whiskers. "Ardita is my greatest find, my lovely ingénue. And the rudely silent gentleman to your right is Tom Valentine."

Tom Valentine gave her a generous smile and, with an exaggerated flourish that didn't deny the genuine chivalry of his actions, half stood and planted a kiss on Sally Jean's hand. Ardita clapped with delight.

"And I am Brett Blakely."

The table turned and Brett stood there, looking like a boy scout who got run through the wrong wash cycle.

"Sally Jean's fiancé."

Awkwardly Brett pulled up a chair and introductions were made. Mr. Whiskers ordered another round of drinks. The men started to talk of the Great War and Sally Jean had a moment to look at Ardita. What she saw made her lose an ice cube down the front of her dress. Ardita had one blue eye and one green eye. It wasn't the kind of thing you couldn't see from the audience, but up close it was undeniable. Sally Jean stared into those eyes and the rest of the room disappeared. She wanted to swim in them; get drunk in them; vanish into their blues and greens. Ardita smiled and Sally Jean smiled back; an infant hypnotized by the most beautiful mobile.

"Hi," said Sally Jean.

"Hi," said Ardita. And her eyes flickered with that same strange look Sally Jean had seen on stage. Was it passion? Anger? Resignation? All Sally Jean knew is that she wanted her own eyes to be blue and green and hard and full of secrets.

The next half-hour passed as in a dream. The band picked up their instruments and decided to play for their own enjoyment. The music was wild and fantastic. The air was thick with smoke. One song ended, and before the next began, Sally Jean heard Brett talking confidentially to Mr. Whiskers.

"All I can figure is she's getting something out of her system. After all, once we're married—"

Sally Jean interrupted, "Sorry, honey. But I'm not getting something out of my system at all. In fact I do believe I just got something into my system."

Brett took in a breath. Since when did Sally Jean talk like that? Since when was she so bold, so hard?

"Sally Jean, darling, you've had too much to drink."

"I know, isn't it grand?"

Brett stood up and pulled Sally Jean by her elbow. "Not so much, Sally Jean. Not so grand as you think." And then with the uncomfortable smile of a parent whose child has just thrown a tantrum in a public park: "Good night everyone. It was a pleasure to meet you. I'm sorry about all of this. She's just not used to drinking, that's all."

"Don't be ridiculous." Ardita stood up. "She's an absolute gem, Brett."

"I've got to say just one more thing," said Sally Jean. "This"— she gestured to the room at large—"all of this. This is what I want. I want to be on stage."

And then Brett tugged Sally Jean by her elbow one last time and pulled her out the door, up the reeking staircase, and into his car outside. The ride home was dreadful. Brett sulked and Sally Jean was forced to wait. As many drinks as she had had, her mind was still calculating. A scene was inevitable, sooner was probably better than later, and she knew enough about alcohol to realize its potential as a social lubricant for all occasions. Breaking off one's engagement wasn't an ordinary social situation, but she knew that it would ease the wretched words out of her mouth and then blur the whole episode, like a watercolor left in the rain, so that neither of them would remember it too clearly in the morning.

Morning brought a horrible knocking at her door and a puffy-eyed ex-soldier who called her some unprintable names and then tearily professed his eternal devotion. These two strategies were employed by Brett in alternation, growing to a rapid-fire rhythm, like a marching-band drummer beating two sides of his thundering drum as he marched down a hopeless street right into a brick wall. Sally Jean comforted Brett as best she could and returned the engagement ring in a moment when she thought he was too tired to heave it out the window. He pocketed it, kissed Sally Jean on her soft blond head, and, in a final torrent of swears and endearments, disappeared out her door.

Sally Jean spent the morning in bed and soon fell back asleep. When she awoke, instead of feeling blue, she felt clean and well rested. She looked out the window of her hotel room, truly seeing the city for the first time. The light was sharp, and everything seemed terribly alive. She dressed and went for a walk around Manhattan and felt the energy of the other pedestrians enter her blood like a strong cocktail. People were everywhere, moving, going places, doing things. And those were just the people she saw; she knew now that there were people below the earth, terrific parties full of glittering people and magical music.

She kept walking through the streets, enjoying the fresh summer air. She made her turns at random, attracted by a tree whose leaves were just starting to turn or a barbershop with a spiraling pole, but she adopted the pace of the crowd around her, hustling as if she had somewhere to go. She walked until her lungs ached and the soles of her feet were flat and hot. When she finally stopped to rest, she looked up and saw a row of familiar brownstones. It couldn't be. And yet, crossing the street and reading the brass 333, she knew that it was. She thought for a moment, and any passerby would have taken her for a lost young woman trying to get her bearings—which she was, in a way. *What else can I do?* she thought, and opened the door and went down the stairs.

Soon autumn came in earnest, and though Sally Jean knew the leaves were dying, were dead as they fell to the sidewalk, they seemed to her, in their vibrant reds and yellows, more alive than ever. She had been at Mr. Whiskers's for five weeks now and had been performing in the revue for nearly a week. Mr. Whiskers had been impressed with how quickly she picked up the routines. For the month before she had been allowed to perform, Sally Jean had watched from a stool backstage, her soft, white arms moving in sync with Ardita's rangy limbs, memorizing her every move. During rehearsals, Sally Jean had worked herself exceedingly hard, pushing against fatigue and biting back tears when she missed a step. And when the girls were sent home, Sally Jean begged Ardita to teach her more, to tell her what she was doing wrong. She wanted to be Ardita's pupil, her slave, and when Ardita praised Sally Jean, she felt like a millionaire.

When Sally Jean graduated to the stage, she experienced the thrill of applause for the first time in her life. Although she was sure that Ardita had earned most of it, she was nevertheless grateful to bask in its warmth. Life was good. She got along well with the other dancers and had even allowed Bernard the martini juggler to take her out for a dinner at a fine restaurant where the meal cost more than a week's salary. She rarely thought of Brett. When she did think of him, he was a storybook character in her mind, a soldier who had been in the war and then mysteriously faded away. At some point she realized that she had always assumed he would die in the war and that she was vaguely disappointed that he didn't, as if by surviving he had shown his intrinsic weakness.

Sally Jean's parents were very sorry to hear that the engagement had been broken off. Somehow they had gotten the impression from Sally Jean's letters that it was Brett who had thrown her over and so were more than willing to send money until a reconciliation could be made. This money kept Sally Jean in a small apartment on Bank Street and her legs in silk. The letters to her parents also served a second purpose of reminding Sally Jean of who she used to be. Sally Jean realized that this aspect of her character, this old sweet nonthreatening Sally Jean, was terribly useful. So even while she nourished the new Sally Jean—the silken legged, cosmopolitan flapper—she kept her old character in play. It was this character who chatted sweetly with Ardita whenever she got the chance. It was this character who asked for Ardita's advice on new dresses and begged Ardita to teach her how to smoke cigarettes. It was this character who amused Ardita with her exuberant innocence, holding tight to her hat as Ardita sped them along Broadway in her lime green Opel Reinette. It was this character who gasped with admiration when, after asking Ardita why she didn't have a driver, Ardita replied that no one could drive fast enough to suit her taste.

And it was this character, this aspect of Sally Jean, who rapped softly on Ardita's dressing room after the show one Friday night. Ardita called for her to come in, and though when Sally Jean opened the door she found her only vaguely dressed, wearing a tangerine-colored kimono that appeared to have lost its belt and ashing a cigarette into an empty glass of champagne, Ardita was not the least embarrassed.

"Sally Jean! At last!"

Sally Jean nodded enthusiastically and clutched her pocketbook to her stomach modestly.

"Well come on in. Be a sport and help me with this champagne won't you? It's the real McCoy."

Sally Jean nodded again and, consciously tipping her head down so that her big brown eyes were at their most sincere, asked if Ardita wanted to join her for a little supper later. Ardita laughed and Sally Jean laughed too, as if the invitation was a bon mot.

"Can't, but do hang on and have a drink? I'll be back in a sec."

With this she threw her lanky body off the settee and swished out of the room. Sally Jean was left alone. Slowly she took in the small dressing room, her soft eyes flashing like a camera. On Ardita's dressing table, she found a small basket filled with jewelry. She rooted among the baubles until she found the necklace with the black and white pearls. She held it up to her neck and admired herself in the mirror. She arched an eyebrow and laughed softly.

"These?" she replied to the mirror. "Oh they're nothing, doll. Just something I throw around my neck when I haven't got anything better to do."

She dropped the necklace back into the jewelry basket and examined the items tucked into the dressing table mirror. There was a snapshot of Ardita with Mr. Whiskers that must have been taken some time ago. In the picture Mr. Whiskers looked the same, but Ardita was young—she couldn't have been more than fourteen years old. The young Ardita wore that same strange expression that Sally Jean couldn't place. There was an ink drawing of Ardita and the girls in their sapphire costumes; a map that appeared to be an old drawing of New York with odd markings made in red pen, surely some inherited document; and tucked into the mirror frame, a brittle old rose gone black with time. The rose had a small card attached with ribbon and Sally Jean opened it with one finger. "You say when and I'm yours. Tom." She read it over twice and crossed the room.

She opened a teak armoire and found Ardita's shoes. Dozens of them, lying in wait for Ardita, black and silver and red, with buckles and heels and silky bows. She pulled out a worn silver slipper and touched it gently, fingering the satin. She put her hand inside, feeling down to where Ardita's toes had strained against the fabric, stretching out the satin so that the shape of her ghostly foot remained. After a moment she carefully replaced the shoe next to its mate, and closed the door. She opened another, smaller closet and had to catch her breath. She leaned in. This closet was filled with weapons—knives mostly; they looked like they might be artifacts from Africa or China or somewhere far off. Some were made of metal, most of wood. She reached out slowly and touched the tip of a wooden knife, pressing her finger hard against its point. She took a deep swig of champagne. How terribly exotic! Leave it to Ardita to have a thrilling hobby like collecting knives. She wished she had thought of it herself. She closed the door and drained her champagne.

She drifted back across the room to the dressing table. She opened a jar of cream and spread some on her cheek. She picked up Ardita's bottle of perfume, noted its label, and absently spritzed it on her neck and on her wrists. It smelled exhilarating, musky, just like Ardita. And then, as if intoxicated by the perfume, she quickly reached up to the rose, deftly untied the ribbon, and slipped the card from Tom Valentine into her purse. At that moment the door opened and Ardita returned.

Sally Jean looked into the mirror and fluffed at her hair innocently.

Then to Ardita's reflection, "Do you think I should bob my hair?" she asked quickly.

"Why?" Ardita smiled and stretched languidly on the settee.

Ardita had returned wearing what appeared to be men's black pajamas and diamond earrings. Sally Jean tugged at her cocktail dress.

"I don't know. I feel like a change I guess."

"You shouldn't, you know. You should stay innocent Sally Jean Baker for as long as you possibly can."

"Why?" asked Sally Jean, sounding to her annoyance like a whining child. "You're not innocent."

Ardita laughed. Sally Jean was feeling more and more frustrated. She pulled at her hair in the mirror, approximating what it would look like short. Then the door nearly pounded down, and before Ardita could respond, a troupe of glamorous madmen poured in, bearing more liquor, a bottle of champagne, and a basket of oranges. These were some of Ardita's friends; Sally Jean had met some of them in passing and they all seemed to be displaced nobility, counts and archdukes, or polo players or heiresses from Chicago.

"Oranges all around!" bellowed a tall bespectacled gentleman with hair the color of the fruit he bore and a curious galaxy of freckles sprawled across his face.

He began to toss oranges to all the various guests; some caught them and some let theirs fall to the floor. A voluptuous woman with unnaturally blond hair picked up three oranges and began to juggle them. She was better than Bernard, thought Sally Jean. Sable coats and silk wraps were tossed to the floor, thrown over the dressing table, and piled on the settee as the guests prepared themselves for a party. Sally Jean recognized Tom Valentine among the crowd and giggled happily as he knelt before her, kissing her hand. And then another man, whom Sally Jean thought might be one of the counts, knelt beside her as well and took her other hand in his.

"Who, pray tell," he said looking up into her eyes, "is this vision of loveliness?"

Tom introduced them, and the count clutched his spare hand to his chest.

"Maude, be a good girl and kill me now, will you? I can't stand to exist in the presence of such beauty."

Maude, the voluptuous blond juggler, snorted with laughter and flicked her fingers against the count's skull. Before Sally Jean could think of a witty response, the count was on his feet, ripping the foil off a bottle of champagne. She stared at the people around her with amazement. This was it; this was the center of things! Then Sally Jean felt Ardita's warm, strong arm around her shoulders.

"Sally Jean, doll, you'd better go."

Her heart sank to her feet and hardened into stone.

"Why? I . . . I don't want to."

"This crowd. They're a little odd, that's all. I just wonder if you'll have a good time."

Someone put on a record and the room filled with jazz.

"I'll be fine," insisted Sally Jean coldly, and danced away from Ardita toward the count.

The champagne cork popped, exploding like a bomb, and Sally Jean squealed. The count laughed and pulled her into his arms.

"How gorgeous you look when you scream," he murmured into her ear. "You should be in the pictures."

Flattered to no end, she blushed sweetly, but then Tom took arm and danced her away. The party grew like a well-kindled fire, roaring and roaring and then fading until someone poked it with a funny remark or a new bottle of booze and the sparks relit and it roared again. Glasses filled and bottles emptied. Ice cubes made music that echoed in the tinkling laughter of the women and the soft flirting of the men.

At one point Sally Jean found herself seated on the floor next to a brunette who looked like Theda Bara. She asked her about Tom. He was so well off and yet he never seemed to work. He had mentioned that he was often in the South and in Canada, too. Was he, could he be a rum runner?

The brunette howled.

"A rum runner? No, I'm afraid the old boy hasn't the sea legs for that. Mr. Tom Valentine is just your plain old run-of-the-mill millionaire bootlegger."

And the next thing Sally Jean knew, she was dancing with Tom again. The whole crowd danced and they drank and the night came heavily upon them. The conversations looped and turned; Sally Jean understood phrases and then lost the strand as the words bent and twisted together like a woven sea grass basket. She stopped trying to follow the lengths and just admired the pattern as it twisted on and on into the night. At one point, just before the sun came up, Sally Jean awoke to find herself curled on the settee, a bottle still clutched in her hand. When she looked around, she couldn't find Ardita. The count was gone too.

"She's gone out," explained Tom. And Sally Jean took his hand in hers.

The trees blossomed with their dead orange leaves and slowly released them, letting them fall like pennies from an old man's hand, until the branches were bare and Central Park was full of skeletons. Sally Jean enjoyed the coming of winter, appreciated the pink the cold pinched into her cheeks, and anticipated eagerly the fireplaces near which she would sit with her new friends, Ardita's friends, and drink hot drinks and sing cheerful songs.

Her confidence as a dancer had grown and she no longer asked Ardita for her help or watched her out of the corner of her eye as she had when she first performed on stage. Offstage, she still watched Ardita though, more than ever. Each night after the performance, Ardita would go directly back to her dressing room. Then she would stay there and entertain her friends; go sit with Mr. Whiskers; or go out on the town, often by herself. No matter the night, Ardita always mysteriously disappeared sometime after one or two o'clock. Sally Jean's theory that Ardita was in love with the count didn't seem to be panning out; after that party, he had never returned to the theater. So Sally Jean decided that Ardita must have a dozen secret lovers and felt irked; how could her idol treat Tom Valentine like that?

And coincidentally, or perhaps not quite so coincidentally,

Sally Jean fell in love with Tom Valentine too. He was the perfect man, she had realized. Strong, capable, rich as Creoeses, Tom knew all the best places in the city. And he had such a way about him—it was like he was a soldier all the time. She told him that once, and he had laughed and kissed her on the ear and told her that if anyone was a soldier it was Ardita. Sally Jean had screwed up her pretty face.

"Well, she can't be a soldier can she? She's a girl."

"You silly Southern Belle," he had said, and she might have been offended except for the way he said it was so admiring.

Sally Jean had never set about courting a man. Where she came from that was a ludicrous idea. But up in New York it was different, and so she went right to work. She hosted an indoor picnic at her apartment on Bank Street and made sure to tell Tom that she'd be much obliged if he stuck around a little afterward. When she finally went to get her hair bobbed, she had Tom come, and held tight to his hand as if she were afraid the barber's scissors were going to slit her throat. And when she performed, she kept her eyes locked on his and kicked her legs as high as they would go.

One night after the show, Sally Jean was gratified to find three separate bouquets waiting for her. Ardita, she counted, had only two that night. Sally Jean took a circuitous path back to her dressing room, carrying around the flowers as if they were a cumbersome baby whose mewling was getting at her nerves. She sat backstage with Bernard a moment, and when he inquired, rolled her eyes at the flowers, as if to suggest her growing popularity was a burden. Back in the dressing room she shared with another of the chorus girls, Sally Jean slowly opened the cards. The first was from an only vaguely familiar admirer, a man called Ivan D'Mengers whom she thought might be one of the counts or at least an archduke. The note asked if she would accompany him to dinner sometime. Sally Jean would have shown off the card to Ardita except she could predict the response. Ardita had lectured her as if she were a schoolgirl about the dangers of counts and men like them. Apparently it was all well and good for Ardita herself to disappear with them into the night, but not poor, sweet, soft Sally Jean.

She ripped open the card on the second bouquet and saw that it was from none other than Tom Valentine. Her heart beat a bit faster and she read this note several times.

"*To Sally Jean.*

My silly Southern Belle.

Yours, Tom Valentine."

She was so interested in this note, in the nuances of meaning just beyond the surface—was the fact that he signed his full name a good sign or a bad one?—that she nearly forgot about the third card. Could it possibly be from Tom too? She tore it open and recoiled at what she read. "My Sally Jean. I'm waiting for you, waiting for you to be mine. Eternally Yours, Brett." Brett! She had forgotten about him almost entirely; did he still live in New York? How completely disgusting! She ripped his card into tiny pieces, and, feeling like her dressing room had been contaminated, hurried into her clothes and left without putting any of the flowers in water.

She raced over to Ardita's dressing room and was about to burst in when she heard low voices through the door. She paused a moment, deciding, and then bent down to fiddle with her shoe strap.

"I have to go Tom, and I know you don't like it, but it's just the way things are."

"Not tonight, please Ardita. Just once, please, do what I want!" His voice was loud.

Soon after, Sally Jean heard something crash against a wall inside, something heavy like an ashtray, and she hustled away from the door. Bernard was in the hallway coming toward her, a bunch of small roses in his hand.

"Why hi, Bernard," said Sally Jean, casual as could be.

"I . . . well, these are for you Sally Jean." He held the flowers out awkwardly as if they were in some running race together and he was passing her the baton.

"You don't say? I wonder who they're from. There's no card." She buried her face in them.

"Oh they're those roses that don't smell," she said, disappointed.

"Actually, I . . . they're from me Sally Jean."

Before she could reply, she heard Tom Valentine exit Ardita's dressing room and come toward them. She turned.

"Tom, I was just looking for you!" she said, her voice bright and happy. "I'm hungry as a tiger; won't you please take pity on me and escort me to some supper?"

"Sure, Sally Jean," he said, sounding half-hearted, and then, oblivious to the martini juggler's stricken face, added "You have a good evening Bernard."

And she tucked her arm through his and they exited down the hall, leaving the unhappy juggler in their wake.

Tom was quiet all through supper and Sally Jean was at her wit's end trying to get his attention. She tried to talk about the day's newspaper, but since she had only caught a glimpse over someone's shoulder backstage, she was limited to headlines and the day's weather, which by this point in the night wasn't particularly news-worthy. She moved on to talk of her childhood, a subject that usu-ally amused and comforted Tom, but this too proved futile. She wracked her brain and found it empty as the trees outside.

"I'm not sure about this whole winter arrangement," she tried brightly. "It was fun when it was coming, but now that it's here it's so, I don't know, cold and endless."

Tom nodded and returned to his dinner.

"I don't like seeing my breath rise up in the air like a spirit. I don't like gray skies and I don't like dead trees. I don't like dead things," she said enthusiastically.

"Me neither," he agreed, looking at her full in the face for the first time that evening. "I don't care for them one bit." And then, leaning encouragingly close, "You're wearing Ardita's perfume, aren't you?"

"Oh, does she wear this too? I didn't know," she lied.

And then dessert came and Sally Jean ate it with enthusiasm, trying to keep the momentum going. But Tom was a million miles away, tired and spent, and soon Sally Jean retreated into herself, trying to figure out what was wrong. She lacked something. Clearly she lacked something that Ardita had in spades. What was it? Ardita was beautiful, but so was she, in her different, softer way. Ardita was a terrific dancer, but hadn't Mr. Whiskers told her how well she was doing? And hadn't she received three bouquets—four, if you counted the roses from Bernard—that very night? What was it? Sally Jean licked the whipped cream from the back of her fork. Well, she'd just have to figure it out and beat Ardita at her own game. Sally Jean wiped the corners of her mouth with her napkin and folded it resolutely on her lap.

For the next week the question of Ardita was all Sally Jean could think of. She had taken hold of this thought like a pitbull with a rat, and she wrestled it constantly, unable to relax the jaws of her mind. And then one night during the Egyptian number Sally Jean looked over at Ardita and caught that mystery that had flickered in those blue and green eyes. She understood what Ardita had, what she was. Ardita was sad. Sally Jean's smile grew and she kicked her legs higher. All she had to do was cultivate melancholy.

And so she tried. She walked around the gloomy city, past

beggars and one-legged women. She stared up at the gray sky and thought of dead people, kittens with broken necks, and losing her looks. She thought of everything in the world that could possibly depress her. She thought of Brett, but that didn't do any good. She only felt pity and even that was eclipsed by disgust. She thought of her long dead grandmother, but that didn't work either. She thought of Peony, and that was the closest she came, but mostly what she felt was jealousy that her younger sister might be riding her at that very moment.

Giving up on actual emotion, Sally Jean set about affecting sadness. When Tom asked her what she was doing one evening, she smiled a closed lip smile and sighed.

"I'll go wherever the wind blows me, I figure."

"Well, a gang of us are heading over to Silveri's for steaks. Want in?"

"No, I don't guess so," she said mournfully.

And when he said, "Suit yourself. You'll be missed," she could have kicked herself.

"I guess I could probably be persuaded," she amended, skipping after him down the hall. "I can't promise I'll be much entertainment though. I'm feeling awful blue for no particular reason."

And then she forgot all about being blue and ended up dancing on the table while Ardita clapped and laughed her church bell laugh.

Weeks passed and spring began to taunt New York, playing peek-a-boo with crocuses that then were frostbit and warm mornings that turned ugly before a girl could fetch her overcoat. Sally Jean saw a lot of Tom Valentine, more than Ardita saw of him. She felt that just one good night could make him hers forever. When he was in the audience, she could see that he was watching her for most of the show. She kept him in her gaze and counted the number of times his eyes flicked toward Ardita, using the glances as a measure of her battle.

One night, looking out into the crowd, she saw a familiar man. She saw the feathered hat and her heart went right into her slippers: Brett Blakely sitting all alone, staring at her with those cold gray eyes. As soon as the curtain fell, she ran back to Ardita's dressing room and threw herself on the settee waiting for her to return. When Ardita came in, Tom Valentine was right behind her.

"You have to help me!" Sally Jean shrieked. "He's come! That dreaded old fiancé of mine was here tonight and I'm sure he's out there waiting, waiting to—"

"Calm down," said Tom, sitting beside her. "You stick with us, right, Ardita?"

Mr. Whiskers opened the door without knocking and just looked at Ardita. She grabbed her black pajamas and was heading toward the door before he had to say a word.

"Oh, dolls, I've got to run!" she said. "There's someone that I have to . . . deal with."

Tom's nostrils flared, and Sally Jean felt frustrated that he was still stuck on Ardita when clearly she carried on with a number of men.

"Tom'll take care of you, won't you Tom?"

"If it's not too much to ask, Tom, I'd be so grateful."

"Ask me for the world, Sally Jean. Nothing's too much for you."

He put his fingers under her chin and kissed her on the lips, right there in front of Ardita.

Ardita left and Sally Jean was left alone with Tom. This was good, this was very good, but Sally Jean still couldn't relax. She felt like she had to seal the deal. She wanted Tom to see Ardita with her clandestine lover and have it imprinted in his mind that Sally Jean was the only girl for him.

"Let's go out!" she suggested.

"Aren't you afraid of that old fiancé of yours?" asked Tom.

"Not with your arm around me," she insisted.

And so they went out into the damp and foggy night. They managed to exit the theater without encountering Brett, and Sally Jean led them uptown, hurrying along the street after Ardita's shadow. To explain their pace, Sally Jean claimed she was afraid it would rain and spoil her hair.

"Also I just feeling like moving fast," she said. "Know what I mean?"

"Are you hungry Sally Jean?"

"Not yet. I just feel like walking."

Ardita crossed the street a few blocks up and Sally Jean followed, keeping Tom in distracted conversation.

"I didn't know you followed baseball, Sally Jean."

"Why sure I do. I think it's terribly fascinating, Babe Ruth and all. Don't you? All those uniforms and rules and men running hither and thither."

Ardita was heading toward Central Park. Sally Jean and Tom followed. The wet grass licked at their ankles and shadows leaked from the dark trees like slicks of gasoline. There was something frightening about this strange island of nature surrounded by stone. The birds that called were haunted and the wind whispered Sally Jean's name in the air. But still she tugged Tom along, determined to end this, once and for all. Somewhere around the boat house, Sally Jean lost sight of Ardita and their pace slowed.

"Why are we here, Miss Sally Jean?" asked Tom. "Are you going to put the moves on me?"

Sally Jean laughed lightly and then changed tack. "I don't know, it's just so beautiful and melancholy here."

"And dark as hell."

Where had she gone? Sally Jean was sure Ardita was around somewhere with her mysterious lover. She didn't want to give up yet. She scanned the horizon. Only darkness, shadows, black like the bottom of a well.

And then the darkness took the form of dark figures. Was this the assignation? Then the figures distilled into the outline of three large men walking directly toward them. Sally Jean's breath turned sharp and Tom pulled her closer.

"You know, let's get lost, Sally Jean. Walk fast."

She did as he told her, but the men kept coming, half-running toward them. Sally Jean and Tom began to run, jumping across paths, heading toward the street. She was running in earnest now, fast as she ever had. A heel broke from her shoe and stuck in a puddle of mud and she continued to run, her eyes peeled open with terror. But there was no escaping. The men hurtled toward them like three loose train cars on a steep grade. Faster and faster they came, thrashing through the underbrush, until Sally Jean and Tom were surrounded. Sally Jean looked up and what she saw terrified her. They weren't men at all; they were monsters.

Their faces were warped and scalded as if they'd been burnt in a gas fire; their upper lips pulled back like snarling dogs', and the teeth that filled them were sickening, yellow, sharp as sabers. And their eyes: hollow, yellow and shining, and no pupils—just slivers like a snake's. Inside these eyes was death.

Sally thought she would be sick and then thought she would scream. But she didn't and she couldn't. She just stared. One of the creatures was talking to them. Its voice was like a poison let loose from hell, sharp and searing.

"Looking for us?" it said.

"No, we're just—," Tom began.

"We're not talking to you."

Their soulless eyes were fixed on Sally Jean.

"I'm not . . . I think you're mistaken," she squeaked. "I'm just Sally Jean."

The creatures came closer, as if fascinated by her.

"You can't pretend; we know your smell."

The words disgusted her, and again she thought she was going to be sick.

"It's nice to look at you," one of the creatures said, coming closer still. "I've never seen the Slayer up close. You look so soft. So tender."

"Stay away from her!" shouted Tom, finally finding his voice and stepping in front of Sally Jean protectively.

"Move," one of them said, and the moon went behind a cloud.

"And if I won't?"

In an instant, one of the creatures leaped at Tom, swiping at him with one arm. Sally Jean saw a flash of the monsters' claws. Red on Tom's cheek. And then he was on his back. Unconscious.

"You will."

Sally Jean closed her eyes then and, for the first time since she was a little girl, started to pray. She was going to be killed, she was sure of it. What would her parents think?

"What's going on?"

Sally Jean opened her eyes and saw the most wonderful thing in the whole crazy world. Brett Blakely.

"Brett," she cried and ran toward him, throwing herself into his arms.

He looked at her with love in his gray eyes.

"Sally Jean," he said and his voice was so calm and safe. He looked right at the creatures and didn't balk or even shiver. Sally Jean let him hold her tight, pulled him closer. She was astonished by his bravery; maybe she had misjudged him. She looked up into his face for comfort. There he was, good old Brett Blakely from Asheville who drove an old Model T and wore a feathered hat and wanted to marry her. And then his face began to melt.

Right before her eyes he transformed, his features dissolved, wrinkling in on themselves until he had the same scalded skin, the same wolf mouth, and the same horrible snake eyes as the others. She tugged away from him, but his arms were stronger than they had ever been. He laughed at her struggle and, with one hand, tore the top of her dress, exposing her neck.

He addressed the other creatures. "This one was mine. You knew that." And then to Sally Jean, with his fangs at her neck, "Mine eternally."

And then something was upon them, a black cloud knocking them back, bringing them to the still-frozen earth. The rest came in flashes, moments of luminescence separate but strung together like pearls—like black and white pearls. Ardita in black silk with a wooden sword in hand. The white moon breaking from beneath a blue cloud. Ardita atop Brett's prostrate body, outlined by the moon, stabbing him in the chest. Dust. Dust blowing in the wind. The monsters on Ardita, all atop her. A flare of teeth. The wooden sword. A bird calling, calling. Dust in the air, like stars, like a galaxy. The moon like an orange, dust like bubbles in champagne. A monster arm in arm with Ardita like they were dancing, like he was a count. And then more dust, raining over her like ashes from the dead. And nobody left. Just Ardita's eyes, blue and green like black and white like pearls and bubbles and oranges.

The next thing she knew, she was sitting in Tom's parlor in front of a roaring fire. She didn't know how long she had been sitting there, but she knew that Ardita had been there and now Ardita had gone and Tom was holding ice wrapped in a towel to his head. They were silent for a long time. Sally Jean didn't know where to begin: the monsters, Brett, Ardita. The fire warmed her body, but her mind still felt frozen and her heart felt cold.

"Who is she?" she heard herself ask, on the verge of tears.

Tom looked into the fire and touched the swelling claw marks on his cheek.

"She's Ardita O'Reilly, just like she says. She's a girl. A girl who also . . . I've known her a long time." He lit a cigarette and then threw it into the fire. Sally Jean saw tears thicken his eyes. "She's a girl," he continued, "who was chosen to fight a war."

And Sally Jean listened quietly as he told her about vampires and how they were everywhere, how they thrived in the dark corners of life. He explained how they could be killed and how Ardita had been trained for years by Mr. Whiskers to know how to do it. He told her how someday Ardita would die in the battle against this evil. And yet she kept doing it. She went out, every night, into the dark where monsters waited to kill her. And she did it knowing that she would die.

"I thought she was a flapper," Sally Jean said weakly, unable to express anything bigger. She had known, somehow, that Ardita was something else. She wasn't careless and wild and decadent like the others; she had a purpose. Sally Jean didn't want to be a flapper anymore and she didn't want to be like Ardita either. She began to cry. The tears flowed from her eyes like water from a well-primed pump. Tom moved toward her and put his arm around her, holding her tighter and tighter as the tears continued to come. He kissed her face and she kissed his and they held each other there in a salty sad embrace.

"Do you love her?" she asked through her tears.

He didn't answer.

"Do you love me, Tom?"

"Yes," he said, kissing the tears from her eyes.

"Do you chose me?" she asked. "Do you chose me?" He nodded and her tears slowed into jerking sobs.

"It's going to be okay," he told her, and she saw that he was crying too.

"It's going to be okay, it's going to be okay," she repeated. "We're going to be together, aren't we?"

He nodded and smoothed her hair.

"Forever and ever?"

He nodded again and smiled at her. "Forever and ever."

And his eyes filled again with tears.

"And we can get married and go back to Charleston and Peony can wear a garland of flowers?"

"A bright, beautiful garland of flowers."

He kissed her soft shoulder and she felt different. She had changed and she felt a kind of sadness she had never fathomed: bottomless, hopeless, hollow, and hard. She had Tom. She had won, hadn't she? She smiled unhappily and sat passively and let him kiss at her sweet soft arm.

Stakeout on Rush Street

Max Allan Collins
with Matthew V. Clemens

CHICAGO, 1943

I missed Bobby.

My husband, Bobby, that is—Robert Winters, a captain in General George Patton's Third Army, currently slogging through North Africa somewhere.

I'd done my best to keep the home fires burning, by taking over Bobby's detective agency while he was overseas. But frankly that hadn't been working out as well as I'd hoped. Divorce work was on the slides. After all, most of the men were off fighting the Germans or the Japanese, and those not-able-bodied men that were left behind seemed prejudiced against a dick in high heels and lipstick.

Even other women seemed hesitant to trust a female private eye, particularly one as (let's face it) attractive as yours truly, or as young (twenty-two); but I managed, now and then, to convince a few of them—the open-minded (and self-confident) ones. Plus I still had a couple of Bobby's old clients throwing me some business—like Mutual Fidelity Insurance and Boeheim Security—and there was the occasional credit check for Carswell National Bank.

Things might have been a little tough, but they weren't impossible, and I figured I still had it easier than Bobby did.

Looking down at my new black shoes with the classy ebony high heels—at the end of some shapely stems, courtesy of my folks and God—I realized that things weren't completely horrible. I had had my eye on these spiked babies for nearly a month before I finally bought them, when a couple of deadbeat clients had finally come through with the money they owed, after I had a little heart-to-heart with them.

Like Al Capone said, you can get more with a smile and a gun than with just a smile.

My office on the fourth floor of the Danton Building, just a couple of blocks outside the Loop, kept the Winters Agency close to the action with the banks and insurance companies. Sitting behind the mammoth oak desk Bobby had picked up second hand, I put my feet up on the foot stool I kept on the left side of the desk and admired my new shoes again in the morning sun. The row of three windows faced east and the spring sunshine poured through the open Venetian blinds like melted butter looking for a lobster.

On the wall to the right of my desk, two doors kept company, side by side—one led to a side hall so my clients could exit quietly without being noticed, and behind the other was a tiny but sufficient bathroom. The wall on the left contained a Murphy bed, which I almost never used, and a photo of Bobby looking businesslike and professional in his best gray fedora.

The door the desk faced—and most of that wall for that matter—was pebbled glass up top, dark wood below. Beyond the door, in the outer office, my secretary, Judy, sat punching out a letter on the typewriter. I couldn't see her, but I could hear the *clack click clack* of the Olivetti.

I'd been skeptical of Judy when Bobby hired her. An old girlfriend of his, about my age, she was a real looker, and I wasn't too happy when I'd first met her. But when Bobby entered the service, it would have been easy for Judy to ditch me for a steadier paying job; but she hadn't, and over the last few months we'd become pals.

When the typewriter stopped its racket, I looked up just as Judy was knocking before coming in without waiting for a response, closing the door behind her. Maybe a couple of inches shorter than my five-four, Judy had bobbed blond hair; mine was dark brown and fell in gentle natural waves to the midpoint of my back. Her eyes were blue as the sky, mine brown. Judy had a cute little Alice Faye pug nose, while mine was long and straight, Joan Crawford-ish.

Otherwise there was a bit of a resemblance, actually—we both had full lips and high cheekbones. We were both slim and had Grable-worthy shapes—today Judy showed off hers in a tight yellow floral dress while I wore a red dress with a black belt, a black necklace and earrings, and my wonderful new black heels. I loved the shoes so much that I forgave them for being impractical for either detecting or my other mission.

"Betty, that man is here again," Judy said, her voice low, her face sour. "I'll throw his keister outta here, if you want."

My secretary was in almost as good a shape as me . . . even though she wasn't The Chosen One.

Which I was—and even Bobby didn't know that his blushing bride was that one woman in each generation placed on the Earth to kill vampires. But my husband was off fighting evil in his own way, while I was fighting it on the home front.

"Who's here?" I asked, actually kind of teasing. From her expression I knew exactly who she meant.

"That . . . weirdo." She jerked her head toward the outer office. "You know, that combination Lugosi and Karloff." I couldn't help but smile. She meant Redmond, my watcher. Judy had no way of knowing that I had met Redmond when I was but fifteen, and that this "weirdo" had trained me in the slaying of the undead. To my secretary, Redmond was just this flaky guy in strange apparel who showed up every now and then, demanding to see me.

"Show the man in," I said.

Her face screwed up even more. "Is he going to pay this time?"

"Judy," I said, not unkindly, "that's my concern, isn't it?"

"Yeah . . . yeah, I guess."

But I knew what she was getting at; if we hadn't become such good friends, it wouldn't have been an issue.

"Wait a second," I said, stopping her as she turned to go. I opened the top desk drawer and withdrew her check. "We got a little cash in . . . so we're caught up." She looked at the total and gave me a tired but grateful smile. Judy was long overdue for a raise.

"Nice," she said, glimpsing my new shoes. "Black goes with most everything."

I nodded; even with the pay boost I'd given her, I felt suddenly uncomfortable that I had allowed myself this small pleasure. I felt myself blushing and quickly said, "You want to get Mr. Redmond?"

"If you insist," she said, her voice sounding faraway.

Soon Redmond strode in, closing the door behind him. I walked around to my side of the desk and sat down as Redmond parked himself in one of the two chairs across from me. Tall and thin, unseasonably attired in a tan overcoat and deerstalker, giving him a Sherlock Holmes aspect, Marcus Redmond wore his reddish sideburns long and his salt-and-cayenne pepper mustache thick.

The curly red mop that peeked out from beneath the deerstalker constantly looked to be in need of a trim and his nearly albino complexion announced to the world that he spent little, if any, time in the sunshine, preferring instead to stay huddled among the antiquated tomes in his used bookstore on Clark Street. In that pale visage his radiant blue eyes were startling, and his long thin nose—Holmes again—split his face like an ax blade.

Glancing over his shoulder to make sure the door was still closed, Redmond turned back to me, and said, "We have a live one."

"By which you mean a dead one."

He nodded, his demeanor at once grave and excited. "A very lively dead one. He approaches the level of a master. No telling how far his power will spread."

"Ye gods, Redmond," I said. "It's a good thing you don't do press relations for the government. You'd have surrendered after Pearl Harbor."

"I know you consider me an alarmist," he said, trying to look wounded, but coming closer to amused.

"I consider you a worry wart."

And he was a worry wart; he knew it, I knew it, and it really wasn't that bad a thing to be for either a slayer or a watcher. In that line of work—that line of duty—your first mistake was generally your last one.

Things remained a tad tense between my watcher and me. He had still not forgiven me for marrying Bobby. ("The Chosen One," he'd intoned, "should stay unattached!") But I had no regrets about that, other than the too-short honeymoon prior to my man heading overseas.

"Our prospect's name, my dear Elizabeth, is Radu Hunyadi, though we can expect him to be using an alias."

"And where is Radu at the moment?"

"In Chicago."

"Could you be more specific?"

"No. You are aware of an altercation in the local underworld, my dear?"

The newspapers had been trying to play the gang war down, but word on the street was this was more than a minor set-to over turf—the worst since the days when Big Al took over. "If by 'altercation' you mean dead bodies in ditches and gutters, I am aware."

"Donny O'Brien's gang has . . . I believe the underworld jargon of the moment is 'rubbed out' . . . several of Frank Nitti's underlings."

"Since when is one gangster killing another gangster a vampire killing?"

Redmond closed his eyes, shook his head, and a hand went to his temple and pressed. "Child, I taught you to think, so think. Would one not assume a ganglord of Frank Nitti's stature might not strike back?"

"You know he has. I know he has. The whole city knows."

"But no corpses from the O'Brien faction have been found," Redmond said, his eyes still closed, the hand still pressing on his temple.

"So, Nitti's guys are better at disposing of the evidence. Cement overshoes and Lake Michigan go hand in glove. I still don't see . . ."

Redmond's eyes popped open and he sat forward in the chair. "But you should see! I taught you to see, child. See."

I shook my head. The old boy had always been eccentric; was he losing his marbles, now? But I went along, saying, "You think a vampire made those bodies disappear?"

The glowing blue eyes tightened. "I know a vampire did that, and not just any vampire. Radu Hunyadi himself."

"How do you know, Redmond?"

With a sigh, he shook his head again, as if he were in the presence of a thick-headed child. "Because I'm the Watcher. It's my role, my duty, my destiny, to know."

Now I pressed a hand to my temple. When Redmond got like this, half John Barrymore, half put-upon parent, it was my turn to have the headache. "I simply was wondering if you have any evidence."

"Until last night, it was just a supposition. Now I know for sure."

I prodded. "Because . . . ?"

He withdrew some photographs from the folds of his coat and tossed them onto the desk in front of me. I glanced down at the top one, which showed what looked like the cornerstone of a new building with the top half of a body sticking out of it like a ghastly swizzle stick.

The next photo was a closeup of the victim's face: a white man with a thin scar over his right eyebrow, a nose that had been broken a time or two, and wide thin lips. The black-and-white photo gave him a ghostly pallor starkly white against the dark gray of the concrete.

"Tommy Brannigan," I said. "A low-life stiff who works for O'Brien."

"Worked for O'Brien."

"This doesn't prove a vamp—" My voice caught in my throat as I looked at the next picture. The photographer had pulled back a little, and I could now see a vicious, gaping wound in the gangster's neck, the bloody edges black against the pale flesh.

Redmond said, "You see my point."

"Both of them. And of course he looks so white because he's been . . ."

". . . drained of blood," the Watcher finished for me.

Redmond had a number of Chicago cops on his private payroll. To them, my watcher was just another source of graft; they had no idea why the strange character wanted them to apprise him of bizarre doings like the ones in this crime scene photos.

"We were fortunate," Redmond said, "that one of my contacts on the force was among the contingent of Chicago's finest who interrupted the . . . uh . . . burial."

"So you think Frank Nitti has hired himself a vampire hitman?"

"I do."

"And it's this, this . . ."

"Hunyadi. Radu Hunyadi."

"A vampire on the Outfit's payroll?"

"Stranger things have happened."

"Not many." I shook my head. "I'm surprised Nitti is involved in this kind of gang war at all. He's a business executive."

"He's only retaliating, my dear. And I doubt he's aware his new best hitman friend is one of the undead."

From another fold, another photo appeared, this one smaller, taken by a Brownie or something similar. Redmond held it out to me. I took it.

I recognized the dapper man known as the Enforcer, the barber who had become Capone's favored gunman and who had risen to Big Al's right hand. With Capone in stir, Nitti was the top of the Outfit ladder now. To civilians he could be a fairly benign figure—particularly compared to Capone—and my husband Bobby had even done a few noncriminal jobs for him.

In the nighttime photo, Frank Nitti stood on a corner in a dark suit, immaculately attired and groomed (as always), his black hair slicked down and parted on the right, his mustache a trim black shape on his upper lip. In his hands the former barber held a dark Homburg. Next to him was a thin, angularly handsome associate.

"Note the face of that Nitti crony carefully," Redmond advised.

"All right," I said with a shrug.

Pulling something else from his mysterious overcoat, Redmond laid a small panel of wood on the desk. It contained the portrait of a warrior from the middle ages, battle helmet atop a head of long, flowing brown hair that trailed down his shoulders. The man had a thick beard, a bushy mustache, and some sort of strange light behind his green eyes.

This vintage portrait appeared to be of the same man Nitti had been speaking to on a Chicago street corner, not long ago.

"Radu Hunyadi," Redmond announced.

"When was this panel painted?"

"Despite my expertise in ancient documents, I can't be certain. My guess is about 1642. He was, of course, not a vampire yet."

"Really?" Looking into the eyes painted on the wood panel set something loose inside me, something that burned, cramped, and stabbed all at the same time. Most slayers merely sensed a vampire: my built-in warning system was strictly four-alarm, and currently in screaming mode.

Redmond's face clouded in concern. "What's the matter, child?"

"When this was painted, Hunyadi was already a vampire— already an extremely powerful one, I'd wager."

"What?" Redmond looked confused.

I pointed to my stomach. "Gut never lies. This isn't just a bad guy, Redmond. This is evil incarnate."

Redmond picked up the panel and gaped at it. I could tell he wanted to argue, but he knew better than to question my personal alarm system.

Then his face changed as, finally, he saw it too. "You're right. There's something . . . abhorrent . . . in the eyes. I can barely see it, and no one other than a slayer would ever get more than a glimpse of it. You're right, my dear. And I am proud of you for this insight. Of course, this makes it even more important that we act quickly."

"Do we know anything about him?"

Sweat seemed to bead instantly on Redmond's forehead, tiny glistening blossoms of fear. He looked even more colorless than usual. Finally, letting out a long breath, he seemed to get control of himself.

"Hunyadi's discreet. That's how he's stayed in business and out of sight for so long. He hires himself out as an assassin and he feeds on the victims. Before he worked for these gangsters, there hadn't been a sighting of him since 1896, when he assassinated Nasr-ed-Din, the Shah of Persia. In 1769, he was among Russian troops who occupied Moldavia. What brought him to the States remains a mystery."

"Not really," I said. "Population here's growing, crime is rampant—he doesn't have three hundred years of history to overcome. Life was probably getting difficult in Europe; he had competition from homegrown evil bastards, over there. What do we know about him?"

"Other than this ancient portrait, we don't have any idea what he looks like—not today."

I nodded.

"But this picture"—Redmond picked up the Nitti photo—"was taken outside Franco's, an—"

"Italian restaurant near the river on Rush," I said. "I know the neighborhood. Guess that's as good a place as any to start."

"Franco's?" Redmond asked. "You're not just going to . . . breeze in there."

"You know I'm more subtle than that."

His only response was an arched eyebrow.

"I think it's time," I said, "for a little stakeout on Rush Street."

• • •

I sat in my black '39 Chevy, half a block down from Franco's. A cool breeze blowing off the Chicago River, less than a block behind me, wafted through the open driver's window and made the warm night feel a little less muggy. I had changed to flats and a pair of Bobby's old blue jeans, along with a sleeveless print blouse.

After all, I wasn't going into Franco's and I sure as hell wasn't out to impress anybody tonight, so I was dressed casually. That didn't mean I was casual about my mission; a black bag loaded with stakes lay on the seat next to me.

A number of men in pinstripe suits, with bulges under their jackets, came in and out of the restaurant throughout the evening. Most of them had dolls on their arm and generally the women looked pretty but cheap—flashy dames with slit skirts and low necklines that flaunted the only features these men were interested in.

But it was the faces of the men I was interested in, as they paraded in and out of the restaurant, with its mirrorlike black-glass façade. I wanted to capture Hunyadi on film, or in a way I wanted not to capture his image. . . .

Oh, a vampire's mug could be caught on film, all right—like in that photo Redmond showed me of Hunyadi and his boss, Nitti. But the creature would not cast a reflection in the restaurant's sleek glass facade, and my camera would record that *lack* of image as well.

I had just changed to a new roll of film in my Leica when Frank Nitti strolled through the door of the restaurant, his wife on his right, a tall man who might be Hunyadi on his left. The crime boss surprised me. I hadn't seen them go in, so I sort of sat there numbly when they walked out. Nitti wore a dapper dark suit, his hair slicked back and parted on the right, the

Homburg again in his hands. Nitti's wife, Antoinette—his second wife actually—walked ahead of him as the little group moved unknowingly in my direction.

Mrs. Nitti, shorter and squatter than her husband, wore a high-collared gray dress that nearly touched the sidewalk when she walked. She had black hair streaked with gray and wore it swept back in a severe bun. I had seen her a couple of times around town, and she perpetually looked as if her best friend had just died.

The tall man walking next to Nitti had his black fedora pulled low, leaving his face in shadow; but I could see by the street light that he had a very pale complexion, a pointed chin, and—despite his height—a muscular physique.

Hunyadi, all right.

Snapping out of my surprise, I clicked off half a dozen pictures before the Nittis climbed into a black Cadillac, two cars in front of mine. They pulled away and the tall man walked off in the opposite direction . . . without ever letting me get a better look at that mug of his.

Just as I settled back into my seat, a meaty paw poked through the open window and turned into a fist just into time to slam into the side of my head, so hard I saw stars, and I don't mean Sinatra and Crosby. The camera dropped from my hand and clattered to the car floor.

"What the hell you doin'?" a deep voice asked as slowly, inexorably, he dragged me by the head through the open window like a big fish he was hauling onto the deck of a boat.

My mouth was closed and he held me so tight I couldn't even open up to bite him. All I could do as I squirmed was smell his cheap aftershave and snatch up the bag of stakes from off the rider's seat. Then he dumped me unceremoniously on my behind in the middle of the street.

Finally I was able to draw a breath as he backed up a couple of steps and reached toward the bulge under his coat. It was an ugly brown coat that went beautifully with his ugly brown pants and shapeless tan fedora. He had a wide empty face, like a gingerbread man's, right down to the raisin eyes, no discernible neck, and shoulders that looked like he was wearing football pads under the shabby suit. His thighs threatened to tear through the pants and his chest bulged the buttons of his white shirt. A vile striped tie had come out and swung over his shoulder when he'd been manhandling me.

"You're a broad," he moaned slowly, as if accusing me of something.

"No, I'm right here in Chicago, you dumb ape," I said as I looked up into his empty brown eyes.

It took me a second, but I finally figured out where I'd seen him before. He was Tommy Merloni, a low-level Nitti lieutenant that Bobby had dealt with on more than one occasion. If memory served, the short white scar that ran over Merloni's right eyebrow was courtesy of my husband.

As I rose, the black bag swinging loose from my right arm, he pulled his rod, a large blue-black automatic that made my knees seem suddenly weak. I decided to put on a brave front.

"You better put that away," I said, "while we're still friends."

Tommy grinned; his teeth were big off-white Chiclets. "Or whaddaya gonna do about it—hit me with your purse?"

"Not a bad idea," I said.

He frowned in thought even as I swung the bag down across his wrist and knocked the pistol free. It skittered across the street down into the sewer and his eyes turned to watch it disappointedly, a kid losing his favorite toy, as I backhanded him across the face with the bag full of stakes. I heard the distinctive squishy crunch as his nose broke.

Tommy roared in anger and muttered an obscenity or two, but they got lost in the flow of blood down his face. He managed one step toward me before I smacked him two more times with the bag—another forehand and another backhand.

He sagged, staggered drunkenly for two steps, then fell in a heap in the middle of the street. Thinking that waiting around for any of Tommy's friends to join the party might not be the best strategy, I jumped back into the car, started her up, and stomped on the gas. I was careful not to hit Merloni with the car, but before he had returned to relative consciousness, I was well on my way back to the office. The camera on the floor I hoped would hold the evidence I would need to convince Frank Nitti of just who—or what—he was in bed with.

After spending most of the night in the dark room, I had developed the pictures, learned what I could, and come up with a plan. By ten o'clock the next morning, I was on my way to Frank Nitti's office.

Today I wore a white dress with black polka dots, the black belt and necklace, and the ebony heels again. They were a little tight, but I knew I looked good in them, and if I was going to get help from the Enforcer, I'd need every edge I could get.

Like his absent boss, Al Capone, Nitti kept an office in the Lexington Hotel at the corner of Michigan Avenue and Cermak Road. I showed up there about ten-thirty, my bag of stakes down in the car, my little black purse holding my wallet and my only weapon: my lipstick. Normally I'd have at least one stake tucked in my purse, but I figured I'd have to stand for a frisk and preferred not to have to explain myself.

The lobby was a forest of marble columns dotted with plush leather chairs, a few sofas, and ashtrays on dark-wood end tables. The place was substantial, with a sweeping staircase off to the left and a bank of elevators to the right. A tall, thin man with slicked back hair, a pencil mustache, and a holier-than-thou look on his face leered at me as I crossed, but I avoided him and went straight to the elevators.

Though I'd never been there before, I knew exactly where I was going. Bobby had been there more than once and, in telling me tales of his dealings with the Outfit, had shared with me most of the details.

I stepped into the elevator, and the uniformed operator, a little old man of maybe seventy with silver hair and almost enough strength to close the door, asked, "What floor?"

"Fourth," I said, and smiled when he glanced at me in surprise.

He didn't say anything as we rose to the fourth story, and when he opened the door he managed only to announce the floor.

I got out and turned to my right. Halfway down the hall, Tommy Merloni sat on a wide sofa on the right side of the hall. His face was heavily bandaged and he seemed to like looking at my legs as I approached him. I don't even think he knew it was me until he looked up and I smiled at him.

"Jesus Christ," he muttered, though with the bandage over his broken nose, the profanity came out thick and practically unintelligible.

I could see he wanted to get up, but his fat ass was pretty much sinking into the sofa, and as he struggled to rise, I placed a hand on his chest and grinned down at him. "Are you sure you wanna do that?"

He let himself slip back onto the sofa.

"I'm here to see Mr. Nitti."

"You . . . you got an appointment?"

"You just tell him Bobby Winters's wife is here to see him."

"Is that who you are?"

"Yeah. Also, the hundred-and-five-pound female who kicked your ass last night. But I'm willing to keep that to myself if you make things go smooth, right now."

He tried to look tough, but having been bested by a woman didn't leave him with much room to argue. "I should at least pat you down," he said, trying to win back a piece of his pride.

I put my hands on the hips of my skin-tight dress. "In your dreams."

He lumbered up off the sofa and went to a nearby door and knocked. A thug in a gray pinstripe suit opened it. He had short brown hair, a reddish tie with tiny white and blue stripes, and a starched white shirt.

"Mrs. Robert Winters to see Mr. Nitti," Merloni said, but I just swept past him into the suite.

I paused and turned to watch the goons trade looks; Merloni managed only a shrug before the pinstriped guy shut the door in his face.

The living room was at least slightly smaller than Wrigley Field, if better furnished. Two Louis XIV sofas faced each other across a coffee table wider than my desk. The oriental rug under my ebony heels cost only a little more than the family Chevy. The walls were a pale pink, the ceiling high and white, the curtains spread enough to let in the sunlight . . . but not enough to make anyone in the living room an easy target from the building across the street.

I crossed the room, the well-dressed thug in my wake saying, "Mrs. Winters, I know Mr. Nitti and your husband are acquainted, but—"

"I'm glad," I said over my shoulder as I crossed the room to a sliding door closed to what I presumed to be the dining room.

The thug came running up and grabbed me, rather gingerly actually, by the elbow.

"You can't go in there, ma'am," he said, his voice low.

His dark eyes were wide with surprise as if no one had ever questioned his authority before. He smelled of fresh cologne, something citrusy, and small beads of sweat decorated his wide forehead.

"I didn't intend to," I answered.

"But—"

"I thought you would go in, get Mr. Nitti, and tell him I'm here."

"Mr. Nitti can't be disturbed," the man said, his voice exasperated and loud now, and unfortunately for him, he'd done exactly what he said couldn't be done.

The sliding door banged open and Frank Nitti stood in front of us, his face a mask of irritation. "What the hell is going on out here, Johnny?"

Johnny didn't seem to know what to say. His eyes went from Nitti to me, back to Nitti, then down to the floor. "I'm sorry, Mr. Nitti, this broad—"

"Broad?" I interrupted.

Nitti turned to see me for the first time and the anger melted from his face a little. "Hey, I know you, don't I?"

"We've met," I said quietly.

The dapper little mob boss seemed to suddenly remember that the dining room door was open and there were people in there. He turned to them, a couple of gombahs I didn't recognize seated at the large oak table that dominated the room, and said, "I'll be a minute." Then he slid the door closed.

Nitti bestowed a small smile, almost but not quite flirtatious. "Now, why don't you tell me where we've met before?"

Smiling back, I said, "You know my husband, Robert Winters—Bobby."

The crime boss's smile widened. "Yeah, I remember Robert. He's a good boy—reliable. How is he doing?"

"As best he can. He's overseas."

He nodded somberly. "You should be proud."

"I am."

Touching my elbow with his hand, he led me toward the two sofas. "And why is it you've come to see me, Mrs. Winters?"

We reached the couches and he gestured for me to sit down. I did, and he dropped onto the sofa across the table from me.

"Where are my manners?" he said. "Coffee, tea?"

I shook my head. "I won't be here that long, but thank you."

He nodded and waited, waving for Johnny to leave us alone.

"I've come to see you about a problem," I explained. "A serious one."

Another nod and I could almost see the wheels turning as Nitti tried to figure out not only where I was heading, but how he could turn it to his advantage.

He said, "And you believe I can help you . . . with your problem."

I shook my head and he looked like that RCA dog, head tilted; he was staring at me like I was speaking another language.

"Mr. Nitti, the problem isn't mine. It's yours. And I've come to help you."

Folding his hands in front of him, the crime boss stalled for time as he tried to comprehend this. I was supposed to end up in his debt, not the other way around.

"And what problem do you believe I have?"

"You're using a . . . clean-up man . . . to settle scores in this current disagreement among you and certain of your peers."

My euphemisms amused him, mildly.

"And this . . . clean-up man . . . is a little, well . . . unusual, let's say."

The crime boss shrugged, not anxious to confirm any of this.

I pressed on. "His victims disappear and no one ever sees them again."

Nitti's face tightened. "If cleaning up was my goal, wouldn't that be a good thing?"

"It would, unless the killer is disposing of the bodies to hide how he killed them."

"Wouldn't that be the idea, Mrs. Winters?" He seemed to be losing patience.

"If he were doing it to cover your tracks, yes, but I'm saying he's covering his own. Hell, your clean-up boy doesn't even want you to know how he's killing these clowns."

Another shrug. "And why would it matter to me?"

"Because, Mr. Nitti . . . Frank? Pardon my poetry, but it seems you're in bed with the undead."

Nitti looked at me as if I were bughouse and his eyes searched the room for Johnny. I tossed the photo I'd taken at Franco's on the table. Unable to find Johnny, Nitti glanced down at the print.

"So you got a shot of me and my wife and one of my boys," he said, with another shrug. "And not a very good one."

"Notice anything else about it?"

He shook his head. "Nothin' except as a picture, it stinks."

"It was taken just last night."

"Yeah," he said. "I put that together."

"And did you leave the restaurant alone last night?"

He thought about that. "Me, Antoinette, and . . . one of my associates. And there we are."

He gestured to the photo.

"Check the reflection," I said, "in the restaurant's glass front."

"All right. There's my wife and me and . . ." His voice trailed off as he looked down at the photo. "I don't get you, Mrs. Winters."

"If you're looking for the third member of your little dinner party," I said, "he isn't in the reflection."

"I told you it stinks as a picture."

"Frank, this Hunyadi . . . that's the name I know him by, anyway. . . ."

"That's his name."

No alias, after all.

"Hunyadi," I continued, "doesn't cast a reflection in a mirror. You know of anybody—anything—that carries that unusual characteristic? Not that any of you Outfit guys are terribly reflective."

His eyes had narrowed. "No reflection in glass . . . or in a mirror . . . ? And that's what you mean by . . ."

"Undead, yes. You're from the old country. You know the stories—or maybe you know that they aren't all 'stories.'"

The gang boss looked as pale as a vampire's victim.

"You've got a bloodsucker on your payroll, Frank. And I don't mean somebody's embezzling."

The grave expression Nitti wore told me he was a believer. I didn't need a hard sell with this European immigrant.

I shoved in the needle. "And here I thought you were a good Catholic, too."

Nitti nodded, forehead tight now. "I am."

"Then you see why I said you've got a problem."

He swallowed thickly. His eyes had a pleading quality few would ever see in Frank Nitti's face. "And you think you can help?"

"Yeah, it's sort of a . . . sideline for me."

"What is?"

"Let's just say I have a client who's hired me to do some cleaning up of my own."

"Where"—He could barely say it—"vampires are concerned?"

"Let's just say, I can take care of this problem . . . or you can continue aiding and abetting an undead fiend and face eternal damnation. Which is it gonna be, Frank?"

Obvious as the answer might seem, Nitti considered his choices for a long moment. He didn't give away what he was thinking, but I thought I knew the man well enough to know that vampires were a whole different level of illegality than anything he wanted to get involved with. Crime was one thing; evil another.

He ran a hand quickly over his mustache and said, "So, if you really can take care of this problem for me, what's it going to cost me?"

"A thousand," I said.

"You said you had another client you were cleaning up this . . . problem . . . for."

"Yeah. But this time it was more like . . . a referral. You want this problem to go away, Frank?"

"Oh, yeah."

"Well, my business is a little off right now, so I'm going to charge you a small fee. We both know it's much smaller than this job is worth."

Our eyes met and he nodded.

"Let's just say then," he said slowly, "that I'll also owe you a small favor sometime in the future."

"Seems fair to me. There's just one thing."

"Yeah?"

"I need you to point me in the right direction."

He thought that over. Then he said, rather affably, "Okay, Mrs. Winters. You know the Chicago Tunnel Company?"

"Sure. They run freight beneath the city."

Nitti looked at me with hard cold eyes. "Hunyadi's down there somewhere." He grunted a humorless laugh. "I thought he picked that hideout was just because hardly anyone goes down there."

"Now you know it was to avoid having to come out in the sunlight."

He sighed, half embarrassed, half spooked. "Now I know."

I sat forward. "Any idea where? Those tunnels run beneath most of the city."

Shaking his head, Nitti said, "We always met at Franco's at night, but he could've gotten there from anywhere."

"Think, Frank," I pressed him. "Did you notice anything or did he ever mention anything?"

The crime boss's eyes glazed over as he seemed to go over every conversation he'd ever had with the killer. "Wait," he said finally. "We were talking once about the city, the sights. You know, guy's new in town, after all."

I nodded.

"Anyway, Hunyadi mentions how quiet the Field Museum is at night. And I thought that was kind of an odd thing to say, y'know . . . since the Field isn't open at night."

That was a good lead. Damn good lead.

I stood slowly, smiling at my host. "Don't worry. I'll take care of this, Frank."

He looked skeptical. "You don't mind my saying, Mrs. Winters—you don't look so tough."

I smiled. "But you don't have to look tough to be tough, now do you, Frank?"

"Good point," he said. "Good point. But this Hunyadi? He's tough too."

"Yeah?"

"Yeah. And he looks it."

And the dapper mobster, ever the gentlemen, showed me out.

Normally, I would have gone back uptown and changed into something better suited for the potential fight ahead—creature comfort, let's call it—but I didn't want to go down into those tunnels with night time closing in, nor did I want to wait another day and let Hunyadi feed on even one more soul, even one that might already be damned. Criminals or not, no one deserved to go out under the fangs of a monster like Hunyadi.

I parked between Michigan and Wabash on Fourteenth, picked up my sack full of stakes, and made my way down into the tunnel at the corner. Forty feet below the surface the freight tunnels held a two-gauge electric railroad and nearly sixty miles of track. I was at the extreme southern end of the network and decided to work my way east toward the Field Museum. If that failed, then I would start on the daunting trek north.

The tunnel—barely six feet wide and just over seven feet high—was constructed of concrete that glowed white under the occasional incandescent lights. I knew the tunnels better than most since my father had worked down there for years. I remembered him telling me there were 3800 lights strung through the sixty miles of track, roughly one every eighty-four feet. They provided some light and made for tons of shadows, especially near the curves.

The air down here was far cooler than back up on the surface, and suddenly my short-sleeved dress didn't seem heavy enough to stave off the chill. I could hear a train or two clattering along in the distance, but before I'd gone very far, the sound faded to silence.

I was alone. Or anyway, I was the only living soul down here.

Walking carefully so as not to break off a heel—or, more importantly, not to stumble into the third rail of the electrified tracks—I made my way up a block to the corner of Thirteenth and Wabash, then turned east. My heels clicked against the concrete floor that rose like narrow sidewalks on either side of the rails. The tunnel got darker as I moved deeper in that direction, and it became obvious that someone had broken out most of the bulbs in this wing. A lonely offshoot of the main system, this single tunnel ran to the museum but was hardly ever used.

The deeper I got, the more shadows I encountered, and my progress slowed even more. I was careful not to let the bag of stakes move around too much. Jostling it would cause the stakes to rattle like dancing skeletons, and in the tunnel that sound would echo all the way to the end.

After a while I couldn't tell if I'd gone a hundred yards or a thousand as the darkness closed in like an ever tightening shroud. My heartbeat accelerated; I could feel it pounding in my chest, and my breathing became rapid and more shallow. I started wondering if I was worried about what I might find or if I was just becoming scared of the dark. Then the first cramp hit.

As it did a shape appeared out of the shadows and loomed over me, blocking out any light from the few bulbs left ahead of me. It growled like a wounded animal, and, as it closed in, the shape became that of a man, not Hunyadi, but a wide shaved-head monster with his fangs bared and his breath strong enough to kill, even if he never laid a pearly white on my neck.

It took a powerful vampire indeed to form alliances and attract followers.

Taking two quick steps back, I dropped into a combat stance—Redmond had taught me well—and yanked one of the stakes from the bag. The vampire lumbered toward me, and when he reached out, arms spread, I ducked, stepped in, and jammed the stake up and into his heart, flesh and tissue tearing, blood burbling. Screaming in anger and pain, he grabbed for the stake instead of me, and his momentum almost took me with him as he tumbled forward and hit the ground in a shower of dust.

His noise served as a warning to his ghoulish buddies, and four more of the creatures filled the cramped tunnel in front of me. The only thing I had going for me was that the small tunnel made it impossible for them all to come at me at once.

The first one, a skinny guy in a baggy suit, charged at me; I swept him past as I jerked out another stake. The second one had greasy hair and wild eyes; he stepped forward and, as if accepting an unexpected award, took the stake right in the chest. Spinning, I kicked the first one in the head and dropped him to his knees. As the last two came at me, I pulled out a stake and, to their surprise, I charged them. I tripped the one on my left as I rammed home the stake in the one on the right. Pulling my last two stakes from the bag even as I spun around, I threw one at the first vampire as he rose and caught him in the chest.

He died instantly and fell like a snipped-stringed puppet, dissolving to dust, his buddies already just mounds of powder where they'd fallen.

I had one stake left, with a vampire blocking my path out of the tunnel and Hunyadi was still somewhere down here to boot. Suddenly I didn't feel like rushing down here had been such a good idea.

The remaining vampire got up and turned to face me. He was muscular, olive-skinned, and looked to be a fairly recent recruit judging from the fresh scabs on his neck. Baring his fangs, he stepped toward me and I backed up a step. We kept up this bizarre tango for four or five steps until it became evident to me that he wasn't going to attack; he was merely guiding me to his master.

My breath caught and I decided that discretion might truly be the better part of valor. Time to ice this underling and get the hell out. His boss could wait until I was better armed; the vampire slayer who gets herself killed is not doing anybody any good . . . particularly herself. Just as I'd made my decision, I felt an arm curl around my neck and tighten.

Hunyadi!

The vampire in front of me took a step forward and I tried to lunge with the stake, but Hunyadi swiped it out of my hand, the wood clattering on the pavement as it bounced away. Hunyadi lifted me, my heeled feet leaving the pavement, my air supply dwindling. Stars started shooting off in front of my eyes, and as those stars began to turn to blackness, I felt the killer's grip loosen, and I could feel his hot breath on my neck as his fangs came closer.

Struggling not to pass out, I went limp, hoping my sudden relaxation would convince Hunyadi that I had no fight left in me. Seemingly secure in the feeling that he had the upper hand, the vampire moved me farther away to give himself easier access to my neck.

That was a mistake.

Forcing my weight down, I slipped through Hunyadi's arm, dropped to the ground, and came up with a kick that caught the underling in front of me between his undead legs. He yowled and howled and backed up a step, while I felt around the darkened tunnel for the stake.

I couldn't find the damned thing and the light was so dim I couldn't see it anywhere.

Hunyadi caught my hair in his hand and jerked.

I screamed, and when he pulled me toward him, I backed up even faster, practically leaping into him, the back of my head smashing into his face. He bellowed and let go of my hair. I scrambled away just as the other vampire charged. I managed to stick out a foot and trip him, and he rolled into Hunyadi, knocking both of them to the ground, sparks shooting up from the third rail.

I crawled around on the concrete, my hose ruined for sure now, searching frantically for the lost stake. Out of the corner of my eye, I saw Hunyadi and the other one wrestling to get away from each other and get to their feet. I crawled forward, my hands scraping off the rough cement, my nails getting as tattered as my hose. Then, just as I was about to give up and simply try to outrun them, I touched something: the stake.

Only it slipped away. They were rising now, and I scrambled along, touched it again, and this time pulled the stake to my chest.

Turning, I threw it at the nearest figure. The stupid damned tertiary vampire yelped and dissolved to dust. That left Hunyadi royally pissed . . . and me fresh out of stakes.

He leaped forward, covering the distance between us in an instant. I finally got a look at him in the dim light. He had a full head of thick, curly black hair, angry bloodshot yellow-set brown eyes, ghostly pale flesh, and thin, colorless lips. He wore a black undertaker's suit with a vest over a white shirt and blood red tie.

"So," he said coldly, his voice deep and regal. "The Slayer has finally found me. How I've waited for this moment . . . and how I will savor it."

He punctuated the remark by slapping me so hard I flew backward, rolling off the concrete onto the tracks, my hair crackling as it touched the third rail, burning the ends away. My ribs hurt—something was cracked, if not broken—and my breath came in short, raspy gulps.

"You're going to die so very slowly," he said, leaping to my side again.

He yanked me up by the hair, my insides hurting so much I didn't think I could scream out loud, though I certainly heard the wail in my head as he flung me in the direction of his lair. I bounced once on the concrete, smacked my head on the wall, and came to rest in a heap near the end of the tunnel.

Hunyadi walked slowly toward me, clearly relishing all this. Obviously he was just going to keep throwing me around like a doll until he got tired of it, and there wasn't a damned thing I could do about it. Every fiber of my being hurt, and I knew I only had enough strength for one more move. If only I knew what that move would be. . . .

I managed to roll over on my back and I watched as Hunyadi closed in. As he stood at my feet and began to bend down, I raised my knees to my chest, my feet coming up so I could try to roll him over the top of me; but my heel caught up in his tie and we both just hung there for an impossible second until I remembered I was wearing my new ebony heels.

Ebony wood!

I smiled at him and drove my foot forward, the heel of the right shoe breaking off as it plunged into Hunyadi's heart. He grimaced, coughed once, then closed his eyes and—much too quickly—died in a shower of death dust.

This time, maybe it would take.

Judy, bless her heart, was still at her desk when I finally trudged back into the office.

"Oh, God," she blurted. "What happened to you?"

I gave her a tired smile and limped through the office on my one good heel. She rose to follow me, but as I reached the inner door to my office, a small, dark man in an ill-fitting suit walked through the door.

Judy looked from the man to me. I nodded toward the man, who gaped at my appearance, then I trudged through the door and closed it behind me. I wanted a shower, I wanted to cry, I even wanted to laugh; but I settled for plopping into my chair and putting my feet up on my footstool.

A second later, Judy poked her head into the room. "Okay to come in?"

I waved and she came in holding what looked like a check.

She held out the check from across the desk. "It's a thousand dollars."

I nodded.

"And . . . it's signed by Frank Nitti!"

I nodded again.

Judy's eyes were huge. "You're going to explain all this to me, right?"

I looked down at my one bedraggled shoe, then looked up at her, and gave her all the explanation I intended to. "I busted a heel doing a job for Mr. Nitti."

Again

Jane Espenson

SUNNYDALE, CALIFORNIA, 1999

"Anya? Anya, what's going on?"

Xander was mumbling, still half-asleep. Maybe even three-quarters. But not entirely. And he absolutely knew something was wrong.

Part of it was the light. Even face-down, face smooshed in to the pillow, blankets up around his ears, he could sense it was wrong. The light was too bright, and even stranger, it was coming from the wrong side. "Anya?" She was probably responsible somehow, like maybe she moved the bed while he was asleep. Some bizarre prewedding preparation? Everything she did these days was about the wedding. The very thought of that made him want to bury himself even deeper in to the bed. *Warm, warm delightful bed . . .*

Except something was still wrong. *The light. Right.* And more than the light. Like . . . where *was* Anya? Still face-down, eyes still closed, he sent one sleepy hand out on a reconnaissance mission. Anya wasn't in her half of the bed. And, in fact, her half of the bed was missing entirely. That didn't normally happen.

He flipped over and sat up in one panicked motion. His heart kicked in his chest. He looked around the room with suddenly clear eyes. He found himself in a twin bed, narrow and too soft and extremely familiar. In fact the whole place was familiar. He was in his old room. Not the basement, but the room upstairs, the room that was his from first grade through twelfth grade. It had never really been a great place to be, but now, now it was positively alarming.

He took it in quickly. Everything was there. The olive-colored shag carpet. The poster of Tyra Banks in unlikely swimwear. His skateboard, leaned against the wall next to a pile of untended laundry. His old bulletin board with his name doodled messily across the cork. On the dusty bookshelf, next to an abandoned pizza box, his Spider-man action figure recoiled from an imminent attack from G. I. Joe. "Whoa . . ." It was all Xander could manage. "I was pathetic."

It was obvious that something supernatural was going on. In Sunnydale it was almost always easiest to just start with that assumption. *Time travel. Gotta be. Someone sent me back, years back, probably because they're evil and somehow this is part of their plan, which probably ends with me all eviscerated and dead.* It wasn't a comforting thought. He got up and went to the dresser. He might end up eviscerated and dead, but he wasn't gonna be eviscerated and dead and naked. Not in front of Tyra. The top dresser drawer was full of comic books. *Right.* He sighed and turned to the pile of laundry. *Oh yeah, this routine.*

Willow's hair was tangled. Her eyes were squinty and they had little crusty bits at the corners. Her cheek was imprinted with a diagonal crease from her pillow. And she wore flannel PJ's with pictures of tiny purple pigs on them. She wasn't at her sharpest. She was, in fact, at her unsharpest.

Willow's bedroom was on the ground floor of her parents' house. So the knocking on the front door had awakened her right away. She stumbled out of bed, ran into an unexpected wall, ricocheted, then finally careened to the door, which was in entirely the wrong place, and opened it. And found Oz. Absurdly, the first thing she registered was that his T-shirt read "Robot Baby Cat."

"Hey," he said.

When Willow imagined the human brain at work, she always pictured it as a kind of machine. Not a computer, but a sort of H. G. Wells steam-powered cogs-and-gears kind of machine. And right now the gears were locked up and the steam valves were backing up. She couldn't fathom how she'd come to be here, in the doorway of her parents' house, in purple pig pajamas, looking at her high school boyfriend-slash-werewolf.

"Um. Maybe I should come back when you're less . . . comatose," Oz suggested.

Willow blinked at him, which made her aware of the crusty things at the corners of her eyes. She rubbed at them while she stumbled through, "Um . . . Oz . . . what the heck's going on?"

"Willow?" Suddenly Oz didn't even sound so sure she was really herself. Which was understandable, since she was a little vague on that very same point.

The phone rang. The laboring machine of Willow's brain recognized that sound right away.

"How 'bout I go ahead?" Oz volunteered.

The phone rang again as Willow nodded at him blankly. Oz turned to walk away. Willow closed the door and stepped to the phone. She picked it up cautiously. "Hello?"

It was Xander.

They walked toward the high school as they talked.

"It's just so weird. And why'd we get our old bodies back, anyway? I mean, what kind of time travel is this? It seems all nonstandard if you ask me," said Willow. She felt better just having Xander to talk to.

"Gimme a sec to look it up my *Big Book of Time Travel*—oh yeah, don't have one."

"Right. Sorry, Xander. Hey, what's the last thing you remember?"

"Me and Anya, going to bed. Like every night."

"Me too." She hesitated. "Only, you know, not with Anya, obviously. Alone."

"Oh. So when do you think we are, Will? Exactly, I mean."

Willow watched as Xander idly kicked at a rock on the sidewalk. She answered slowly.

"Three years ago. Senior year. A couple months before . . . you know, graduation. I saw my calendar at home. I forgot I used to cross off the days. Neat little Xs and small notes about papers being due. Then I'd go back and write down what grade I got on each one."

Xander looked at her. "Wow. I'm glad I didn't know that then. New heights of teasing would have been scaled."

Willow glanced at Xander. "It's weird how weird you look."

"I didn't realize how much the construction work kinda changed me. I mean, look at this arm. It's all scrawny. How'd I live like this?"

"I don't know. Oh, Xander, watch this. I noticed right before you came by." Willow pointed at a passing dog-walker and muttered something Xander couldn't hear. Obviously a spell. Xander looked at her.

"What did you do?"

"I turned the dog into a turnip."

Xander looked at the dog. It was small and fluffy and not very much like a turnip.

"Xander, I can't do magick, I mean, not *well*. It's like *that* went back to how it used to be too! I don't even get how that happened! Isn't that creepy?"

"Oooh. Yeah. That's by far the creepiest part of unexplained nonstandard time travel."

"Shut up. I think it's plenty creepy." She instantly regretted that. "Sorry. Little bit cranky."

"'S'Okay. Maybe it's like jet lag. Losing three years probably does that. Or maybe it's gaining three years, depends how you look at it, I guess."

They walked in silence for a few steps, deep in thought.

"You tried reaching her?" Willow asked.

"I told you. Only like a dozen times. There's no answer. Maybe she's still in the present—I mean, the future."

"Wait, that doesn't make sense. Xander, even if she's still in the . . . even if she wasn't sent back like us, she still exists in this time. I mean, it would just be, like, high-school Buffy. She's got to be around."

"So where is she, Will?"

"I dunno. Let's hurry up."

Xander and Willow moved along the residential Sunnydale street. They walked fast, as if something was on their trail. Which maybe it was. When magick happens and the world goes wonky, it was often good to make oneself in to a moving target. Because sometimes something evil was watching.

A tree stood in front of the Summers house. And stretching away from the foot of the tree was its dark shadow. Other things in the yard had shadows too. The mailbox had a shadow. So did the tennis ball abandoned there by the neighbor's spaniel; it had a little shadow. But if you looked close, you might notice that these weren't quite as dark as the tree-shadow. The tree-shadow was very dark. When the wind moved the branches of the tree, the shadow moved too. At exactly the same time. Until it didn't. Until it twitched. Until it shifted on its own. Until it turned its attention to the house. Until it thought. *Now. I will move now.*

Buffy was vaguely aware that she'd been sleeping through the ringing of the phone. And some part of her mind was a little pissed off that no one had been picking it up. *House full to burstin' with people, after all, Willow and Dawn and Giles.* The place was a commune. Then it registered that it didn't *feel* like a house full of people. Not this morning. Maybe it was slayer-sharp senses picking up different acoustics from different furniture, or a different pattern of air moving through the halls, or a different scent from different human bodies. Or maybe it was just because she knew really well what it felt like to be alone.

Then there was a sound. *Outside. The front porch.* Someone or something was at the front door.

Buffy was on her feet immediately, lunging for her weapons in one smooth motion. But her weapons chest wasn't where she left it and she ended up slamming her hand into the nightstand. *Crappity-crap!*

She found the weapons chest, unable to take the time even to wonder why it was there, against the opposite wall, where she used to keep it. She grabbed a stake and flew for the bedroom door, down the stairs, even as the front door began to swing inward. Out of time.

Buffy launched herself down the stairs, stake braced in front of her.

She came to a rest with the tip of the stake pressed against her mother's chest.

Joyce looked frightened and startled. Buffy looked back. At her mother. Who was obviously completely alive.

There were a thousand things Buffy wanted to say to her, to ask her. *Are you real? Will this last? Can I tell you much I love you?*

She opened her mouth, half-wondering which of them she was going to hear.

"Were you at the gallery?" That wasn't one of the ones she was expecting to pick.

Frowning, Joyce moved the stake away from her heart. "Yes, I was. The alarm went off and the company called me. False alarm. We don't open till ten, so I figured I'd head back here, grab a shower, and maybe get impaled by my teenage slayer daughter."

Unsure what else to do, Buffy nodded, wondering if she looked as freaked out as she felt.

Willow was still aware of a pressing instinct to hurry, but right now that was out of the question. Right now there was more of a need to do this. To stand next to Xander and stare open-mouthed.

"There it is," she heard him say, very softly. "Then. Now. You know . . . before it blew up."

Sunnydale High. Not an unsafe charred hulk left damaged by a Mayor-snake, then devastated by a Mayor-snake-killing explosion, but a solid building that looked like it would stand forever. They stood and looked up toward the main entrance. Around them students crowded and swarmed, hurrying to get inside before the bell.

"It looks smaller," he continued. The building, the parking lot, the bike racks. "Even the buses."

Willow turned to look. "Xander, that's the special education bus. It *is* smaller."

"Oh . . . right."

"Oh my God! Look! Over there." Willow jabbed him in the ribs hard and pointed, picking one figure out of the crowd. A blond head shone among the rest. Not Buffy, someone else.

"Ow! Who? Oh, Harmony." Xander squinted at the girl who would be turned into a vampire. Soon. She was bitten during the graduation melee. It felt strange seeing her, knowing what was going to happen.

"In the sunshine. How strange is that? She has no idea . . ."

Xander looked blankly at Willow. "So, do we, what? Do we warn her? Are we here to like, keep that whole thing from happening? Like a Quantum Leapy thing? Or, you know, not?"

Willow turned and headed for the main entrance. "I don't know. But I bet Giles will. Maybe he's even like us, you know, from the future or whatever, and he can help us figure this out."

Willow and Xander walked through the halls, making their way to the school library. Xander kept being distracted. His old locker. The fliers on the walls. The display case in the hallway, the one with that cheerleading trophy that always gave him a funny creepy feeling. The halls were emptying as students made their way into their homerooms. That's what Larry was doing when Xander saw him. Larry was a football star, and he was one of the many students who would die at the upcoming graduation ceremony. Xander got the strangest feeling watching Larry disappear into a room and close the door behind him, like he was watching Larry die right then. He shuddered.

"This is really weird, Will. I don't like this. It's like we can see what's gonna happen to everybody."

"I know. I used to think I'd love to be able to see the future, know all that stuff. But not if it's like this."

"You there!" A familiar voice rang out behind them. "Why aren't you in homeroom, you nasty little vagrants?"

Willow looked back, knowing already who it was. Principal Snyder, every scant inch of him. He would also die soon, swallowed whole in front of the entire student body. Willow and

Xander stopped and gave in to the unique and sad experience of being lectured by a ghost.

"Let me see your hall passes!"

Buffy looked at the waffle iron and tried to figure out if the waffles were done. She was pretty sure the light was supposed to go on. Or maybe it was supposed to go off. It was definitely one or the other. She tried to remember if the light had been on when she poured the batter on. Maybe it was and then the light went off and she didn't see it. Or maybe not. "Mom?"

Joyce entered the kitchen. "What? Haven't you left for school? Oh, Buffy."

Buffy looked at what her mother was looking at: bowls and spoons on the counter, some spilled waffle batter, and the uncooperative waffle iron which was starting to smoke a little around the edges. No matter what Mister Light said, they were probably done. Really, really done.

Joyce hurried to rescue the waffles while Buffy tried to explain.

"I was trying to make you something nice for breakfast. You know, for us to have together before you have to go back to the gallery. And I knew waffles were your favorites. *Are* your favorites. I promise, I promise so much that I'll clean up the mess."

Joyce was using a fork to try to scrape a half-raw, half-scorched waffle off the surface of the waffle iron. "Buffy, you really should've asked me about this. Did you even grease this thing at all?"

"Um . . . grease it?"

Joyce sighed, exasperated. "Sit down over there, out of my way, and let me fix this."

Buffy sat.

"Aren't you going to be late for school?" Joyce asked.

"There's lots of time. They pushed first period back a half-hour this week." The lie came easily, and it made Buffy feel like a criminal. So few sentences, a finite number of sentences she'd ever spoken to her mother. How many of them had been lies?

She watched in silence as her mother moved around the kitchen. Cleaning up Buffy's mess, making food for the two of them to share, humming softly. The humming wasn't a song. Anyone else might call it tuneless. But, with a jolt, Buffy recognized it as her mother's own *particular* tunelessness, the same little nonsong she always hummed to herself. When she died, the nonsong would go with her. Buffy let the tears fill her eyes. She wasn't going to lie about that, about the tears. If Mom saw, she saw.

Buffy knew there were things she should do. She should call Giles and say "Hey, I've been sent careening three years backward in time. How 'bout you?" She should round up Willow and Xander and Anya and Tara. *No, no, Anya and Tara aren't my friends yet.* But she *should* round up Willow and Xander and they should figure this out—find out why it happened, what the threat was. Kill it. And go back to the right time.

The right present. When Mom is dead.

Joyce was making omelets. Buffy watched, marveling at how easy she made it look. Where did her mother get that grace, the ability to make things look easy? Back in the present, Buffy was running a household now—trying to, anyway. She never felt graceful, never felt able. She'd had her mom in her life for such a short time, and she'd never really appreciated her, not this part of her anyway. Maybe this was a gift. A chance to do it again, do it right.

A thought occurred to Buffy. "Um . . . Mom? Where's Dawn? Did she go to school?"

Joyce looked up from the omelet. "Dawn? Who's Dawn?"

• • •

A bird flew over Sunnydale. Its small shadow hopped and glided along the ground. Over streets and sidewalks. Over lawns. For a fraction of a second it crossed the Summers' front yard. The shadow flicked from a corner of the driveway to a corner of the house before it leaped to the roof and on over the town. And while it crossed, almost too fast to be seen, something rode with it, skittering along the ground to the deep shade of the bushes at that corner, near the front door. The something dark was moving closer.

Finally free of Snyder, Willow and Xander burst into the library, startling Giles, who was just crossing the room with a thick book in one hand and a cup of tea in the other.

Xander slumped with disappointment. "It didn't happen to him."

"How can you tell?" Willow asked.

"Well, just look at him. Look how young he looks. His skin is much tighter. This is Giles from three years ago."

"Xander, we all look young. If our skin was as old as his we'd be tighter too! These are our bodies from three years ago, remember?"

"Oh yeah. So maybe it is him."

They both turned and stared at Giles. After a second Willow realized something.

"If it happened to him, he would've said something by now."

"Mmm." Xander nodded in agreement.

Giles cleared his throat impatiently, which made them both jump.

He spoke. "Oh yes, absolutely. If it had happened to me I would undoubtedly know what in the bloody hell you two were on about and then perhaps I wouldn't be watching you stare at me like an exhibit in a bloody wax museum."

Willow blushed. "Oh."

"Sorry," Xander mumbled.

"It's possible we're not thinking too clearly right now, Giles. I mean, I was asleep and then I woke up and there were pajamas and my old house and Oz was there . . ."

Giles shifted his weight to the other foot, taking it all in. "Hmmm. Yes. Again, I'm sure I'd be extremely understanding if I, well, understood. One of you, for God's sake, tell me what's going on."

"Time travel." Xander explained. "For us, last night was November 8, 2001. And today we're partying like it's 1999."

"Extraordinary." Giles took off his glasses and cleaned them as he sat down at the library's central table.

Willow and Xander followed him to the table.

"You believe us, right?" Xander asked, anxiously.

Giles met his eyes. "Yes, yes, I do, actually."

"Um . . . can I ask . . . why?" Xander asked.

Giles thought a second, then said, "If you live on a Hellmouth and you question the unlikely, I find that it just slows everything down."

"We thought maybe it happened to you, too," Willow volunteered. "But I guess not."

"No, no, it certainly did not. What . . . have you talked to Buffy?"

"No." Xander turned a chair around and straddled it backward. "We tried to call, but there's no answer."

"We walked past her homeroom on the way here and she wasn't there either. So I guess we know a little more . . . nothing. We know nothing." Willow had tugged the ends of her long sleeves over her hands, twisting them nervously.

"Hmm, yes."

"But we're okay," Xander said hopefully. "I mean, we're not

injured, and, you know . . ." He shot a glance at a nearby patch of floor, "The Hellmouth looks like it's neatly shut. It could be worse."

Giles was startled, and his nerves were thin. "Xander! Time has been disrupted! Something very powerful did this for motives we can hardly begin to guess. The Slayer hasn't been located. She may be in danger. We all may be in danger. And on top of this it's starting to look like the Mayor is up to something—"

"Giant snake on graduation day," Willow said simply.

"What?"

"It's okay. We kill it." Xander supplied. "Blow up the school in the process."

"So you might want to start getting your favorite books out of here."

"Stop it!" Giles was on his feet now, almost shaking with alarm. "Stop! It's vitally important that you not tell me any more about the future!"

"Oh. Okay." Willow nodded. "You don't want to influence it. I get that."

Xander nodded too. Then stopped. "Wait. I *don't* get that. I mean, we know stuff that could really help you right now. And it's not like, oh no, if we influence the past we change our present, because, frankly, there's a lot of problems in our present and a little changing might be, you know, just what we need."

"No." Giles was firm. "It's too risky."

"Um, Giles? I'm kinda with Xander on this one. I mean, I don't get the what's-so-risky."

Giles cleaned his glasses again. "Well, any knowledge of the future could affect me in unforeseen ways, my choices and emotions. For example, if I know that we will defeat the Mayor, then perhaps I don't work as hard to make it happen."

"You might take it for granted," Willow supplied.

"Yes. Just knowing the outcome might make the outcome fail to happen, you see? And, for another thing, we have no way of knowing if you're from *this* future."

Xander thought he was following along pretty well, but that part threw him. "What?" he asked. "Which future?"

"The events you remember, they might have happened on a different timeline from this one, making your information dangerously misleading. Or they may not have happened at all. Perhaps someone has magickally implanted three years of false memories into your brains, although that's a stretch."

"Ooh. Not really a stretch," Willow said, thinking it through. "It's kinda like what the monks did with Dawn."

Giles looked at her. "What monks? Who's Dawn?"

Willow and Xander exchanged a look.

Xander cleared his throat. "Um . . . I guess that's one of the things, one of the things we're not supposed to tell you about."

Giles looked at the two of them searchingly. Obviously curious, but resisting. After a moment he went on: "Well, one thing is certain. We have to find Buffy. We need her, and she may be in some kind of danger. If something sentient did this, then it did it with a purpose."

The darkness at the corner of Buffy's house lay flat against the ground. Sometimes it rippled at the edges, agitated by the closeness of its goal. She was in the house, on the other side of the door. It didn't know her name. It didn't even know she was the Slayer, although it sensed the power. All it knew was that it had to do this. It had to clean it all up. Put things right. Others would clean up the rest of the Violators. They were probably closing in on them now. But that wasn't its concern. It just had to get rid of her. To start to put things right.

The knowledge of its closeness to its goal made it bold. It rippled itself forward, creating a shadow where none could be, on the unshaded stoop—a deep stain of shade. It pushed forward, elongating, reaching for the door. It inched itself forward, slowly.

It was paper thin. Thinner. It slipped under the door without effort. It did not know what effort was.

It was inside the house.

Buffy stood at the bathroom sink. She stared at her own reflection, the reflection of how she'd looked three years ago. Her hair had been lighter that year, and her face a little younger, more unformed, still half child. It was distracting, leading her mind down paths of choice and regrets. She shook her head, looked down, and gripped the edge of the sink, trying to force herself to think.

She had her mother back. Alive. Buffy wanted to cry with joy at the very thought. She had her mother.

But she lost her sister.

But she had her mother.

Buffy heard her mother downstairs now, crossing the entryway from dining room to living room, probably looking for her purse, her keys, getting ready to head out to the gallery again. And Buffy knew she should go to school. She'd ducked her mother's question earlier with a lie, but now it was clearly time to leave. She needed to seek out her friends anyway, talk to Giles, start working on making her way back into the future . . . except that the future wasn't necessarily where she wanted to be.

Here, she had no sister. She had a mother.

I could take her to the hospital, Buffy thought. *It's so early. If they caught it now, caught the tumor now, they could fight it maybe, cut it out of her. There'd be no fatal hemorrhage.* Maybe it wasn't over after all. Maybe the last three years were best forgotten, discarded. But Dawn—*How do you weigh a sister against a mother?*

The phone rang. Phones rang for a lot of reasons. It could be anyone on the other end of that line. But what were the chances . . . what were the chances that it was Giles calling, or Willow? Someone who would make her do the "right" thing? Someone who would say, *You can't do this. Can't step out of time this way, accept the mistake, take back the three years.*

Buffy ran from the bathroom, back into her bedroom. She picked up the receiver and immediately dropped it down onto the cradle again, severing the connection. Then she reached under and behind the bed, groped for the phone cord, where it snaked into the jack. With a violent wrenching pull, she unplugged the phone from the wall. She'd have to disconnect them all, all the extensions. But that was easy. And it was the right thing to do. She needed time to think. Time to spend with her mother.

Buffy stepped out onto the landing. Joyce was in the doorway, hand on the knob. Heading out. She looked up the stairs toward Buffy.

"Buffy? Did you get the phone?"

"Yeah. Wrong number."

"Oh, all right. You want me to drop you at school, or—"

"Mom?"

Joyce paused and looked at her daughter. Buffy continued, "I think I'm sick. I suddenly feel terrible."

Joyce frowned, concerned. "Terrible how?"

Buffy looked away as she answered. "Kinda hot. You know, fevery. And my skin hurts. Not serious sick but still . . ."

"Oh, Buffy. Well, I suppose you can stay home, if you—"

"No. Mom. I really . . . do you think you could stay with me? For a while?"

Joyce hesitated.

• • •

The something dark was curled around the bottom post of the banister at the bottom of the stairs, a round black shadow that listened and waited. It was content to wait now. Now that she was in sight. It needed to be done, but it needed to be done neatly. If the other one stayed, that would be all right for now. Because at some point the Violator would be alone and then she could be taken away. And the others would be gone too. It could be clean again. Everything could be put right.

Willow waved her hand and pointed. She knew without even looking that nothing had happened. When you did magick, really *did* it, there was a kind of surge. It started as a kind of surfacy thing, a crackle in the fingertips and a sort of carbonated feeling that sizzled up your arm. And then, right after, as the magick took hold, you could feel something deeper in your chest and belly—a feeling, just for a moment, that felt a little like panic and a little like joy and little like anger. And it felt as good and clean and strong the hundredth time you felt it as it did the first time. There was no feeling like that now.

Xander leaned over and asked, "What did you try to do?"

They were sitting together at the central table in the library. Willow inclined her head toward where Giles was standing in the stacks, looking for texts that might help them understand what was happening. She spoke softly to Xander, respecting Giles's desire to be kept uninformed about their current lives. She figured that included her improved magickal abilities. "If it worked, all the books that mention time travel would have turned red. Then we could only worry about the red ones." She glared absently at her hand as if the lack of magick was somehow its fault.

Giles returned to the table, carrying a book. He handed it to Xander. "I think this one may be helpful." The book was red. Xander looked Willow, his eyes wide.

"Hey! Maybe it worked!"

Willow glanced at the book. "I've looked at that one before. It was always red."

"Oh." Xander sounded defeated.

Willow had a sudden thought. She looked to Giles. "Xander and I, we need to go to class."

Giles was surprised. "Surely you—we have research to do."

Willow realized that this Giles wasn't used to her being so forceful. She explained: "We're not getting anywhere here. I think we should go try to figure out if we're on the right time line or not, by, you know, *living* here . . . just till we can tell."

Giles hesitated. Xander didn't look that certain either. "Exactly how can we tell that?"

Willow closed the book on her lap. "We want to know if we've lived this day before, right?"

Giles, clearly picking up on the idea, answered, "You'll want to look for independent events, things that aren't influenced by the different ways you're going to interact with them—a science exam, a lecture or class project, or a fire drill . . . something."

Xander nodded, thinking that it was a pretty impossible job. Who remembered a fire drill from three years ago? But it was better than sitting here feeling helpless. He nodded and said, "Giles, while we're doing that, maybe you should try to find Buffy. I think we've let this go too long without her."

Giles nodded. Xander was right. This Xander and this Willow both seemed more confident, less likely to be led. Stronger. A part of him felt very proud.

Buffy was propped on the living room sofa, a blanket draped over her. She smiled as Mom handed her a bowl of Chicken and Stars soup, then adjusted the blanket as she sat down by Buffy's feet. "Thanks, Mom."

"Oh, honey. You're welcome. I know how it is to suddenly feel yucky."

Buffy felt a shiver of alarm. "Do you? I mean, have you been feeling sick?"

"What? No, of course not! I just mean that when you feel sick, it's just such a helpless feeling, like you're young again and you just want your mother to take care of you."

Buffy looked into the soup, moving stars with the tip of her spoon, hiding her emotion. "Yeah, that's it. That's exactly how I feel."

Willow slipped into History class, late. It had taken her some minutes of walking the halls, peeking into classrooms, for her to recall her senior schedule. But this was right—Mr. Harten at the front of the class, Oz in a desk to her left.

"Miss Rosenberg, nice of you to join us." Willow remembered that Mr. Harten had never been an original guy. He'd decided, years ago, on an appropriate quip to address tardiness, and he saw no reason to change that habit.

"Sorry Mr. Harten. Couldn't be helped," she said back to him as she took her seat. She noticed a few heads turning toward her in surprise, including Oz. It took her a moment to realize what they were reacting to. She was out of character. High school Willow didn't have that confident off-hand voice. She wouldn't ever have shown up late for class, and certainly not without a notebook, and if for some reason she did, she would have been blushing like a radish from having the eyes of all the students on her.

After a moment Mr. Harten started talking again. Willow listened hard, trying to remember if she'd heard this lecture before, a discussion of the role of accident in history. It was interesting, and some of the facts sounded familiar, but she wasn't sure. Maybe this part—

"Pssssst!"

Willow looked around to see who was hissing. Oz, in that desk to her left. Probably worried about her after her strangeness this morning, and now . . . *He probably thinks I'm ignoring him. Which I kind of am.*

She looked at him, met his eyes. He smiled at her, one of the little smiles he reserved just for her, the faintest twitch of his lips. To her surprise she *felt* that smile, felt the warmth that it caused. She smiled back at him, almost involuntarily. A connection. She felt her pulse speed up, blood rush to her face. She looked away, fast.

Whoo. She was one confused little kitty. At first this world had felt terribly foreign. But there were parts of it that were beyond familiar. She had just been patting herself on the back for having moved beyond the scared, radishy teenager that she had been, and suddenly here she was, scared and red-faced—radish deluxe.

And desperately homesick. She didn't want to be here any longer. Her world in 2001 was kinda screwed up, with Tara getting so strange on her, moving out . . .

And now with this reaction to Oz . . .

What do I want?

Tara.

She knew she'd rather be there with Tara, even an angry Tara, than anywhere in this old landscape where she felt herself losing ground, slipping back into what she used to be. She still loved Oz, and she'd never lied to herself about that, but not like how she loved Tara. And she didn't want to be back in the life that Oz-love belonged to.

She slumped a little lower in her seat and tried to concentrate on the lecture. Maybe she'd remember this section on scientific accidents. She didn't look toward Oz again. She didn't notice his confused frown. Or the dark dark shadow that his desk made—darker than the other shadows.

Xander looked at the parallelogram on the blackboard. Geometry. It suddenly occurred to him that perhaps this wasn't time travel, perhaps it was one of those hell dimensions, and he was going to be enrolled in remedial ninth grade geometry forever. But it didn't matter, he supposed, if he understood anything now. He was just here to play "Do I remember this?"

Mrs. Holland was drawing a rectangle on the board. She labeled one vertical side A and the top B. "So who can tell me the area of the rectangle?"

Xander knew that. A times B. He nodded to himself, a little self-satisfied. A person didn't take geometry twice without learning something. Someone else in the class gave the answer and Mrs. Holland continued. She pointed at the parallelogram. Its top was Y units long and it was X units tall. And the length of its oh-so-slanty side was Z. What was its area?

Xander started looking around the room at the other students, no sense in even listening to this. Then he looked back. Something had suddenly struck him. What if that parallelogram was made of wood? What if it was part of a carpentry project? He imagined sawing off triangles from both sides, leaving a square. Then you could put those triangles together . . . another square, put them next to the first square. He could see it in his mind. It was a rectangle. A Y-by-X rectangle. And he knew how to do that.

"The area is X times Y!" He stood up and shouted it. Everyone turned to stare at him.

He sat back down, smiling sheepishly, while the teacher, obviously startled, explained to the class why Xander's answer was right.

They went on, discussing areas of circles, volumes of pyramids . . . Xander wielded a mental saw, rearranging the shapes, building huge structures in his mind. It was simple. Could it really have been this easy all along? All the torture, all the years of feeling stupid . . . unnecessary. Well, that was just terrific.

Xander was having a breakthrough about cutting the area under a curve into infinitely small rectangular slices when he saw a shadow flit across the floor, but he barely noticed it. He was moments away from understanding the basic principle behind all of calculus.

Willow and Xander sat, heads together, at lunch. They discussed the total absence of any progress, except that Xander was now convinced he was a misunderstood geometrical genius.

There weren't two shadows following them anymore. They had merged into one. It lay, spread like a manta ray, under their table. It didn't care who they were or what they were talking about. It just needed to clean them. They didn't belong there.

Willow was talking over the babble and rumble of the cafeteria. "But, Xander, I told you all that! Every time I tutored you I talked about cutting up that parallelogram!"

"But you didn't say it was made of wood!"

"*Wood?* For God's sake, Xander, how does that make any diff—"

She broke off and Xander stared at her.

Then she screamed.

She slumped in her chair, silent now, and started to slide to the ground. Xander, scared and confused, jumped up and hurried to grab her. He picked her up in his arms, ignoring the stares from the students in the crowded lunchroom.

There was something on her leg. It was clinging to her shin. A dark film. Xander had never seen anything like it. And whatever it was, it was clearly hurting Willow. She whimpered, semiconscious.

Xander carried her out of the lunchroom, toward the library. Giles would know what to do. *He has to.*

Giles stood on Buffy's front stoop. He knocked again, getting impatient. Finally Joyce opened the door.

"Oh! Mr. Giles . . . Rupert."

"Um . . . Joyce. Hello."

The two of them had been awkward with each other ever since a candy-addled encounter on the hood of a police car the previous year. He cleared his throat, willing himself to soldier through the tense moment.

"Is, um . . . is Buffy here?"

"Well, she is, but the thing is, I'm afraid she's not feeling very well today. Unless the world is at stake, I think it would be best if you waited to see her tomorrow, or, you know, whenever she feels better."

Giles met Joyce's eye and set his jaw. "I'm afraid the world might be at stake, at least a bit."

Startled by his determination, Joyce took a step backward and Giles brushed past her, turning left into the living room.

Buffy was on the sofa, feet up, blanket to her chin. A can of soda with a bendy-straw protruding from it sat on the floor next to a celebrity tabloid. She blinked up at Giles.

"Giles? What's going on? Is it Faith and the Mayor?"

Faith and the Mayor. Giles hesitated, thrown off balance. Was it possible that the time phenomenon affecting Willow and Xander had left Buffy untouched? But there was something about Buffy's open, guiltless face. Strikingly unblinking. It wasn't ringing true.

"When you're really innocent, your eyes aren't quite that wide. You're not telling the truth. I know what's happened, Buffy. I know where you're from."

Joyce was in the doorway. "What do you mean? Where she's from?"

Buffy sat up and pushed the blanket aside. "Mom, I have to talk to Giles, if it's okay."

"Oh, well, all right, if it's slaying business. I'll be upstairs." Joyce reluctantly turned toward the stairs.

Giles sat heavily on the sofa next to Buffy. He didn't know how to begin this conversation. Directly, he supposed, was best.

"You have to go back to where you belong, Buffy."

"I don't know what you're talking about. Go back where?"

"Buffy, please. This is serious. I know what's happened."

She looked at him sharply, genuinely curious. "How? Did it happen to you too?"

"No, but Xander and Willow were affected. They're at the school, trying to figure out what happened. We were all quite concerned when we couldn't reach you."

Buffy tossed the blanket aside and walked to the fireplace. She leaned her forehead against the mantelpiece. She took a deep breath. With her head still down, she said, "I don't want to go back."

The shadow on the mantelpiece fluttered. She was so close.

Giles wanted to come closer, to stand near Buffy, but something told him not to get too close, that her composure couldn't take it. He gave her a moment, then he asked softly, "I understand that your life in the future isn't perfect, but it is your life, and you have to go—"

Her head snapped up and she fixed on him angrily. "It isn't

perfect?" she mocked. "What I'm dealing with is way beyond 'isn't perfect.' You want to hear about it? The fabulous parade that is my future?"

"I can't." He hastened to stop her. "It's important that I not know what's going to happen."

She took a step toward him and he backed up involuntarily. Buffy never used her superior strength to intimidate him, and he was alarmed and frightened, frightened for her. What had happened to her to harden her this way? He was afraid he was about to find out.

"Here's my life, Giles. My lovely, miraculous life. First, Angel leaves me. Then I meet a new man, Riley. But he leaves me too. Oh, and I get a little sister, did they tell you about that one? I get the little sister I've always had but who never existed. And then my mother dies."

Giles took another step backward and steadied himself with a hand against the wall. Joyce was going to die?

"That's right, Watcher. She dies. A brain tumor. It's probably in there now, cooking away."

"Buffy, please, don't go on. I can't—"

"Can't what? Can't hear it or can't take it? Because it's not over. We're not even at the part where I die again to save the world. But I go to heaven, until Willow brings me back, pulls me out of paradise. Then you leave forever, which, by the way, thanks oh so much in advance. And I'm so alone, Giles. You can't image how alone I am. I'm so alone I'm having sex with Spike just because it's the only way I can feel anything."

Giles's face was a frozen mask, incapable of registering the amount of shock he was feeling. Could this really be the future? How could Xander and Willow have kept this to themselves? And how could Joyce be dead? How could Willow bring Buffy back from the dead? And could he leave Buffy alone in such a state? It didn't make sense.

"I'm so sorry." It was all he could manage, and he was deeply aware of how ridiculously inadequate it was.

"So that's why I don't want to go back. I know it's wrong and selfish, but God help me, Giles, it's what I want. I think . . ."

"What? What do you think?"

"I think maybe someone gave me a do-over."

Giles sat down, polished his glasses, and thought about that.

Xander burst into the library, Willow a slight weight in his arms. "Giles! Damn it, Giles, you have to be here!"

Willow was gasping for air, fighting obvious pain. "He's not here, Xander. Put me down."

On the verge of a screaming panic, Xander decided instead to listen to his friend. He set her gingerly onto a chair. "Maybe I should take you to the hospital."

Willow winced and closed her eyes. "Right, because they're so good with killer shadow demons."

Xander knelt in front of her and looked at her leg. "Is that what this is, Will? A shadow demon?"

"I dunno. Maybe."

It looked to him more like a sheet of dark thick plastic that had been burned onto her. Where it had touched the skin of her ankle it had clung and seared itself right to her. Where it had touched pant leg, she'd had some protection, but it had still worked through in places and adhered to her. He tugged at the cuff of her jeans, trying to pull the substance or demon or whatever it was away from her. But he could feel it resist, pulling tighter against the pressure he was exerting.

"Xander! Stop that! It hurts!"

He pulled away and sat back on his heels. "I don't know what this thing is, Will. I think it's probably good that a lot of it's just touching the fabric. But I don't know how to fix it."

"I do."

He looked up at her, confused. Her eyes were open now, bright with pain but very focused. She continued, "We have to get back home."

"But Giles isn't here. And he said we'd need to know more so we could figure out what spell did this."

"This thing is doing something inside me, like it's put in little roots or something. It's spreading and we don't have time to do this Giles's way."

Xander blanched. Willow was making it sound like she was dying or something. "What other way is there?"

"My way. Can you . . . um . . . push me over to the table . . . or . . ."

Xander didn't like the sound of trying to maneuver her across the room, not with her in such pain. He pushed the table to her. She continued talking as she paged through one of the books Giles had piled on the table. "A spell sent us here, right? What Giles wanted to do was find our what spell it was and then undo it. Like untying a knot. What I'm talking about is stronger. I want to cancel any hold that any magick has over us. It's more like . . . like breaking a chain."

"Is it harder?"

"It takes more force, yeah."

"But, Will, you're already weak, and we've seen that your magick isn't exactly working its best here—"

"That's why . . ." She paused, and Xander realized she was fighting constant pain. "That's why you'll have to help me."

Xander shifted his weight from one foot to another. He was getting impatient, watching Willow read.

Something was killing Willow, and he had no idea where Giles and Buffy were.

• • •

Buffy watched Giles as he polished his glasses and thought. She'd missed him terribly since he'd returned to England, and she found herself absurdly grateful to have him here again. Even if she wasn't going to like what he was going to say.

Finally he took a deep breath and put his glasses back on. "You've put me in a difficult position, Buffy. And the truth is that I can't know for certain that the right answer is to send you back to your time. But I cannot help but feel that something is terribly—"

Buffy felt something hit her bare right arm. Something heavy and very, very painful. At first she thought she was being burned. Then it was worse than that. She screamed.

Giles leaped to his feet and ran to her. "Buffy! What is it? What is that thing?"

Buffy spared a fraction of a second to look at her arm. The thick dark film looked like it was grafted over her skin. And now . . . now it felt like something was burrowing in, digging its way into her flesh. She leaned heavily against the mantel again. The pain was making it hard to remain standing.

Willow felt terrible. The pain in her leg was fresh and sharp, and it was spreading. She had this mental image of tiny vines growing from a seed. The tiny vines were pain, and they were working their way up inside her leg. She found herself closing her eyes for longer and longer stretches of time, and it was getting harder and harder to pull herself back to the task at hand: getting home.

She was jolted back one more time when Xander plonked something onto the table in front of her: a small plastic bag full of herbs.

"I found this one in Giles's desk too. Bottom drawer behind a bunch of other stuff."

Willow forced herself to lean forward and examine the contents.

The first bag Xander had brought to her had turned out to be Giles's stash of English tea. Useless for performing spells. But with any luck . . .

"This is it," she declared. The cured leaf of a rare tropical plant, it had one very valuable trait: whatever magick she and Xander might manage to conjure up, this herb would make it stronger. Now there was nothing left to do but try to give it something to act on.

Xander asked, "So what do we do with it? Burn it or . . ." Willow looked at him and managed a smile. Xander was doing great, especially at not asking constantly if she was okay. The dark thing had spread, was halfway up her thigh, but Xander was being very cool about it.

"Just scatter it around. Make a circle around us."

So Xander pushed the table away again and scattered the chopped and wilted leaves around Willow's chair in a circle. When he finished he knelt in front of her. "What now?"

"Hold my hands. That'll focus my energy too."

Xander held her hands. Willow closed her eyes and leaned her head back. She concentrated on bringing the power of the universe around her, to use it to pull her back into her real time. If it worked, she and Xander, and anyone else nearby who was in the wrong time, would all be returned to where they belong.

She felt the power. Felt it building. She visualized it like a tower, growing from the ground up within the circle of her and Xander's arms. It grew, strong and bright. But the pain in her leg was strong too.

She opened her eyes. "Xander? I don't think it's gonna work."

Buffy held her arm out away from her body. Whatever this thing was, she didn't want it spreading to her torso through her own carelessness.

Giles was standing beside her now. Steadying her with one hand on her opposite shoulder, bending over the arm, examining it. Taking too long.

"Stop looking at it." She gasped. "Get me a knife."

Giles hesitated. Buffy locked eyes with him. She gave him a look that said, *Don't argue.*

Giles hurried to the weapon's chest and within a second he was handing her a wicked-looking hunting knife.

"What are you going to do, Buffy? Try to peel it away—"

Buffy plunged the knife through the clinging entity and into her inside arm, halfway between wrist and elbow.

Stunned and horrified, Giles jumped back.

The dark thing on Buffy's arm had a three-inch slit right through its middle. It loosened its grip as Buffy's blood coursed through and splattered on the floor, leaving fat red circles.

"Buffy! What have you done?!"

"I don't know. I just . . . I needed to cut it. I thought maybe it would let go."

"I don't think it's that kind of—"

"Wait. Look!"

The dark thing was moving, contracting and thickening on Buffy's arm. Over the wound. Over the blood.

It tasted the blood. It was dirty—foreign blood from the future. It had to go. It all had to go. The person. The blood. But there was more blood. Blood got away. The foreign body was scattering. That couldn't be allowed. Where was the blood?

On the floor.

The dark thing let itself gather, contract, and drop.

Buffy and Giles watched in amazement as the dark thing dropped to the floor. It flattened out to a shadowy skin and moved to the spots of blood. It moved over them, moved on. . . . Two spots gone. It moved on.

"Giles, look. It's drinking the blood. What is it? Some kind of horizontal vampire?" Buffy was almost dizzy from the sudden lack of pain. Blood continued to run down her arm from the knife wound.

Giles was staring with sudden realization. "It's . . . cleaning. I think it's getting rid of you."

"What?"

"You don't belong in this time line. This . . . thing . . . it's cleaning up the time line by getting rid of you. All of you, including the spilled blood. I've read of such a thing, but I disregarded it." He looked sharply at Buffy. "We're not done. When it's done with your blood it has to take you out."

Buffy still held the knife. She fell to her knees by the shadowy creature. Stabbing it hadn't worked, but years of being the Slayer had taught Buffy something very important: Almost nothing could survive being cut into a hundred tiny pieces. It was a remarkably consistent law.

She hacked at it. Making deep cuts one way, then the other. It was in five pieces, then eight, then a dozen. She kept going.

Finally she felt Giles's hand on her shoulder. She looked up, a little dazed from what she'd been doing, and weak from loss of blood.

"You're done, Buffy. It's dead."

She kept her eyes on his face. She knew she was pleading, but she hoped it didn't sound that way. "If it's dead, can I stay? Can I please stay here?"

Xander lifted Willow into his arms. She'd finally passed out from the pain, and he'd decided it was time for the hospital. Willow might not think it could help, but he had to do something.

He lifted a foot to step over the patchy ring of dried herb. His foot hit something that felt like . . . all he could think of was . . . an electric sponge. He stepped back. And, as he looked, a glowing cylinder formed around him.

"Man, I hope this is a good thing."

The world seemed to fade around him. "Oh my God, we built a transporter. No, wait, I mean a time ma—" And before he finished the thought, he was gone.

As Giles looked into Buffy's face, he was searching for a way to say yes to her, a way to tell her it was okay to stay here. Then she began to fade.

SUNNYDALE, 2001

Buffy, Willow, and Xander were in the Magic Box. It was one day after they all materialized back into their beds. Willow had no evidence of ever having been attacked. Buffy bore a thin silver scar from her own knife.

They hadn't talked to Giles yet. Buffy thought he probably had ended up with no memory of their visit to the past. How could he possibly have known everything she'd told him and not let it show, all this time? Willow wasn't so sure. Giles could be very strong.

Willow asked a question, though, that they *should* know, one that had been bothering Buffy. "So who did it?"

Xander looked confused. "I thought it was that shadow monster thing. Right?"

"No." Buffy'd thought about it a lot. "They were just doing what they do—cleaning up. Something else actually sent us back there."

"So who?" Xander asked. "I mean, who would do something that, like, weird?"

Warren looked at Jonathan and Andrew. "Wait. Say that again?"

Jonathan cleared his throat nervously. "It didn't work."

Andrew piped up. "Well, dude, not true exactly. It did work. *Bam,* time displacement. But then, *Bam.* They're back."

Warren nodded. "That's okay. It's a good start. And we've got lots of other surprises for 'em."

Buffy sat alone in the training room and thought about what had happened. Willow and Xander's spell had worked just in time. They'd done it again. She'd seen Giles's face as she'd faded back into this world and faded out of the world in which her mother was alive. *Go Xander. Go Willow.* They'd pulled her out of heaven.

Again.

ABOUT THE AUTHORS

Scott Allie writes and edits comics and stories, primarily for Dark Horse Comics and Glimmer Train Press. His series The Devil's Footprints, with Buffy cover artists Paul Lee and Brian Horton, debuts this March. He lives in Oregon with his wife, Melinda, and their phantom cat, Shadow.

Laura J. Burns and **Melinda Metz** are obsessed with *Buffy the Vampire Slayer*. In fact, it was the chock-full-of-subtext writing on *Buffy* that inspired them to try their collective hand at television-writing. So far they have written two pilots and spent a season as staff writers on the late, great TV show *Roswell*. In the book world, they created the Roswell High series written by Melinda and edited by Laura. They have relished this opportunity to contribute to the world of *Buffy*.

Max Allan Collins and **Matthew V. Clemens** have collaborated on over a dozen published short stories, and the latter assists the former on CSI and Dark Angel tie-in novels. Max Collins is the author of the *New York Times* best-selling graphic novel *Road to Perdition*, from which the Tom Hanks/Sam Mendes movie derived; his Nathan Heller historical series is much honored, and he has written and directed three independent films. Matt Clemens is the co-author of the regional best-seller *Dead Water*, a true-crime account, and owns his own small publishing company.

Greg Cox is the *New York Times* best-selling author of numerous Star Trek novels, including *The Eugenics Wars, The Q Continuum, Assignment: Eternity,* and *The Black Shore.* He has also written for several other media franchises, including X-Men, Iron Man, Roswell, Xena, and Farscape, and recently completed the novelization of the movie *Daredevil.* A diehard Buffy fan, he can't believe that nobody had done a pirate slayer yet. Then again, he is also perversely proud of having edited the novelization of *Cutthroat Island.*

Kara Dalkey, a recent transplant to the Pacific Northwest, has had fifteen fantasy novels and twelve short stories published. Among her recent works are *Genpei,* a historical fantasy novel set in Japan, and The Water Trilogy, which she describes as "Atlantis and Arthurian Myth in a blender." Her hobbies include her two cats, Ultima Online, and playing electric bass guitar in an oldies rock 'n' roll band.

Jane Espenson has been on the writing staff of *Buffy the Vampire Slayer* since the third season of the show. She is currently the show's co-executive producer. She has also written a number of comic books and episodes of other programs, including Buffy's brother-show, *Angel.*

Rebecca Rand Kirshner is a bon vivant. Ask anyone.

ROSWELL™

ALIENATION DOESN'T
END WITH GRADUATION

Everything changed the day Liz Parker died. Max
Evans healed her, revealing his alien identity. But
Max wasn't the only "Czechoslovakian" to crash
down in Roswell. Before long Liz, her best friend
Maria, and her ex-boyfriend Kyle are drawn into
Max, his sister Isabel, and their friend Michael's
life-threatening destiny.

Now high school is over, and the group has
decided to leave Roswell to turn that destiny
around. The six friends know they have changed
history by leaving their home.

What they don't know is what lies in store…

SIMON PULSE
Published by Simon & Schuster

Aaron Corbet isn't a bad kid—he's just a little different.

On the eve of his eighteenth birthday, Aaron is
dreaming of a darkly violent landscape. He can hear
the sounds of weapons clanging, the screams of the
stricken, and another sound that he cannot quite
decipher. But as he gazes upward to the sky, he
suddenly understands. It is the sound of great wings
beating the air unmercifully as hundreds of armored
warriors descend on the battlefield.

The flapping of angels' wings.

Orphaned since birth, Aaron is suddenly discovering
newfound—and sometimes supernatural—talents. But
not until he is approached by two men does he learn
the truth about his destiny—and his own role as a
liason between angels, mortals, and Powers both
good and evil—some of whom are bent on his own
destruction....

a new series by Thomas E. Sniegoski
Book One available March 2003
From Simon Pulse
Published by Simon & Schuster

Todd A. McIntosh is a twenty-five-year veteran of the makeup industry. His credits include projects in television and film, as well as years spent instructing makeup students all around the globe. Todd's home is in Los Angeles, but he often returns to his former residence, Vancouver, British Columbia, Canada to instruct. Todd was Makeup Department Head on *Buffy the Vampire Slayer* for six years, from the presentation to the end of the sixth season. Once again freelance, Todd found the time to pen a fun little adventure for this book between film projects and cuddling the cats!

Michael Reaves is an Emmy award-winning television writer and a *New York Times* best-selling novelist.

Kristine Kathryn Rusch writes in several genres under many pen names. She has won major awards in science fiction, mystery, and romance, and has been nominated for major awards in fantasy and horror. Her latest science fiction novel is *The Disappeared from Roc*. Her latest mystery novel, published as Kris Nelscott, is *Thin Walls* from St. Martin's Press. Her latest romance novel (which is really a fantasy novel) is *Simply Irresistible* written as Kristine Grayson and published by Kensington. She also writes novels in her favorite media universes, including Star Trek and Star Wars, and is happy to write a story in the Buffy universe.

IT'S BACK!

She slays, she sings, she kicks demon butt – and now Buffy's mag is back for round two!

Buffy the Vampire Slayer magazine takes you on a joyride through the streets of Sunnydale and right up to the doorsteps of your favorite *Buffy* and *Angel* characters.

Including:

- **Exclusive interviews with the cast and crew**
- **Behind-the-scenes set reports and photography**
- **Latest news in front of and behind the cameras**
- **Reviews of all the latest *Buff*-stuff!**

To subscribe, E-mail: **buffysubs@titanemail.com**
or call: **847-330-5549**

AVAILABLE NOW AT
NEWSSTANDS AND BOOKSTORES

Giles (to Buffy): "What did you sing about?"

Buffy: "I, uh . . . don't remember. But it seemed perfectly normal."

Xander: "But disturbing. And not the natural order of things and do you think it'll happen again? 'Cause I'm for the natural order of things."

Only in Sunnydale could a breakaway pop hit be a portent of doom. When someone magically summons a musical demon named Sweet, the Scoobies are involuntarily singing and dancing to the tune of their innermost secrets. The truths that are uncovered are raw and painful, prompting the question, "where do we go from here?"

Now, in one complete volume, find the final shooting script of the acclaimed musical episode "Once More, With Feeling." Complete with color photos, production notes, and sheet music!

The Script Book: Once More, With Feeling

Available now from Simon Pulse
Published by Simon & Schuster

Everyone's got his demons....

ANGEL™

If it takes an eternity, he will make amends.

Original stories based
on the TV show
Created by Joss Whedon
& David Greenwalt

Available from Simon Pulse
Published by Simon & Schuster

2311-01